# Behind
# the
# Net

# Behind the Net

STEPHANIE ARCHER

ORION

**Stephanie Archer** writes spicy, laugh-out-loud romance. She believes in the power of best friends, stubborn women, a fresh haircut, and love. She lives in Vancouver with a man and a dog.

For spicy bonus scenes, news about upcoming books, and book recs, sign up for her newsletter at:

https://www.stephaniearcherauthor.com/newsletter

**Instagram**: @stephaniearcherauthor

**Tiktok**: @stephaniearcherbooks

To check content warnings for any of Stephanie's books, visit www.stephaniearcherauthor.com/content

*For Bryan, Alanna, Sarah, Helen, and Anthea,*
*who clap the loudest when I win*

An Orion paperback

This edition first published in Great Britain in 2024 by Orion Fiction
an imprint of The Orion Publishing Group Ltd
Carmelite House, 50 Victoria Embankment
London EC4Y 0DZ

An Hachette UK company

3 5 7 9 10 8 6 4

A CIP catalogue record for this book is
available from the British Library.

ISBN (Mass Market Paperback) 978 1 398 72425 9

Printed in Great Britain by Clays Ltd, Elcograf, S.p.A.

MIX
Paper | Supporting
responsible forestry
FSC® C104740
FSC
www.fsc.org

www.orionbooks.co.uk

THE LEFT WINGER skates toward the net and slapshots the puck at me. There's a *thwap* of the puck in my glove, and my blood flares with competition and satisfaction.

"Streicher shut out," my new teammate calls as he breezes past, and I toss the puck onto the ice with a quick nod. The fans back in New York used to chant that during games. When I won the Vezina Trophy last year, awarded to the best goalie in the NHL, they referenced it in the speech about my performance.

Near the bench, the coaches watch, make notes, and discuss the team's performance. A puck gets past me and my gut tightens. The head coach's gaze flicks to me, expression indiscernible.

Two weeks ago, I signed as a free agent below my value so that I could play for the Vancouver Storm. After the panic attack that caused her car accident, my mom insisted she was fine, but I know that if she kept them from me, it must be getting worse. Now that the team has signed me for a lower price, I'm an asset. They could trade me for more money and I wouldn't have any say in the matter. I'm like a house they just got a deal on, and if they decide to buy something better, they'll sell me.

Worry flows through me. My mom's dealt with depression and anxiety for years, ever since my dad passed in a self-inflicted drunk driving incident when I was a baby, but while I wasn't looking, it turned into something so much worse.

Leaving Vancouver isn't an option, and I'm not giving up the sport I love, so this season needs to go well. I need to play my best and maintain my top status so they don't trade me. This year, I need to focus.

The players run drills as practice continues, and I reference what I know about them from previous games. I've played against the Vancouver Storm in the past, and I recognize their faces, but I don't know these guys like my old team. I played for New York for seven years, since I was nineteen. I don't know these coaches, and this city hasn't felt like home since I left for the juniors, but Vancouver is where I need to be right now.

Something strains in my chest. It's only the first day of training camp, but I've never felt more pressure to play my best.

The whistle blows, and I skate toward the bench with the other players.

"Looking sharp out there, boys," the coach says as we gather around the bench.

At the end of last season, one of the worst in the Storm's history, Tate Ward made headlines after he was announced as the new head coach. The guy's in his late thirties, not much older than some of Vancouver's players, and he had a promising career as a forward in the league until a knee injury ended it. He coached college hockey until last year, and from what I've read in hockey news, the fans are skeptical. Head coaches are normally older, with more experience coaching at the pro level.

Ward glances at me, and under my goalie mask, my jaw tightens.

"We have a lot of work to do over the next few seasons," he says, surveying the group of players. "We finished last year near the bottom of the league."

The air feels heavy as players shift on their skates, bracing themselves. This is the part where a lot of coaches would point out players' flaws and weaknesses. What the team fucked up on last year. This is where he'll tell us that losing is not an option.

And don't I fucking know it.

"Nowhere to go but up," Ward says instead, crooking a grin at us. "Hit the showers and rest up. See you tomorrow."

The players head off the ice, and I pull my mask off with a frown. I'm sure this pleasant, supportive facade of Ward's will end as soon as the season starts in a few weeks and the pressure becomes real.

"Streicher," Ward calls as I head down the hall to the dressing room. He heads over to me and waits as the remaining players shuffle down the hall, giving them nods of acknowledgment. "How are you settling in?"

I nod. "Fine." My apartment is filled with boxes that I don't have time to unpack. "Thank you, uh, for setting up the apartment. And the movers."

Tension gathers in my shoulder muscles and I drag a hand through my hair. I hate accepting help from others.

Ward waves me off. "It's our job to help players settle in. A lot of players ask for an assistant, actually. They can help you unpack, get you set up with meals, get your car serviced, walk your dog, whatever."

"I don't have a dog."

He chuckles. "You know what I mean. We're here to provide you with whatever you need so you can focus on the ice. Anything you need, just let us know."

I don't need help focusing on the ice. I've refined my life down to the two things that matter—hockey and my mom.

"You bet," I say, knowing full well I'm not going to ask for anything.

I've always been the guy who takes care of himself. That's not about to change.

Ward lowers his voice. "If your mom needs any help, we can provide that, too."

When I requested a trade to Vancouver, he was the one who called me to ask why. I told him everything. He's the only one who knows about my mom.

Anxiety spikes in me, and this is why I shouldn't have opened my fucking mouth. Now people want to get involved. Every instinct in my body revolts, and my shoulders hitch.

My schedule this year will be grueling. Eighty-two games, half at home in Vancouver and half away, with team practices, training with the goalie coach, and my own workouts. On top of that, I'll have sessions with my physio, massage therapist, sports psychologist, and personal trainer.

Something flares in my chest, a mix of competition and anticipation. I've been competing at hockey since I was five years old, and I thrive on a challenge. Pressure fuels me. Years of training have made me into a person who loves to push my limits and win.

This year? Between how stubborn my mom is and how intense my schedule will be? It's going to be a fucking challenge.

Nothing I can't handle, though, as long as I stay focused.

"We're good." My words are clipped. "Thank you."

It's always just been me and my mom. I've got it handled. I always have.

———

After I shower and change, I leave the arena to grab lunch and head home for a nap before hitting the gym. I'm walking through an alley from the arena to the street when a noise by the dumpsters stops me.

A fluffy brown dog's butt is sticking out of a box. As I walk past, the dog lifts its head out of the box and looks at me. There's macaroni and cheese all over its snout.

The dog wags its tail at me, and I stare back. Her eyes are a deep brown, bright with excitement. Her breed is hard to tell. She's forty or fifty pounds, maybe a mix between a Lab and a spaniel. One of her ears is shorter than the other.

The dog takes a step forward, and I take a step back.

"No way," I tell it.

The dog flops to the ground, rolls over to expose her belly, and waits, tail sweeping back and forth over the pavement as she asks for belly rubs.

Where's her owner? I glance up and down the alley, but we're alone. My nose wrinkles as I study her. No collar, and among the macaroni, her snout is dirty and greasy. Her fur is too long, falling into her eyes, and even though she needs a haircut, I can see how skinny she is.

There's a twisting feeling in my chest that I don't like.

"Don't eat that," I tell her, frowning as I nod at the garbage. "You'll get sick."

Her pink tongue flops out the side of her mouth.

"Go home."

My words come out stern, but she's still waiting for belly rubs.

My heart strains, but I shove the feelings away. *No.* This isn't my problem. I don't do distractions. I don't even date, for fuck's sake, because I know from experience that people want more than I can give them.

I can't leave her here, though. She could get hit by a car or injured by a coyote. She could eat something that could make her sick.

The SPCA will take her. I pull my phone out and, after some Googling, call the nearest location.

"There's a dog behind the arena downtown," I tell the woman when she answers. There's only one arena in downtown Vancouver, so she'll know where I mean. There are dogs barking in the background on her end. "Can someone come pick her up?"

The woman laughs. "Honey, we are so understaffed. You'll have to drop her off at one of our locations."

She lists the locations that are accepting dogs before hanging up. The ones nearby are all full, so I'll have to drive a couple hours outside the city to drop her off. I stare at the phone, brow furrowed, before I look down at the dog.

She jumps to her feet, still staring at me, wagging her tail. It's like she thinks I'm going to give her a treat or something. There's an annoying pull in my chest.

"What?" I ask the dog, and her tail wags harder. Something in my chest warms, and I swallow past a thick throat.

I can't just leave her here.

In the back of my brain, the rigorous, disciplined part of me scoffs. What about my insane schedule? I can't handle a fucking dog. I can't even handle having a girlfriend without fucking everything up. I sure as shit can't take care of a dog. I'm traveling half the season.

But I can't just leave her here.

Her tail is wagging again, and she's looking up at me with those brown eyes. I'll take her to a shelter, but I'm not going to keep her.

That evening, I'm sitting in my car outside the shelter, surveying the small but well-maintained building. I can hear barking from inside. There's a fenced-in field beside the building with dog toys and some plastic equipment, like at a playground.

In the passenger seat, the dog stares out the window, curious. I roll down the window and let her sniff.

After scouring lost dog ads online, I found a highly rated farm that takes in strays and places them with new owners. They vet their owners carefully, and the dogs are well taken care of.

This is the best shelter I could find. I drove three hours to get here.

My gaze sweeps over the place, and I swallow past the knot in my throat. I picture leaving her here, and a weight forms in my gut.

The dog looks at me and pants, her tongue hanging out.

"I can't keep you," I tell her.

She stands up and tries to climb into my lap, and I sigh. She kept trying to do this while I was driving. She crawls into my lap and rests her head on the armrest.

Fuck. If I knew how hard this would be, I wouldn't have taken her to begin with.

That's a lie. No way was I leaving her in some dirty alley.

I run through the reasons I can't keep her. I've never even had a dog. I have no idea how to take care of one. My mom is dealing with some serious mental health struggles and needs me, whether she can admit it or not. I need to focus on hockey. After my ex, Erin, and I broke up when we were nineteen, I don't do commitments. This dog is a major commitment, and I would need to work my demanding schedule around her.

And yet, hesitation rises in me. I study the building, looking for flaws. There are a few weeds in the garden. The outside trim needs new paint. In the field, there are a couple holes that dogs have probably dug. I can't handle a dog, but I can't leave her here.

This place isn't good enough for her.

I rub the bridge of my nose, knowing my mind is already made up. Fuck.

"Hey."

Her head pops up and she looks up at me, bright-eyed. My heart tugs.

"You want to live with me?" I ask her, and she continues to stare at me with that cute look. "Oh. You want a treat."

She wiggles up and jumps off my lap into the passenger seat, waiting. I reach over to the back seat and open the bag of treats I bought for her, giving her a few, watching as she crunches them up.

My mind is made up, and I ignore the little voice in my head telling me this isn't a good idea. I watch as the dog curls into a ball in the passenger seat and goes to sleep. I have the money to bring an assistant on this year, and the dog will be well cared for.

On my phone, I scroll through my contacts until I find who I'm looking for.

"Streicher," Ward answers.

"Hi." I rub my jaw as that bad feeling snakes through my gut again. "I changed my mind. I'm going to need an assistant."

# CHAPTER 2
## PIPPA

MY HEART HAMMERS while I stand outside Jamie Streicher's apartment building.

The last time I saw him in person, I had just spilled a blue Slurpee all over my white t-shirt in the high school cafeteria. His cold look of disinterest replays in my head, his green eyes flicking over me before turning back to his conversation with the rest of the hot, popular jocks.

Now I'm going to be his assistant.

He was always an asshole, but god, he was so gorgeous, even then. Thick dark hair, always just a little messy from playing hockey. Sharp jawline, strong nose. Broad, strong shoulders, and tall. *So tall.* Unfairly dark lashes. He never hit that awkward teenager phase that seemed to span my entire teens. His silent, intimidating, grumpy thing both unnerved and fascinated me, along with every other girl and half the guys in school.

Oh god. I drag in a deep breath and enter the number on the keypad outside. He buzzes me up without answering. In the elevator, my stomach wobbles on the way to the penthouse.

I'm not that dorky band girl anymore. I'm a grown woman.

It's been eight years. I don't have a teenage crush on the guy anymore.

I need this job. I'm broke and crashing on my sister's couch. I quit my terrible job at Barry's Hot Dog Hut with zero notice after a week. Even if I wanted to go back—which I don't, I only took that job as an emergency way to pay bills and help Hazel out with rent—they'd never rehire me.

Besides, there's no way he remembers me. Our high school was huge. I was the dorky music girl, always hanging with the band kids, and he was a hot hockey player. I'm two years younger, so we didn't even have classes together or friends in common. He's one of the best goalies in the NHL, with the looks of a freaking god. The fact that he's known for not doing relationships seems to make people even more feral. Last year, someone threw panties on the ice for him—it was all over the sports highlights.

He isn't going to remember me.

I watch the number climb higher as I approach his floor.

He'll be busy with practices and training. I won't see him.

And I really, really need this job. I'm done with the music industry and its famous assholes. I went to school for marketing, and it's time to pursue that path. The only Vancouver job postings in marketing require at least five years' experience, so I wouldn't even be considered. According to my sister Hazel, who works as a physiotherapist for the Vancouver Storm, a marketing job with the team is opening up soon. They prefer internal hires, she said.

This assistant job is my way in. It's temporary. If I prove myself in that job, that's my foot in the door to the marketing job with the team.

The elevator opens on the top floor, and I walk to his door, taking a deep, calming breath. It doesn't work, and my heart pounds against the front wall of my chest.

Need this job, I remind myself.

I knock, the door swings open, and my pulse stumbles like it's drunk on cheap cider.

He's so much hotter grown up. And in person? It's actually unfair.

His frame fills the doorway. He's a foot taller than me, and even under his long-sleeved workout shirt, his body is perfection. The thin fabric stretches over his broad shoulders. I'm vaguely aware of a dog barking and racing around the apartment behind him, but my gaze follows his movement as he props a hand on the doorframe. His sleeves are pushed up, and my gaze lingers on his forearm.

Jamie Streicher's forearms could get a woman pregnant.

I'm staring. I jerk my gaze up to his face.

Ugh. My stomach sinks. That teen crush I had years ago bursts back into my life like a comet, thrilling through me. His eyes are still the deepest, richest green, like all the shades of an old-growth forest. My stomach tumbles.

"Hi," I breathe before clearing my throat. My face burns. "Hi." My voice is stronger this time, and I fake a bright smile. "I'm Pippa, your new assistant." I smooth a hand over my ponytail.

There's a beat where his features are blank before his eyes sharpen and his expression slides to a glower.

My thoughts scatter in the air like confetti. Words? I don't know them. Couldn't even tell you one. His hair is thick, short, and curling a little. Damp, like he just got out of the shower, and I want to run my fingers through it.

His gaze lingers on me, turning more hostile by the second, before he sighs like I'm inconveniencing him. This is how he seemed in high school—surly, irritated, grouchy. Not that we ever interacted.

"Great." He says the word like a curse, like I'm the last person he wants to see. He turns and walks into the apartment.

I knew he wouldn't remember me.

I hold back a humorless laugh of embarrassment and disbelief. I don't know why I'm surprised by his attitude. If I've learned one thing from my ex, Zach, and his crew, it's that gorgeous, famous people are allowed to be complete assholes. The world lets them get away with it.

Jamie Streicher is no different.

I take the open door as a sign to follow him. The dog sprints to my feet and jumps on me. She's wearing a pink collar, and I love her immediately.

"Down," he commands in a stern voice that makes the back of my neck prickle. The dog ignores him, hopping onto my legs and wagging her tail hard.

"Hi, doggy." I crouch down and laugh as she tries to give me kisses.

She's full of goofy, wild energy, doing these little tippy-taps with her paws on the floor as her tail wags so hard it might fall off. Her butt wiggles in the cutest way as I scratch the spot above her tail.

I'm in love.

Jamie clears his throat with disapproval. Embarrassment flickers in my chest but I shove it away. I'm here to help him with his dog; what's his problem? When I straighten up, my face feels warm.

Also, his apartment? It's one of the nicest places I've ever been inside. It's one of the nicest places I've ever *seen*. Floor-to-ceiling windows span two stories and overlook the water and North Shore Mountains, filling the open-concept living room and kitchen with light. The kitchen is sparkling and spacious, and even though the living room is cluttered with moving boxes and dog toys, the enormous sectional sofa looks so comfy and welcoming. There are stairs, which I assume lead to the bedrooms. Through the windows, I can see North Vancouver and the mountains. Even on a stormy day in the worst of the rainy, bleak Vancouver winter, the view will be spectacular.

I bet this place has a huge bathtub.

"What's her name?" I ask Jamie as I pet the dog. She's leaning against me, clearly loving all this attention.

His jaw ticks and the way he stares at me makes my stomach dip. His green eyes are so sharp and piercing, and I wonder if this guy has ever smiled. "I don't know."

On the floor near the couch, there's a giant fluffy dog bed, and about a hundred colorful toys are scattered throughout the living room. A water bowl and empty food bowl sit on the floor in the kitchen, and on the counter, there's a giant bag of treats, half-empty. The dog runs over to one of the toys before bringing it to Jamie's feet and looking up at him, wagging her tail.

"I have to go to the arena, so let's get this over with," Jamie says, like I'm wasting his time. He stalks past me, and as he passes, his scent whooshes up my nose.

My eyes practically cross. He smells incredible. It's that un-pin-downable scent of men's deodorant—sharp, spicy, bold, fresh, and clean, all at the same time. The scent is probably called Avalanche or Hurricane or something powerful and unstoppable. I want to put my face in his shirt and huff. I'd probably pass out.

As he moves around the kitchen, showing me where the dog's food is, I'm struck by the way he moves with power and grace. His back muscles ripple under his shirt. His shoulders are so broad. He's so, so freaking tall.

I realize he still hasn't even introduced himself. This is something famous people did on Zach's tour when they came backstage, like they expect you to know who they are.

"All our communication will be through email or text," Jamie says. "Walk the dog, feed the dog, keep her out of trouble. I've already taken her to the vet and for grooming." He glances at her again.

I offer him a reassuring smile. "I can handle all of that."

"Good." His tone is sharp.

Wow. Mr. Personality, right here. I swallow with difficulty. He's so bossy. A shiver rolls over me, and my skin tingles. I bet he's bossy in bed, too.

"Because it's your job," he adds.

A sick feeling moves up my throat but I shove it down. I'm not sixteen anymore. I know better, and I know his type. After Zach, I know not to fall for guys like this—famous guys. Guys with an ego. Guys who think they can do whatever they want without consequences.

Guys who will just get tired of me and cast me aside.

"On game days, I have a nap after lunch," he says over his shoulder as I follow him upstairs. "I need total silence."

It takes all of my willpower not to salute him and say, *sir, yes, sir!* Something tells me he wouldn't laugh. "I'll take her out on a long walk during that time."

He grunts. That's probably his version of crying tears of joy.

In the upstairs hallway, he stops at an open doorway. The room is empty except for a handful of large boxes and a mattress wrapped in plastic.

"This will be my room?" I ask.

He frowns, and my stomach squirms.

"I mean, this will be the room where I sleep when you're away?" I clarify so he doesn't think I'm trying to move in full time or something. "When I'm taking care of the dog."

He folds his arms. "Yes."

The way he stares at me, it's making my stomach do tippy-taps like the dog's paws on the floor. My nervous reaction is to smile again, and his frown lines deepen.

"Great." My voice is practically a chirp.

He tilts his chin to the bathroom down the hall. "You can use that bathroom. I have my own en suite."

His eyes linger on me, and I try not to shift under the weight of his gaze. This guy does *not* like me, but I'm going to turn that around once he realizes how much easier I can make his life. Besides, he'll never even see me.

Losing this job is not an option.

# CHAPTER 3
## JAMIE

PIPPA HARTLEY IS STANDING in my living room, playing with the dog, and I can't breathe. When I opened the door, I thought I was hallucinating.

Her hair is longer. Same shy smile, same sparkling blue-gray eyes that make me forget my own name. Same soft, musical voice that I'd strain to hear back in high school while she was talking and laughing with the other band kids.

Grown up, though, she's fucking gorgeous. A knockout. Freckles over her nose and cheekbones from the summer sun and strands of gold in her caramel hair that's neither brown nor blond. Although her braces were cute back in high school, her smile today nearly stopped my heart.

*I'm Pippa,* she said at the door, like she didn't remember me. I don't know why that made me so disappointed.

"Do you want me to help you unpack?" she asks, playing tug-of-war with the dog. "Or I can get groceries or meal prep for you."

I watch the pretty curve of her mouth as she speaks. Her lips are soft-looking, the perfect shade of pink. They always have been.

Fuck.

"No." The word comes out harsher than I mean, but I'm rattled.

I can't fucking think around Pippa Hartley. It's always been like this.

In an instant, my mind is back in that hallway outside the school music room, listening as she sang. She had the most beautiful, captivating, spellbinding voice I'd ever heard—sweet, but when she hit certain notes, raspy. Strong, but at certain parts, soft. Always controlled. Pippa knew exactly how to use her voice. She never sang in public, though. It was always that fucking Zach guy singing, and she'd play guitar as his backup.

I wonder if she still sings.

I wonder if she's still with him, and my nostrils flare. Over the summer, I saw his stupid, punchable face on a billboard and nearly drove off the highway. *That* guy is the opener on a tour? He could barely play the guitar. His voice was average.

Not like Pippa. *She's* talented.

Eight years later, I still think about that moment in the hallway all the time. I don't know why—it doesn't matter.

The dog shakes the toy while Pippa holds on, and she laughs.

I need to get out of here.

"I have to go to practice." I snatch my keys off the counter and haul my bag over my shoulder.

"Bye," she calls as I step through the door.

———

After practice that afternoon, I'm about to open the front door when a noise in my apartment stops me with my hand on the door handle.

Singing. Fleetwood Mac plays inside my apartment. Over the tune, her voice rings out, clear, bright, and melodic. She hits all the notes, but there's something special to the way she sings it. Something uniquely Pippa.

I can't move. If I go inside, she'll stop singing.

Alarm rattles through me, because this is exactly what I shouldn't be doing. She was supposed to leave before I got home.

I can't have Pippa around this year. It's only been a few hours, and she's already gotten inside my head.

When I open the door, my new assistant is unpacking the kitchen boxes, reaching up to set a glass on the shelf, leaning forward on the counter, giving me a clear view of her incredible ass.

Irritation tightens in my chest. This is the last thing I need.

My gaze sweeps around the apartment. Most of the boxes are unpacked. She's set up my living room, and the photo of my mom and me sits on the bookshelf. She's arranged the living room furniture differently than my apartment back in New York. The Eames chair faces the windows, overlooking the city lights in North Vancouver, across the water. The dog is sleeping on the couch, curled up in a ball.

I fold my arms over my chest, feeling a mix of relief and confusion. The apartment looks nice. It feels like a home. I was dreading unpacking, but now it's almost done.

I don't even mind that the dog is on the furniture.

Her singing stops and she glances over her shoulder. "Oh, hi." She gasps and looks at her phone on the counter before her eyes dart to mine. "Sorry. I didn't realize what time it was." She dusts her hands off and walks to the door. "How was practice?" she asks while pulling her sneakers on.

The sweet, curious way she asks makes my chest feel funny. Warm and liquid. I don't like it. I have the weird urge to tell her how nervous I am about this season.

"Fine," I say instead, and her eyes widen at my sharp tone.

Fuck. See? This is why this isn't going to work. I care too much about what she thinks.

"Daisy and I went for a two-hour walk around Stanley Park, and then I spent most of the evening training her to do tricks."

My eyebrows pull together. "Daisy?"

She shrugs, smiling over at the dog on the couch. "She needs a name." She picks her bag up. "I took her out an hour ago, so you don't need to."

I try to say something like *thanks,* but it's just a low noise of acknowledgment in my throat.

She smooths a delicate hand over her ponytail, blinks twice, and gives me that bright smile from before, the one I thought about during my entire practice.

Her cheeks are going pink and she looks embarrassed. "I'll get out of your hair." She loops the strap of her bag over her shoulder and gives me another quick, shy smile. "I'll be here tomorrow morning after you leave for practice. Good night, Jamie."

My gaze drops to her pretty lips, and I'm tongue-tied. She probably thinks I've been hit in the head with the puck too many times.

She leaves and I stand there, staring at the door.

Maybe I don't have to—

I crush the thought, like slapping a mosquito off my arm. Pippa has to go. I know from my mom and from the one relationship I attempted in my first year in the NHL that if there are too many balls in the air, I'm going to drop one. I always do.

The second she leaves, I pull my phone out and call Ward.

"Streicher," he answers.

"Coach." I rake my hand through my hair. "I need a new assistant."

# CHAPTER 4

"YOU'RE LETTING ME GO?" I repeat into my phone the next morning, blinking at nothing. I'm at Hazel's front door, putting my shoes on to leave for Jamie's place. My mind reels, and my forehead wrinkles in confusion. "I don't understand."

The woman in the team's office sighs. "Don't take it personally. These guys can be so particular."

My stomach sinks. Fired after one day. This isn't going to look good when I apply for the marketing job with the team.

I really thought I killed it yesterday. I unpacked most of his things, and Daisy was nice and tired by the time he got home. It was actually fun, walking her and playing music in the apartment while she followed me around.

Panic starts to bleed through my thoughts. Shit. I need money *now*. I need to move out of Hazel's tiny studio. I can't go back to the Hot Dog Hut—I gag at just the memory of the creepy way the owner looked at me. Not to mention the way I smelled after my shifts.

Fired. My parents are going to flip out. After wasting my life following Zach around on tour for two years, they desperately want me to have a career in marketing—what I went to school for. They're obsessed with me having a stable, consistent job. A desk job. Something with benefits. Something *not* in the music industry. They worked really hard to pay for my education. My parents aren't rich or anything, and they sacrificed a lot for me and Hazel to have what they didn't.

I want them to be proud of me.

I thank the woman, hang up, and stare at the floor. Reality hits me, and my shoulders sink. This sucks.

Beside me, the door opens and slams into me. I scramble to move out of the way, but trip over one of my moving boxes, landing flat on my ass.

"Sorry!" Hazel's eyes are wide as she helps me up. "Are you okay?"

I rub my arm, wincing. "I'm fine. I shouldn't have been standing in front of the door."

Her apartment is a tiny studio because Vancouver is expensive as hell. Hence why I need this job if I'm going to move out.

"How'd it go yesterday?" She heads to the corner with the kitchen and pulls out smoothie ingredients.

When I got home last night, she was teaching a yoga class. Outside of working as a physio for the team, teaching yoga is Hazel's true passion. She had an early morning class today before work.

I fill her in on the disappointing news I just received, and her jaw drops. "And they didn't even say why?"

"Nope." A prickle of rage pokes me between my ribs, and my stomach tenses. "He was a real dick, though. Barely said two words to me the whole time. He just did this smoldery, glowering thing with his eyes." I narrow my eyes and grunt.

Hazel raises a dark eyebrow. Her hair is darker than mine, a chocolate brown against my dishwater blond. "Do you think he remembers you?"

"No. Not at all." I slip my shoes off and set them in the front hall closet. "He didn't even introduce himself."

She makes a face from the kitchen area. "Rude."

"Right?" I shake my head as I flop back down onto the couch. "So rude. Like, I know he's a hot, rich celebrity, but I'm still a person, you know?"

"Totally." Hazel's nodding vehemently, ponytail bouncing. "You're a person. You deserve respect."

"Respect?" I sputter. "He doesn't know that word. He treated me like I was a flea who belongs in the garbage."

Hazel bares her teeth. "I hate him. Hockey players." Her eyes narrow. "They're the worst."

Hazel dated a hockey player in university, but he cheated on her. It was a whole thing. I don't bring it up.

"The worst," I echo, folding my arms over my chest. My foot taps a staccato rhythm on the floor, and knots form in my stomach. I did great yesterday, and I'm perfect for this job.

After Zach, my confidence took a hit, but now this? Way to kick a girl when she's down.

My mind flashes back to a month ago, in the airport, waiting for my flight home. The tour manager had arranged my Uber, which I thought would take me to the meeting spot for the tour bus so we could all travel to the next location. Instead, it went to the airport, and when I started phoning people in confusion, no one answered.

Finally, Zach called me back.

"Ah, shit," he said. "Did she already send you to the airport? I was going to talk to you first."

He dumped me over the phone. He said we were different people now, that we weren't teenagers anymore, and that he wanted to see who he was apart from me. We dated for eight years, since grade ten, and he had his employee send me away.

When he was offered the tour in our last year of university, he arranged for me to work on it, assisting the tour coordinator so we didn't have to do long distance. When he was stuck on a song, we worked through it, me on my guitar, helping him with lyrics. I put my whole life on hold to follow him around while he lived out his dreams.

My face burns, thinking about how I cried in the airport bathroom, feeling so lost and alone. So unwanted, like a bag of trash on the side of the road.

Guys like Zach and Jamie? They think the world revolves around them. They think they can dispose of people after they lose interest. Shame surges in my stomach, followed immediately by fury.

I'm so sick of being that girl, the one who gets disposed of.

I sit up straight, feeling fired up. "I'm going to confront him."

"Um." Hazel's eyes go wide, hands paused on the blender. "I don't think that's a good idea."

My pulse races at the idea of telling off Jamie Streicher. I'm sick of getting stepped on by men.

"You're always saying that I need to tell the universe what I want," I tell Hazel.

"Yeah, the *universe*. Not him. He'll probably call the police."

"He won't call the police." I picture him physically removing me from his home, throwing me over his shoulder. A weird twinge hits me between the legs. Oh. I like that idea.

Whatever. Not the point. He's king of the assholes, but I need this job.

Hazel barks a laugh. "This is how you end up on the front page of the newspaper. *Local Hockey Star Accosted by Insane Stalker.*"

"I'm not going to stalk him. I'm going to get my job back."

Maybe she's right and going in with guns blazing isn't the best approach. She turns back to the counter to make her smoothie, and when she opens the cupboard, I spot the muffin tin I used last week.

An idea hits me. Hazel's right—if I show up and demand my job back, he'll think I'm a psycho.

If I show up with *cupcakes*, though, I'll just be reinforcing what a great assistant I'd be. No one calls the police on someone who brings cupcakes.

When I tell Hazel my plan, she laughs. "I'll keep my phone on in case I need to bail you out."

Two hours later, the cupcakes are cooled and decorated. On the outside, they're perfectly iced, topped with fun, colorful sprinkles. These cupcakes are filled with my rage, though. I really beat the shit out of the batter while I made them, pouring all my frustration from Zach and Jamie and my crappy life situation into it.

From the schedule Jamie gave me, I know he'll be home in ten minutes, so I pack the cupcakes into a container and get ready to leave.

Hazel grins at me as I slip my shoes on. "Go get 'em, tiger."

On the walk to Jamie's apartment, it starts to rain. I forgot that Vancouver's weather can turn on a dime, so I'm not wearing my coat with the hood. At a stoplight, I chew my lip, wondering if I should turn back and get my other jacket.

No. I can already feel the hesitation wavering in my stomach. If I turn back, I won't go through with this.

I *need* that job. I need the money. I need to give Hazel space at the apartment, and I need an in with the team so I can get the marketing job and move on with my life. This is happening.

I'm getting my job back.

I'M TRYING TO NAP, but I can't stop thinking about my pretty assistant.

*Ex*-assistant.

Fuck. I stare out the windows of my bedroom, where it's pouring rain to match my mood. I've been thinking about her all day. Why do I care? She'll get snapped up by someone else in a heartbeat.

An ugly feeling spikes in my chest. I hate the idea of her setting up some other guy's apartment, smiling for him and singing in his kitchen.

There's a knock at my front door, and I frown. I wasn't expecting anyone. When I reach the door, Daisy is already there, sniffing under it and wagging her tail.

I open it and freeze.

Mascara runs down Pippa's face. She's been crying? Pain shocks my chest, but her eyes are clear and her hair is soaked, bangs sticking to her forehead, and my chest muscles ease. At the sight of me, she straightens up, nostrils flaring. In the back of my mind, I notice how cute that is.

"Hi," she says, and the long column of her throat works. She blinks.

She's nervous. She's holding a plastic container. There are cupcakes inside.

I frown again. "How'd you get upstairs?" She needs a key or to be buzzed in.

She waves me off. "The guys from yesterday remembered me, and I gave them cupcakes."

Of course they let her up. This woman could talk a cop into handing over his gun. All she'd have to do is smile and flick her ponytail, and he'd be like, *you want the bullets, too?* There's a weird, funny pressure in my chest, and for the first time in so long, I feel the urge to smile.

She shoves the container into my hands. "These are for you."

I raise my eyebrows, staring at them through the clear plastic lid. "I haven't had a cupcake in over a decade."

Her eyes bug out. "What? That's so sad." She catches her reflection in the mirror behind me, which she must have hung yesterday. "Oh my god." She wipes a finger under her eye to clean up the makeup. "Is this what I look like? Jesus."

She *does* know that I fired her, right?

She turns back to me and takes a deep breath. "I did a good job yesterday."

I hesitate. She's not wrong.

"No." Her cheeks are flushed. "A great job. I can handle everything you throw at me, no problem. And you didn't even introduce yourself." Her mouth tightens. "Who do you think you are, Ryan Gosling? You can just fire me like a dickhead?"

I know Ryan Gosling. I met him at some NHL party last year that the team had to go to. He's a nice guy. Way nicer than me.

Is that her type? My jaw tenses. I don't like that idea.

"Dickhead," I repeat.

"Sorry." She winces. "I'm a person, you know. I deserve to be treated with respect."

Her eyebrows pinch together and she blinks rapidly, looking like a kicked puppy. Oh, fuck. My heart sinks. I hate this feeling. I hate her feeling like this, and I especially hate knowing that I did that.

She's right. I was an asshole yesterday. I didn't mean to be, though. I don't know how to be normal around her. She showed up looking like a Disney princess, and I could barely say two words to her.

She points at Daisy, who's waiting by her feet, gazing up at Pippa with adoration. "I get along great with Daisy. I'm sorry I was still here last night. I lost track of time, and it won't happen again. I promise you'll never have to see me." Her voice wavers. "I'll do whatever it takes to get my job back."

The air thickens with tension, and we both stare at each other. Is she...? In my head, images appear of us tangled up in bed. She's beneath me, head tipped back, eyes closed, with an expression of pleasure on her face as I thrust into her.

I'm going to be thinking about that later with my hand around my cock, and I hate myself for that.

"That's not what I meant," she says quickly, cheeks flushing a deeper shade of pink. "I said that weird. I just mean, I really need this job, so whatever I did that made you think I'm not a good fit, please let me know."

There's no way I can tell her the truth—that she's the girl I was obsessed with for two years in high school. And everything she said? She's right. I like the way she set up my apartment. She tired Daisy out yesterday more than I could have. I can already tell this dog needs a ton of mental stimulation as well as physical exercise. Deep down, I trust her with this dog.

I should let the team find me another assistant. Pippa's problems are not my problems. I have enough on my plate.

Just like at the shelter with Daisy, I ignore that hesitation. The way Pippa's looking at me now, with a mix of determination and worry, her head held high like that? It gets me right in the middle of my chest.

I stare at her, studying her face. Even though she looks like a drowned rat, her eyes still sparkle. Her cheeks are flushed, so full of life and vibrancy, and my chest feels weird, like I have heartburn.

I raise an eyebrow at her. "You call me a dickhead, and then you ask for your job back?"

She shifts, wincing. "Yes, I did." She flattens her lips, looking up at me with a guilty expression, and the determination in her eyes plucks at a muscle in my chest. "Sorry."

I like this girl. She's scrappy. It took a lot of guts for her to show up and call me a dickhead. No one talks to me like that.

I can't screw her over like this. I'll find a way to focus this year. I always do. I've had years to practice discipline. This year, I'll just have to practice harder.

I can't fire her, but I can keep her at arm's length.

I fold my arms over my chest, shifting on my feet against the doorframe. The back of my neck feels warm. "Okay."

She lights up, and for a moment, I'm terrified she's going to throw her arms around my neck. "Really?"

Terrified or excited. I don't know.

"Don't keep anything here," I add quickly.

She claps, and that riles Daisy up. She starts zooming around the apartment. Pippa beams at me, smile stretching wide across her face, and I feel like I'm about to be sick.

"Thank you." She clutches her hands together. "I promise, I'll be great."

That's not the problem.

"I have training," I tell her. It's not for an hour, but I'm not going to sit around the apartment, staring at her.

She's already taking her jacket off. "No problem. I've got everything under control here. Need any groceries?"

I pull on my shoes and hesitate. I do need groceries.

At whatever my expression is, she nods. "I can get them. What do you like to eat?"

"Uh." The dietician for the team has detailed meal plans for every player, but I don't want to rely on Pippa more than I need to. "I don't know. Stuff."

She nods, smiling. "Great. I can totally get that."

I pull the door open. I need to get out of here.

"Wait," she says, handing me the cupcakes. "Take these with you. You can give them to the team or whatever."

I give her a strange look. If I show up with cupcakes, I'll never hear the end of it. Nevertheless, I take them. I can't see that look of disappointment on her face again.

On the street outside, I open the container and shove one into my mouth. My eyes roll back in my head as the sugar hits my tongue, and I nearly moan in ecstasy.

It's the best fucking thing I've ever tasted.

# CHAPTER 6

"I CAN'T BELIEVE the cupcakes worked," Hazel says as we walk along the mountain path.

It's been two weeks since I confronted Jamie, but between me taking care of Daisy and Hazel's physio job and yoga classes, we've hardly seen each other. Today is our first chance to catch up.

Daisy sniffs something in the bushes before bounding ahead. We spent the morning doing recall training until Hazel and I felt confident letting her off the leash on a leash-optional trail in North Vancouver. As we ascended the trail into the mountains, the temperature dropped, but the sun is out, the forest is serene and peaceful, we have warm jackets on, and Daisy's having the time of her life.

I think back to when I confronted Jamie. He looked like he was going to throw me out, or worse, call the team and ruin my chances for a future job.

But he didn't. When I said *I deserve to be treated with respect*, he almost looked... remorseful.

"I don't think it was the cupcakes," I muse.

I haven't seen him since he left for practice that day because he's been busy with training, and since the season started a few days ago, he's been traveling. His apartment is like something out of a design magazine, and sometimes, as I gaze out the windows at the mountains, it feels like I'm staying in a vacation home, totally separate from my real life. The apartment is always filled with light, so this week, I bought a few plants to make it feel more personal.

The apartment is gorgeous, and yet it's kind of lonely, just me and Daisy. I've never lived alone. In university, I always had at least four roommates, and then on Zach's tours, there were always people around. There was always someone to chat and laugh with.

I need to make more friends in Vancouver. All my friends are in the music industry.

My stomach sinks. I need to make new friends because I'm done with music.

Something I said to Jamie has replayed in my head constantly since that conversation with him. *I'll do whatever it takes.*

I cringe. "I accidentally insinuated I would sleep with him to keep my job." Hazel squawks with laughter, and I groan. "I clarified right away. But still. Awkward."

"Has he figured out you went to the same high school yet?" Hazel's one year older than me, one year younger than him.

"Definitely not. Have you worked with him yet?"

"Nope." She slides a glance to me. "Are you going to bring it up?"

"Hell, no. How awkward would that be? He'll want to know why I didn't say anything the first time I met him."

"Well, it won't matter soon enough. Emma set a mat-leave date, so they're putting the paperwork together for the internal job posting."

Right, the marketing job. My stomach twinges with nerves and I nod eagerly. It feels a bit forced. "Great."

"They'll probably start interviewing in December or the new year."

"That's good. That gives me enough time with the team to prove myself."

"Yep." Hazel raises her eyebrow. "And then we can both work stable, responsible jobs for the rest of our lives, forever and ever." Her voice takes on an airy, sarcastic tone.

I give her a flat look. Hazel's dream is to open her own yoga and physio studio, a place where people of all body types and sizes feel comfortable, but our parents would choke if they heard that.

Risky, they'd say.

I stare at my shoes as we walk. "I mean, they're not wrong. Having a stable job does make life easier."

She breathes out something that sounds like *fuck.* "Yeah, but they're, like, *obsessed* with it."

"They want the best for us."

Our parents didn't grow up *poor,* but they were both from low-income families. Our dad was a mechanic, and our mom was a ballet dancer until she didn't make it into a ballet company. Then she started her own dance studio. She taught ballet until they retired to a small town in the interior of British Columbia a few years ago. Although she was an amazing teacher, I think it served as a reminder of what she hadn't accomplished. Growing up, when I'd make comments about pursuing music, she'd use herself as an example of why I shouldn't.

*Failure is really hard,* she always says. *Set yourself up for success instead.*

They want us to live comfortable, happy lives, and to my dad, that means having a job with a biweekly paycheck and benefits. To my mom, that means something that won't be too disappointing if it doesn't go well. Like Hazel's physio job. Like this marketing gig.

*Not* anything in the music industry. That's why I studied marketing in university with a music minor. I wanted to major in music, but they talked me out of it.

They were right, it turned out. The music industry is brutal. I remember playing a song I wrote for Zach, and how he and his manager laughed after. Zach said it was *cute*.

My stomach clenches with shame. I think about that moment and my heart hurts. I'm not tough enough to withstand that.

Hazel turns to me. "Does Dad keep asking you about Streicher?"

On top of our parents wanting us to have solid jobs, our dad *loves* hockey, and he's a lifelong Vancouver Storm fan. He's thrilled that we both now work for the team. When he found out a guy from our high school was traded to Vancouver, he lost his mind with excitement.

I groan. "Yes."

We laugh, and Daisy sprints ahead to greet a yellow Lab coming down the path.

"She's such a good dog," Hazel says, linking her arm through mine.

I smile at Daisy. "Yeah, she is. I love that part of my job."

We walk, watching the dogs, saying hello to the owners as we pass them, and enjoying the time in the forest. A river flows through the trees, rushing over the rocks. There are clearings along the path with shoreline, and Daisy darts in and out of the water before returning to the path.

"You haven't touched your guitar since you got home."

My throat constricts, and I swallow with difficulty. "I've been busy."

That's a lie, and she knows it. My entire life, songs would

float into my head. Zach and I would hang out, and I'd goof around on the guitar, and when I hit a certain combo of chords, the song would show up in my head. It was like opening a door. Like, oh, there you are.

Since Zach dumped me, nothing. Dead silence.

Our boots crunch along the path and I picture my guitar sitting alone in Hazel's apartment, waiting for me. A weird guilt moves through me, like I'm neglecting it. I bought that guitar back in high school. It's not the nicest or most expensive guitar—far from it—but I love it, nonetheless.

And now I'm avoiding it.

Every time I think about playing my guitar, I think about Zach arranging to have me sent to the airport. I think about all the times I played guitar while Zach and I worked on lyrics. I think about him laughing at the song I wrote.

Hazel's mouth twists to the side, a pinch forming between her eyebrows. "Does this have anything to do with Herpes?"

I choke out a laugh. That's what she calls Zach. "We can't call him that."

"I tell everyone I know that he has it."

My chest shakes with laughter. "Herpes is forever."

She narrows her eyes and taps her lip. "Right, and Zach is long gone. Let's call him Chlamydia instead." Her expression sobers. "So, does it have anything to do with him?"

I lean down to give Daisy a scratch as she trots beside me. "Probably."

Hazel's quiet, and there are probably a hundred things she wants to say. She never liked Zach, even back in high school.

"I wish you knew you were the fucking best." She says it quietly. A muscle in her jaw ticks. "I wish you knew how talented you are. You'd be unstoppable."

When she uses that quiet, serious voice, it makes me feel

like crying, and I don't know why. We walk in silence with only the sound of the river rushing beside the path.

"Well," she shrugs, "you'll just have to meditate him out of your head."

"Herpes," I say in a commercial voice, like I'm selling spa packages. "Meditate it away!"

"Chlamydia," she corrects, and we laugh. "Seriously. Meditate that guy the fuck out of your mind."

Her brash, no-bullshit approach to wellness has me smiling.

She chuckles. "And if meditation doesn't work, you need to get laid."

My face heats.

"The best way to get over someone is to get laid. Especially —" she puts extra emphasis on the word, turning to me and staring hard "—when you've only slept with one guy in your entire life."

I squirm, tucking my hands in my jacket pockets. Yep. It's true. I lost my virginity to Zach and haven't hooked up with anyone else.

Another flicker of shame burns in my stomach. That was probably part of the reason he wanted to move on, because I can't—

I can't, uh, get there. I can't have an orgasm with a guy. I admitted once to Hazel that every time Zach and I slept together, I faked it. I did it once, and he was so happy and relieved. I think he thought it was his fault that I couldn't get there. And then I just kept faking it. I kept telling myself, *this will be the last time*, because it's lying. But in the end, I wasn't hurting anyone, so I kept doing it. If I couldn't come, it stressed him out, which stressed me out. It was just easier to fake it.

The idea of sleeping with someone new is daunting. I've never gone on a formal date, and I've never been on a dating app. Zach and I had been friends since grade eight band class and we got closer and closer. Until one day near the end of grade ten, he held my hand and I let him. Then he started calling me his girlfriend. Everyone around us acted like it was no surprise, so I didn't make a big deal of it.

Over the years, I just got swept away in his current, I guess. I frown, not sure how I feel about that. I can't imagine being as familiar with someone else as I was with Zach.

Especially with my little *issue*. I'll have to fake it all over again for someone new.

Hazel gives me a flat look, like my worries are written all over my face. "What?"

"I can't—" I wave my hand around in the air. "You know."

She snorts and copies my gesture, overexaggerated. I let out a nervous laugh.

"Orgasm?" she prompts.

I make a strangled noise. "Yes. It's just my body. And now I have to tell a whole new person about it?"

She sighs, her head falling back. "It's not your body. Your coochie knew Zach was a colossal loser."

"Stop talking about my coochie."

"Your coochie wants action!" she shouts at the forest, and I sputter with laughter, trying to cover her mouth. "Give your coochie what she wants!"

A couple passes us and we smile at them. My face is bright red. When they're gone, we dissolve into giggles again.

Hazel throws a stick for Daisy, and Daisy takes off after it. For the rest of the walk, Hazel tells me about her snooty coworkers at the yoga studio, and by the time we return to her car, my face hurts from laughing. Daisy's coated in a layer of mud from running through puddles, but she has that exhausted, happy dog look on her little face.

"Come on," I say to her, gesturing to the towel-covered back seat. "Jump up."

She stares at me before she launches into a full-body shake, tossing mud and dirty puddle water all over me. I throw my hands up, but it's too late.

On the other side of the car, Hazel's laughing her ass off. She takes a photo of me and smiles at the result.

I give her a strained smile. "The mud is in my hair, isn't it?"

"Yep." She grins.

———

An hour later, Daisy's clean and curled up on the couch in the living room while I'm in the shower, washing the dirt out of my hair. Jamie won't be home until later this afternoon, so I'm singing a Coldplay song. I sing it the way I would have recorded it, soft in some parts and raw in others.

The bathroom acoustics are amazing, and there's something about the hot water running down my skin and the smell of my conditioner that makes me feel like this is my own little world, all by myself, where no one can touch me.

I finish the song, turn off the water, and towel-dry my hair before I wrap it around me and step out of the bathroom to check on Daisy.

Jamie Streicher is standing in his living room, staring at me in my towel.

## MY BRAIN ISN'T WORKING.

That's the only explanation for why I'm just standing here, staring at an almost-naked Pippa in a tiny towel. Her wet hair cascades around her shoulders, and above the towel she clutches to her chest, my gaze snags on her cleavage. Freckles dot across her collarbone, just like on her face.

She was singing in the shower, and it was the sweetest sound I'd ever heard. I couldn't move.

Something rushes in my blood—arousal. Attraction. Sparks skitter down my spine as I take in her legs. Her skin looks so soft.

Whether I want to be or not, I'm still so attracted to this girl.

Her face is going bright red. Her toenails are painted mint green. Why is that so fucking cute? I stare at her bottom lip. Was it always so plush like that? Blood hurries to my cock, and I turn around.

"What are you doing?" I demand. It comes out harsher than I mean.

"Daisy got mud all over me, and I didn't realize you'd be home so early—"

"It's fine." She wasn't supposed to be here when I got home. This can only work if I never see her.

Who the fuck am I fooling? It isn't working. I've been thinking about her for two weeks, wondering what she and Daisy were doing. She's been sending me daily emails with updates, and even though I never respond, I look forward to them. I wait for them, refreshing my email while I'm sitting on a plane or between training sessions.

I thought if I didn't see her, she couldn't distract me. I was so wrong. I make a frustrated noise in my throat and head to the door.

"I can be out of here right away," she calls after me.

"I'll be back at four." That's the time I was scheduled to be home, but one of my trainers had to reschedule. I yank my boots on and don't look back.

In the elevator, I close my eyes and blow out a long breath in a pathetic attempt to center myself. My phone buzzes in my back pocket, and when I pull it out, I see a photo of me and my mom flashing across the screen with her incoming call.

It's the reminder I need. I can barely handle hockey plus taking care of my mom, let alone losing my head over some girl. It's not worth it.

"Hey, Mom," I answer.

# CHAPTER 8

JAMIE LEAVES and I stare at the door, stunned.

He's *such* a dick. He's the one who was home early. I was just following the schedule he gave me.

I head up to the room where I stay when he's away so I can get changed and get out of here. I don't even bother blow-drying my hair. I just throw my clothes on, head downstairs to give Daisy a kiss on the head goodbye, and lock up.

Hazel's teaching an online yoga class from home until this evening, and I'm trying to give her space, so I head to the coffee shop downstairs to write my daily update. Jamie never asked for them, but I'm trying to do a good job.

I have a text from Hazel from earlier in the afternoon. I missed it while I was in the shower.

*What the fuck is this?* she asks, and I open the link she sent.

My stomach drops through the floor when the video starts. I scramble to connect my headphones as Zach plays a recent show, smiling at the woman beside him on stage. She looks about the same age as me and Zach, with long, wavy platinum hair. Her clothes are stylish and bohemian, and she's smiling and singing alongside Zach while he smiles back at her.

She looks like she belongs on stage. She's so comfortable up there, so flawless and charismatic.

My headphones connect, and my jaw drops. They're singing a song that Zach and I wrote together. I mean, I didn't get writing credits because we just played around with the tune on one of our off days, but still.

I didn't just get dumped—I got replaced. By a newer, shinier model. My eyes sting and I blink the tears away.

*You don't have it*, Zach said to me once when I floated the idea of trying to write my own album. I've always wanted to. *Being in the spotlight is really hard*, he told me, like he was protecting me from it.

He wasn't always like that. Or maybe he was, and it just surfaced more in the past couple months. When things were good, when Zach turned his charisma on and shone his light on me? It made me feel so special and warm. When it was just us, we'd laugh so hard. He knew me better than anyone. His smile made me feel like a million bucks.

In the video, he smiles at her the way he used to smile at me, and my chest aches. My eyes well up again, a tear falls, and I wipe it away fast.

He never asked me to come out on stage with him. Not once.

This sucks.

I'm sitting in a coffee shop with a hundred and twenty-three dollars in my bank account, living on Hazel's couch when Jamie's in town, and my ex is moving on.

Through the glass, my gaze locks with Jamie's. Seriously? It's like the universe keeps finding the worst time possible for me to run into him.

I put my head down, hoping the glare on the glass hides me. If I just pretend I didn't see him, maybe he'll go away—

Nope. I peek over at him. He's at the coffee shop door. He's opening it. Shit. Maybe he's just getting a coffee.

Nope. He's heading toward me.

## CHAPTER 9
# JAMIE

SHE'S SITTING at a table beside the window, wiping at her eyes, trying to hide her tears. Alarm shoots through me, and my protective instincts flare. In a shot, I'm inside, in front of her.

I glare at her. "Is this because I saw you in your towel?"

She frantically wipes the tears away, blinking rapidly. "No." She laughs at herself, but it feels hollow. "That didn't even register on my list of embarrassing experiences." She clears her throat and forces a smile. "I'm fine."

My chest hurts, watching her like this. I hate this.

"Tell me why you're crying." I cross my arms.

"I'm *fine*," she says again, not meeting my eye. She reaches for her phone and her bag like she's about to get up.

I lean over her, setting my hands on the table. I'm being an intimidating jackass, but I need to know why she's crying so I can fix it.

"Tell me." My voice is low, and her breath catches.

She slides her phone across the table before hitting Play. On the screen, that fucking Zach Hanson guy she dated in high school is singing on stage beside a woman.

I raise an eyebrow at Pippa.

Her eyes flash with anger. "He *dumped* me last month and

now he's on stage with someone new." A fresh wave of tears spills over. I want to kill that guy for making her feel like this.

I glance back at the video, at that stupid asshole's face. So they were still together until recently. He was scrawny in high school, and now, I can't make out his build under his jacket, but he still looks small. I'm stronger, I bet.

"Stop crying," I demand.

"I'm trying." She takes a shaky breath. "Everything is totally shit right now. He has this shiny new muse, and I'm a loser living on my sister's couch and begging for my job back." Another tear rolls down her face.

My hand lifts and I catch myself just in time. What the fuck? Was I just about to wipe her tear away? I sit down across from her. My knee bounces as I figure out what to do about this.

I hate that guy. I hate him so fucking much. He has a soft, squishy, punchable face. Goalies almost never get into fights, but if that guy were on the ice at my game tomorrow, I wouldn't hesitate.

My thoughts snag on what she said about living on her sister's couch.

"So get your own place," I tell her.

When she looks at me, she's irritated. Good. At least it's helping with the crying. Angry is better than sad. I can't handle a sad Pippa.

"Vancouver's expensive. I want to find something close to your place so I can get over there quickly if you need me."

In the back of my mind, I like the way she says *if you need me*. A funny prickle moves over my skin, and I frown harder.

"You should go home."

"I *can't*." Her face crumples, and I panic. Her sister's teaching an online yoga class, she explains. "Why am I even talking to you about this? I'm okay. I just need to cry this out."

I hate everything about this. Every protective instinct in my body surges with the need to make things better for her.

"Move in with me."

We stare at each other. I don't know where the fuck that came from. I'm not supposed to be spending *more* time with her; I'm supposed to be avoiding her.

Living with her isn't keeping her at arm's length.

She's stopped crying, though. That's something. She's staring at me with a confused look.

The idea of her living in my apartment eases something in my chest.

"It'll be easier on Daisy." I'm scrambling.

I remember her singing when I got home, and my heart thumps harder. If she's living with me, maybe I'll hear her sing again.

Across the table, she's chewing her lip with an uncertain expression. "I don't know."

My pulse is picking up. I picture her in my apartment, lying on the couch, reading a book with Daisy at her feet. Playing her guitar like she used to with her friends back in high school. My chest warms. I like that image.

I don't care if this is a bad idea. I can't let it go. Besides, I'm busy with hockey and visiting my mom in North Van. I won't even see her.

And I won't be worrying about her, so that's something.

"You can't be crying in public," I tell her. Again, my voice comes out sharp and stern. *Jackass.* "It's unprofessional. You'll move in tomorrow."

I watch her for any sign that she doesn't want to do this, any fear or repulsion. But instead, she lets out a long breath and her face relaxes like she's relieved.

My heart lifts.

The corner of her mouth curves up, and her eyes soften. "Okay." She nods. "Thank you, Jamie."

Something sparks down my spine. I like the way she says my name, sweet like that. I like the way she's looking at me right now, like she likes me.

I jerk a nod at her and stand up.

"Tomorrow," I repeat.

She nods, wiping her smeared mascara off. "Tomorrow."

As I head upstairs, my pulse races like I'm in the middle of a game. I just threw a wrench into the well-oiled machine that is my life. Pippa is intoxicatingly pretty, and around her, my mind blanks, but I feel a twinge of excited anticipation that I haven't experienced in a long time.

THAT EVENING, just before sunset, I park in the driveway of a suburban home in North Vancouver, bag of Greek food sitting in the passenger seat. There's an informal dinner for the players tonight, a get-to-know-you type of thing for the new guys, but I ignored the invite. From the back seat, Daisy wags her tail, curious and excited. I take a deep breath.

I can't fucking believe I told Pippa to move in with me. With her watching the dog, though, I'll have lots of time to keep an eye on my mom.

From the back seat, Daisy leans her head on my shoulder, sniffing me, and I send her a side-long glance. A weird feeling grows in my chest.

Am I... starting to like this dog? I frown at her, and she pants and wags her tail. I snort.

"Come on." I get out of the car, let Daisy out, and walk up to the small home.

The house is modest—firmly middle class. I tried to buy my mom something bigger when I went pro, but she refused. She said she didn't want to leave the neighborhood she'd lived in for years. That she liked the neighbors and didn't want to make new friends.

As I near the front door, movement on the roof catches my eye and my heart stops.

My mom is on the roof, wearing thick gardening gloves. She waves with a big smile. "Hi, honey."

Blood beats in my ears. She can't be up there. My mind races, picturing her having a panic attack up on the roof, slipping and falling, cracking her head open on the pavement.

"What are you doing up there?" I demand. Daisy barks up at my mom, wagging her tail.

My mom grins wide at me. "Cleaning the gutters."

"Get down. Now." I'm using my firmest voice. "It's getting dark out."

"I can see just fine. I'm just finishing up, anyway." She chuckles and drops a fistful of leaves on me. They flutter down to my feet, and Daisy jumps and tries to bite one.

"Jamie, honey? Whose dog is that?"

I raise an eyebrow at Daisy, who's sitting with her tail sweeping back and forth on the pavement. The corner of my mouth twitches as her eyes widen. She thinks she's getting a treat.

Maybe a little part of me is starting to like this dog.

"Mine," I tell my mom. "I got a dog."

My mom lights up, clapping. "You did? Oh, Jamie, that's great. That's exactly what you need."

"Can you please get down?" I'm feeling twitchy with her up on the roof, so high. "I'll hire someone to do this."

"Stop treating me like a child. I'm not incapable of living my life."

Irritation rises in my gut. Irritation and something else, something angrier. I hate that she pretends she's fine when she's not. She's always been like that. We never, ever talked about her depression or anxiety when I was growing up. We still haven't talked about the car accident last year. My gaze sweeps to the open garage. Her car is fixed, and I wonder if she's been driving. She's not allowed to until she gets help.

She was driving friends home from the bar when she had the panic attack and rear-ended another car. Because of my late father's struggles with alcoholism, she's always the designated driver. I think one of her friends smelled like booze, and combined with driving at night, when my dad's accident happened, it just set her off.

I don't remember him—I was only a baby when he drove drunk and wrapped his car around a pole—but I resent him for leaving my mom with all this baggage. If not for him, maybe she wouldn't have had depression while I was growing up. Maybe she wouldn't have panic attacks.

"You're not even clipped in." My chest feels tight. "You could slip and fall."

She rolls her eyes, making her way over to the ladder. "A meteor could bonk me in the head and kill me." She descends the ladder, and my heart rate slows. "You worry too much."

Internally, I deflate. Sometimes, I wish I was like her, but then who would hold our family together? Who would swoop in and answer my mom's calls when she's having an episode?

Daisy loves her immediately, of course. We head inside, and my mom putters around the kitchen, setting out the Greek food I brought while I grab plates. Daisy sniffs every square inch of the house.

"How are you settling into your new place?" she asks.

I feel the weird urge to tell her about Pippa. What would I even say? My assistant is a drop-dead gorgeous songbird who I had a crush on in high school. Who's incredible with my dog. Who stocked the fridge with all the foods I like even though I barked "stuff" at her as a grocery list. And now she's going to be living with me, sleeping on the other side of the wall.

Maybe doing other stuff on the other side of that wall. The thought goes straight to my cock.

"Fine," I tell her. "It's fine."

She brings the plates to the table. "I want to come to a game."

"I don't think that's a good idea."

She blinks at me like I've slapped her, and I immediately regret my words. I could have said it differently. It *isn't* a good idea, though. The smell of alcohol is a trigger for her, and at a hockey game, everyone's drinking. If something happens, she'll take up my full attention, and I can't lose focus on the ice.

"Jamie." She gives me an indulgent look, but there's irritation beneath it. "I had one little panic attack."

One that she's admitted.

Her eyes are on the lasagna as she dishes it out. "You're treating me with kid gloves."

*That's because you're fragile and you don't have the best track record of keeping it together,* I think. And in my head, I'm ten and making my own school lunch during one of her low points of depression.

"Do you need any help moving in?" She moves to the kitchen, and I'm relieved that she's dropped the idea of coming to a game.

"No. I'm all unpacked."

She gives me a funny look. She knows how demanding my schedule is. "That was fast."

I clear my throat. "I hired an assistant to help with Daisy and other stuff."

My mom blinks at me. A smile stretches across her face. "You? You hired someone to help you?"

"It's not a big deal." I give her a hard look, but the corner of my mouth tugs up.

She laughs. "If you say so." As she passes, she nudges me with her elbow. "That's great, honey."

Warmth spreads in my chest. I duck my head, embarrassed. "Yeah, well." I shrug. "She does a lot of things for me that save time so I can focus on hockey."

"She?" Her head tilts and her eyes sparkle.

My gut dips, and my gaze darts to my mom. I shrug again. "Yeah."

The back of my neck heats.

"What's her name?" My mom's eyes are like lasers, and there's that little twitch at the corner of her mouth.

I hold my face neutral, not wanting to give anything away, even as my pulse picks up at the thought of my pretty assistant. "Pippa."

*Please don't ask where she's from*, I beg silently. I'll blurt out that we went to the same high school and then it'll all come tumbling out.

She makes a pleased, humming noise. "Pretty name. How old is she?"

She smells blood in the water.

I'm twenty-six, which puts Pippa at twenty-four. "I don't know."

"Guess."

My skin tingles. She knows. She so fucking knows. "A little younger than me."

"Hmmm." She smiles, nodding, watching me. "Interesting."

I stay silent.

"Is she pretty?"

I rake a hand through my hair. "I don't know."

"I mean, you have *eyes*, don't you?" She asks it so innocently, like she doesn't know the answer.

I blow out a long breath, frustrated with my mom but also with myself, because I shouldn't have this inconvenient crush.

And I sure as shit shouldn't have demanded she move in with me.

"Yes, okay?" I rush out. "She's very pretty and she has a beautiful singing voice and Daisy loves her."

My mom rolls her lips to hide a smile, but her eyes are bright.

"What?" I demand.

She bursts out laughing.

I groan. She has a way of getting things out of me.

She smiles at me as she takes a seat across the table, tilting her head. "Erin was a long time ago." She says it quietly, and my lungs tighten. "I saw her on a new TV show. She's the star."

My jaw tenses so hard my teeth might crack, and I think back to seven years ago, during my rookie year. Erin Davis, the supermodel on her way to the top who shocked the fashion industry when she left modeling abruptly. Over the past few years, she's been acting. I look her up once in a while to see if she's still working.

My mom thinks Erin and I broke up because I couldn't handle hockey *and* a relationship, which is technically true. She doesn't know that when Erin told me her period was a week late, I panicked. Erin was so excited, and I had terror written all over my face. We were nineteen, for Christ's sake. It was my rookie year and I was working harder at hockey than ever. Every chance I could, I was flying home to visit my mom. My best friend growing up, Rory Miller, wasn't interested in being friends now that we played for separate hockey teams. Everything was different and I was barely holding it together. Adding another commitment to my life was terrifying. I would have done it, though, no matter how hard it was.

She got her period a day later, but the damage was done. We both knew the relationship was over, and a week later, I saw the news about her leaving modeling. She fell off the face of the planet for almost five years.

Guilt squeezes my lungs. That's why I don't do relationships anymore. Because Erin wanted so much more than I was able to give her. Because it was casual for me, and I broke her fucking heart and blew up her life. She was so traumatized, she left a promising career.

I did that.

Maybe I wasn't in love with her, but she was a nice person, and she deserved so much more than the half-assed attention I was able to give her. If we had ended up having a baby, that kid would deserve so much more than the limited time I could give them.

I'll never hurt someone the way I hurt Erin.

When I retire from hockey, I'll have time for that stuff—a relationship, maybe getting married, maybe having kids. If I stay fit and keep my head in the game, I can play until my mid-thirties. Until then, those other things aren't part of the plan.

"Jamie?"

My head whips toward my mom. She's looking at me with a curious, soft expression.

"There's more to life than hockey, you know."

I nod and make a noise of acknowledgment, but she doesn't get it. After seeing Pippa cry the other day, it's not going to happen. I know I don't have time for her, and I can't crush her like her ex did, and like I crushed Erin.

"And I still want to go to a game." She widens her eyes at me in an affectionate *I mean business* way. "I'll sit in the nosebleeds if I have to."

# CHAPTER 11

# PIPPA

A WEEK LATER, I set a framed picture of me and Hazel on the bookshelf in my room. I was fine with moving into a room that was basically empty except for the bed and dresser, but over the past week, furniture kept arriving. I wasn't even here when this bookshelf showed up—it just appeared, put together, this morning after I got home from Daisy's walk.

My stomach flutters. I know he put it together.

He's almost never here. Sometimes, I hear the front door open when he gets home late. Daisy sleeps in my room every night, but she likes to greet him when he gets home, so I crack the door and let her run out, but I don't say hi because I want to give him space.

In my room, I slide my guitar case out from under the bed to make room for a box. I'm about to push it back under when I hesitate. My hands linger on the case before I snap it open.

My guitar gleams at me, and my heart twists. I love this thing, and now I'm shoving it away to collect dust. I reach out and pluck a string.

The last time I played was in front of Zach and his manager on the tour. I didn't even want his manager there, but Zach pulled him in, and they listened while I played the skeleton of a song I'd been working on. Even back in high school, I loved writing music.

Deep down, I dreamed of having a career like Zach's.

When they smiled at me after, in that condescending way, I actually chuckled with them to hide my embarrassment. The worst part was that until that moment, I thought I had what it took to make music my career. I can sing, I can play guitar, and I can write music. I always wanted to write an album, even if just to see if I could.

The marketing job is going to be so much easier in the end. No one gets their heart broken over a desk job.

There's a noise at my bedroom door, and I inhale sharply. Jamie's standing there, frowning at me.

"Jesus." I snap the guitar case shut and slide it under the bed. "You scared me. I didn't hear you get home."

He frowns harder. "Sorry."

"It's fine."

His gaze flicks down to the edge of the guitar case sticking out from under the bed, and he looks like he wants to ask me something, but before he can say anything, I stand.

"I was just about to take Daisy out. I'll be out for a while to give you some space." I breeze past him, and my pulse is still whistling through my veins.

I wish I didn't have this reaction to him. To him, I'm probably like a gnat—tiny, insignificant, and slightly annoying. The way he frowns every time I'm around tells me everything I need to know.

I head downstairs to get Daisy ready to go, and as I clip her leash and harness on, Jamie walks into the living room, crossing his arms over his chest, watching. His presence in the apartment is intense—he's towering and broad, and his green eyes make my skin prickle, they're so sharp. Our eyes meet and I smile nervously, trying to summon that version of myself who demanded her job back and called him a dickhead.

"I've been taking her to the dog park near here," I tell him. If I act like I'm unaffected by him, maybe my body will get the hint. "There's this guy who has a dog who looks a lot like Daisy. They like to play together. I think his name is Andrew."

I'm rambling as I pull my shoes on. I can't seem to get my nerves under control around this guy.

"Andrew." He says the word like it tastes bad.

I meet his piercing gaze, blinking in confusion. "Yeah. He's young. Probably my age. He's a personal trainer."

Jamie's gaze turns cold before he prowls to the door. "I'm coming with you."

My lips part in surprise as he yanks his shoes on. "You don't have to. I know you're probably tired." He usually has a nap at this time, exhausted from practice.

"I'm not tired." He pulls his jacket out of the closet and slips it on before taking the leash from my hand. "I'm sore, and I need to move. Let's go."

Before I can protest, he opens the door and gestures for me to step into the hall.

THE WALK to the dog park is silent and tense. When we arrive, Jamie scans the fenced-in area before his shoulders relax and his frown lessens. I wave and smile at a few people before I let Daisy off the leash to greet the other dogs.

Does he not trust me with Daisy? I chew my lip as I run through possible reasons he came with us. The guy's been avoiding me for a week.

"This park is really safe," I tell him. He's leaning on the fence, arms folded over his chest, with a scowl on his face. "I'd never bring Daisy somewhere unsafe."

His scowl softens. "I know. I trust you." The corner of his mouth twitches, and his eyes almost look... amused? "I wouldn't have asked you to move in if I didn't trust you."

I make a dubious face. "You didn't ask."

He coughs and looks away. Was that a laugh? It's so hard to tell with him.

"We should get to know each other better." His eyes are back on me, and it's tough to look away. They're the color of Douglas fir trees. Of the earthy green moss in Stanley Park. Of a deep green rock at the bottom of a creek.

"Um." I blink stupidly in surprise, feeling shy. "Okay. What's your favorite food?"

His eyebrow goes up. "That's your question?"

"I had zero warning you were going to want to talk today, or I would have prepared a list of questions." My smile turns teasing.

The corner of his mouth twitches again, and his eyes almost look soft. I like this look on him.

He watches me for a long moment. That girl who demanded her job back surfaces, and I stare back at him.

"Christmas dinner," he says, still watching me in that unnerving way that makes my stomach flutter. "Turkey, mashed potatoes, gravy, broccoli casserole."

"Cranberry sauce?"

He nods. "Homemade, not canned."

"Of course." I smile. "Are you crazy about Christmas?"

"Not really, but my mom loves it." He looks over at Daisy, who has a stick in her mouth and is trying to bait another dog to chase her. "We spend most of the time cooking together and watching Christmas movies."

The way he says it makes me think that he just likes seeing her happy.

He slides a glance at me, studying my face. "I liked those enchiladas you made, too."

Pride fills my chest at a job well done. "Great. I'll make them again."

Daisy sprints past us, chased by a golden retriever, having the time of her life, and I smile at Jamie. His mouth twitches as our eyes meet.

Every time I smile, his mouth twitches. That realization makes my stomach warm and liquid, and I smile wider at him.

Maybe he's not such an asshole, after all.

"Next question." My hands are getting cold, so I tuck them into my jacket pockets. "Why hockey?"

Looking around the dog park, his eyes narrow as he puts his answer together. "I don't even know where to start."

"Start at the beginning."

He snorts. "I got my first stick at two years old."

"Wow." My eyebrows shoot up. "Your dad's a big hockey fan?"

His expression changes, barely perceptible, and he frowns. "He was. He died."

"Oh." My heart drops, and now I remember reading this. Shit. I should have remembered. "I'm so sorry."

He shakes his head. "It's fine. I don't remember him. It happened when I was really young. He was a drunk, and he wrapped his own car around a pole."

"Shit," I breathe. That's so tragic. I study Jamie, but he seems unaffected by this.

"Seriously." He stares at me. "I don't remember him. It's always just been me and my mom. That's enough for me." He glances away, rubbing his sharp jaw. "Hockey's fast-paced, more than any other sport, and the feeling of being focused on the game, shutting everything else out, it..." The corner of his mouth twitches again, and his gaze comes to mine. "On the ice, it's like nothing else exists."

My heart squeezes. That's how I feel when I'm writing songs. Or when I used to. Like everything fell away.

"I like being part of a team," he tells me, arching a brow. "But I like being the only guy in the net, too." His big shoulders lift in a shrug. "I like the pressure."

"Do you like your new team?"

"I've played against them before, but I'm not friends with any of them."

"What about those cupcakes?"

His gaze shoots to mine in confusion.

"The container was empty. You gave them to your team-mates, right?" He freezes, a guilty look crossing his handsome face, and my jaw drops. "Oh my god. You threw them out."

He shifts, glancing around the park. The guilty look intensifies.

"Jamie." I'm giving him an appalled look, and when I say his name, he turns and gives me his full attention.

It's intoxicating.

"Did you dump those cupcakes in the garbage?" I cross my arms, but I can feel the smile twisting on my mouth. "They were terrible, weren't they?"

Our eyes are locked, and the side of his mouth isn't even twitching; it's curving up. God, his eyes are pretty. The way he's looking at me, amused and intense, it's making my stomach flutter like crazy.

Are we *flirting* right now? I can't look away from him.

"They were incredible." His gaze drops to my mouth, and my eyes widen a fraction.

We are *so* flirting right now. What?

I blink about twelve times, memorizing this moment so I can analyze it with Hazel later. "So you didn't dump them."

He shakes his head, still giving me that smirky half smile. "I ate every last one."

I'm melting. That's the only explanation for what's happening to my insides right now. "Oh."

"Yeah." He's dropped the smirk, but his eyes are still sparkling, amused, almost happy, even.

"If I make more, are they going to make it to the team?"

"Probably not."

I laugh, and the corner of his mouth twitches.

God, I want to see a full smile so badly. I bet it would knock me off my feet, make my hair flutter with the force of it.

"You brought your guitar," he says, changing the subject.

My stomach drops. I can't tell him the truth.

"It's nothing." I force a smile and shake my head. Then I roll my eyes. Too much, I tell myself. Too fake. "It's my old guitar that Hazel doesn't have room for. I bought it for myself after graduation." Alarm bells ring in my head as I veer closer to the topic of high school. I roll my eyes again, trying to convey a *no big deal* vibe, which I've never been able to master. "I don't even play anymore."

He's doing that staring thing again that makes me feel like I have no clothes on. "Why not?"

"Um." All I can think about is Zach on stage with that new woman, and how easily replaced I was. With a better model, too. New and improved.

"I don't know." I frown at my sneakers. "I learned when I was twelve, and then I met Zach—" I glance at him. "My ex."

He makes an unhappy noise of acknowledgment.

"We would always mess around with music and stuff. I'd play a tune, and we'd sing it together or something." I play with the hem of my jacket. "Even when we were on tour, sometimes I'd play if it was just me and him hanging out." Shame settles in my stomach, and I worry my bottom lip with my teeth.

I hate being the girl who got dumped. I hate that Zach left an ugly mark on me. The breakup is like a weight holding me down.

I lift my gaze to Jamie's, and there's something in his expression as he listens to me talk. Something sweet and sharp, and it makes me want to stay here in this dog park for a whole day, talking.

"Whatever," I say, putting on a smile to shove away the weird Zach feelings. "It's in the past."

His eyes move over my face. "You have a nice voice."

My face falls, and embarrassment weaves through me. "You heard me singing?"

His Adam's apple bobs as he nods. "That day I..."

Oh, right. The day he nearly saw me naked. Cringe. My face heats. "Everyone sounds good in the shower."

"No." He gives me a hard look. "They don't."

Jeez, he's so intense. A tiny shiver rolls down my back at his firm tone. Is he this firm in bed? I try not to bite my lip at the arousal that shimmers through me. The idea of Jamie Streicher on top of me, naked, sweating, and wearing a look of agonized ecstasy, is very, very hot.

"You have a great voice," he tells me again. "You know you do."

When my grade twelve music teacher said that to me, Zach made it seem like the teacher was being nice. Like the teacher felt sorry for me.

"I'm not going to do anything with it."

He glares at me.

"I'm not performer material," I tell him, echoing the words Zach said years ago.

*You don't have it*, he'd said. Oof. It's still embarrassing that I even tried. Especially when my mind flicks to his new manic pixie dream girl.

"It's okay," I reassure Jamie.

"Your ex is a fucking loser to let you go," he bites out.

My breath catches. His eyes flash with fury, and I tilt my head, studying him. He frowns harder. He's about to keep going, but I cut him off.

"Let's go." My tone is bright. I don't want to be sad, hurt loser girl right now. I just want to forget.

His gaze lingers on me for a moment before he nods and drops it. As we walk home, I ask him about his upcoming schedule and fish for other ways I can help around the apartment. He's resistant, though, and besides taking care of Daisy and ordering groceries, he doesn't ask for much.

I make a mental note to buy more cupcake ingredients, though.

We're a block from the apartment when something in the window of a music store catches my eye, and I stop short.

Oh my god.

The guitar of my dreams sits on display in the front window, gleaming. The photos in the guitar magazine I flipped through a couple months ago didn't do it justice. In person, I can see the fine craftsmanship, the details in the grain of the wood, the shape that I can practically *feel* resting on my leg as I play. It's beyond beautiful. My gaze traces every line, each string, every fret, memorizing it.

It's made from a mix of walnut, mahogany, and spruce wood. In the video I watched, the guitar sounded warm, rich, and full. The company only made a thousand of them, and there's one right in front of me.

I bet the inside of that guitar smells incredible. I think this is what they call *instalove*.

I want it. I want it so freaking badly. I can't afford it, though. If I get the marketing job and I'm very, very good with my money, maybe I can find one in a year or two.

I catch myself. Why am I pining over my dream guitar when I can't even pick up the one I have? There's a sharp ache in my chest.

I realize Jamie's watching me watch the guitar, wearing a curious expression.

"Sorry," I chirp, turning away from the guitar. "Let's go."

———

When he leaves for his game that evening, he actually says goodbye.

"Break a leg," I tell him, sitting on the floor of the living room, training Daisy to "leave it."

His eyebrow goes up in alarm. "*Good luck* is fine."

I picture the brutality of hockey and how breaking a leg isn't that unrealistic. "Sorry. Good luck."

He nods once before he's gone.

That evening, I'm lying in bed, thinking about the conversation we had at the dog park. I replay Jamie's facial expressions, the amused spark in his eyes as he listened to me talk, the piercing gleam as he talked about hockey and why he loves it.

I wish I could see him smile. I picture it, and my stomach flutters.

And there it is—a trill of notes in my head. I sit up in the dark bedroom. It's just a few notes, but it's that same feeling as before, when I'd sit with Zach on a couch with my guitar and we'd goof around. It's a sparkling pressure in my chest, like fizzing bubbles. I place my hand over my sternum, smiling out the window, and I'm so relieved I could cry.

Zach didn't break me. That girl I used to be is still in there. I just have to find a way to get her out.

I think about Jamie again, and I wonder if it has anything to do with him.

# CHAPTER 13

# JAMIE

"STREICHER," Ward calls as I head to the dressing room after practice. "My office when you're done."

My gut pitches as I give him a quick nod and head to the showers. Getting called to the coach's office is like going to the principal's office. In the shower, I run through my recent games and practices. If Ward's going to bring up my weaknesses, I need to be ready.

His office door is open when I arrive, and he looks up from his computer.

"Hey." He stands. "Let's get some lunch." He tilts his head to the street below his office window. "I know a place."

A weight gathers in my gut. If it was something easy, we'd just talk in his office. Lunch means a bigger conversation, and whatever it is, I'm not excited to hear it.

Ward makes small talk as we leave the arena and walk through the streets of downtown Vancouver.

"This way," he says, stepping down an alley.

I raise an eyebrow and glance down the narrow lane, but he's walking with purpose and direction, so I follow him to a green door. Above it, a weathered sign reads *The Filthy*

*Flamingo.* He hauls it open, and classic rock spills out at a low volume.

"After you, Streicher."

I step inside. It's a bar, with warm wood paneling on the walls, vintage framed concert posters, Polaroid photos behind the bar among liquor bottles, and string lights across the ceiling. People sit in the booths, eating lunch.

"You took me to a dive bar?" I ask Ward as the door closes behind us.

"Hey," a woman snaps, holding a tray of drinks behind the bar. She's in her late twenties, with long dark hair in a high ponytail. She's wearing an old-looking band t-shirt and a scowl. "This isn't a dive bar."

"It isn't a dive bar, Streicher," Ward says loud enough for her to hear.

The bartender glares at him before carrying the drinks to a table.

Ward leans in. "It's a dive bar, but we don't say that in front of Jordan. This place is her baby."

We take seats at the counter as I take the space in. Three lunch options are written on the chalkboard behind the bar, and I get the impression that those are my only options.

I kind of like this place. It's weird. When traveling to Vancouver over the years, I'd either be in North Van with my mom or in a hotel room. This crappy bar feels like a small connection to the city that will hopefully be my home for a while again.

I wonder if Pippa knows about this place.

"Jordan hates hockey." Ward's voice is low. "So no one will bug us here." He crooks a grin at me, and his eyes follow the prickly bartender with interest before he drags his attention back to me. "Still settling in okay? There was that hiccup with your assistant. Is that all taken care of?"

"Yes," I say quickly. "Everything's great. She's a huge help."

Ward smiles, pleasantly surprised. "Glad to hear it."

Jordan takes our orders, and when she leaves, Ward slants a curious glance at me.

"You didn't make it to dinner the other night."

He's talking about the informal dinner I skipped. "I had to check on my mom."

He nods in understanding, surveying the Polaroids behind the bar. A pause. "You don't spend much time with the guys after games."

On my barstool, I shift in discomfort. Some guys in the NHL make friends with their teammates, and some don't. My New York coach didn't have a problem with me staying focused and out of trouble. The last thing a franchise needs is their players in the media for partying. I wasn't top goalie in the league last year because I was out drinking with my teammates.

My thoughts snag, and I picture Rory Miller and me playing hockey as teenagers. His dad, NHL Hall of Famer Rick Miller, would arrange extra ice time for us at the local arena, and we'd spend hours practicing shootouts, laughing, and chirping at each other.

That guy was my best friend. My jaw tenses, and I fold my arms over my chest. I don't do that kind of thing anymore.

"I focus on hockey," I tell him, offering him a shrug. "It hasn't been a problem until now."

His mouth hitches up. "Streicher, your focus is second to none." He pauses a beat. "But I want you to spend more time with the guys off the ice. Team camaraderie is just as important as training on the ice."

My brows snap together. "I don't have time."

"Make time." His smile is easy, but the determination in his eyes leaves no room for uncertainty.

My knee bounces with frustration. Keeping the coach

happy is a critical part of staying on the team. I've seen coaches with major egos trade players for petty reasons. Pissing him off could jeopardize everything.

I meet Ward's gaze. The guy doesn't seem to have an ego, but I don't want to take any chances.

"You got it," I tell him.

THE ARENA IS empty except for the players on the ice. Half wear white jerseys over their pads, and half wear blue jerseys, and they run drills while Jamie and the second-string goalie guard each net. The coaching staff stand on the side of the ice with clipboards, calling out feedback to the players.

I take a seat in the stands behind the bench, clutching the keys Jamie forgot on the counter this morning.

Jamie's in the net, blocking pucks that players shoot at him. He's fast as lightning. I don't even see the puck and he's already caught it. Between drills, he gets on his knees and does these hip-thrusty moves to stretch. In my head, I hear seventies porn music and hide my smile behind my hand.

The whistle blows, and the guys skate off the ice before filing through the hall to the dressing room, pulling helmets off and talking to each other. A few of them send me curious glances.

A big blond guy with a charming, boyish grin leans on the railing separating us. His damp hair is cropped short, and he has the bluest eyes.

"Are you lost?" he asks.

"No." My cheeks go pink. "I'm Pippa, Jamie's assistant."

His smile broadens. "Streicher didn't say anything about a pretty assistant."

A laugh bubbles out of me. Some guys can't pull this vibe off, but he can. Despite his size, he feels like a big golden retriever, goofy and fun.

"Dude," I tease, wincing at him. "Is that your line?"

He chuckles, not even a little embarrassed. "How come I've never seen you at one of the games?"

"I don't really like hockey." I make a face and shrug. "Sorry."

"Pippa."

At the sound of Jamie's voice, my stomach fizzes. Jamie strides toward us with an expression like a storm cloud. His hair is also damp with sweat, which should be gross, but it's weirdly hot on him. He stops between the blond guy and me like he's trying to shield me.

My face heats even more. I hope he doesn't think I'm here to scope out players or something.

"You forgot your keys," I tell him, holding them out. "I didn't want you to get locked out while I'm walking Daisy."

"Thanks." He takes them before shooting the blond guy a weird look. A lock of dark hair falls into Jamie's eyes, but he doesn't notice.

The blond guy smiles even wider at me. For a hockey player, he has surprisingly nice teeth. "I'm Hayden Owens."

"Pippa."

"Hi, Pippa." Hayden looks at Jamie. "How come you don't invite her to games?"

Jamie frowns and flicks a glance at me.

"I take care of the dog in the evenings, usually," I say quickly, not wanting Jamie to be in an awkward position.

Hayden leans on the railing, and Jamie's jaw tenses. "Pippa, do me a favor, okay?" He jerks a nod at Jamie. "Make this guy come out with us after a game. Half the team is afraid of him because he doesn't talk."

A laugh bursts out of me, and Jamie turns his glare to me.

"I can see it," I tell him. "You glare a lot."

Hayden chuckles.

The corner of Jamie's mouth twitches, and my stomach has that fizzy feeling again. I smile wider—I can't help it. I'm getting used to being around him, and that starstruck feeling I had is slowly melting away.

So I had a crush on him in high school. That was years ago. I've learned so much since then—mainly to never, ever date one of these superstar guys who has everything at their fingertips. Nothing will *ever* happen with Jamie Streicher. Knowing this bolsters my confidence.

Hayden walks backward to the dressing room, pointing at me. "Pippa, nice meeting you." He points at Jamie. "Remember what I said."

Hayden leaves, and I get to my feet, tucking my hands into my jacket pockets. "Alright, I'm going to go."

"Hold on a sec." Jamie rubs the back of his neck, and I'm curious. His throat works.

It's like I'm seeing a hidden layer, one where he's nervous.

"I was wondering," he says, and I wait. "My mom. She's been bugging me to come to a game."

"Oh, that's so nice." A smile lifts on my face, and I wonder what his mom is like. "You want me to arrange the tickets with the office?"

"Uh, no. I can do that." His eyes meet mine. "I was thinking you could go with her."

My expression is dubious. "You know I don't know anything about hockey, right?"

His face relaxes, and he makes a noise that's *almost* a laugh.

Almost. Like an amused hum. "That's okay. She doesn't care. Just keep her company."

"I can do that. Is she grumpy like you?"

I blurt it out without thinking. The more Jamie and I hang out, the easier it is to tease him like this. This is a hell of a lot better than the tense, awkward silences.

He arches an eyebrow, and something bubbles up inside me. It feels like delight. "No."

Even though he isn't smiling, his eyes glitter, encouraging me. I make an overexaggerated face of relief. "Good. That would be a long night."

He stares at me, and I flatten my mouth so I don't laugh. It feels like he wants to smile, and my heart is bouncing around in my chest like a ping-pong ball. If I had seen *this* version of Jamie in high school, I'd have been a full-out stalker.

"Very funny," he says instead.

I roll my eyes. "I know, I'm hilarious. Okay, I'm gonna head home."

"Thanks for dropping off the keys."

"No problem." I take two steps before I stop and turn to him. He's still standing there, watching me leave. "Jamie?"

He waits, watching me intently.

"You should go out with the team. I bet it would be fun."

His gaze roams my face, and it feels like he wants to say something, but he just nods once. "I'll think about it."

# CHAPTER 15

# PIPPA

A SAN JOSE player slams Hayden into the boards in front of us, and around us, fans are screaming, slamming their hands against the glass, rattling it. A roar of *boo*s rises up from our end of the arena.

"That's a fucking penalty!" a guy behind us shouts at the ref.

Jamie's mom, Donna, glances at me with bright eyes, the same deep green as Jamie's.

"This is very exciting," she says, smiling. "It's easier to say that when my son isn't the one getting slammed into the boards."

She fiddles with a string of beads around her left wrist, twirling them. She's been doing that since we got to the stadium.

I smile at her, and my eyes catch on Jamie in the net near us. Watching Jamie Streicher play a game is a totally different experience than sitting in on a practice. When he blocks the puck, the crowd around us cheers for him, although it doesn't even seem like he notices or cares. Just like in practice, he's faster than I can follow, but now, there are five guys trying to sink the puck in while another five fight them off. Jamie's body bends and contorts in the net in sharp motions, but he makes it look easy. It's fast-paced, brutal, and charged with energy.

I love it.

I thought hockey was boring, but maybe I never paid attention until now. My dad will be thrilled, of course.

My gaze drops to Donna's fingers as she twirls the beads. "Can I get you anything? I can grab another drink or some food. Whatever you like."

She shakes her head with a smile. "No, thank you, honey. I'm okay." She tilts her head, studying me. "Are you from Vancouver?"

"North Vancouver," I say without thinking.

"That's where I live." She lights up, and I freeze. "What neighborhood?"

I can't lie to her—she's too nice—and the longer I try to think of something, the more thoughts fall out of my head, so I just blurt out the truth. "Berkley Creek."

"No *way*. That's where Jamie grew up."

"No way." I force a smile as my pulse picks up.

Her brow wrinkles in curiosity. "What high school did you go to?" There are a couple in the area, and it's not uncommon for students to go to schools outside their catchments for special programs.

"Um." Here we freaking go, I guess.

Someone taps us on the shoulder before pointing at the Jumbotron above. The game is stopped for a moment, and Jamie's mom is on screen.

"Please give a very special welcome to the woman behind the *Streicher shut out*," the announcer calls. "Donna Streicher!"

The arena cheers, and Donna laughs and waves at the camera, glancing up at us on the screen. She points at Jamie and blows kisses at him. A chorus of *aww*s rises around the arena.

I grin so hard. Jamie's mom is so nice and cute, and she's so proud of him.

And thank fucking *god* for that interruption.

"Jamie tells me you have a pretty singing voice," Donna says a few minutes later while the players gather for a face-off.

He said that?

"Are you a musician, too?"

My stomach dips. "I don't really do that anymore."

Her mouth hitches in a wry, crooked smile. "Oh, darn. I'd love to hear a song eventually. If *Jamie* says you're good, you must be." She pats my hand on my knee. "No problem, honey."

We both pause as San Jose skates toward Vancouver's net. The energy around us rises as their forward slapshots the puck at Jamie. It hits the back of the net, and the crowd lets out a collective groan.

"He'll be pissed off at that one." Donna's still fiddling with the beads. "He's so hard on himself, but that's how he got here." She gestures at the ice. "Ever since he was a kid, he's taken on all the responsibility. I worry about him." A smile lifts on her mouth, and she glances at me. "I'm really glad he has you to help out. He takes on too much."

I nod. "Yeah, I've noticed. But he did join me on a walk the other day."

She arches a brow, and her eyes sparkle. "Oh?"

"He said it helps with muscle soreness, moving after practice like that."

Her eyes linger on my face, interested and amused like she has a secret. "Oh. Yes. That makes sense. How did you get into being an assistant?"

I tell her about my degree, Zach's tour—leaving out the details of how I left—and how I want to get a job in marketing with the team.

She smiles affectionately. "That's great, Pippa. I'm certain that whatever you want in life, you'll make it happen."

I shoot her a weak smile. Marketing isn't my dream, but it's my best option. I can hear my parents' voices in my head. *There's nothing wrong with a stable job, Pippa!* Guilt weaves through me. They paid for school for me when so many people have to either scrape student loans together or skip university altogether. Who cares if it's not my dream?

I've already learned my lesson about pursuing my dream. My gaze flicks over to Jamie as he watches the puck at the other end of the ice.

Some people are meant to pursue their dreams, but I'm not one of them.

———

While the players change and talk to the press after the game, we head to the box reserved for friends and family. The box is filled with people—players, coaches, spouses, kids, and friends. I recognize a few coaches and players, including Hayden, who gives me a friendly wave.

I show Donna pictures of Daisy while we wait for Jamie.

"Oh my goodness." Donna's hand covers her mouth as she smiles at a photo of Daisy mid-sprint. "This is just too cute."

Behind Donna, a server passes with a tray of drinks.

"I love the ones with her tongue hanging out." I scroll through the images, grinning. "I take about twelve pictures a day."

Out of the corner of my eye, I see a player accidentally bump the server. The server's eyes go wide, and she scrambles to right the tray, but it's too late. The drinks tip and spill, splashing over Donna's sleeve. The glasses crash to the floor, and everyone in the box turns to look.

"I'm *so* sorry," the server gasps.

Around us, people pick up the shards of glass, pass us napkins, and clean up the spill on the floor.

"I'll get more napkins," the server tells us. "Stay right there."

"Oops." I pass Donna a hand towel with the Vancouver Storm logo on it.

Donna dabs at her sleeve, not saying anything.

"Are you okay?" I ask.

She clears her throat before her eyes dart around the room. She's gone white as a sheet, and it doesn't seem like she heard me. She blinks and looks toward the door leading to the hallway.

"Donna?"

"Hmm?" She whirls around to look at me. Her chest rises and falls fast.

Something's wrong. I have that feeling in my gut. She's acting different.

"Are you okay?" I ask again softly, placing my hand on her arm. "Can I get you something?"

At the contact of my hand on her, she turns to me with a baffled look, like she forgot I was there.

"I need some air. I need to get outside." The tone of her voice has changed completely.

The silly, warm woman from moments before is gone, and now she sounds petrified. She forces a smile, and I know it's forced because I do that all the time.

"Ladies' room," she says, sounding breathless. She's already stepping away. "Be right back."

There's a bad feeling in my stomach as I watch her make her way to the door. I heard once that people who are choking often run to the bathroom to avoid making a scene, when it's the most dangerous place to be since no one can help them.

Donna's not choking, but she's definitely not okay.

I hurry after her. When I push the ladies' room door open, she's in front of the sink, splashing water on her sleeve. She's wheezing, breath shallow and rapid. Eyes wide as saucers.

My mind whirs—I don't know what to do. I don't know what's happening. Her eyes are darting around the small space as she tries to pull in more air.

"What's going on?" I ask, rushing over to her side.

"I'm fine." Her voice shakes as she turns the water off, and she's wheezing harder than ever, clutching the side of the sink for support. She leans against the wall, and alarm bells ring in my head.

She can't breathe. She's having a panic attack.

# CHAPTER 16

# PIPPA

"DONNA." My voice is strong and firm as I step in front of her. "Look at me."

Her gaze flicks up, terrified, as she gasps for air.

I point at my eyes. "Right here."

She nods frantically.

"We're going to breathe together." I scramble to remember what Hazel does in her yoga classes. "In, two, three, four," I say, slow and steady, holding eye contact with her. "Out, two, three, four, five, six. Great. Nice job. In, two, three, four."

She's shaking, trying to drag in breaths with my slow timing. She's slumping over more on the wall, and I'm worried she'll slip, so I help her to a seated position on the floor and take the spot beside her.

"You're doing great." I launch into another counted breath.

"This never happens," she says, shaking her head.

I nod with understanding. "No problem. We're just going to breathe through it."

Her eyes lock on mine, full of fear. "It's the smell of bourbon. It just makes me lose it."

"It's okay." My voice is calm, and I count her through another breath.

The door opens, and a woman takes one look at us sitting on the floor and walks back out. I lead Donna through more breathing exercises. I don't know what I'm doing, but this seems to be helping. After five minutes, it seems like she's okay. Shaky, but she can breathe on her own. Her breaths are deep and strong.

"I'm okay," she says, nodding with closed eyes. "I'm so sorry."

My eyes go wide. "Donna, don't apologize. Please. This is just..." I shrug. "This is just life."

The corner of her mouth turns up as she offers me a grateful smile. "You're amazing, do you know that?"

I shake my head, laughing. "I don't know what I'm doing."

She laughs. "Me neither."

We're quiet for a moment. I can hear people chatting in the hallway, heading home. My mind flicks to how often Jamie visits his mom. She said *this never happens,* but she headed to the ladies' room fast enough to tell me otherwise.

"Does Jamie know you get panic attacks?"

She sighs. "Yes." She glances at me with a pleading look. "Please don't tell him about this. He has enough to worry about with hockey."

I grimace with discomfort. He's my boss. I can't keep secrets from him. Then, I think about Zach arranging to have me sent to the airport. I know what it's like to be embarrassed by something that isn't your fault.

"Okay." My mouth twists. "But I think you should tell him."

She snorts. "He'll try to move in with me again."

There's a commotion in the hallway. Raised voices.

"Where is she?" Jamie's voice booms.

My pulse skyrockets, and I jump up, exchanging a look with Donna before opening the door. Jamie's standing outside the door to the box, arms folded and jaw set, while the woman who walked into the bathroom gestures down the hall toward the washroom. Jamie's face is flushed from exertion and his eyes are bright, and there's a shift in my chest. God, he's so freaking gorgeous, even when he's furious. Jamie meets my gaze, and the flashing anger in his eyes drains away. His shoulders inch down.

"Hi," I say brightly. "We just had to use the washroom," I lie.

He storms over, staring at Donna, who appears behind me in the hallway outside the washroom. "Someone said there was a woman in the bathroom having a panic attack."

Donna blows out a breath and rolls her eyes at me. "So much for that."

"Mom." His tone is sharp, worry written all over his face.

She waves him off. "So I got a little excited."

"What happened?" Jamie demands. When his mom just blows out another frustrated breath, he turns to me. "What. Happened?"

"The server accidentally spilled booze on me," Donna admits. "Pippa helped me collect myself, and now I'm just ready to go home and read my book. I'm booking an Uber."

He's already shaking his head. "I'm driving you."

Her phone is out, and she's tapping away on the app. "No."

I see where he gets his stubbornness from.

"Yes."

She glares up at him with the corner of her mouth curling up. "*No.* I'm perfectly alright now, thanks to Pippa." She shoots me a warm smile, and this time, her eyes sparkle.

I don't know what to say. I can't believe the breathing exercises helped. "It was nothing."

She shakes her head. "No, it wasn't." She winks at me.

After Donna promises to text him the second she's home,

Jamie relents, and we all head downstairs to wait for her car. When it pulls up, she wraps me in a warm hug.

"I'll see you soon," she tells me, and she has this way of saying it like we're old friends. When she hugs Jamie, she tilts her head in my direction. "Don't let her get away."

My face heats. I know she means as his assistant, because I make his life easier, but I can't help but hear it the other way. The romantic way.

*No*, I tell myself. We're not going there. The last thing Jamie Streicher is thinking about is dating his assistant, and I'm not getting *any* ideas about dating another famous guy.

"Text me when you're home," he reminds her as she gets into the car, waving at us.

We watch the car drive away before his eyes settle on my face. They don't have the hard edge they usually do.

"Thank you. I don't know what would have happened if you weren't there. Last time, she was driving, and—" His eyebrows pull down. "She crashed her car."

"Shit." My mouth falls open.

"She was okay," he adds quickly, crossing his arms. His jaw ticks, and pain stabs in my gut for him. He looks so worried.

"She's okay," I tell him with what I hope is a reassuring smile.

"Yeah." His eyes trace my face, my hair, which is loose around my shoulders tonight.

The way he's looking at me is making a warm weight settle in my stomach.

He gestures at the parking garage. "Let's go."

"Oh. I was just going to walk."

His eyebrow arches. "Why? We're going to the same place. Besides," he says, glancing around us, "it's not safe for you to walk home alone."

I let out an amused huff. "Jamie, compared to some of the places I've been with the tour, Vancouver is *very* safe."

He looks down at me with a set jaw. "No, Pippa."

The way he says my name, all stern and demanding like that, sends a shiver down my spine.

Before I can even answer, he puts his hand on my lower back. A pulse of something warm and liquid hits me low in my belly, and my breath catches.

When we reach his car—a black luxury crossover probably worth more than my parents' house—he holds my door open before getting in the driver's side.

His clean, masculine scent hits my nose, and my eyes almost roll back. He smells incredible, and being in a confined space with him was a huge mistake. My gaze slides over to his hands on the steering wheel as we exit the parkade.

He has big hands.

*God, Pippa.* I tear my gaze away and stare out the window as he drives.

"That's why I moved home," he says quietly.

His eyebrows knit together, and I have a feeling he's still worrying about his mom. I think about what Donna said during the game, how Jamie takes on everyone else's problems.

None of it is fair. It's not fair that Donna gets panic attacks, and it's not fair that Jamie feels the need to fix it for her. I understand that's how family works—you take care of your loved ones. Still, I wish Jamie left more space for himself. Who takes care of him?

He's quiet, watching the road. I notice how good a driver he is—confident but cautious. Like he doesn't have anything to prove.

His gaze connects with mine before going back to the road. "Thanks for coming to the game."

"I had fun." The way Jamie moved on the ice replays in my

head. "You're so fast out there. You're meant to be a hockey player."

There's something funny in his gaze, and it seems like he wants to say something. The car feels too small, suddenly, and there's a warm tug in my heart.

"Thanks, Pippa," he says, voice low.

When we get home, Daisy runs over to us, tail wagging. I say hello to her and reach for her leash to take her out one more time before bed, but Jamie's fingers brush mine as he takes the leash from me.

"I'll do it."

"I don't mind," I tell him.

"It takes me a while to unwind after a game. I'll be up for hours."

An image flashes in my head—him unwinding in a different way. Standing in the shower, late at night, one hand on the shower tiles as water rolls down his perfect, chiseled chest and abs, the other hand fisting his cock. I bet his lips would part and he'd wear a tortured expression as he came.

"Okay." My face is going red as I shove the image out of my head.

I can't be thinking things like that.

"Good night." His gaze drops to my mouth, and my pulse stutters as he frowns.

I'm frozen, locked in place, as he glares at my mouth like it offends him. Daisy's waiting at our feet, but it doesn't seem like he even notices. His eyes burn, and I'm more aware than ever of how big and broad this guy is.

Low in my stomach, arousal blooms.

"Good night." My voice is a squeak as I hurry off to my room.

Later, as I'm lying in bed, I'm lost in thought, thinking

about how Jamie takes care of everyone. But who takes care of him?

A dirty thought sneaks into my head. It's Jamie and me, tangled in the sheets, him on top of me, his thick arms supporting him on either side of my head, caging me in. He's pushing inside me. His mouth drops open and his eyes go deliciously hazy. There's a warm thrum of pressure between my legs, and my pulse picks up.

*That's* how I would take care of Jamie.

He's totally out of my league, and I've been burned by guys on his level before. I shouldn't want to fuck Jamie, but I really, really do.

ON SUNDAY MORNING, I lie in bed, staring out the window at the mountains across the water. It's only October, but after a recent cold snap, there's snow at the top of them, a dusting of white on the trees.

I'm also thinking about Pippa and the sweet curve of her mouth. It's been like this all week. I can't get one particular thought out of my head.

I really, really want to fuck my pretty assistant.

A groan of frustration slips out of me, and I close my eyes. I know better. Everything about Pippa is dangerous—her lush mouth, her smile, her sweetness. Back in high school, she was just the girl I was fascinated by, but as I get to know her, it's turning into more. I can feel it.

I'm not going to do anything about it, though. Messing around with the woman working as my assistant is a fantastic way to fuck up both my life and hers. After Pippa helped my mom during her panic attack, I trust her. Daisy's grown on me, and I look forward to coming home to her wagging her tail, excited to see me. Without Pippa, I'd either need to get a new assistant or find another home for Daisy.

I don't want either of those things.

And after what happened with Erin? I know better. Getting involved with someone isn't part of the plan. My mind drifts to Erin and her devastated expression when she realized I wasn't ready for more. I hurt her so badly she left her whole career. She deserved so much more than what I could give her.

Pippa does, too.

She and my mom have plans to take Daisy on a hike in North Van next weekend. I actually like her living here. Hearing her move around the kitchen to make her morning coffee is the best way to wake up.

I picture Pippa's mouth around my cock, her gray-blue eyes looking up at me, gauging my reaction. Blood rushes to my dick, and I'm hard.

*Almost* the best way to wake up.

I picture her soft-looking lips again, her silky hair that I'd love to wrap around my fist as I feed my cock into her tight pussy. Arousal tightens in my groin and my cock aches. I pull myself out of my boxers and give my length a stroke. A bead of pre-cum appears at the tip, and I drag in a breath, letting it out on a groan.

I shouldn't be doing this.

I'm only thinking about her, another part of me counters. Better this than acting on it.

While I stroke myself, images of Pippa roll through my head. Her hair across my pillow, her back arching as I lick between her legs. The way her stomach muscles would clench as she came, eyelashes fluttering. I bet she'd bite her lip while I fingered her.

My balls tighten. Jesus Christ. My hand works fast, and I fist the sheets in my other hand. I think about how warm and soft her mouth would be, how fucking incredible she'd look with my cock between her plush lips. The teasing spark in her eyes as she slowed down, keeping me right at the edge.

The pressure and heat at the base of my spine boil over, and I come, spilling all over my abs and chest with a low moan.

Fuck. I'm breathing hard, staring at the ceiling, wishing it was Pippa I just came all over instead of myself.

After a shower, I head out into the apartment—to a front-row seat of Pippa's ass in yoga leggings.

My cock twitches as I stare at her, bent at the waist, cleaning coffee grounds off the floor. She turns and straightens up with a smile.

"Good morning." Her eyes linger on my damp hair before she gestures at a mug on the counter. "There's coffee for you here."

My eyebrows snap together. Pippa does this—makes me coffee—and I don't know how I feel about it. I'm not used to someone doing these things for me.

A funny warmth spreads through my stomach, and I jerk a quick nod at her.

"Thanks."

When I reach past her, her scent surrounds me. Vanilla, maybe coconut? Something light and sweet, like her. My balls tighten.

How am I horny again? I *just* jerked off.

Pippa tilts her head at me with a patient look. "Wow. You must really need that coffee."

I'm glaring at her, I realize. I clear my throat and walk toward the door, sipping the coffee.

Fuck. That's good.

"Daisy," I call. "Let's go for a walk."

She's curled up on the couch in the living room, sleeping. She opens her eyes halfway before going back to sleep.

"I've already taken her," Pippa says, finishing her coffee.

I frown. "It's your day off."

She shrugs, smiling at Daisy. "I like taking her out first

thing in the morning. The streets are quiet, and we wander through the park. It's nice, and I don't mind." She places her mug in the dishwasher and heads to the door. "Okay, I gotta go. I'll be back around noon."

My eyes are on the curve of her thighs in the yoga leggings, thinking about what they'd feel like around my head. "Where are you going?"

"Hazel's teaching hot yoga today." She pulls her sneakers on. "The other teachers at her studio are kind of bitchy, so I like to go to support her."

There's a weird feeling in my chest, like I don't want to say goodbye. Without thinking, I set my coffee mug on the table and nod once at her.

"Alright. Let's go."

She stares at me in confusion.

I pull my sneakers on, ignoring the warning feeling at the edge of my consciousness. It's just yoga, I tell myself. I'm already in workout clothes since I was planning to take Daisy on an easy run this morning. I'll do this instead.

"I'm sore today. Yoga helps with my flexibility."

She bites her lip, and my gaze traces the curve of her mouth. "Are you sure?"

"Yes." I open the door. "After you."

When she offers me a shy smile in the elevator, the warning feeling goes silent. Maybe she wants to spend more time with me, too.

"WE'RE BREATHING," Hazel reminds the class, walking slowly around us to make adjustments to our poses. She rests her palm on my lower back, and I deepen the downward dog stretch.

Sweat drips off my nose and onto the mat. I know this class is called *hot yoga*, but I forgot *how* hot it really is. I've chugged two bottles of water in forty minutes. Sweat pools in my sports bra, and as I tilt with the pose, reaching for the sky with my right hand, it pours out. My underwear is damp, and not in the fun way.

I glance over at Jamie, and our eyes meet. His cheeks are flushed from the heat. His shirt came off a few minutes into class, and I can't seem to focus on the poses or Hazel's voice. There are only three other people in the class, but I barely notice them.

Jamie Streicher's body is perfect. Beads of sweat roll down his washboard abs. A smattering of dark, neatly trimmed chest hair spans his broad chest. Thick, muscular arms hold him up during poses. His pecs and calves? Chiseled from stone. Down his stomach, a trail of hair leads into his shorts, and my mind snags on it again and again.

Every time he moves, his muscles ripple. Combined with his bright eyes and intimidating strength, he's the perfect picture of vitality and power.

Arousal thrums low in my stomach, and I'm picturing him picking me up and throwing me over his shoulder.

Maybe I spoke too soon about my underwear.

He's also insanely flexible. From the depth and balance to his poses, he's done yoga before.

"*Child's pose,*" Hazel says beside me in an emphasizing tone, like this isn't the first time she's said it. She widens her eyes at me, a silent question of *dude, what are you doing?* in her eyes, and I hurry into the pose.

Letting Jamie come with me was a terrible idea. I can't stop staring at him. He's a flawless Olympian—my dad told me he played in the last Winter Olympics for Canada—and right now, I look like a sewer rat.

We hang out in child's pose for a while, and Hazel refills our water bottles. When I glance over at Jamie, his back muscles don't look as tight as before.

He has a lot of back muscles. I clench my eyes closed and put my head down, deepening the pose. It's not like that with Jamie, and no good can come from ogling him.

I remember the low groan I heard from his room this morning. I keep telling myself it was just him stretching, waking up. He said he was sore. It was probably that.

It doesn't stop me from picturing what else that groan could have been from, though.

Hazel pokes me in the ribs. The rest of the class is in chair pose, and I'm still in child's pose.

"Focus," she murmurs as she passes.

I'm focused, alright. Focused on the shirtless hockey player who's miles out of my league.

———

After class is over and I take a quick shower in the change room, I head back to the lobby. The students from class are taking a photo with Jamie. The two yoga teachers who were at the front desk when we checked in are waiting, eyes on him, and when it's their turn, they're at his side in a flash, arms around his waist. Something pinches between my ribs.

He isn't smiling, but he also isn't glaring. One of the women nestles closer to him, and his gaze flicks over to me.

A muscle yanks in my stomach and my shoulders tense. I have no reason to be pissed. I have zero claim on him. He's my boss and roommate and that's it. I just... really don't like them touching him like that and looking at him with stars in their eyes.

"What the fuck?" Hazel hisses at my side. "You brought him here?"

We didn't have a chance to talk alone before class. "He didn't give me a choice."

We watch the other teachers take a flurry of pictures. "He's really flexible." She slides a coy glance at me.

"Stop it." I hide a laugh.

Her expression is all innocence.

Jamie finishes taking photos and heads over to us.

"Good class," he tells Hazel with a nod. "Thanks." He holds his hand out. "I'm Jamie."

She takes it warily. "Hazel."

"You work with the team."

Surprise flicks over her features. "Yes." She mentions the senior physiotherapists she works with, and Jamie nods.

"The other players could benefit from something like this."

Hazel just shrugs, but I can tell she's trying not to smile. She can be guarded, especially with men, but deep down, she wants people to walk out of her classes feeling good, even if they are pro hockey players.

"Join us for lunch," he tells her.

Yoga, and now lunch. My stomach flutters, and I tell it to shut up. He's probably starving and doesn't know how to ditch me, or he doesn't want to be rude. I stare at Hazel, and she stares back at me. In our gazes, we're having a full conversation.

"She'd love to," I say, smiling at Jamie.

———

Jamie takes us to a strange, dingy bar in an alley in Gastown.

"*The Filthy Flamingo*," I read on the sign above the door.

"Don't say it's a dive bar," he tells us as he holds the door open.

Hazel and I pause at the front door, letting our eyes adjust. They're playing "Tangerine," my favorite Led Zeppelin song. The inside of the bar is cozy and warm, and I immediately love this place—the vintage concert posters, the photos behind the bar, the twinkling lights stretching across the ceiling.

Behind the counter, a woman mixes drinks. She's gorgeous, actually, with this nineties grunge look that I immediately love.

She glances at Jamie. "You again."

He makes a noise in his throat that sounds like a stifled laugh. The bartender nods hello at me and Hazel. "Sit wherever."

My gaze lands on a poster for The Who's *Quadrophenia* album. "Hazel!" I point at it. "Look."

Hazel smiles at it. "Cool."

"You like *Quadrophenia*?" the bartender asks.

We slip onto bar stools. "It's our dad's favorite album," I explain. "We grew up on that record."

She offers us a small, pleased smile. "Good taste." A beat. "I'm Jordan."

"Pippa." I like her immediately. "That's Hazel. And Jamie."

She nods at Hazel, and when she turns to Jamie, she arches an eyebrow. "No hockey talk in here."

He makes another noise that might be a laugh. We order lunch, and while we eat, Jamie actually makes conversation with Hazel about yoga.

"I'd love to do a class for injured athletes," Hazel's saying. "Something that goes at a slower pace."

"Hazel wants to open her own studio one day," I explain for Jamie. "A space where people of all body types feel comfortable, instead of just skinny people."

His eyebrows rise and he regards Hazel with something that looks like respect. "That's a great idea. The world needs more people like you."

She stares at him. "I thought you were supposed to be an asshole."

Jamie looks at me, and something glints in his eyes. "Did you tell her that?"

"Um." I blink. "No?" Very convincing, Pippa. I wince, but I'm smiling. "I mean, you did fire me."

Our eyes lock, and my stomach does a slow, warm roll. There's that fascinating twitch at the corner of his mouth. I have the urge to reach out and brush my finger over it. Hazel's glancing between us with a funny look on her face. Our gazes meet, and her eyebrows bob up and down once.

She's really trying not to like him, but between his thoughtful questions, his interest in her profession, and how little ego he has, she doesn't stand a chance.

I don't know if I do, either. Who is this version of him? He's nothing like the surly asshole I thought he was.

Jamie finishes his sandwich and leans back in his chair. "Do you do private classes?"

Hazel looks concerned. "Yes?"

He nods once. "My trainer will contact you."

Later, when Jamie heads to the washroom, I smile at Hazel. "You're right. All hockey players *are* evil."

She rolls her eyes but she's smiling. "Whatever." Her eyes narrow at me. "He likes you."

I flush with happy, buzzy feelings. "He can hardly stand me."

She chokes. "Are you kidding?"

"Hazel, the guy *fired* me. He only rehired me because he felt bad for me. And then he saw me crying, and that made it ten times worse." I lower my voice. "He pities me. I'm just the dog walker, basically. He doesn't like me."

She holds my gaze with a knowing look. "He likes you."

I hate the flurry of butterflies in my stomach at her words.

On the counter, Hazel's phone starts buzzing. "I have a ton of notifications," she mutters, frowning at the screen. "Dude," she says a moment later in a flat tone, scrolling through comments.

She's been tagged in one of the photos with Jamie that the other students posted. It's going viral on social media because he almost never takes photos with people. An email pops up on her phone, and she reads it.

"My class next week is full," she says, sounding dazed.

My jaw drops. "That's incredible."

She shakes her head, reading on. "The whole month. My Saturday hot classes for the whole month are booked up. The studio wants to add a second class in the afternoon."

I'm beaming. She turns to me with a funny, surprised smile, and gratitude for Jamie squeezes in my chest. I love seeing Hazel so happy and proud like this.

When he returns, Jamie insists on paying for lunch to thank Hazel for the class, and after we say goodbye to her, we head back to our apartment building.

Something occurs to me, and I turn to him with narrowed eyes. "You knew going to Hazel's class would help her."

He shrugs, but the corner of his mouth lifts. My heart swells.

"Oooooh." I nod, smiling at him. "Okay. I see it now."

"What?" His expression is concerned.

I just continue smiling at him. "You're *nice*."

He looks at me like I've grown another head.

I nod. "Yeah. You are. You take care of your mom, you took in a stray dog that needed a home, and you made me move in." I hitch my thumb over my shoulder in the direction we came from. "You bought us lunch. Jamie, you're nice."

He beeps his key fob at the entrance of our building and opens the door for me, not meeting my gaze. "It's not a big deal."

"I told you Hazel's coworkers were bitchy, so you came with me to help her out."

His eyes rest on me as we wait for the elevator, and there's something warm in his gaze. "Maybe I just wanted to hang out with you."

I chuckle. "Mhm. I'm sure. You probably have supermodels on speed dial, so it makes perfect sense that you'd spend your day off with *me*."

We step into the elevator. Amusement twitches on his lips. "Speed dial?"

"I said what I said." My chest shakes with laughter. Something about the way he's pinning me with his gaze, and how maybe I'm amusing him, is making my stomach do excited backflips.

Our gazes hold, and there's a drop in my stomach that I'm

going to attribute to the elevator ascending. His eyes glitter, and I can smell his fresh, sharp scent.

Oh, wow.

He isn't smiling, but his gaze is warm. Delight sparkles in my chest, and I fight the urge to rub my sternum. This feeling is new.

"I owe you one for today." My voice is barely above a whisper, and I'm aware of how small this elevator is and how much room he takes up.

His throat works as he swallows, still holding my gaze. "You want to make it up to me?"

My lips part, and a shiver rolls down my spine. There's heat in his eyes, and I blink at him, stunned.

His words sound suggestive. An intimate muscle tugs between my legs. Oh god. I can't get turned on in an elevator. I'm not that kind of girl.

The corner of his mouth slides up into a smirk, and my heart beats faster.

I *am* the kind of girl who gets turned on in an elevator. It's too late. It's happening. We're there. I'm horny for my hockey player boss in an elevator.

I really can't be doing this. Jamie is totally off-limits. He's too hot, too nice, and he smells way too good. Letting my crush balloon into something more will only end in heartbreak for me.

"Okay," I say, still holding his electric gaze.

"Play me a song."

I flinch. A heavy weight extinguishes my horniness as my thoughts freeze.

"Any song," he says, and my skin prickles at the low tone of his voice. The elevator door opens. "One of your favorites; I don't care."

I open my mouth to tell him I can't, but he dips his head

down to meet my eyes so we're on the same level. His arm is holding the elevator door open.

"Yes, you can," he says in a firm, demanding tone. The corner of his mouth is curling, and I wonder if I were to sit down and play a song for him on my guitar, would I get a full, high-watt smile from him?

It's tempting.

I'm standing there frozen, but his hand comes to my lower back, and he gently guides me out of the elevator. His warmth permeates my layers of clothing, and I want to lean into his hand.

Inside the front door, Daisy jumps up and runs over to greet us, and he grabs her leash from the side table. I still haven't said a word.

"It's settled then." He clips her harness on before straightening up. "Thanks for a fun morning, Pippa," he murmurs.

It's *settled*?

At whatever my expression is, his mouth slides into that sexy smirk again.

"Bye," he says, stepping out the door.

I stand there for a long moment, replaying his slow smirk, the press of his hand on my lower back.

He wants a song, but every time I think about picking up my guitar, my stomach churns with worry and hesitation.

*Yes, you can*, he said, and he sounded so certain. Maybe he's right. Maybe I can. I lean against the door, blowing out a long breath.

A FEW DAYS LATER, I'm standing in my kitchen in my boxers, staring out the window. It's midnight, and the kitchen's dim, only lit by the city lights.

I can't sleep.

I've barely seen her all week. When I get home, she heads to her room or leaves to meet Hazel. I pour a glass of water and down half of it, thinking about the charge of electricity between us on Sunday afternoon. I wanted to kiss her so fucking badly.

I still do.

"Fuck," I mutter before draining the glass.

The fear in her eyes when I asked her to play a song for me made me sick. Her ex fucked with her head, and now she can't do the thing she loves.

I want more for her. I don't want her to live with this fear. I want her to crush it and feel proud. Pippa's strong—I saw it when she helped my mom with her panic attack.

I rub the bridge of my nose. I want *more* for her? I'm no one to her. She works for me. She doesn't remember me. A twinge of guilt gets me in the gut. Maybe telling her to play for me was over the line.

There's a noise behind me, and Pippa's standing in the dim kitchen, looking just as surprised as I am.

She's wearing pajamas, a silky mint green shorts set. The shorts are short, and her legs are long and smooth. Her hair is messy, like she's been tossing and turning, and I don't know why I like that idea so much. When my gaze snags on her top, lust surges in my blood.

Her nipples are peaked. Oh, fuck. My teeth grit, and it takes all my willpower to drag my gaze up.

"I couldn't sleep," she says with a nervous smile.

I nod. "Me, neither."

She moves past me and turns the kettle on before pulling her favorite tea out of the cupboard. Decaf vanilla chai. The wrappers are always in the garbage; she must drink a ton of that stuff.

"You've been avoiding me this week," I say, and her hands falter as she rips the bag open.

"Um." She blinks at the counter. "No, I haven't."

I stare at her, and finally, her gaze flicks to mine. A smile ghosts over her face and she laughs a little.

"Okay." She sighs with a guilty wince. "I have."

"Mhm." I lean on the counter, and her gaze lingers on my abs.

Is it appropriate for me to be standing in front of her in my underwear? Probably not.

Do I care? I watch as she pulls her bottom lip between her teeth, tracing my abs with her gaze.

No. No, I do not. My blood hums with satisfaction as her eyes linger on my body.

"I didn't take you for the kind of person who doesn't pay their debts," I tell her.

She huffs a laugh. "I wouldn't say it's a *debt*."

"'I owe you one.' That's what you said."

"Jamie." She rolls her eyes at me, smiling. I love the way she says my name in that teasing way.

I fold my arms over my chest, and her gaze lingers on my biceps. "What's the holdup?"

She turns, busying herself with her tea. "You've had games and stuff."

Not more than normal.

My mind wanders to a couple nights ago, after I got home from a game. When I turned on the TV, it was already on the sports channel. Was she watching my game?

Pride bursts in my chest at the thought of it.

"You're stalling."

Her eyes are on her tea, and the smell wafting off it is the same as her hair products—sweet, spicy, and warm. Comforting but sexy and intriguing. I have the urge to bury my face in her neck and huff.

She lifts her gaze to meet mine, and her eyes are full of vulnerability. "The last time I played for someone, they laughed at me." Her voice is quiet.

Rage surges through my veins. I'll kill them. "Who?" I demand in a low, lethal voice. "Tell me. Names. Now."

She rolls her eyes. "Jamie."

"*Now.*"

"It was Zach." Her face is going red, a patch of pink on each cheek, and my fists clench while folded over my chest. "And his manager." She blinks like she's reliving it before she blinks again and she's back here in the kitchen with me.

Just when I think this guy can't get worse, he does.

I nod once. "That's the song I want to hear."

I'm such a fucking asshole.

Her eyes go wide. "What? No."

"Yes." My voice is firm and demanding. I'm a pushy, arrogant dick, but I don't care.

Her hands twist, and she tries to cover up her nervousness with a fake smile. She's scared, and it's making my chest feel tight.

"Hey." I lean down so my eyes are level with hers, and my hands come to her upper arms. There's that incredible chai smell again. "When I was nine, I got hit with the puck."

Her eyes widen. "Really?"

I nod and point to my wrist. "Right here. The puck pinged off the pipe, and I had forgotten my gloves, so I was wearing spares that were too big, so they shifted. It hurt like a motherfucker."

Her expression is sympathetic. "I bet."

My hand returns to her arm. I can feel her warmth through the silky fabric. My thumb strokes back and forth over the fabric, and her lips part.

"I didn't want to get back on the ice. I was scared of getting hit again."

Her eyebrows pull together, and the way she looks at me makes me want to scoop her up into a hug and never put her down. I'd never let her go. The way she's looking at me makes me want to protect her from the world and assholes like her ex.

Her mouth slides into a rueful smile. "I don't want to get back on the ice," she whispers, nose wrinkling. Even in the dim light, her freckles are so pretty. "I'm scared of getting hit again."

This moment in my kitchen feels like we're the only people on the planet. In the back of my mind, a warning bell rings, but I ignore it. I'll deal with that later. Right now, Pippa needs me.

I give her a squeeze. "You can do it. I got back on the ice, and it was okay. Remember when my mom had a panic attack? You nailed it, songbird. You did everything right. You're tough as nails deep down, I know it."

Her brow rises. "Songbird?"

I didn't mean to call her that—it just slipped out. It's perfect for her, though. "Mhm."

She bites her bottom lip. She wants to do it. I know she does.

"Tell you what." I give her arms another squeeze while I study the blue of her eyes. "Half a song. That's all."

The long line of her throat moves as she swallows, gaze locked on mine like I'm a life raft. I want to be that for her.

I let her go and straighten up. "Come on." My tone has turned authoritative. "Let's go."

"Now?" Her eyebrows go sky-high. "Like, right now?"

"Yep." I stride to the couch and drop down, slinging an arm over the back. "Now."

Her gaze lingers on me on the couch, on my abs, my pecs, my arms, and for a brief moment—my crotch. My dick twitches with interest, and there's a pulse of something hot low in my gut.

Let her look all she wants.

"Quit stalling."

"You're so bossy," she says, shaking her head as she disappears up the stairs to get her guitar. She says it in a resigned way, but there's something else in her voice. Something amused by my bossiness.

I lean back and lace my hands behind my head, and when she returns, guitar in hand, she stops short at the sight of me.

"Yes?" I ask.

"Can you put a shirt on?"

Her gaze snags on my stomach, and I feel like smiling again. I know what I look like. "Why?"

I know why, but I don't care. Watching my pretty assistant get flustered is fun.

She gives me a flat look and gestures at my torso and arms. "All of that."

There's a pressure in my chest, warm and crackling, like laughter. My mouth hitches into a smirk. "No."

"Stubborn, too," she mutters, and I smile at her.

She freezes, watching my face with a funny look. Like awe or something.

"What?"

"You're smiling." Her pretty lips curve into her own smile. Her gaze roams my face, and my skin prickles with awareness.

Suddenly, I want her a lot closer. In my lap. Straddling me, maybe. Her hands in my hair, and mine in hers.

She tucks her chin down, cheeks going pink again. "Alright, Jamie Streicher. Your smile makes me feel like playing." She takes a deep breath and strums. The opening notes ring out.

She starts to sing, and something in my chest locks into place.

JAMIE STREICHER'S smile captivates me. Even after his mouth is back to the normal cruel slash, the warm glint remains in his eyes.

I strum the chords, pluck the strings, and sing that song I wrote months ago about getting older and changing. The one Zach laughed at.

My voice is gritty from sleep. I haven't warmed up, and there's a rasp to the notes, but I like how it sounds. I keep hearing their laughter, seeing the look on Zach's face, so baffled and embarrassed but entertained, but I shove those thoughts away.

*You're tough as nails, deep down. I know it.* That's what Jamie said.

He also called me songbird.

His eyes are on me the entire time, warm and steady, and he pulls me back to the present. To this moment, sitting in his living room in the middle of the night while I play my guitar for the first time in months. It isn't as hard as I thought—in fact, it feels natural, like no time has passed. Through the windows, the city lights twinkle from across the water, and the moon is bright in the night sky.

My shoulders ease as I move into the chorus again, and something unfurls inside me. This song is fun. It feels like Fleetwood Mac with a modern Taylor Swift spin, and then one more element that's all me. It has a quick tempo and a hooky melody. It's why I couldn't get the tune out of my head once it showed up. I had to do something with it, had to weave it into a song.

I pause after the second verse, narrowing my eyes at Jamie as I try to remember the next part. He raises an eyebrow at me, intrigued.

The next verse rushes back at me, and I launch into it. The corner of Jamie's mouth tugs up into a lazy grin.

God, he's fucking gorgeous. My eyes drop to his torso, so distracting with all the ridges and deep lines of muscle. The way he's spreading his legs like that, in his black boxers?

I yank my gaze up, and his eyes flash with interest. Oh god. He saw me looking at his crotch.

The song is about becoming a new person, and my mind wanders back to Zach as I sing the last third, leaning into the music. I thought Zach and I would be together forever. At the airport, I waited for my flight in the terminal, feeling so fucking crushed. The person I trusted most had shipped me away, out of sight, and I felt like I'd never feel that closeness that I had with Zach with anyone again.

Now I wonder if we ever had that closeness to begin with, or if it was all in my head.

Jamie's still watching and listening. Something glitters in my chest, just a pinch of it, fine but sparkling. Zach wasn't the one for me, but the way Jamie's making me feel right now, so safe and special and supported... maybe I'll find that feeling again.

Not with Jamie, of course. Even if he did date, he'd go for

someone in his league. We've always been on two different levels, even back in high school. I'm not naive. I know better.

But that doesn't mean I won't find it with someone. Maybe. One day.

I finish the song, and pride moves through my chest. My mouth twists as I hide a smile. It's embarrassing, being proud of myself for something so dumb. Something's flowing through my blood, a burst of excitement from playing something I love. Passion and challenge and pride all mixed together. It intoxicates me. Or maybe that's from being this close to Jamie while he's almost naked.

Jamie leans forward, eyes on me. "You wrote that?"

I nod. My heart thumps in my chest.

He studies me before he growls and shakes his head, almost to himself. "That guy was never good enough for you. Not in high school and not now. I hope you fucking see that."

His words melt into me. If what Zach did put a crack in my heart, Jamie's words smooth something cool over it to fill it in. Like aloe over a sunburn. It means something, what he said.

"Wait." My eyebrows snap together, and I tilt my head, replaying it. "I didn't tell you Zach and I went to high school together."

Jamie's eyes widen a fraction, and my lips part in surprise. Is it possible that he remembers me from high school? No. No way.

A guilty look passes over his face, and my jaw drops. "Jamie." My tone is accusing, and I wear a curious smile.

"Fuck," he mutters to himself, rubbing the back of his neck. His expression is sheepish, and it's adorable. "You probably don't remember, but we went to the same high school."

A laugh bursts out of me. Don't *remember him?* How could anyone *not?*

"I'm a couple years older, and I missed a lot of school for hockey," he goes on, and his embarrassed expression sobers me immediately.

Oh. He's serious. He actually thinks I don't remember him.

"I'm sorry I didn't say anything before," he goes on, and his knee bobs up and down in a distracting way. "You took me by surprise when I saw you the first time, and then I just..." He trails off, and his eyes meet mine. "I didn't want to make it weird."

I could go on pretending, but why? It's exhausting. And the fact that he remembers me is making my heart do Daisy's excited tippy-taps against the front wall of my chest.

"I remember you," I admit. "Of course I remember you."

His expression stills. "You do?"

I can't help but roll my eyes. "Jamie. Come on. You were on your way to the NHL. You were one of the popular kids. All the girls swooned over you. You were gorgeous, even back then—"

His eyebrow goes up, and there's that look again. Teasing, focused, and determined. "You think I'm gorgeous?"

Sparks dance up my throat, and I swallow. I'm blushing. "Uh," I say stupidly.

The corner of his mouth twitches. "You said *even back then*. That means you thought I was gorgeous then, and you think I'm gorgeous now."

My pulse beats in my ears and I can't look away. His gaze pins me like a butterfly under glass. My lips part and close as I scramble for what to say.

Busted. I'm *so* busted, and now that he clearly knows I've had the most massive crush on him forever, it's going to be awkward.

He leans forward with a confident, teasing smirk that makes my heart pound harder.

"I thought you were gorgeous, too," he murmurs, looking at me in a way that makes me feel like I can't breathe. "Even back then."

It can't be true. I study his eyes, searching for the lie, but come up with nothing. No one's ever called me gorgeous except my mom, and that's different.

Something weird is happening inside my head; I'm rapidly reconsidering everything I thought to be true.

"Oh." The word falls from my lips, and the corner of his mouth tugs up. "Okay." I sound dazed.

Our eyes are locked, and there's a zing of tension between us. My stomach rolls, and for a moment, I want Jamie to be that guy, the one who makes me forget Zach ever existed.

His gaze drops to my lips, and focused hunger flares in his eyes. My nipples pinch, because I've never been looked at like that, and definitely not by a guy who looks like Jamie.

Predatory focus rises in his eyes, and between my legs, I clench.

It feels like we're about to kiss.

A tiny part of me is freaking out, waving her arms around and snapping her fingers to get my attention. This is crazy, and it isn't real. The energy in the air is heated, tense, and dangerous, and I don't want anything to do with it. I don't even want to *imagine* that Jamie likes me.

He'll devastate me. After Zach, I'm full of cracks. I can't have feelings for Jamie, because if it ends like it did with Zach—which it will—I'll smash.

I shoot to my feet, holding my guitar like a shield. "We should go to bed."

He watches me with that look that makes my insides squirm. "Good night, Pippa."

Leaving him in the living room, sprawled on the couch like

that, I run up the stairs, back to my room, where I set my guitar in its case and climb back into bed.

My heart races while I stare out the window at the dark sky, thinking about how Jamie watched me while I played.

"THEIR FIRST-LINE DEFENSE is weak since Hammond is out with an injury," Ward tells our defensemen a couple nights later in the dressing room. Hayden Owens and Alexei Volkov, an older defenseman, nod.

Ward continues to talk us through game strategy. The energy in the room is heightened, crackling with intensity. Even down here, we can hear the fans excited in the stands.

The Calgary Cougars are our biggest rival, and tonight is the first game against them this season.

Ward runs through the drills we practiced this week, but my mind is elsewhere.

My mind is on my pretty assistant, sitting in her tiny sleep top and shorts, smooth legs tucked beneath her as she played the guitar in the middle of the night, looking like an angel sent from heaven.

Or maybe she was sent from the devil, because Pippa is tempting as hell.

*Gorgeous, even back then.*

Something pleased floods my chest. She remembers me, and she thinks I'm hot.

I've been thinking about her since I woke up this morning.

Throughout practice, my mind was on her singing. In the shower, I pictured her with me, naked and wet and smiling up at me with sparkling eyes. When I picked lunch up from the Filthy Flamingo, I remembered how her eyes danced, taking in the string lights across the ceiling.

After she played guitar for me, I wanted to kiss her so fucking badly. The way her nipples pinched under her top has been tormenting me for days. I can't remember the last time I was so attracted to a woman.

I am so fucked.

I catch myself—I'm not fucked. I'm fine. I've trained with the best sports psychologists in the world, and I know how to block out distractions. Pippa isn't an option. She's not part of the plan, and there's no room to slip, because if Pippa and I start messing around, I have an ugly feeling that we won't be able to stop.

One of the sports psychologists in New York liked to appeal to my competitive nature. *Challenge yourself*, she'd say. Keeping my distance from Pippa—my high school crush, the girl I can't seem to say no to—is proving to be a challenge. Nothing I can't handle, though.

I remember the smile that grew on her face as she kept playing and singing, like she was proud and surprised. My heart twists and I rub my sternum over my hockey pads. Fucking hell, she was so beautiful, and knowing she was afraid to do it made me so proud.

I hope she knows she isn't broken. I hope she realizes what she's capable of.

She's here again tonight with my mom. Sparks pop in my chest at the idea of Pippa watching my game. Maybe biting her plush bottom lip in tense moments.

"Streicher."

My head snaps up. Ward and everyone else in the change room are staring at me.

"You okay?" Ward tilts his chin at where I'm rubbing my sternum.

I let my hand drop. "Yeah." I nod. "Fine."

On the way to the ice, he pulls me aside.

"Is tonight going to be a problem?" he asks as the other players shuffle past. Music pumps in the arena as players hit the ice to warm up.

Shit. My distraction with Pippa is written all over my face. *Get it together, Streicher.* I shake my head. "Nope."

Ward studies my face. "Don't let Miller get in your head." He glances around, waiting until the equipment manager steps out of the hall. "I know you guys have history."

My thoughts screech to a halt. Rory Miller was traded to Calgary recently. I knew this and I completely forgot.

*That* is how bad this thing with Pippa is. I forgot that the guy I grew up with, who used to be my best friend until he turned into a total fucking asshole, is going to be on the ice tonight.

I frown at Ward. "How do you know about that?"

"It's my job."

Seven years into his career, Miller has a reputation for partying, girls, and being a fucking asshole on the ice. As he developed into an incredible right winger, his ego grew. Coaches keep him around because he scores goals, but he's far from a fan favorite.

I hate playing against him. Calgary's one of the closest teams to Vancouver, geographically, so we play them six times this season.

He has one of the best scoring averages in the league, and he's going to be slapping pucks at me all night. This is the kind of thing I should have been thinking about all week, preparing and reviewing game tape.

"You've played with him," Ward says. "You know his weaknesses?"

Miller's the star. Always has been, since we were kids. He's the most competitive person I've ever met. We never would have been friends if I wasn't a goalie.

I think back to past games. He doesn't listen to the coach's plays. The starting line will think they're running a certain play, and Miller will take it off the rails for the chance to score. And because he often succeeds, he gets away with it.

I know to keep my eye on him, even if his teammates are setting up for a different formation. I know not to trust him.

I nod at Ward. "Yeah. I know him."

"Good." He slaps me on the shoulder. "Let's get out there and have a great game."

I hit the ice, and the back of my neck prickles. On the other half of the rink, our opponents warm up, skating and shooting pucks at the goalie. The arena's already packed, brimming with energy.

Rory Miller's standing there, wearing a smug, cocky grin that makes me want to hit him. He tilts his head, turns, and skates for the net, sinking the puck in before he spins around. His smile stretches from ear to ear, and my gut seizes up with irritation.

He's trying to get to me. This is what he does.

I head to my net, centering myself. In front of the goal posts, I warm up, and my gaze locks with Pippa's. She's sitting behind the net with my mom and my mom's friend.

Pippa's wearing a Vancouver Storm hat. I blink, staring at her in it, and those sparks ignite in my chest all over again.

She lights up, lifting her hand in a quick, shy wave that makes the corner of my mouth tip up. I wave back, and the frustration I felt moments before melts away. She points at her hat, and I nod, letting myself smile at her. I like seeing her in my team's gear.

Beside her, my mom is chatting away, smiling. She says something to Pippa, who nods and laughs. My mom likes Pippa and asks about her every time I call, and I like that, too.

I like that after the game, Pippa and Daisy will be at home.

———

The whistle blows and the third period starts. My blood pumps hard as Calgary takes the puck.

Pippa's gaze rests on my shoulders like a blanket, calming me, keeping me focused. I've blocked every shot, and the fans are chanting *Streicher shut out*.

Their left winger passes to Miller, who swings around Owens. He's on a breakaway with the puck, skating hard, eyes on me. That fucking smug smirk on his face. His team gets in position, but I ignore them.

He's frustrated. His smug smile is forced. I'm getting to him. He showed up here tonight to score against me, to prove something to me, maybe that he doesn't need me or that I'm just another player to him.

His gaze flicks to something behind me, and his eyes go wide in surprise.

Pippa. My heart stops. He knew I had a thing for her in high school. I never told him, but he knew.

By the time I realize what he's done, the fans are groaning in disappointment and the puck is in the net.

Miller skates past me with a catlike smile. The fans boo him, and he turns that grin on them, which riles them up more. My stomach sinks, my teeth grit, but I shove all the thoughts away as the game resumes.

I was focused on his weaknesses when mine sits right behind me.

———

We win, and after the coach reviews the game in the change room, I shower and head upstairs to the box.

My heart stops when I see Rory fucking Miller grinning down at Pippa, predatory gaze locked on her. He says something, she laughs, and he grins wider, stepping closer to her.

Primal protectiveness rises in me. It's not uncommon for players from the other team to visit the box, especially if they have friends or family on the opposing team. I sure as fuck don't like him being here, though, talking with her. My teeth grit, and I'm in front of him, placing myself between them, staring him down.

His dark blond hair is still damp, and he's in his suit. Is he trying to fucking impress her or something?

He eyes me with smug amusement. "There he is."

"What the fuck are you doing here?" I bite out, glaring at him.

His grin broadens, and I want to fucking kill him.

"Just catching up with the lovely Pippa," he says before gesturing over his shoulder, where my mom, her friend, and Ward are talking. "And I wanted to say hi to Donna."

"I was telling Rory how I work as your assistant now." Pippa gives him a shy smile, and my glare intensifies.

I don't like her smiling for him.

"And you guys live together," Rory adds, narrowing his eyes at us.

My skin crawls. He sees right fucking through me.

"Don't talk to her," I snap, and people in the vicinity glance over at my tone.

He has the fucking audacity to laugh. "Buddy."

At my sides, my hands make fists. My pulse whooshes in my ears. On the ice, this is all fair game, but up here? With my—

With my assistant, I remind myself, dragging in a deep breath.

"I should get going," he tells Pippa, smiling down at her like he's found buried treasure. "Early flight tomorrow. Great seeing you again, Pippa. Maybe next time, you can show me around Vancouver."

She laughs. "You're from here."

His eyes sparkle. "I'm sure the city's changed in a decade. And I'd love to keep catching up." His gaze slides to mine, and the suggestive undertones make my blood roar.

No fucking way.

He tilts a grin at me. "Maybe you'll get your *Streicher shut out* next time, huh?" Miller walks away before I can respond, waving at a few people before disappearing out the door.

Before I can say anything else, Owens is in front of us, slapping my shoulder. I try not to flinch.

"Great fucking game, bud."

"Thanks." My tone is terse.

I just want to get home, get the fuck out of here. Maybe Pippa will play another song for me tonight.

Pippa shoots Owens a sympathetic smile. He took a puck to the ankle in the second period. "How's your ankle, Hayden?"

For some reason, when she smiles at him, it doesn't cut as much. Maybe because my gut tells me he's a good guy, and he's this friendly to everyone.

He reaches down to lift his pant leg, showing her the red welt and growing bruise. "Pretty gross, but I'll live." He puffs out his chest in an exaggerated way. "I'm tough, Pippa."

She laughs. "Okay."

A couple of the players are at the door. One of them waves to Owens and he makes a *one moment* gesture.

"We're going out," he tells us, and unlike Miller, he's not just talking to Pippa. He points at me. "Coach said you had to hang out with us."

I roll my eyes with a snort, but I can't argue. In every practice, Ward brings up team building and bonding and has called me out specifically a few times. Even though my blood is still rushing after the game and I won't sleep for hours, I don't feel like going out.

I just want to hang out with Pippa. Maybe we can watch a movie at home.

Pippa's smile is hopeful, and her eyes are bright. "What do you say? Do you want to blow off some steam?"

My eyebrow arches. "You actually want to go?" I tilt my chin at the players congregating by the door. "With them?"

She shrugs, and her sheepish smile is so cute. "Yeah, I do."

Owens isn't an asshole like Miller, but I still don't want a bunch of single hockey players circling Pippa like sharks.

"Come on." Owens punches me lightly in the stomach, and I push him off with a snort. This guy is like Daisy in human form, excited and full of energy.

In an instant, my mind changes. I want to see this girl outside the walls of my apartment. I want to see her laughing and having fun.

I nod once. "Okay."

Pippa lights up, and I can't look away. "Great."

# CHAPTER 22

# PIPPA

OUTSIDE THE ARENA, Donna promises to text Jamie when she gets home as she and her friend pile into the Uber, and we follow the team out to the Filthy Flamingo.

Jordan gives us a flat look as we pile in. "Are you fucking kidding me?" she asks Hayden.

"Hey, sunshine," he says, laughing, grabbing her in a big hug. "We won tonight."

She elbows him in the gut, and he pretends it hurts. "I don't care." She sees me and gives me a small smile and a nod. "Hey."

"Hi." I gesture at the hockey players as they take up the back half of the narrow bar. "Is this okay?"

She snorts. "Yeah, it's fine. I'm used to these assholes."

Chairs and tables scrape as the guys rearrange them so we can all sit together. At the back of the bar, a guy stands in front of a mic, tuning his guitar. He looks up and winks at Jordan.

"You hired live entertainment?" I smile wide at her.

She rolls her eyes. "No, that's just Chris."

Chris waves at us. "I'm her boyfriend."

"He's not my boyfriend," she says, loud enough for Chris and everyone between the two of them to overhear. "We just have sex."

A laugh slips out of me. "Nice."

Maybe I can get to the place where I can have casual sex with a guy I don't care about.

Jamie's hand lands on my lower back, and he leads me to a seat in one of the booths before slipping in beside me. His arm comes over the top of the booth, his thigh presses against mine, and his scent surrounds me. His position around me feels possessive, like I'm his.

I think about the other night, how he remembers me from high school. How he said I was gorgeous. My throat feels tight. I can't stop thinking about the intense way he looked when he said it.

A tiny shred inside me wonders if Jamie's attracted to me. I've been the quiet, invisible girl in the background for so long that it feels unfathomable.

Hayden slides into the other side of the booth, along with Alexei, a gruff defenseman in his mid-thirties who doesn't say much. His nose is crooked like it's been broken before, but like all these guys, he's handsome, just in a rougher way.

"Miller gave us a run for our money tonight, huh?" Hayden asks, and Alexei grunts his agreement.

To my surprise, Rory also remembered me from high school. He made me show him pictures of Daisy, so I showed him one of Daisy, Hazel, and me the day we went hiking in North Van, and he studied it with interest. He only started acting like an asshole when Jamie showed up.

Jordan drops off our drinks, and I study Jamie, who studies me right back over his beer.

I know Rory isn't interested in me *that way*. I only got platonic vibes from our conversation, but he was trying to piss off Jamie.

The image of Jamie in the upstairs box, jaw clenched tight and jealousy flashing through his eyes, makes me smile up at him. I want to see how this thing with Rory and Jamie plays out. I wonder if they'll ever be friends again.

"Something funny, songbird?" His voice is a low murmur, and a shiver runs down my back.

I smile wider. "Nope."

His eyes dance, and even though his mouth is in a flat line, his gaze is warm and amused. "Good. Keep it that way."

I chuckle. In my jacket pocket, my phone buzzes. I pull it out and read the text from my friend Alissa, who I worked with on the tour.

*Girl. We're gonna be in Vancouver next week. Last stop on the tour before the break!*

My stomach sinks. The faces of everyone from the tour roll through my head, and shame rises in me. With a close-knit group of people who work insane hours, side by side, secrets don't exist. No one from the tour texted me after I mysteriously didn't show up at the next stop, and I have no doubt everyone knows exactly what happened.

I frown at my phone. I hate being reminded of my old life.

My phone buzzes again.

*There's a wrap party on Tuesday night, and your name is on the list! Jenna said she hasn't gotten your RSVP yet.*

I stare at her message in disbelief. No fucking *way* am I going to a wrap party with everyone. How fucking shameful would that be? I can't. I won't.

I read her text again, frowning. I never got an invite. I open my email and scroll through the unread messages.

There it is. Oh god. The email went out to everyone on the tour, and Jenna always forgets to blind carbon copy people, so everyone can see my email on the list. Everyone knows I've been invited.

Jamie brushes my arm. "What's going on?"

"Nothing." I blink, tucking my phone away.

He stares at me in that way that makes my stomach flutter. "Tell me."

"Bossy."

"Mhm." The corner of his mouth slants, and I can feel my own smile starting.

On the small stage at the back of the bar, the guy starts playing guitar and singing. The players mostly ignore him, but he doesn't seem to mind. I take a long sip of my drink and hum with appreciation because Jordan makes good whiskey sours. I lick the foam off my top lip, and Jamie's gaze drops to my mouth. His eyebrows slide together in a focused frown.

"Are you going to tell me why you look like you saw a ghost?" he asks in a low voice. Around us, the players are talking, laughing, and horsing around, but Jamie doesn't even notice.

I chew my lip, taking in his handsome face. His cheekbones are still flushed from his game, and he watches me with patience and curiosity. Something in his deep green eyes makes me want to tell him things.

"There's a wrap party for the tour next week."

His gaze pins me, his jaw tightening. "The tour you got fired from?"

I laugh without humor. "I mean, when you put it that way, I sound stellar."

"Pippa."

"I know, I know." I sigh, take another sip of my drink, and there are his eyes on my mouth again. Heat pools low in my stomach. His hand brushes my arm again, scattering goosebumps along my skin.

I wish I didn't have this reaction around him. It's getting harder to hide.

"Everyone saw that I was invited," I tell him, blowing out a long breath. "If I don't go, it's like…"

"Defeat."

My gaze rises to his. "Exactly. Like I'm hiding from them." My throat feels tight, and I shake my head. "A part of me wants to hide and forget them all. But there's this other part of me that feels like—" I swallow. My pulse is beating harder. "Like, *fuck him*, you know? Fuck him for firing me and picking someone new." My stomach churns, and I roll my eyes at myself. "Sorry."

"Don't." His tone is sharp. "Don't apologize." He takes a drink of his beer. "You should go."

I snort, giving him a flat look. "I'm sure that'll go great. If I show up looking super hot, they'll think I'm trying to get him back, but if I show up looking like garbage, it'll seem like I'm falling apart without him. Besides, he'll probably be making out with his new muse all night."

I down the rest of my drink. I don't want to think about this anymore.

On the stage, the guy finishes his third song before setting his guitar down. "I'm going to take a quick break, folks."

Jamie's thumb taps my arm, and he tips his chin at the stage. "Your turn."

My smile is indulgent. "Right. Very funny."

"I'm serious." His gaze bores into mine, filled with determination. "What did I tell you about getting back on the ice?"

The authority in his deep voice makes my face heat.

"Jamie." My mouth is quirking into a rueful grin. "This isn't getting back on the ice. I haven't performed on stage since high school."

"I remember."

Awareness shimmers through me, along with... something sparking in my stomach. I wish I could see inside his head.

He pins me with his gaze. "I know you can do it."

The way he looks down at me, the certainty in his voice, it makes my insides warm.

Hayden turns back to us from where he was talking with the booth behind him. "Pippa, are you a singer?"

I roll my eyes. "Not really."

"Yes," Jamie cuts in. "She sings and plays guitar, and she's good."

Hayden leans his chin on his fist, looking at me like it's Christmas Eve and I'm Santa. "Pippa."

"*No.*" I stare at Jamie. "Thanks a lot."

Hayden gathers the guys' attention. "Pippa's going to sing for us." He starts clapping.

They all react at once, clapping and hollering and moving chairs out of the way for me, but I stay seated. I glare at Hayden, but I can't be mad at him. My heart is racing but I'm laughing.

"Tell you what, songbird." Jamie's mouth brushes my ear, and there's that low tug in my belly again. "If you sing a song up there, I'll go with you to your wrap party. We'll show your asshole ex who came out on top."

I meet his gaze, and electricity pulls between us like a cord. I picture walking into the party with Jamie's arm around me, maybe his mouth brushing my ear the way it did a second ago.

I picture the look on Zach's face—disbelief, shock, and jealousy.

I like that idea.

"Deal."

EVERYONE IS STARING AT ME. This guitar is out of tune, but there isn't time to fix it.

I'm scared. My heart beats out of my chest. My thoughts are everywhere, whizzing around like bees. I readjust the strap on my shoulder and strum a soft chord. The motion is effortless.

The Filthy Flamingo goes quiet, but I can hear my pulse in my ears. Jordan leans on the bar counter, watching. What am I going to play? I scramble for a song.

If they laugh, I'll be so embarrassed. I could never go to another game.

I meet Jamie's eyes, and my mind pauses. He looks like he did the other night, when I played for him. The watchful, patient expression pinning me.

I could play that song.

The sound of Zach and his manager's laughter echoes in my head, and my lungs tighten. Playing for Jamie alone is different than playing for a bar full of people.

Across the bar, Jamie's mouth tips up as he watches me, and he winks. Right. Getting back on the ice. I'm not ready to play my own music, though.

Everyone's waiting. I hold Jamie's gaze, and I hear a song in my head. A song by Roxy Music that my dad used to play when Hazel and I were kids.

I play the opening notes and start singing. My heart is still banging like a drum, so I look at Jamie while I sing, because something about him makes me feel like this is going to be okay.

After the second verse, my jitters fizzle out. While I play, I remember my dad playing this song in the living room as Hazel and I danced around to it. Our goofy dance moves made him laugh.

During the chorus, I let my voice fly higher, testing the response. I launch into the next verse, and the stage feels steadier under my feet. The other players listen with rapt attention. Hayden's grinning his boyish smile at me, and I smile back. My gaze swings back to Jamie, and his eyes are so warm, they make my breath catch on one of the notes.

I finish the song, and the bar explodes with noise—cheering and applause. My face is on fire while I set the guitar back on the stand.

I can't believe I just did that.

"You want to play another?" Jordan asks, arching a brow at me, but she's smiling.

I shake my head. I feel like I could, though. "Not tonight, thank you."

Everyone is staring at me, smiling. They aren't laughing, so that's good. My gaze darts around, looking for an anchor, but I'm swarmed by people congratulating me. It's overwhelming.

"Just a moment," I breathe before walking to the hallway with the washrooms.

I need to catch my breath, to let my heart settle down. The wall is cool and solid as I lean against it, closing my eyes and dragging in those deep yoga breaths Hazel's always going on about.

Footsteps make my eyes open. Jamie stalks toward me with a furious look on his face.

"Wha—" I start.

His eyes flash with heat. "That was fucking amazing."

His hand comes to the back of my neck and he drags my mouth to his.

JAMIE'S MOUTH takes mine hard, like he's been wanting this for years. He grips the back of my hair and tilts my head back, dragging his tongue along mine, and my knees go weak. His movements are urgent, hungry, insistent, and demanding. His intoxicating, masculine scent is in my nose, and I can barely breathe. I don't even *want* to breathe if this is the other option. My hands move up the firm planes of his broad chest, and he groans into my mouth.

Oh god. He licks into my mouth like he wants to fuck me.

I've *never* been kissed like this.

"Fuck," he mutters between kisses, and my whole body pulses with heat.

I'm wet. He's made me wet from a kiss.

I'm not sure if my eyes are open or closed. I can't feel anything except the needy pressure between my legs, Jamie's demanding mouth, and the light pull of my hair in his fist. He grips my hair like he owns me. His other hand rests around the base of my neck, heavy and huge. He doesn't apply pressure, but just the contact of his big hand holding me in such a vulnerable position, it makes me never want to move. I like this way too much.

His stubble brushes my mouth and I moan into him. Something about that noise sets him off, because he presses his entire body against me, pinning me to the wall.

His hips push into me, and I gasp against his lips.

He's hard. The thick steel length presses into my stomach. Warm pressure twists between my legs, and I moan. Jamie's kissing me, his erection is huge, and I've definitely lost my mind.

"Jesus fucking Christ, Pippa," he growls, pulling back to look at me with dark eyes. He's breathing fast, glaring at me, towering over me. He releases my neck, and I almost whimper in protest, but he rests his forearm on the wall above my head, staring down at me with a glazed look that sets my underwear on fire.

Jamie Streicher is so fucking hot.

"What's happening?" I breathe.

He blinks and frowns, and then his gaze shutters. "Shit." He straightens up, and I want to yell *no!* "I'm sorry." He drags a palm down his face. "I lost my head. I wasn't thinking."

There are a hundred things I want to say. *I liked it* and *do it again* come to mind.

He takes a step back. Without his body heat, I'm cold. The hunger and urgency are gone from his expression, leaving only his typical cranky surliness. But unlike normal, I don't feel like teasing him about it.

I just feel hurt. An ugly realization hits me—this is exactly how I felt at the airport.

What am I *doing*? He's hot, protective, and secretly sweet. Kissing him was like nothing I've ever experienced. He's nice to his mom, for god's sake. He's the whole package. If I let him, he will *devastate* me. What Zach did will be a tiny scratch compared to what Jamie could do.

It's like I've thrown a bucket of ice water on my thoughts, and my head clears.

Jamie's mouth is a hard line as he shoves his hand through his hair. "I only do casual stuff, and with us working together—"

"I know." I play with the ends of my hair as I look away, getting my breathing under control. "This isn't a good idea."

I meet his gaze, and he studies me, looking torn. "You're my assistant," he says.

A weight lands in my stomach, and I'm angry with myself, because he's right. Everything about this is a terrible idea. I step toward the ladies' room and force a smile, like what just happened was nothing.

"I'll be out in a minute," I tell him, pushing the door open before he can answer.

I take a long moment to wash my hands, wetting a paper towel with cold water and pressing it to the back of my neck. My skin is still hot from Jamie practically fucking my mouth with his tongue.

Against my will, I picture Jamie fucking my mouth with that steel rod that pressed into me. My eyes close and I groan.

*This isn't a good idea*, I told him.

I can't be picturing it, then.

# CHAPTER 25

# JAMIE

MY JAW IS tight as I stalk back to the group. Something about my gait makes the guys move out of my way.

Fuck. Kissing Pippa was incredible. It's like she was made for me.

I shouldn't have done that, but something about Pippa makes me lose control. I can't give her more than casual, and I know that's not enough for her. That isn't enough for *me* where she's concerned, and that terrifies me.

At the booth, I down the rest of my beer, watching the entrance to the hallway, remembering how her soft mouth felt under mine, how her curves pressed into me, and how she gasped and rubbed against my cock. I don't think she even realized she did that. The hazy, drugged look in her eyes lit my blood on fire. Every cell in my body wanted to throw her over my shoulder and carry her home before I fucked her into the mattress.

If Pippa and I were together, I'd never let her rest. The thought curls around the base of my spine, and my balls ache.

I stare at my empty beer glass. My pulse is still racing. Every nerve in my body is on high alert. I wasn't even this amped up during my game tonight.

I can't believe I did that. My eyes close. I said *you're my assistant,* but what I meant was *you're special and I don't want to hurt you.* She's been through the wringer. If I crushed her the way I crushed Erin, I couldn't live with myself.

"You okay, buddy?" Owens asks, raising an eyebrow at me.

I nod and drag a sobering breath in. "Fine."

Behind him, Pippa meanders through the players to her seat. They're calling out praise for her performance, and she's giving them shy smiles. My chest tightens, and the bar feels too small.

Owens glances between Pippa and me. "Oh."

I glare at him, daring him to say something, but he just smirks.

Pippa reaches the table. "I'm going to go." Her gaze darts to mine before she looks away.

I stand, pull out my wallet, and slip a few bills out, setting them on the table.

"Don't leave on my account," she tells me. "I'm going to walk."

"It's dark," I say before I can catch myself. The idea of her walking down dark alleys makes my shoulders tense. "And I'm tired."

Her gaze flicks to mine, and I regret leaving that hallway a few minutes ago. "Okay." She puts on a bright smile for Owens. "Hayden, thanks for inviting me."

He stands and gives her a bear hug. Her feet lift off the ground, and she laughs into his broad chest. "Anytime. We're going to make you sing again."

Something pinches in my gut as I watch them, and my teeth grit. I know he's like this with everyone, but I don't like it. I want to touch her like that.

When he puts her down, she's flushed. "Maybe."

Everyone gives Pippa hugs as we leave, and when we step out the door, she's smiling her normal smile again.

"That was terrifying," she tells me. "But I'm happy I did it."

"Playing for everyone?"

She nods and glances at me. "Thanks for encouraging me."

My throat tightens as we walk. When she sang tonight, she looked like she was on top of the world. She smiled and sang and played like that fuckface Zach never happened. Like no one had hurt her, or like she had healed from it.

I want that for her. I want it so fucking badly.

That's why we can't do more of what we did tonight. She deserves so much better than me.

We stop at a crosswalk and wait for the light to change, and she rubs her arms, shivering. My eyebrows snap together.

"Cold?" I ask.

It's early November. It isn't raining, but the temperatures have dropped. She's wearing a light rain jacket with no insulation.

She nods. "We'll be home soon."

I slip my jacket off.

She rolls her eyes. "Jamie. I'm fine."

"Put this on. Now." My voice is low, and I see her breath catch.

"Bossy," she whispers, pulling it on. It's huge on her. The sleeves are way too long.

She looks fucking adorable.

We walk home in silence, listening to the sounds of the city —the car horns, peoples' conversations as we pass, noise from restaurants and bars. Inside the apartment, Pippa gives me a quick, tight smile before disappearing upstairs. I take Daisy on a long walk, thinking about Pippa the entire time, and when I climb into bed, certain that she's sleeping, I pull my aching cock out and stroke it to the memory of her moaning into my mouth.

I broke Erin's heart because I wasn't careful, and I know better than to take chances.

This is as close to messing around with Pippa as I'll get.

THE NIGHT of the wrap party, Jamie's jaw drops as I walk down the stairs.

A ping of delight hits me square in the chest, and I try to hide my grin. I know I look good. My hair is loose in long, undone waves. My dark teal velvet dress hugs my slight curves. Jamie's eyes linger on the thin straps, the neckline dipping into my cleavage, and the embroidery running down the dress to my thighs.

"That's what you're wearing?"

The words are sharp and short, like he doesn't approve, but the heat in his eyes tells me a different story. My face heats.

*This isn't a good idea*, I told him after we kissed. *You're my assistant*, he said.

This past week, we've been acting like the kiss never happened. He joined me on a few dog walks around Stanley Park and in North Van, and Donna joined us once when we hiked Seymour Mountain. It didn't seem like she picked up on any weirdness between us. I have a feeling she'd say something or tease us if she did.

"You look great," I tell him, taking in his charcoal suit. "You're going to have women falling all over you."

Good lord, he looks good. The suit must be custom, because it fits him perfectly. He isn't wearing a tie, and instead, the top two buttons of his white dress shirt are open.

He holds my eyes, and a muscle in his jaw ticks. I chew my lip, trying not to remember the sound I heard the night we kissed.

I can't help it, though.

That night, I lay in bed, tossing and turning, trying to fall asleep, but all I could think about was Jamie's lips on mine, and his tongue stroking into my mouth like he owned me.

When Jamie went into his room, I heard it through the wall —his low groan. The same low groan I heard a few weeks ago. He was stretching, I had told myself.

He wasn't stretching.

The second I heard it, my eyes went wide with shock, and the apex of my thighs heated. For the first time in... I don't know how long, I slipped my hand into my panties and touched myself—quick, light strokes. I came in less than a minute. A new record. I couldn't believe it.

Actually, looking at Jamie now, in his charcoal suit, I can believe it. I can believe it so hard.

My gaze drops to his mouth, pressed in a flat, unhappy line, and I remember how consuming his kiss was. A shiver rolls down my back.

"You're going to be cold," he mutters.

"I'm bringing a jacket, bossy." I roll my eyes at him, and his jaw ticks again. I stride past him to the front door, and when I lean down to put my heels on, I stumble over Daisy's leash.

Jamie sighs and walks over.

"I'm fine," I tell him, but he crouches at my feet and takes my shoe from me.

"Put your hands on my shoulders."

"I'm *fine*."

"Pippa."

I sigh and set my hands on his shoulders before he slips my shoe on and buckles the delicate strap.

"You're surprisingly nimble."

I crook a grin at him, and as he looks up at me, something hot and smug flashes through his weird mood tonight. "I'm very good with my fingers."

My breath catches in my throat. He's kneeling in front of me, big hand circling my ankle, telling me how good he is with his fingers, and I picture this scenario going in a very dirty direction. Sparks burst between my legs, and our eyes are locked.

If I were braver, I'd say something bold and sexy like *show me* or *prove it*, but instead, I just stay quiet, looking down at him with heat pulsing between my legs.

He breaks eye contact first, looking down to put on my second shoe, and when he's done, he stands and pulls my coat out of the closet, holding it for me to slip my arms into. I feel weirdly shy after having his hand brushing my ankle, but I blink it away and give him a quick smile.

"Ready?" I ask.

He nods once. "Bye, Daisy," he calls, and she opens her eyes halfway before going back to sleep.

We ride the elevator to the parking garage in silence. He opens my car door, and I thank him, but he just nods at me with a grunt. I watch him circle the car to his door. His jaw is tight again, and he's wearing his displeased frown.

He regrets saying yes to this, I realize. He made the deal with me before we kissed. My stomach plummets. What if he thinks *I think* this is a date?

"This isn't a date," I tell him when he climbs into the car.

He stares at me like I'm a bug on the sidewalk. "I know." His tone is pissed and resentful.

He pulls out of the parking garage and onto the street. It's raining, and Jamie's bad mood is making me feel like tonight is already a mistake.

"We haven't talked about having overnight guests," he says out of the blue.

I whirl toward him, giving him a strange look. "Huh?" I choke out a laugh. "What are you talking about?"

I can't even *imagine* bringing a guy home. Where would I find one? After what happened with Zach, the idea of taking my clothes off for a guy, letting him touch me... My stomach churns. I hate that idea.

My mind flicks to the guy beside me, all broad shoulders, thick hair, sharp jaw. His delicate fingers brushing my ankle. The low, needy groan I heard through the wall.

I didn't mind him touching me.

His nostrils flare as he shoulder-checks and changes lanes. His eyes are on the road, and the air in the car is thick with tension. "Daisy wouldn't like it."

I'm speechless. I don't know whether to laugh or punch him in the face. "Daisy loves visitors," I say without thinking.

The look he gives me could burn my skin off.

I don't even know what to say to him right now. We drive the rest of the way to the party in a weird, tense silence, and I'm regretting this more by the second. This party is going to be so awkward. On the street in front of the restaurant where the party is, he finds a parking spot.

"Stay there," he barks before getting out and opening the trunk.

I'm getting irritated. He agreed to come with me, and now he's being a dick. I don't want to do this—I just want to go home.

He opens my door, and I'm about to inform him that we're going back, but he opens an umbrella and gestures for me to step out. He holds it high above my head, frowning at my hair.

"Don't want your hair to get wet."

Something in my chest lifts at the picture of him standing there, waiting for me. I'm a grown woman who can take care of herself, but between him helping me with my shoes, putting my coat on me, and now trying to keep my hair dry, I'm melting into a puddle.

I hate to keep comparing him to Zach but can't help myself —Zach expected everyone to take care of him, and it only got worse as time went on. My throat tightens as I remember Zach asking me where his coffee was one morning, like I was his employee. I guess I was, because I worked on the tour, but that wasn't my job.

"What's going on with you?" I ask as rain taps on the umbrella above us.

His throat works as he looks down at me. We're standing close, and he smells delicious.

"I'm sorry." His eyes pin me, raking over my hair, my face, my collarbone. "You look beautiful."

Something in me relaxes, and I smile up at Jamie, looking so handsome. I literally *am* his employee, and yet he's the one treating me with care and attention.

*He's this way with everyone,* a wry voice reminds me. Jamie Streicher takes care of everyone in his life, and I'm not special.

"Let's go," he says, guiding me to the front door of the restaurant with his hand on my lower back.

My stomach dips, and it's hitting me now. Zach is inside, and I have to pretend what he did didn't bother me at all.

I feel sick.

"Hey." Jamie looks down at me, studying my face. "Don't let them see you scared, songbird."

My throat tightens as I gaze up at him. Whatever weirdness

there was back in the car falls away, and the look he's giving me is just like when he encouraged me to get on stage in the bar. Like he believes in me.

I nod at him. "Yeah. Okay."

"I'm your goalie," he says. "I'll block all your shots tonight."

A chuckle escapes me, and I smile at him. The corner of his mouth ticks up, and his eyes fill with affection.

For a split second, I wish he'd kiss me again.

WE STEP INSIDE to a wall of sound—thumping music, laughter, conversation. The door guy checks our names off on a list before a woman takes my coat.

A ripple of curiosity moves throughout the dim space and my skin prickles under the weight of interested gazes. My pulse whooshes in my ears as I glance around, giving a tight smile to a few people I recognize. On the second floor, more people gather, and there's someone at the top of the stairs letting people in and out. That would be the VIP section.

A flash of pale blond hair catches my attention up there, and my stomach freezes. In the dim lighting, I can just make her out, laughing and tossing her hair over her shoulder. Zach will be nearby, no doubt.

Jamie's warm hand lands on my lower back.

"How about a drink?" he murmurs in my ear, and I nod. He leads me over to the bar and orders a whiskey sour for me and a beer for himself.

"I'm just going to have one." His eyes flick to my hair. "I'll be fine to drive."

"I know." I laugh quietly. "You're Mr. Responsible."

His gaze drops to my mouth, and my blood spikes with electricity. "Not always," he mutters, taking his beer from the bartender before thanking her.

"Pippa!" Alissa shrieks, and I flinch as she throws her arms around my neck. "You made it."

I force a smile. "Of course."

She turns to Jamie, staring at him like he's a piece of cheesecake she's about to devour. "Hi."

"This is Jamie," I tell her.

He shakes her hand, and she's practically drooling. There's a crackle of pleasure in my chest, but when she bats her lashes at him, the back of my neck prickles with irritation.

"How do you two know each other?" she asks, still gazing at him.

His hand returns to my lower back. "I'm her boyfriend."

My thoughts drop off a cliff. His hand slides up my back, over the bare skin of my shoulders, before it rests on the part where my shoulder meets my neck. It's a possessive gesture that makes my heart beat harder, and every brain cell in my head stumbles.

"Yeah," I say stupidly, staring at him.

He winks at me. He *winks* at me. His mouth curves up on one side, and I'm fascinated by the movement.

"Wow." Alissa tilts her head at me, blinking. "So soon." She glances up at the VIP section, and we all know exactly what she's implying.

Anger drips into my blood, but I don't let it show. I bet no one fucking said *wow, so soon* to Zach and his new friend.

Jamie tucks a lock of my hair behind my ear. I can't breathe. I just stare at him in disbelief and awe. He's *so* good at this.

"With the right person," he says, holding my gaze, "you just know."

I could kiss him right here. In one sentence, he's solidified the impression I make tonight as well as implied that Zach wasn't the right guy for me. Give this guy an Academy Award.

More people from the tour swarm us, and Alissa introduces Jamie to everyone as my boyfriend. One of the tour electricians is a hockey fan, and that sets off another round of questions and curious but impressed glances at me.

"Can I buy you a drink?" the hockey fan asks Jamie.

His hand slips down, taking mine. "Thank you, but I'm driving us home."

His hand is huge, warm, and calloused, and I lean against the bar counter for support. This is a lot, pretending with him like this, and I'm starting to like it too much.

"We live in Gastown." His eyes meet mine and there's a flash of humor in his gaze just for me.

"You live together," one of the makeup artists repeats, and she stares at one of the hair stylists with meaning.

Every woman knows this look. It's the one I shoot Hazel sometimes that means *we will gossip about this later*. My chest squeezes and I tamp down my smile.

A few minutes later, a staff member for the event appears at my side.

"You've been invited upstairs," he says imperiously, like I've been summoned by a king.

Jamie's mouth is by my ear again. "We don't have to do anything you don't want to do," he murmurs, and his breath tickles my neck. It's hard to think when he does that. I can smell his aftershave, and it makes me feel like pulling him down a dark hallway and reliving our kiss.

He pulls back to look down at me, and mischief sparks in his eyes. I'm so intrigued by this version of the surly goalie. "Or we can have some fun," he whispers, glancing at my mouth.

I wilt out of pure horniness. Jamie Streicher is going to kill me tonight.

A rueful smile twists onto my mouth as I nod at him. "Okay."

Alone, this would be god-awful and *terrifying*. With Jamie, though, it feels like we're in it together. Like we're at a costume party where our costumes are so good, no one can recognize us. Playing a couple feels like a shield, a private joke just for us.

With him by my side, I'm okay. I've got this.

The staff member leads us up the stairs to the VIP section, and I feel eyes on us the entire way. Jamie's hand is on my arm, helping me in these tottering heels. Halfway up, my steps falter as hesitation claws up my throat.

Panic begins to pound in my chest and I can't take a full breath. I'm back at the airport, crying in the terminal after I was thrown out like yesterday's trash.

"Hey." Jamie looks down at me, concern crossing over his expression. "Remember what I said."

Right. Outside. *I'm your goalie tonight. I'll block all your shots.*

I nod at him. Meeting his eyes settles my racing heart. "You won't let him get between my crease?" I whisper, smiling. It's a phrase I heard one of the commentators say while I watched one of Jamie's away games. It means to score a goal, and it sounds dirty as hell. I'm trying to make him smile.

His lip curls like he's disgusted, and I laugh.

"*In* your crease," he mutters. "And no, I fucking won't."

He says it sharp, with jealousy, but maybe that's wishful thinking on my part. As I step onto the landing at the top of the steps, I lean my weight onto his arm.

"Why'd you wear these ridiculous shoes?"

I shrug. "Because they're hot."

His gaze lingers on my legs. "Yeah" is all he says.

The staff member unhooks the velvet rope, and I try not to roll my eyes. Did this stuff ever impress me? I hate that the party is so divided. Zach wouldn't even have a tour if not for all the people on the main floor who bust their asses every night, racing to fix last-minute audio issues or hunt for replacement equipment. He has no clue how half their jobs even work.

"Pippa."

Zach's in my face, wrapping me in a hug. His scent is in my nose, and my heart lodges in my throat. My skin crawls as he embraces me and our ears brush. A repulsed shiver rolls down my back. This is nothing like when I touch Jamie. It's cold and stiff, and the second Zach lets me go, I back away—straight into Jamie.

His arm locks around my waist, pinning me to his side, and I breathe a sigh of relief. That's so much better.

Zach's staring at me with a surprised smile, blinking with a tiny frown like I'm someone he can't place. "Look at you."

"Hi." I still can't really breathe, but Jamie gives my waist a squeeze before he drags his nails over the velvet fabric. I wonder if he likes that sensation, because I sure do.

Pippa. Focus. I force a smile at Zach.

He's wearing a fluorescent yellow hoodie with reflective strips, what people on construction sites wear as safety gear, and I kind of hate him for it. A few months ago, he told me he needed to start dressing to set trends, because he was a celebrity now. He's trying to be fashionable, but it feels insincere, like he's trying too hard.

He swallows, still staring at me in that funny way, before gesturing at my dress with appreciation. "You look amazing."

I can't lie, I'm pleased. This look on Zach's face? It's satisfying as hell.

Just like everyone downstairs, Zach turns to Jamie and balks.

"Jamie Streicher." Jamie holds his hand out. He's way taller than Zach, and I stifle the urge to laugh. "Pippa's boyfriend."

Zach's hand freezes mid-air before he recovers and shakes Jamie's. "Yeah, we went to the same high school," he says, and the words are toneless.

"Right." I nod.

When Zach looks back at me, there are knives in his gaze. He gestures behind him, and his platinum blond appears, gliding forward like she's been summoned. "Have you met Layla?"

Jamie's hand tightens on my waist. No, I have not fucking met her, and Zach knows that.

I hate pretending to be okay with something. I hate how everyone's playing their little roles, including me and Jamie, and I hate that I ever felt the need to show these people up.

Zach doesn't matter, and these people aren't my friends. I realize that now. I knew it before, but it's smacking me in the face tonight.

"Hi." I smile at her and shake her hand. Her hand is so tiny, like a child's, and I try not to roll my eyes. "Pippa."

She nods with wide eyes. "Layla."

The way she smiles at me, though, it's kind and shy, and I pause. I thought she'd be this Cruella type, cackling in victory that she stole my man, but she seems young, small, and quiet. Zach takes a step forward, and her eyelashes flutter as she backs up.

Oh. Pity, or maybe empathy, rises in my stomach at the way she's dismissed. I know how that feels.

Zach waves us over to the group. I recognize a few people from TV shows and movies, a couple guys from a band I like. Jamie takes a seat, and before I can sit beside him, he pulls me into his lap.

He's so warm and solid, and his hands settle on my waist

like they belong there. I know this is just for show, but my face heats with shyness. I think back to standing outside Jamie's building for the first time, psyching myself up to go in. How intimidating he was at first. How handsome I thought he was—and still do. Sitting in his lap is *not* how I thought this would go.

I'm not complaining, though.

Zach's eyes snag on me sitting there, but I turn away like I don't care.

"When you make a deal," I tell Jamie quietly, "you really deliver."

His gaze drops to my mouth, and I wonder how far he'll take it tonight. Heat moves over my skin, and even though my legs, shoulders, and arms are bare tonight, I don't feel cold.

The server brings me another drink and a water for Jamie, and he gets pulled into a conversation about hockey with the guitarist on Zach's tour. I pretend to listen, but really, my attention is on Zach and Layla.

She sits beside him, listening to him talk to the group. He doesn't address her once, and she wears a forced smile. No one talks to her.

I feel bad for her.

I also wonder, was that me? I think back to these parties and how I felt lucky to be there, lucky to have Zach's attention on me. Layla glances over at me and smiles, and I feel the urge to hug her. It'd be weird if I did, I know that, but it looks like she needs one. I showed up here tonight, ready to hate her, but now I just want to drag her with me when we leave.

The guy Jamie was talking to gets up to greet someone, and Jamie's hand slides from my waist to my hip. His gaze is on Zach.

"So that's the kind of guy you go for." His tone is flat and unhappy.

I watch Zach regale the group with a story. He's thriving as the center of attention, and as he says something and everyone laughs, I catch him glancing around to gauge their reactions.

He wants them to like him so badly.

"Not anymore," I tell Jamie.

Our eyes meet, and the chill in his gaze fades a fraction. Is he thinking about when I told him he was gorgeous, or the kiss in the hallway?

"And all this." His fingers squeeze my hip and his gaze roams my face, my hair, my dress. "It's not for him?"

I laugh in disbelief. "What? Jamie," I murmur. "Of course it's not for him."

His nostrils flare, and I have the urge to stroke my finger down his strong nose.

"What the fuck am I supposed to think, Pippa?" His green eyes flash and he grips my hip harder.

Oh. I like that feeling.

"You pulled out all the stops for this guy." He runs his free hand back through his hair, messing it up. "It's the ultimate revenge, isn't it? To make him want you back?" His teeth clench. "To make him beg to fuck you?"

I'm speechless, blinking, jaw dropping to the floor in shock.

"Jamie," I say, but I have no follow-up. I try to turn on his lap, but his big hands anchor me in place.

"Stop moving," he bites out, and a moment later, I feel it— the hard press of his erection into my backside.

My eyes go wide.

I know tonight is fake, and this is probably just his body's reaction to me sitting in his lap. This unsettled, angry side of Jamie is lighting me up, though, sending heat through my blood, and I'm hyperaware of his stiff length against me, his hands on my hips, the way his fingers brush the soft fabric, how they tense when he looks at my mouth.

It feels good to be someone more than the girl who got stepped on.

"That's not the ultimate revenge," I say softly.

His dark eyes meet mine, pinning me. His jaw ticks.

My mouth curves into a smile, and I don't even recognize myself right now. "The ultimate revenge would be fucking you."

I'M the closest I've ever been to hauling this girl over my shoulder, taking her home, and forgetting all the rules I've made for myself.

Her mouth curves up and her eyes glitter with teasing as I replay the words she just said.

*The ultimate revenge would be fucking you.*

I wish.

In the car, I'd push this dress up, tear her panties off, and bury my face between her legs. I'd do it right there in the front seat. I wouldn't care if anyone saw.

No—I'd do it here in front of Zach. I'd make her scream my name in front of all of these people. Drinks would get knocked into laps, people would stare as I thrust into her and made my pretty assistant mine. The girl I've wanted for-fucking-ever would come so hard on my cock.

My erection presses into her backside as I rein in my thoughts. From the second she walked out of her room in this dress, I alternated between fantasizing about tearing it off her and being irritated that she was dressing up to impress the fuckwit who's desperate for attention.

Pippa's eyes are locked on mine, gauging my reaction, and

my teeth clench. I need to get my shit together. I do one of my mental centering exercises from hockey—deep breath, focus on the feeling of my lungs expanding and not the way my balls ache, listen to the music around us, the chatter and conversation, and try not to inhale the sweet scent of her hair. My thumbs brush the soft velvet of her dress, and I let that steal my entire focus.

I open my eyes. I'm still rock hard. I still want to fuck her.

"Pippa," I start, but I don't know what I'm going to say. I can't think around her.

She shakes her head, looking embarrassed. "I don't know why I said that." The long line of her throat moves as she swallows, looking at her hands. "I owe you for this. Thank you so much."

"For what?" My tone is flat with tension.

She gestures around the party, and then between her and me. "For this. For letting me sit in your lap. For going along with this whole charade."

*Letting* her sit in my lap? I actually feel like laughing. Pippa's ass pressed into me is the most erotic thing I've experienced in years, and I'll be jerking off thinking about it for weeks. Also, the poisonous look Zach gave me the moment Pippa wasn't looking made the whole night worth it.

Whether she realizes it or not, Pippa doesn't need him anymore. Zach realizes it, though. A burst of smug male satisfaction hits me in the chest as I lock eyes with Zach across the party. He pauses mid-conversation before resuming, and I know I'm right.

Fucking asshole. The urge to protect Pippa expands tenfold.

She squeezes my knee, and sparks shoot up my leg, straight to my cock. This is sweet torture, having her in my lap like this.

The only reason I'm not moving her off to give my dick a break is because I'll never get this chance again.

I glance between her eyes and her mouth. "Promise me you'll never sleep with Zach again."

She chokes. "What?"

"Do it," I demand. I sound like an asshole, and I don't care. "Promise me, Pippa."

She shakes her head, laughing. "I promise. Oh my god. After what happened? I'm not that stupid."

"I don't think you're stupid at all."

"Well." She shrugs, giving me a lopsided, self-deprecating grin. "I did stay with the guy for way too long," she says in a low voice, leaning in. Her breath tickles my ear. "And he was terrible in bed."

"Really." My nostrils flare as I picture them together—him on top of her. No, he'd probably make her go on top each time because he's a lazy fuck.

I fucking *hate* that image.

"Ow," she says, shifting on my lap.

My fingers dig into her hips, and I loosen my grip immediately. "Sorry."

"It's okay." She gives me a small smile.

"Why was he bad in bed?" The question falls out of my mouth before I can stop it. I can't help it. I need to know.

She gives me a look. "I'm not telling you details."

"I put on a suit for this."

"You put on a suit multiple times a week for games," she argues back, smiling, and my chest feels pressurized like a pop can.

I love that she isn't afraid of me, and that she likes to argue back.

The side of my mouth tugs up. "It's past my bedtime."

She chuckles. "Fine. Okay." Her gaze slides to Zach before

coming back to mine. "He would do this thing with his hand," she whispers to me, and I lean in, even though I can hear her just fine. She flattens her fingers and then shifts them back and forth fast, like she's a DJ, and she's baring her teeth.

A rusty laugh scrapes off my chest. "What is that supposed to be?"

She laughs, and when her sparkling eyes meet mine, my pulse trips. "That's Zach rubbing my clit."

My stomach churns. I don't like her using his name in the same sentence as *my clit*.

"It always felt rushed, and I'd worry I was taking too long and then I—" She shrugs with a wince. "I wouldn't be able to get anywhere."

With us, it wouldn't be rushed. I'd take my time. I'd take all fucking night. When the sun rose, she'd still be coming, exhausted from countless orgasms in every conceivable position.

"The whole thing felt like a chore near the end." Her gaze flicks to mine. "Sorry. Too much information."

A feeling surges in my blood, electric and determined. I've been competing in sports my entire life. I thrive on competition. It's woven into my DNA at this point, and it's the best way to motivate me.

Hearing that Zach couldn't make Pippa come? It lights my blood on fire.

I'd make her come. I'd make her come so fucking hard.

My pulse beats in my ears, and in this moment, there's no one here but me and her. I hold her gaze, swallowing with difficulty as I picture sliding my hands up her dress here in the dark restaurant, pressing the pads of my fingers over her damp panties. Maybe she'd grip my knee, maybe she'd bury her face in my shoulder while she shook on my lap, unraveling.

I need to make her come.

"It's not too much information," I manage, and my voice is hoarse. "Was it just with him?" I ask for some stupid fucking reason. "That you couldn't get there?"

I like the pain, I guess. I like the torture of hearing about her struggles with orgasms, even though I can't do a fucking thing about it.

She bites her lip and I follow the motion. *I* want to bite her lip.

Our eyes meet again. "He's the only guy I've ever been with," she admits.

I drag a deep breath in as competition roars in my veins. *Me*, my subconscious shouts. *I'm the one who can change her mind*.

She shifts on my lap, and I clench my jaw as she brushes against my cock again.

"Sometimes I'm successful, um, by myself."

Even in the restaurant's moody, dim lighting, I can see the flush across her cheeks. I wonder if they flush like that while she has her hand between her legs.

"Why are you blushing, songbird?" My voice is low.

"I'm not," she says, breathless. She won't look at me, but her pulse jumps in her neck.

The pretty songbird is thinking about something naughty, and I need to know what it is. One hand is still gripping her waist, but I lift my free hand and press the backs of my fingers against her cheek. Her lashes flutter.

"You're burning up. You don't have a fever, do you?" I arch a brow at her, teasing her.

"I don't think so," she whispers, eyes darting to mine.

"What are you thinking about?"

"Nothing." Her eyes are wide.

Now I have to know. I turn her in my lap so she can't avoid my gaze. "Tell me."

She huffs, half-amused and half-annoyed. "Jamie."

"Now."

She groans. "Bossy. Okay, fine. Last week..."

"Go on."

"This is embarrassing. Okay. Whatever. I usually have a tough time even on my own, but last week I was able to really quickly." Her expression turns mortified. "Oh my god. Why am I telling you this?"

"You were just following orders," I say, but my voice sounds far away because all I can think about is Pippa across the wall that separates our rooms, stroking herself. Gasping. Her toes curling as she comes.

Fuck. I'm so hard right now.

"Jesus," she mutters as my cock pulses into her.

"Stop moving," I grit out.

She gives me a look. "Stop stabbing me with that skyscraper."

I choke out a laugh. Only Pippa could make me laugh in this moment. Maybe I'm lightheaded because all my blood is straining in my dick right now.

"What about you?" Pippa looks at me. "Everyone says you don't date."

"I don't."

"Never?"

Erin's face flashes into my memory—happy, smiling, and I'm flooded with guilt all over again as I remember reading about her pulling out of all of those fashion shows.

"I had a girlfriend when I was nineteen."

Pippa's head tilts as she listens.

"Erin." It feels weird to say her name out loud. "She was nice but..." I shake my head, unsure of what to say. "My schedule is intense, even in the offseason, and my mom needs a lot of attention."

Pippa nods, and her eyes are full of warm compassion. She's the only person who knows the full extent of things, I realize as I study her face.

"I can only handle those two things."

She nods again. "Right."

I meet her eyes, and something shifts in my chest. Playing pretend like this feels too easy. It's different from dating Erin, who always felt more like a friend, and that realization is a sharp kernel in my chest. My hands stroke up and down Pippa's sides, and her eyelids fall halfway, like it's either relaxing her or turning her on, or maybe both.

My attention is pulled to my cock. Again.

Hard. Again.

I'm letting myself act the way I want to with Pippa, and I don't know if I'll be able to stop once we leave. Touching her is fucking magic.

Behind Pippa's back, Zach stares at her while his friend talks.

My cock throbs, and I get an idea. I'm an evil asshole, and I'm taking advantage of Pippa when I'm supposed to be helping her. There are a million reasons why I shouldn't do what I'm about to, but I don't care. The second we walk out the door, everything goes back to normal. We both know this isn't real.

"You really want to drive the stake into his chest?" I murmur, leaning in and letting my mouth brush her ear. She shudders against me.

I wait until she meets my eyes. Christ, her eyes are pretty.

"Kiss me," I tell her.

PIPPA BLINKS.

"He's watching." I arch a brow, and my gaze falls to her lips. I know how soft her mouth is. I've replayed it a hundred times. "Only if you want to."

"Yeah," she breathes, nodding, and when I lift my gaze to hers, she's looking at my mouth. "If he's watching, we should."

"Mhm."

"Okay. I'm going to kiss you now."

My hand comes to the back of her head and I gently pull her forward.

Our kiss is different this time. Less urgent, less frantic, although I feel all those things beating against the front wall of my chest, urging me to take her mouth, but no. I want to savor this one, because just like her sitting in my lap, we'll never get another shot. After tonight, she'll never see that loser again, and my opportunities to touch her will drop to zero.

I kiss Pippa like I mean it. Like she's air and I'm about to suffocate. Her hands fist my collar and pull me closer to her, and I nip her bottom lip before I taste her again.

I kiss her like we have forever. I know we don't. We have maybe thirty seconds more of this if I'm lucky.

She sighs into me like she's been thinking about this all week, too. Everything falls away—the people, the music, everything except the feel of her mouth under mine, her pressed against me, my hands in her hair. She's so fucking sweet. Her tongue slips into my mouth, and I'm leaking pre-cum in my boxers. I suck her tongue, and she whimpers.

I could make her come so fucking fast. I'd do it over and over until she begged for a rest.

"Pippa," I whisper between kisses.

She nods, and her mouth seeks mine again. Desire floods my chest, drowning out everything else. Every bad thing I've ever seen or that has happened to me evaporates into the atmosphere as I kiss her, like she's filling me with light. Her hair is silk, and I tilt her open more, so I can get deeper. I need to get deeper. I need her to be fully mine.

I know this isn't real, but it's still fucking incredible.

I sense a presence in our vicinity, and when I open my eyes, there's a fluorescent hoodie beside us. I'm cradling Pippa's jaw in my hands now, but Zach reaches out and tugs on a lock of her hair.

I pull back, glaring at him, jaw clenching.

"What are you two doing hiding in the corner?" he asks. His smile is wry, forced, and uncomfortable. "It's a party. Come hang out with us." He gestures at the table of his friends. He says it like he's not asking.

Under my hand, Pippa's back muscles tighten. Even without my hands all over her, I'd sense her hesitation, the way she straightens up.

"We have to go." I stare at him. "We've got an early morning and I'm not done with this one tonight." My tone is suggestive, and her eyes flare with surprise and heat. "Right, baby?" I ask, locking my arms around her waist. Her lips are swollen, and she looks dazed as she nods.

Something smug courses through me. Zach's expression is both unimpressed and irritated.

She stands, and when I get to my feet, I take a step closer to Zach to emphasize our height difference. I don't use my size to my advantage often, but tonight, I'll take any opportunity to show this guy up.

"Thanks for inviting us."

"Yeah," he says, forcing a smile. He looks like he's about to be sick. "Really great to see you, Pippa."

She forces a smile right back. "You, too."

I take her hand—it fits perfectly in mine. On the way down the steps, I'm practically carrying her, supporting her arms. She waves goodbye to a few people, and the second we get outside, she deflates. I let her arm go, because now that we've left the party, the ruse is over.

Something in my gut sinks. That all felt too easy, and I know how dangerous that is.

"Oh my god," she breathes, closing her eyes. "That was a lot."

"Pippa." I fold my arms over my chest so I don't do something stupid like touch her hair or waist again. We aren't pretending anymore. "You killed it."

She snorts, rolling her eyes.

"You did."

She smiles up at me. "Thanks to you."

My heart beats harder. "Anytime."

I can't tell her the truth—that tonight wasn't a favor to anyone but myself.

I CAN'T STOP THINKING about her.

"We'll have another round," Owens tells the server, gesturing at our large group. All the players are out tonight in a bar after a loss against Ottawa.

Unease simmers in my gut as I drink my beer. Whenever the whistle blew during the game tonight, I had the urge to look over my shoulder. I couldn't stop picturing her sitting there, smiling and watching me play. I've been away for six days, and it's time to face an ugly truth.

I miss the songbird.

The server places another beer in front of me and I slug back the rest of my drink before handing her the empty glass and thanking her.

"You're in a mood tonight," Owens notes, cocking a grin.

I stare at him.

"How's your girl doing?"

My girl. The words warm my chest. "She's my assistant," I say, but it doesn't sound convincing.

"Yeah." He smirks. "That's what I meant."

I drink half my beer. "She's none of your fucking business."

He lets out a loud laugh, head tipping back. "Streicher, relax. I'm not going after Pippa."

My shoulder muscles ease and I take another pull of my beer.

I think back to the conversation Pippa and I had in the car, where I told her not to bring guys home. So fucking stupid. Could I have been more obvious? She probably thinks I'm a toxic asshole.

And then there was the wrap party. Kissing her, touching her, pulling her into my lap. I've been replaying that night all week.

"You're probably going to bite my head off for saying this," Owens starts.

"So don't say it."

He grins. "Nah. I'm going to say it anyway. You play better when Pippa's at the game."

I fold my arms over my chest. I can feel my nostrils flaring. There's a weird pressure in my chest.

"That's because when she goes to my games, my mom is there," I tell him in a sharp tone. "I worry about my mom."

He shakes his head, eyes glittering. "I don't think that's it."

"You're drunk."

He laughs again. "Yeah, I am, but that doesn't mean I'm wrong."

I roll my eyes. These fucking rookies think they know everything. Down the table, Alexei Volkov calls him over, and when Owens gets up and leaves, I picture Pippa sitting behind the net. My nerves immediately settle.

Fuck.

I rub the bridge of my nose. I'm not ready to look this problem in the eye. It's cowardly of me, and it goes against everything I've learned about grit and mental toughness from my sport, but...

I can't do this for real with Pippa. I can't mess it up and then be in the same category as Zach, the fuckface loser. After hearing her play guitar and sing for me, I know she has what it takes to have a career in music.

She just doesn't realize it yet.

In my back pocket, my phone buzzes. It's a picture of Pippa and Daisy on a hike this afternoon. The sun peeks through the trees, and Pippa's eyes are so bright. Two pink patches bloom on her cheeks from the cold. My heart squeezes. I study them, tracing the lines of her face and her caramel hair with my gaze. She's wearing a light jacket, and I frown.

*Dress warmer*, I text. It gets cold in the mountains.

My full focus is on my phone, watching as the typing dots appear. A twist of excitement hits my chest, like the moments before a player tries to score on my net.

*Bossy*, she texts back.

I huff, leaning my chin on my palm, scrolling back up to the photo of her. The beer is making my head float, and I wonder if she'd say that in bed.

My mind floods with images of us together—naked, breathing hard. Maybe I have her wrists pinned down as I push into her, watching her eyes go hazy.

My cock stiffens and I clench my eyes closed, rubbing my face. Christ, Streicher. Get your shit together.

Pippa's problem with orgasms has nagged at me all week.

I stare at my text conversation with her, wanting to say so many things. *How are you* and *have you been thinking about me too* and *I know a hundred ways to make you come.*

*How are things at the apartment this week?* I finally settle on because it's less personal.

*Quiet*, she responds. *Daisy misses you.*

My pulse picks up. I lean forward, elbows on my knees, staring at my screen.

*I'll be home before she knows it,* I text back.

Pippa's response comes right away. *She's looking forward to it.*

My mouth curves up.

"Holy shit," Owens says down the table, pointing at me. "He smiles."

I shake my head at him, and I think I'm still smiling. "Fuck off, Owens," I call down to him, but there's no bite to my words. He just grins back at me.

*Tell me about the hikes you've done this week,* I text Pippa.

*You want a detailed schedule?*

*Yes. Down to the hour.*

*Demanding.*

I smirk at my phone, knee bouncing as my blood crackles with energy.

Half an hour later, we're still texting, messages flying back and forth. I've lost count of how many beers I've had. I don't drink much—my mom was always worried I'd inherit my dad's alcoholism—but I tell myself that drinking with the team is part of the team bonding thing Ward likes. I'm in that buoyant buzzed zone where everything seems more fun.

*Thank you again for coming with me to the wrap party,* she says.

I left for my away games the morning after the party, so we haven't had a chance to talk about it.

*No problem.*

*I want to apologize for what we talked about.*

My gut tenses. *Explain.*

The response doesn't come right away, and I can sense her chewing her lip on the other side of the continent. *The stuff that I talked about with Zach and me... it was unprofessional.*

I rub the ache behind my sternum, picturing her brow

wrinkling with worry. *Does she regret telling me?* I forced you to tell me.

*Still. It's not your problem and I'm embarrassed.*

I don't know what this feeling is in my chest. It's a blend of wanting to give her a hug that lasts for hours and the fierce need to prove her wrong about this "problem" she thinks she has.

*Nothing to be embarrassed about, songbird.* I hit send before I can think twice about calling her that. I really shouldn't, if we're talking about being professional. I can't seem to stop, though.

*Okay, well...* she replies. *Thanks for listening.*

*You can talk to me about that stuff anytime,* I tell her, like I'm her fucking boyfriend or something. My chest clenches at that thought.

An ugly image wanders into my head. I picture Pippa and me sitting on the couch in the apartment, her talking about her sex problems with a guy she's seeing. Rage whips through me. I fucking *hate* that image.

*I'm going to go to sleep now,* she texts. *Good night, Jamie.*

*Good night, Pippa.*

Long after her last message, I stare at my phone, scrolling through our conversation.

Zach couldn't make her come, and I want to so badly. Not just because of my competitive nature, but because Pippa's lovely, and she deserves everything good. I could see the anguish all over her face when she told me about it. It upsets her.

I need to fix this for her. I need to take care of her.

I bury my head in my hands. There are a million good reasons to forget she ever told me those things. She works for me, and I trust her in my home, with my dog, and with my mom. I like her, and I don't want to screw things up for her the way I did with Erin. And I know from last year, my mom needs me to keep an eye on her, even if she isn't ready to admit it.

"Streicher, when I said you should spend more time with the team," Ward says with a crooked smile, gesturing to me on my phone, "this isn't what I had in mind."

I glance around the table. Everyone is in conversation, talking and drinking and laughing, but my head is back in Vancouver with the woman I'm supposed to keep my distance from.

I slip my phone back into my pocket, and Owens orders me another beer.

———

It's late when I get back to my room. I'm clumsy, fumbling with my key to open the door. After I put my phone away, Owens had us all laughing at stories from his summer trip to Europe. He reminds me of how Miller used to be before he turned into a jackass. Ward even told us a bit about his pre-injury days when he played for Toronto.

The entire time, though, my mind lingered on Pippa's problem.

I yank my shirt and pants off and flop down onto my bed, pulling out my phone and skimming through my conversation with Pippa again.

It's only a matter of time before she admits it to another guy and he wants to help her out, too.

My head falls back onto the pillow and I let out a low groan. The thought of sharing her makes my jaw clench. I like Pippa, and not just because I want to fuck her. I like talking to her, I like hanging out with her, and I like living with her. She makes those cupcakes for me. She's funny, sweet, and beautiful.

We're friends, I think. I don't want her to bake cupcakes for another guy, or sing in the shower while he listens outside the door.

My head spins, and I realize I'm drunk. I haven't been drunk in years.

I let my mind wander back to Pippa, and an idea trickles through my sluggish thoughts. On my phone, I search for a sex toy I've heard about. My pulse beats in my ears and I'm rock hard as I put the toy in my cart, address it to Pippa at the apartment, and pay for it.

THREE DAYS LATER, I'm sitting on the private plane with the rest of the team, waiting for take-off, when I send Pippa a note that I'm on my way.

*Daisy's looking forward to it!* she responds, and I smile at my phone. We've been texting during my entire trip, sending each other photos throughout our days. I catch myself studying her photos, memorizing them, and looking forward to the next one.

An email notification pops up on my screen. *Shipment out for delivery.*

My eyes narrow, because I don't remember ordering something to the apartment. Pippa usually handles that stuff on the credit card I gave her.

*Good news! Your purchase is out for delivery and should arrive later today.*

*(1) Satisfyer - personal toy with clitoral suction for her toe-curling pleasure!*

My heart stops.

I fucking forgot.

Oh, fuck. My pulse restarts at a sprint as the memory

rushes back—lying on my bed in my boxers, hard as steel, buying Pippa a sex toy.

Fuck, fuck, fuck. No. Shit. I can't believe I did that. This is not okay. She works for me. She never asked for this. She's trying to keep things professional. *I'm* trying to keep things professional. My throat closes up.

"You okay, Streicher?" Volkov asks beside me and I nod tersely.

"Fine," I mutter, heart going a mile a minute.

Fuck.

The tracking link says it's due to arrive half an hour after I get home. My skin feels hot, and I'm sweating. If I rush, I might be able to make it home to intercept the package.

I picture Pippa receiving it with a horrified, disgusted expression. All the text conversations this week, the smiles she gives me, the walks we go on—I've ruined it all.

Whatever Pippa is to me, I just blew it up.

"Cabin crew," the pilot says over the intercom, "prepare for departure."

The flight attendants ensure everyone is buckled in and the plane door closes. My pulse races, and I'm stuck on this fucking airplane for five hours, praying Pippa doesn't get the package before I do.

———

The second we land, I'm out of my seat, hauling my bag out of the overhead bin. The guys shoot me wary looks.

"Excuse me," I say in a sharp tone as I head to the front. The plane is still taxiing along the runway, and one of the flight attendants rolls his eyes at my behavior.

I don't care if I'm being rude. I need to be the first one off this plane. If I don't get there in time, I'm fucked, and it's not even about having to find a new assistant. If she sees I sent her a sex toy, I've just lost the only person I actually like in this city.

My stomach knots and nausea rolls through me.

I'm right behind the flight crew as they open the door. If this was a regular flight instead of a private plane, or if I wasn't known for hockey in this city, I'd probably be arrested with the way I'm acting. Instead, the flight crew just look unimpressed as one of them gestures for me to go ahead.

"Sorry," I mutter at her as I rush past. "It's an emergency."

I sprint through the airport. With my height and frame, in *this* city, I'm easily recognizable. People are gawking, taking photos and videos. I must look like the fucking Terminator, running like this. My bag catches on someone's elbow and they stumble.

"Sorry," I yell over my shoulder, still running.

There's a special airport exit for private flights, thank fuck. I wait for the person in front of me, breathing hard, sweat beading on my forehead.

There's no update on the package's location. Still out for delivery. I swallow past the knives in my throat. My nerves are shot, and I've never felt this tightly wound. Not before a big game, not when I found out my mom was having panic attacks, never.

I don't know what that means, and I'm not going to deal with it now.

The person at the exit gives me a long look while they process my passport. The moment he recognizes me, I see it in his eyes. More guilt forms in my gut; if I wasn't a professional hockey player wearing a suit that cost more than most people's paycheck, I'd be hauled into questioning for looking shady as fuck.

"Have a good day, Mr. Streicher," he says, gesturing me through. "Give us more of those Streicher shut outs."

"You got it," I call as I hurry out the doors.

The Uber is waiting for me outside, and I slide in. I left my car at the apartment in case Pippa needed it.

"Five hundred bucks to get me home as fast as you can," I tell the driver, pulling the bills out of my wallet.

The next twenty minutes are excruciating. The driver rides the gas and brake, driving so far over the speed limit I don't even want to look, and is honked at a dozen times. My knee bounces as I grit my teeth, alternating between staring out the window and refreshing the tracking page.

When we pull up in front of my building, I shove the bills at him and race out of the car. The elevator takes a century to arrive, and another century to get to the top floor. A tiny old lady gets off on the tenth floor, and I have to hold back from shoving her out of the elevator to get her to move faster. I'm crawling out of my skin with impatience.

The elevator finally opens on the top floor, and I'm at the front door in a shot.

No package on the floor. My pulse beats in my ears. I'm not in the clear yet—it could be inside or with the concierge downstairs.

Inside the apartment, it's quiet. Daisy trots over, tail wagging, and I absentmindedly pick her up, petting her while scanning the apartment, opening the cupboard below the sink to check the recycling.

No Pippa. No package. No empty box. A quick call downstairs confirms they didn't receive a package either. Relief eases through me, and the knots in my gut untie, one by one.

It hasn't arrived yet. I sigh and lean back against the front door to catch my breath. I just aged a decade. I give Daisy one more scratch before setting her down, and she returns to the couch and goes back to sleep. As my pulse slows, I scrub a hand down my face.

That was so fucking close. Too close.

In the upstairs hallway, I'm heading to my room to change out of my suit when a noise stops me in my tracks. A gasp. I stare at Pippa's door.

A fast, rhythmic tapping sound, like a whir, followed by a breathy moan.

All the blood in my body rushes to my cock. I didn't beat the toy home. It got here before me, and my pretty assistant is currently using it in her bedroom.

WAVE AFTER WAVE of intense pleasure radiates from where I press the toy against my clit. I'm shaking, back arching off the bed, muscles taut, mouth open with my eyes clenched closed as I ride out the most intense orgasm of my life.

When I can't take it anymore, I turn the toy off and collapse back into the pillows, catching my breath.

That was... amazing. I lift my head and stare at the toy Hazel sent me. My mind is blown. Floaty, relaxed feelings flow through my body, and I huff a laugh.

That thing worked, and *fast*. Maybe I'm not broken after all. I bite my lip, grinning to myself. Thinking about Jamie while I used it made everything more intense.

So I have a little crush on him. I always have. I'm not going to do anything about it. I take a sobering breath and get dressed before heading downstairs.

Jamie's in the kitchen, unloading the dishwasher, looking absolutely fucking delicious in athletic pants and a gray long-sleeved shirt. Something about the way the thin fabric clings to his chest and shoulders makes me want to run back upstairs and use the toy all over again.

I break into a huge smile. "You're home."

This week, I texted him that Daisy missed him, but the truth is, *I* missed him.

He watches me with an expression I can't discern as I walk over and wrap my arms around him in a hug. It isn't until my face is pressed against his chest and my eyes fall closed that I realize maybe this isn't how most assistants greet their bosses.

I can't find the energy to care, though. Using that toy wiped me out.

"How was your flight?"

When I step back, Jamie won't meet my eyes, and his cheekbones are flushed. He shifts away from me, folding his arms over his chest. "Fine. Good."

"Good." I smile at him again.

I'm just feeling so relaxed. Hazel will be so smug, and I'm going to buy her flowers as a thank you. No, the whole flower shop. Every damn flower in the place.

I watch Jamie's Adam's apple as it bobs. His gaze darts to mine before he closes his eyes, frowning.

"Are you okay?" I ask.

"Fine," he manages before storming upstairs.

I raise an eyebrow, watching his tall, strong form as he disappears. "Grumpy," I call after him.

His door slams, and when I return to my room a few minutes later to grab something, I hear his shower running. He must be tired from traveling or something.

I open my bedside drawer, where I stashed the toy, and grin to myself. I'm going to use it again tonight.

## CHAPTER 33
# PIPPA

THE NEXT MORNING, Daisy and I are just getting home from her morning walk when we run into Jamie in the hallway outside his apartment.

"Heading out?"

He can barely meet my eyes as he shifts his gym bag over his shoulder. "Yep."

"Have a great practice."

"Thanks." His gaze lifts to mine, and I think he's about to rush to the elevator, but he doesn't move. He clears his throat. "What are you up to today?"

I can't say the first answer that comes to mind. *Riding my new toy while I think about sitting on your lap, grinding against your huge erection.*

Definitely can't say that. My face heats, and my body tightens in anticipation.

I've been using that toy nonstop.

I've never owned one, so I didn't know how incredible they were. On the tour, there was no privacy, so it's not like I could have used one. And even if I had one, I'm sure it would have fallen out of my bag at the worst time, in front of everyone.

"We're going hiking with Hazel." I hesitate. "And I might play my guitar for a bit."

His gaze goes soft and warm, and a funny feeling rises in me. I *like* that look on his sharp, handsome face. I like him looking at me like that.

"That's great, songbird," he says, and the corner of his mouth curves up.

My heart flutters. I'll do anything to make him smile again. His eyes hold mine, and the flutters in my chest intensify.

"Send me a picture on your hike."

I nod, smiling. He just wants to know how Daisy's doing throughout the day, I remind myself.

After we say goodbye, I head to my room and pull my guitar out. I play around with it for an hour, strumming and hovering with my pen above my notebook, ready to write lyrics, but nothing shows up. That's how I used to write music—I'd get a few parts of the song, maybe one verse, the chorus, maybe just an opening line, and then I'd fill the rest in, but today, nothing feels good enough. Nothing sounds worthy of creating a song around. I can't stop picturing Zach and his manager.

I blow out a long sigh of frustration. Some musician I'd make. I can't even do this as a hobby without seizing up in self-doubt.

————

"They're opening up that marketing position next week for internal applications," Hazel tells me on our hike that afternoon.

"That's great."

I picture myself in meetings to discuss brand partnerships, campaign strategies, or a logo redesign. Compared to the insane hours on a tour, an office job will allow me to have a normal life.

Maybe I'll even make friends there. And if someone makes fun of me or laughs at my ideas? I'll be fine, because a marketing idea isn't a piece of my heart the way songs are.

Something makes me pause. If I work for the marketing department, I won't get to see Jamie or Daisy anymore.

My good mood pops like a balloon.

It's for the best, though. I think about trying to write music this morning and how paralyzed I was by the idea of negative criticism. I'm not like Zach, who was always able to ignore the bad stuff.

"You don't have to apply for it," Hazel says quietly. "Just because it's what Mom and Dad want—"

"I want to," I cut in. "It's what I went to school for."

Her gaze lingers on me, wary. She doesn't buy it. Hazel has always been able to see right through me.

I can already hear how happy my parents will be that I even applied. They've been asking nonstop about it.

Besides, I'm just starting to play music again. I don't want to put pressure on myself to make it everything in my life. I just want to love it again.

"Oh, I meant to thank you for the gift," I tell Hazel, changing the subject and shooting her a cheeky smile. "Did it cross boundaries? Absolutely. Do I care? Not really."

She tilts her head, frowning. "Huh?"

"The toy."

"What toy?"

My eyes narrow. "The one you sent me."

She stares at me. "I didn't send you anything."

I blink. "Yes, you did. The Satisfyer."

She chokes out a laugh. "I didn't send you that. Although, that's a great choice. Everyone always goes for the vibrator, but they're like *bzzzzzz!*" She makes a noise like a buzz saw. "It's too much sometimes."

I stop walking. "You sent it to me."

"No," she says slowly. "I didn't."

Then—

Oh god. My mouth falls open. He's the only other person who knows my address. Even the team office still has Hazel's address on file for me, even though they know I'm living at Jamie's.

"What's that look?" Hazel asks.

I'm staring at nothing. My face is the temperature of the sun, and I'm going to die of embarrassment or horniness or shock.

Jamie Streicher sent me a sex toy, and I've been using it nonstop while thinking about him.

The image of him standing in the kitchen, staring at me with discomfort as I walked out in a post-orgasm haze, appears in my head. I press my hands against my cheeks. I'm going to die. Any second, my whole being will just *poof* into the air.

"Oh god," I whisper.

"*What?*"

"I think Jamie sent it."

She crows with laughter. "Awesome."

"No," I protest, wincing. "Not awesome."

Her eyes are bright with excitement. "He *liiiiiikes* you."

"No, he doesn't." My voice is weird again. "He doesn't."

She gives me a look that says otherwise.

He can't. *You're my assistant*, he said. I glance at Hazel, worry furrowing on my brow. My pulse picks up. "He pretended to be my boyfriend at a party Zach was at and got a boner when I sat on his lap," I blurt out.

Hazel's jaw hits the ground but her eyes are smiling. "Tell me everything."

When I'm finished recounting that night, she shakes her head.

"He wants to fuck you."

My skin prickles, and I can't get a full breath. "I don't know what to do."

"Do you want to fuck him?"

*The ultimate revenge would be fucking you.* I can't believe I said that.

"Yes," I squeak out, blushing. "But we can't."

She sighs. "You know how I feel about hockey players, but if *you* want to, and *he* wants to..." She gives me an encouraging look. "Why not?"

Because I already like him as more than a friend. What if I fall for him, only to move out in a few months and never talk to him again? What if I start to like him too much, and he pulls a Zach on me?

I've already been crushed once this year. I can't go through it again. Jamie's so insanely hot and so out of my league, it isn't even a possibility that he won't break my heart.

"Pippa," Hazel says, "just keep it casual with him. Guys are only as faithful as their options, especially these guys." She shrugs. "Don't forget who he is. And leave your emotions out of it."

Easy for her to say. Hazel always keeps relationships temporary and uncomplicated, but I don't know how to do that.

I live with Jamie. I work for Jamie. We text and talk about our day. His dog is basically my best friend. I hang out with his mom.

Nothing about this is uncomplicated. My emotions are already fully involved, and if I let it go any further, it's going to hurt like hell.

———

That afternoon, I get home earlier than expected, and Jamie's shoes are in the front hall closet, but the apartment is quiet. Daisy's tired after our hike so heads to the couch to nap, and I wander up to my room to charge my phone.

As I pass Jamie's door, I hear my name in his low voice, barely above a murmur.

My heart stops. Is he talking about me on the phone? I frown and lean in, listening. This is totally wrong, but if he is, I have to know what he's saying. My skin prickles as I press my ear against the door.

*"Fuck,"* he mutters in the same tone as when we were kissing. A low, needy groan.

My eyes go wide. My skin heats as I imagine what he looks like on the other side of the door, fisting his cock and wincing with pleasure.

*"Pippa."* I hear his low moan through the door and feel a rush of wetness between my legs.

My hot hockey player boss is jerking off while moaning my name. A thrill shoots through me, and I picture us together, all the hard planes of his body while he touches me, urging me on.

Jamie would be so, so different from Zach in bed. *You can do it*, Jamie said when I was uncertain about performing in the bar.

I bet he'd say that in bed, too.

PIPPA COMES HOME the next evening with Daisy and stops short in the kitchen, tilting her head with a surprised smile.

"What's this?" she asks, gesturing at the massive mess I've made.

I rub the back of my neck, feeling stupid. I can't believe I thought this was a good idea.

"Dinner," I manage, meeting her gaze before looking away. "I made dinner for us."

I'm a fucking wreck. I can't stop thinking about her having orgasms in her room with the toy, and I can't stop worrying she'll find out it's from me. She must not know I sent it—it's the only explanation for why she hasn't quit or called HR. When I think about her moving out, I feel sick. When I imagine the look on her face as she finds out I bought it for her, I want to tear my hair out.

I've tried compartmentalizing Pippa. I've tried placing her in a separate box in my mind and saving thoughts of her lush mouth, perfect tits, and round, smackable ass for the moment I climb into bed every night.

None of it's working. She's constantly in my thoughts, and me buying her that toy is a looming axe above whatever we are.

I'm falling apart, so I'm making dinner for us. I don't know why. I don't seem to understand logic anymore. Not where Pippa's concerned.

She blinks. "I didn't know you could cook."

I shrug like it doesn't matter. "You don't have to eat it if you don't want to."

"I do want to," she says quickly. "I'm just surprised." She tips a smile at me, and my nerves settle a fraction. "Pleasantly surprised." Is she blushing? She wanders to the oven and peers in. "Enchiladas?"

I nod. "Black bean, yam, and spinach. Ready in twenty."

She heads upstairs to drop her stuff, and I blow out a long breath as my head falls back. Five minutes later, I'm loading the dishwasher when she returns to the kitchen. She reaches to pass me a bowl, and our fingers brush. Electricity spikes through our touch, and I jerk back.

"What's up with you?" She gives me an amused, curious look. "You're so jumpy."

My shoulders tense. "I'm fine."

She snorts. "Jamie, your shoulders are at your ears. Do you need a massage or something?"

My cock stiffens, thinking about her soft hands kneading into my neck. Jesus fuck. "I don't need a massage," I blurt out.

She puts her hands up. "I didn't say *I* was going to do it. Relax."

I'm fucking *blowing* this. I drag a breath in. Pippa moves in front of the sink to wash a knife, and without thinking, my hands are on her shoulders, moving her away.

"I'll clean up. I didn't make this mess so you can clean up after me."

"I know." She shrugs under my hands. "I'm happy to help. I live here, too."

"Pippa. Sit down."

She sets the clean knife on the drying pad and turns to me with a worried look. "Did I do something wrong?"

"No." I hate myself. "I'm sorry. I'm stressed out today."

Her mouth twists. "Is there anything I can do to help?"

There I go again, picturing her sinking to her knees and taking me between her pretty lips. I'm about to say no, but another image appears in my head. Us sitting in the living room in the middle of the night while she plays the guitar.

"Music." I fold my arms across my chest, leaning against the counter. "That would help."

A smile lifts on her mouth and she reaches for her phone. "I can play DJ, no problem."

"No."

Her gaze snaps up to mine, one eyebrow raised.

"You."

Her mouth twists to the side again, but she holds my gaze. "That was a one-time thing." She smiles like she's kidding, but vulnerability flashes through her eyes, and my chest aches.

I lift my eyebrows at her. "I made dinner." Just like her, I'm teasing, but I'm also not.

We stare at each other, and I feel her resolve fading.

"Come on, songbird," I murmur. "You going to make me beg?"

She huffs, rolling her eyes. "Fine. But only because you're clearly having a bad day." A little smile curves on her pretty mouth and her eyes lose that hesitant expression from a moment ago. She heads to the stairs.

She returns with her guitar and takes a seat on the couch. I stand in the messy kitchen, staring as she positions the guitar on her lap, looping the strap over her shoulder.

It feels almost too good to be true.

"I've been playing around with some stuff," she admits with

a funny, almost-embarrassed smile that makes me want to kiss her again. "It isn't very good."

The breath leaves my lungs in a huff. "I'll be the judge of that."

"Okay." She smiles to herself and begins to play.

Her music fills the apartment, and a warm, tight pressure surges in my chest. The song she's singing is hopeful, sweet, and fun. The lyrics are about getting back up on the horse after falling off. Pippa's voice is soft but strong, and she has control over her notes like a professional. She makes it look easy and effortless.

As she sings about moving on from tough times, I wonder if I have anything to do with this, if the pep talk I gave her before the wrap party about getting back on the ice made any impact.

I really, really hope it did.

She sings a line about finding someone better, and an ugly thought strikes me. What if she's thinking about moving on with someone else? I imagine her swiping on a dating app, and I feel sick. I picture guys knocking on our front door to pick her up, and my jaw hurts from clenching.

The tune ends, and she shoots me an embarrassed smile. "Not a lot of cleaning happening over there," she teases.

I blink, shaking myself. "Did you write that?"

She nods. "I know it needs work."

"Why do you do that?" I ask without thinking. "Cut yourself down like that."

Discomfort flashes across her face, and she shifts her feet beneath her legs. "Um." Her lashes flutter. "I guess I say it first so others won't." She looks over at me, and I definitely want to kiss her again, even just to distract her from the assholes who made her feel like she wasn't good enough.

"I'd never do that, songbird."

She holds my gaze before she gives me a small nod. "I know."

I'm so fucking gone for this girl.

"How can anyone ever say yes to you if you say no to yourself first?" I ask. She chews her lip, watching me, and instead of pushing the issue, I just twirl my finger in the air. "Next."

She laughs, and the tension dissipates. "Demanding."

As I clean up, Pippa continues to play. Daisy snoozes on the couch, and when the timer rings, I dish out and gesture for Pippa to sit down at the table I've set.

The air hums with excitement. This feels like a date. No. Not a date. This feels like... something more. Something natural, easy, and necessary. Like we're a couple or something. Daisy's eating her dinner from the slow-feeder bowl I bought her, and Pippa watches with amusement as her tail wags.

This feels like family.

My stomach tightens. We're not, and I know that. This is just me trying to smooth things over with her so I don't lose someone I really need this year.

Pippa takes a bite and hums with appreciation. "Jamie, this is great."

I smile at my plate. "Thanks. I used to make it for my mom when I was a kid."

She quirks a funny smile at me, half-confused, half-amused. "You were cooking as a kid?"

I nod, gripping my water glass. The memories flood back— my mom's dim room in the middle of the day, curtains closed, her under the covers, fast asleep. All she did was sleep for weeks at a time until she rose out of the funk she was in. That's what she called them—*funks*.

"Okay," Pippa says, leaving it be.

It's her reaction that makes me want to share more. The

way she gives me space tells me she'll keep it between us. She'd never tell the media or her friends.

"My mom had depression when I was a kid. Sometimes I had to cook for myself."

Her concerned gaze meets mine, but there's no pity behind her eyes. "Oh. I'm sorry."

"It's okay. I managed it."

Understanding passes over her features, and a small smile lifts on her face. "That's why you take care of everyone."

I just shrug. "I have no choice."

She reaches across the table, covers my hand with hers, and gives it a warm squeeze. Her skin is soft, and my hand tenses under hers so I don't haul her into my lap like at the wrap party.

"Sorry," she whispers, yanking her hand back at my grim expression.

This is going all wrong. We eat in awkward, tense silence, and when we're done, she gets up to clear the plates, but I stop her.

"I'll do it." My tone comes out sharper than I wanted.

She takes a seat on the couch and picks up her guitar again. She plays another song while I clean the kitchen more thoroughly than ever. If I stop, she'll stop playing, and I'm desperate to hear her voice. Her singing on the couch makes this apartment feel like a home.

Her song ends and she glances over at me with a small smile. "I think you got that spot."

I look down to where I'm scrubbing the spotless countertop.

She bites her lip, her nerves written all over her face. "Sit with me?"

My feet are already moving to the living room. I can't say no to her, it seems. I drop down in the chair facing her.

She pauses, offering me a hesitant look. "Are we okay?"

I jerk a nod. "We're fine, Pippa."

She studies me, chewing her bottom lip, and I can't stop thinking about what that bottom lip felt like between my teeth as I kissed her at the wrap party.

Fucking hell, what I wouldn't do to experience that again.

Silence stretches between us before I shoot to my feet. I'm on edge, and I'm going to do something stupid if I sit down here with her.

I make it all the way to the hall outside my room when her voice stops me.

"Is this about the toy you bought me?" She climbs the last of the stairs, folding her arms over her chest.

My gut drops. Of course she figured it out. "Pippa." I drag in a breath. "I'm so sorry."

She stares at me. I can't read her expression. "Why?"

I shake my head, feeling sick with nerves. "It crossed a line. You told me that in confidence and—" I cut myself off, frustrated. "I don't want to make you uncomfortable. I had too many beers and I'd been thinking about you all day." Shit, I didn't mean to say that. "Because we'd been texting. I'd been thinking nonstop about what you said at the wrap party." My eyes meet hers, and heat roars in my blood. "I like you being here. I like you playing music in the apartment and I like you coming to my games."

Her mouth tips up into a smile. "I like going for walks with you, and you making dinner."

My heart aches. All I can do is nod. I can't believe I almost fucked this up because I was horny.

She tucks her hands in the sleeves of her sweater. "And I like going to your games and hanging out with your mom."

Now we're just listing more reasons why I shouldn't have done what I did.

Her tongue darts out to wet her lips. "I used it."

I stifle a groan at the memory of listening to her coming all over the toy. I can only imagine what it looked like. I can't *stop* imagining what it looked like.

I can't lie. "I know."

"You do?" Her eyes go wide.

"This place isn't soundproof." I rub the bridge of my nose. Now that she knows, maybe she'll be more careful so I don't have to walk around with an erection all day.

She shifts, squeezing her thighs together. "I heard my name coming from your room the other day," she whispers, cheeks flushing.

I freeze. Yesterday, I let her name slip when I was thinking about her, jerking off. Even remembering it sends blood rushing to my cock. "I didn't hear you get home."

We stare at each other for a long moment, and the air between us sparks. She bites her bottom lip and I watch the movement, fascinated. I wonder if she'd do that if I had my fingers buried inside her.

My eyes close. Fuck. No matter how hard I try, I can't get those ideas out of my head. I feel myself getting hard.

"Jamie," she breathes, and I look at her.

The look in her eyes tells me something dangerous is about to happen. She's about to say something that I won't be able to stop thinking about. I know it.

"What?" My voice is low.

"Why did you buy that toy for me?" Her lashes flutter. "The real answer."

I take a step toward her. The thread holding my willpower together is close to snapping. "Because I wanted to give you something he couldn't."

Her gaze drops to my erection, and more blood rushes there.

"Because," I continue, because I can't seem to keep a

fucking secret around this girl, "I wanted to make you come harder than ever, and that was the only way. And I don't want anyone else to do it."

Her throat works and she's blushing again, but her eyes are locked on mine. The tension between us is thick and electric as I take another step toward her.

"Did it work?" I ask, because I can't help myself.

Her breath is ragged as she nods, and my balls ache. I should go to my room. I'm about to snap with her looking at me like that.

My control frays, and I walk forward until her back is pressed against the wall. My chest brushes hers, and I can feel her breath on my neck as she tilts her head up to look into my eyes.

"You need to stop looking at me like that, songbird," I tell her, leaning my forearm on the wall above her head.

"Or what?" she breathes.

"Or I'm going to lose my mind." I say it like it hasn't already happened. "I can't stop thinking about you using that toy."

A tiny smile ticks up on her mouth. Coy, teasing, and knowing, like she sees exactly what she's doing to me.

*Keeping my distance*, I chant to myself. But the voice is getting quieter, farther away.

"You want to show me?" The words fall out of my mouth before I can catch them. My voice is low and thick.

There's a beat between us where that fading voice in my head thrashes for attention, and I slam the mental door on it. This isn't a relationship. Pippa has no experience in bed, and I do. Who better to show her what she's worth than me, a man who thinks the world of her?

In the dim light of the hallway, her pupils blow. "Okay."

My control snaps, and my hand wraps around the back of her neck, pulling her mouth to mine.

JAMIE KISSES like he's mad at me. His mouth moves with urgency, demanding and rough and desperate, like he's pouring every ounce of frustration back into me.

I love it.

I sigh into him in relief, because his mouth back on mine is like drinking water after a marathon. So necessary, so needed, so fucking *good*.

He grips my hair, angling my head back and stroking into my mouth. Sparks of pleasure skate over my skin, and his kiss is drugging me. I lightly suck on his tongue, and he groans.

"You're fucking killing me," he rasps between kisses. He's furious, and delight and desire flicker low in my belly, warming me. His stubble is rough against my skin, his lips are practically bruising mine, but I don't care. I just need more.

He groans again like he's in pain, leaning his forehead against mine. My hands come to his t-shirt, skimming up and down the hard planes of his chest. God, I want to see him shirtless again, like that night in the kitchen.

"Fuck," he bites out, glazed eyes flashing. "I need to see it. I need to see you make yourself come on the toy I bought you."

His lips seek mine, and a heavy ache forms between my

legs as he nips my bottom lip. A soft moan slips out of me. The breath whooshes out of my lungs as his hips pin me against the wall and his thick length presses against my stomach.

Kissing Jamie is hotter than anything I've ever done with Zach.

His lips move roughly down my neck, and I stand there, heart racing like this is a dream. I'm floating, and we haven't even *done* anything yet. He backs away, and I feel his absence immediately.

He opens my bedroom door, glares at me, and points into my room. "Get in there," he demands.

I shiver. Jamie bossing me around makes me feel untethered and completely unlike myself, and I don't mind one bit.

Heart pounding, I walk past him into my room. At my bed, I stop and turn. He follows me into the room and crosses his arms over his chest.

"Well?" he asks.

Oh god. My stomach dips, and the horniness I felt moments before wavers. He's probably slept with a hundred women, and now I have no freaking clue what to do.

He's going to laugh at me. Just like Zach and his manager laughed at me. I blink rapidly, meeting his gaze, and his expression changes.

"Songbird," he says, holding my gaze. "Do you want to stop?"

"No, I just—" I cut myself off, glancing at my bedside table. "I don't know how to do this part."

His eyes turn soft. He steps forward and threads his fingers into the back of my hair again.

God, that feels good. I close my eyes as he presses his lips to mine. The nerves drain away.

"Take your clothes off and get on the bed."

He pulls back and looks down at me, and something about him telling me what to do sends heat rushing back to my center.

"Do you understand?"

I nod, dazed.

"Good." He lets go of my hair, steps back again, and folds his arms.

My pulse picks up again as I pull my sweater off. I reach for the hem of my shirt, and as I pull it up, Jamie's eyebrow lifts.

"Slower."

Another twist of heat between my legs. I like this side of him—primal, bossy, demanding, wanting me. I pull my t-shirt off at a criminally slow pace, watching his jaw tick, his eyes simmer with heat, and his fists clench, tucked beneath his arms.

His gaze drops to my bra, a pale pink lacy thing. His tongue taps his upper lip as his eyes linger on my chest, and my nipples prick. I picture that tongue tracing my skin above the bra, and there's a rush of liquid between my legs.

The way he's looking at me? It feels good.

His eyes meet mine. "All of it," he says, tilting his chin at my pants. Another shiver rolls down my spine.

When my jeans are off, he stares at my lace thong like it offends him, but I know the truth. His Adam's apple bobs as he lets out a long breath, gaze fixed between my legs.

"Are your panties damp?"

I nod.

"Good." He clenches his eyes closed, jaw ticking while he drags in another breath. "Keep going."

My blood whooshes in my ears as I reach back to unhook my bra. I can't believe I'm doing this. I feel like laughing with excitement and nerves, like when I'm on a roller coaster. When I remove my bra, Jamie's eyes are on my breasts. His nostrils flare, and a thrill of excitement shoots through me.

"Jesus fuck," he mutters, looking away before his gaze returns to my chest. "Panties, too, Pippa."

I slip them down. My skin prickles from his gaze between my legs, and he groans and rakes his hand through his hair before tilting his chin behind me.

"On the bed."

He's still fully clothed, and I'm bare-ass naked. This is either the most intimidating thing I've experienced, or the hottest. Or both. I can hear my pulse in my ears as I settle onto my duvet, leaning back into the pillows. My thighs press together, and there's a dull ache between them. My nipples pinch, my skin goosebumps, and a thought strikes me.

What if I can't come?

Worry spikes in my mind. It'd be so awkward. Tension forms in my chest and I chew my lip, looking up as Jamie looms over me, still crossing his arms.

He opens my bedside drawer, and when he sees the toy, he pauses before picking it up. His eyes are dark, lit only by the lamp on my bedside table, and another thrill arcs through me, landing at my center.

He hands me the toy before straightening up, waiting. He's so tall, so fucking broad, and he seems too big for my bedroom.

"Like this?" I breathe, heart pounding. He's just going to stand over me like that?

He nods. "Mhm. Exactly like this, songbird."

I'm nervous, but I don't want to stop. Him watching me like this, not touching me even though I know he wants to—I'm going to be thinking about this for a long time.

My gaze is locked on his as I click the toy on. Its whirring noise fills the quiet bedroom, and his eyes darken.

"What are you waiting for?"

"Bossy," I whisper, and the corner of his mouth twitches.

I press the toy to my clit and my eyes fall closed.

Oh my god.

My thigh muscles tighten. The suction against my clit is perfect, better than anything I've ever felt. Well... I remember kissing Jamie moments before. That was a close contender.

Jamie kissing me between my legs might be the best thing I've ever felt, if it's anything like this.

I sigh, head tipping back, and I can feel his eyes on me. Oh my god, this is so hot, with him standing over me, glaring down at me with that furious look on his face. I never thought I'd be into this.

I sneak a peek at him. Yep. Furious. Absolutely furious. Heat builds around the base of my spine, and I moan and close my eyes again.

"Keep your eyes open," he demands.

I do as he says, gazing up at him. He looks so mad, but when my eyes drop to his pants, his erection strains against the fabric.

My clit aches, a dull throb of heat and pleasure, and I whimper.

"Are you close?" he asks, and I jerk a nod.

He arches a brow, looking down at me like he hates me, but there's a soft affection in his eyes. "Are you going to say my name when you come?"

Another pulse of heat between my legs. I'm soaking wet. "I don't know. Maybe."

"Wrong." His jaw tightens. "You'll say it. Without a doubt."

His confidence makes me huff with quiet laughter. My toes curl at the waves of pleasure radiating from my clit as the toy sucks, and I picture Jamie's mouth there, his eyes burning as he looks up at me.

Oh. That's good. He rakes his hand through his hair,

messing it up. It looks so hot like that. I want to touch his hair so badly.

"Fuck," he mutters again, gritting his teeth. "You're so fucking hot, Pippa. Can't wait to see you come for me."

I nod in desperation, gripping my duvet with my free hand. The heat and pressure build, and pleasure is surging through my body.

Zach pops into my head. I flinch, pushing the image away, but I can't. I picture us in bed, him getting impatient with me.

I'm full-body cringing, and the ache between my legs fades.

No. No, no, no. Not now. I *had* this. I close my eyes, chasing that feeling from a second ago.

Jamie's voice is low, brow furrowed. "What's going on?"

I shake my head. "I don't know."

Embarrassment, shame, and regret whirlpool inside me. This was a huge fucking mistake. I can't believe I thought I could go from sexually broken to basically having an orgasm on display.

Who the fuck do I think I am?

My face is going red, and suddenly, I'm too naked, too exposed. I lift the toy away; it isn't doing anything, anyway. My legs snap together.

"This isn't working." My voice is wobbly. I close my eyes and pull my legs in. I just want to hide. God. How am I ever going to face him again? "I'm sorry. It's taking too long and I'm cold and—" I shake my head. "Sorry."

I'm humiliated. This is going to make things awkward between us.

Jamie sits beside me on the bed, watching my face. His jaw still clenches but his eyes are watchful, and maybe a little worried.

"I'm sorry," I say again.

"Stop apologizing." He reaches to tuck a lock of hair behind my ear, and my heart tugs with the intimacy of it.

I really wanted to do this. It felt fun and sexy and dangerous.

"You're too in your head." His eyes search mine.

"I don't know how to get out," I admit.

His gaze drops to my mouth, and his eyes darken again. He drags a breath in and lets it out slow. "I have an idea."

JAMIE PULLS his shirt over his head, and I'm assaulted with a fantastic view of his rippling torso. Muscles upon muscles. Rounded, toned shoulders. Defined pecs. Stacked abs. They dance and jump as he yanks his pants off, and that warm, tight feeling between my legs pulses once again.

Oh. There it is.

"What are you—" I start.

"We're trying something new. Stand for me."

I slip off the bed as he throws the duvet back and takes my spot. His legs fall wide before he gestures for me to sit between them. There's something so attractive about his tight black boxers. Maybe it's the outline of his cock against the fabric, straining.

"Come here, Pippa."

I shiver at his tone, loaded with tension and heat, but I do as he says, settling between his legs. His erection presses into my backside, and there's a spark of heat between my legs.

The second I settle back against him, I sigh with pleasure. He's so *warm*. He pulls the duvet over us, covering me.

"Better?" he murmurs against my ear, and I nod.

"So much better."

"Good." He inhales me, nose against my neck, and lets it out as a sigh. "It's my turn, okay?"

I nod, letting my head fall against him. He kisses my cheek, my jaw, my neck, and the tension leaves my body.

His hands skim up my thighs, strong fingers digging into the muscles, massaging me. As his hands draw closer to my center, he pauses.

"Put your hands on my thighs, songbird."

I set my hands on his warm skin, and he flinches.

"You're cold," he huffs, laughing quietly.

"Sorry," I squeak.

"It's okay." He presses another kiss to my cheek, and this is the side of Jamie that's the most dangerous. The sweet version of him. "Put your feet on mine."

I do, and he groans like he's in pain.

"Like ice," he says, and I laugh. A little puff of air against my neck tells me he's laughing, too.

I'm relaxing more by the second. His hands stroke up and down my thighs, inching closer and closer to the apex each time, and I'm melting into him as heat builds inside me.

"How's that?" His mouth moves against my shoulder.

"Good," I whisper.

His hands move up to my breasts, and when his fingers find my nipples, I sigh again. He pinches and rolls the peaks, gently at first, but with growing pressure, drawing more gasps and sighs from me until I'm squirming against him. His cock pulses against my back as I arch into his hands. Heat pools at the bottom of my stomach and I can feel how wet I am.

"I'm going to try the toy again," he says, low in my ear. "You think you can handle that?"

I nod, opening my legs, pressing them against his thighs. "Uh-huh."

He shifts under me, reaching for it, and slides it under the duvet, applying it to my clit before he turns it on.

The toy's intense suction on my clit makes every muscle in my body pull taut. "Oh my god."

"Have you played with the settings?"

I'm writhing on him. "No."

Oh god. This is so good. This is perfect, exactly what I need. He's so warm and solid beneath me, all around me, and my nails dig into his thick, muscular thighs. His cock pulses again when I do that.

He turns the intensity of the toy down, and the desperate, aching feeling fades—not completely, but I'm no longer on the brink of coming.

"Hey," I protest, but it's more of a desperate plea.

His teeth scrape my shoulder. "You're not in charge here." His hand comes to my stomach, sliding to the underside of my breast. I want him to touch my nipple again, roll it, pinch it, anything, but he won't, he just keeps stroking my skin, circling the aching point.

"Tell me what you feel right now," he murmurs into my ear, lowering the intensity of the toy another click.

The toy's soft suction pulls me into a comfortable, floaty zone. I can't come like this, but I don't want it to stop.

"Songbird. Pay attention."

I suck in a breath. Right. Focus. "Okay. Um. I can feel the toy between my legs."

"Good." Pleasure ripples through my body, warming me. "What else?"

I close my eyes. "I can feel you against my back. You're so warm."

"Mhm."

"Your legs under my hands."

"Very good. You're doing so well." His low tone is pleased, and my clit throbs at the praise.

My skin feels hot. I need more, but I can't get there with this low setting. My back arches. "Jamie, I need more."

"Not yet." Finally, his thumb slides up, playing with my nipple, and my head falls back again.

"Oh my god."

"Tell me a few more things you feel."

"Um." My thoughts scatter at the way he pinches me. The toy whirs away between my legs, and my chest rises and falls fast as my breathing picks up. "Your hand on my nipple."

"Mhm." His mouth is back on my shoulder, and his stubble scrapes me. "Your tits are so perfect, Pippa. Seeing you in that pretty pink bra is going to make me come for years."

My pussy aches, flooding with heat and liquid. "Wow."

"What else?"

My thoughts float in the air and I try to catch them. "Um. The duvet against my skin."

"Uh-huh."

"Your boner against my ass."

He huffs a laugh. "Sorry."

"No," I breathe. "I like it. It's hot."

He groans. "What else, baby?"

My body clenches, tightening around nothing. I *like it* when he calls me that.

"I can feel your thighs against mine," I say, and my voice is thin.

He clicks the toy up one speed, and when I moan, he pinches my nipple harder. His knees hook under mine so he's holding my legs open with his thighs. The way he has me, I'm powerless, and my pussy thrums with pressure.

"Oh my god," I gasp.

"How's that?"

"Good. So fucking good." My back arches again and I press my lips together to hold in the moan. "More."

"More?" His tone taunts me.

"Please."

A rumbling noise comes from his chest, like he likes me asking nicely. He clicks the toy up again.

"You look so fucking pretty," he says in my ear as I twist in his lap. "So fucking *gorgeous* sitting in my lap as I use the toy on your pussy."

He clicks the intensity up again, and my eyes roll back. I picture him bending me over this bed, pushing that big cock into me. My pussy flutters. Oh god. It's starting.

This is working. I can't believe it's actually working.

"That's so good," I choke out. The pressure builds again, swirling between my thighs. Jamie's so warm against me, against my legs, against my back. His big hand cups my breast, kneading, and the pleasure inside me rises. "Oh god," I breathe. "Don't stop."

His teeth scrape my neck. "What if I did?" He lowers the setting, and the pressure between my legs dies off.

"No," I cry, digging my nails into his thighs. "More."

"Beg me," he demands in a low voice that makes me shiver. "Beg me to let you come, songbird."

"Please." I'm breathing hard. "Please let me come."

"Good." He clicks the toy up a few speeds, and I groan. "Keep talking. What are you thinking about?"

"Your cock." My voice breaks as he clicks the toy up again. "Your cock inside me."

"Is that what you want?"

I nod urgently. "Yes."

"You think you could take me?" He clicks the toy up again, and I'm squirming on his lap.

My body isn't mine; it's his. He owns it. He's wielding it however he pleases, and I'm just along for the ride.

"I don't know," I admit.

His thick arm wraps across my torso, anchoring me to him, and I clutch it.

"I think you could." His voice is a hot rasp in my ear. "I think you could take my cock. It'd be a tight fit in this gorgeous pussy, but we'd make it fit."

I'm just nodding, eyes clenched closed as the toy makes me feel like I'm about to burst with pleasure. The first flutters begin.

"I need to come," I tell him, squeezing his arm.

"Then come, baby. Come on the toy I bought you. Show me how good it is."

His teeth scrape my earlobe, and the pressure boils over.

# CHAPTER 37

WAVES OF PLEASURE pulse between my legs, and I can't think, I can't speak, I can't even breathe—I'm just clamping down around nothing, shaking in his lap as he holds me against him.

"Good girl," Jamie growls. "Such a good fucking girl for me, coming so hard."

A noise I've never heard myself make slips out of me, half-moan, half-cry, and he holds the toy against my clit as intense pleasure radiates through me.

"Oh my god," I cry. "Jamie."

He groans, clicking the toy down one speed. "You're doing so fucking good, Pippa. Keep going. Ride it out, baby."

He lowers the speed one more click, and I'm still there, floating and totally paralyzed in euphoria. I've never come for this long. I've never come this hard. I feel like I'm being turned inside out. Heat spreads out from my center, and I can feel *everything*—the way his hard chest feels against my back, how his big arm locks me against him, the brush of his thighs against mine, his lips on my neck, urging me on.

Finally, I can't take it anymore, and my hand covers his. He pulls the toy away, and I collapse against his body.

Holy shit.

I'm still shaking with aftershocks, hips tilting against his erection.

"Stop that," he tells me, and I laugh, dazed.

"Or what?" I press against him again, and this time, his hips press forward to meet me, cock pushing into my ass.

Something tugs inside me, knowing how badly he wants me.

I pull out of his grasp, turning to kneel between his legs, and our eyes lock as he sits against the headboard, watching me. His deep green eyes are glazed with lust, and there's another twinge of warmth where he pressed the toy moments before. I can see the shape of his cock, distorting the front of his black boxers, and my center heats.

When I drag my gaze up to Jamie's, his expression is pained.

"Don't look at me like that," he begs, nostrils flaring. "This was supposed to be about you."

My eyes drop again to his cock, and it pulses under my gaze. I shoot him a knowing grin.

Busted.

As my gaze traces his torso, all the ridges and valleys, smooth chest and hard lines of his abs, I'm overcome with the urge to take care of him, to provide him with something no one else can. He's so controlled, so careful, so militant about everything, but right now, I just want him to feel overwhelming pleasure like I did a few moments ago.

I reach out and stroke his length over the fabric of his boxers.

"Fuck," he mutters, head falling back against the bed frame. His eyes are half-lidded.

His reaction spurs me on, and I give him another slow

stroke. He's so hard, so thick, and when I think about what he would feel like inside me, my thighs squeeze together.

I already know it would be so good. It might even hurt a bit, and I'm weirdly turned on by that.

On my next stroke, I linger at the head, running my thumb over it. The fabric is damp with pre-cum, and he lets out a low groan, jaw tightening.

"Oh, fuck, Pippa."

His jaw clenches again, and I feel drunk with power. I'm barely touching him, and I have him making all these noises that I'm going to remember while I'm using the toy next time. Something bold streaks through me, and I pull the waistband of his boxers down, letting his cock spring free.

Jamie's cock is gorgeous—thick and long and hard. The best-looking cock I've ever seen. No wonder he gives it so much attention in his room. Pre-cum beads on the tip, and when I drag my thumb through it, he sucks in a sharp breath.

"Is this okay?" I ask softly.

He jerks a nod. I lift my thumb to my lips and suck the salty taste off, and his Adam's apple bobs.

"Jesus Christ," he mutters in a ragged voice. His eyes pin me, so bright and full of intensity that I shiver. "Did you like that?"

I nod, smiling at him before I return to stroking him. "You're fun to play with."

On the next stroke, he moans. "Fun to play with," he repeats, watching me work his cock. He's so thick. More liquid beads at the tip, and when I slip my other hand around his balls, his big thighs tense.

"Shit," he gasps. "If you don't stop that, I'm going to come all over your tits."

Heat rushes to my pussy, and my lips part in excitement

and surprise. I want that. I want that *so bad*. I keep working his cock. Fascinated by his reaction, I give his balls a gentle squeeze. He frowns, lips parted, and I feel like I have him under my complete control right now.

I love it.

"Take your boxers off," I whisper.

As soon as he does, my hands are back on him. I stroke him faster, and he curses again.

"Pippa," he warns. His hands clench at his sides and his eyelids droop like he's about to pass out. His strained abs ripple.

I'm soaking wet, jerking Jamie Streicher off. His shoulders tighten as he sinks his hands into his hair. His expression is strained, his breathing is rapid, and he can't look away from me. I don't need to try to memorize this moment; I know I'll never forget this.

In my hand, his cock pulses, and he nods, letting out a loud moan. "Gonna come, baby. Gonna come all over your gorgeous tits."

My eyes are wide. "Do it."

He hunches over, groaning. Cum shoots out of his cock and coats my chest as I continue stroking him, and when I think he's done, he isn't. He keeps coming, watching me with that agonized expression I love while he sprays liquid onto my breasts. It's covering my hands, it's on my tits, and it's dripping down my stomach.

"My fucking god, Pippa," he mutters, catching his breath, watching me with something that looks like awe. "You made me come so hard." His gaze drops to my chest and the corner of his mouth pulls up into a satisfied smirk. He dips a long finger through his cum before looking at my mouth.

"Open."

I do as I'm told. My face heats but so does the apex of my

legs—I love it when he tells me what to do. He slides his finger into my mouth, and I moan at the taste of him, sucking his finger and letting my tongue swirl around it.

He groans again as he takes his hand back. "Jesus."

I light up with a delighted grin. He rolls his eyes, but the corner of his mouth tugs into a sated smile. He leans forward to press a soft kiss to my mouth.

"I knew you could do it," he whispers. His hand drifts to the back of my neck. It's so warm, so comforting, so *nice*. I'm never leaving this bed.

He kisses me, and instead of urgent and demanding like before, he's soft, sweet, gentle, like he's cherishing me. My thoughts float in the air, my skin tingles, and I sigh into him.

My god. Is that what sex is like for other people? What the hell was I doing with Zach all those years?

"You okay?" he murmurs, pulling back to search my eyes.

"Yes." I nod, breathless.

I'm more than okay. I'm a thousand times better than when we walked into this room.

He gives me one more kiss before pulling away. "Stay there."

He returns a moment later with washcloths to clean me up, and my pulse stumbles at the two sides of him—demanding and bossy versus sweet and caring. I watch his toned ass and powerful thighs as he walks away. When he returns, wearing clean boxers and holding a glass of water, he's still wearing that sated expression, that smirk as his eyes rake over me, and I can't help but grin at him.

"What time is it? I should walk Daisy again."

"I'll do it," he says, digging through his pants pocket for his phone. "You stay here." He pulls his phone out, and his expression changes. "Shit," he murmurs, frowning.

"What's wrong?"

He already has the phone at his ear. "I have six missed calls from my mom."

I SIT UP STRAIGHT, worry sobering me. He props the phone against his ear with his shoulder while pulling his pants on.

"What's going on?" he asks when Donna answers. Concern is etched into his features, which were so relaxed a moment ago.

He pauses, listening, hands faltering on his socks. His eyes widen. I'm already off the bed, getting dressed.

"Okay," he says before listening more. "I'll go over to her place to see if she's okay." He glances at me. "Can you try those breathing exercises Pippa did with you?"

He listens, but his eyes are locked on me, brows knitted together as I pull my sweater on, goosebumps rising all over my arms.

After promising to call her back, he hangs up before scrolling through his contacts.

"What's going on?"

"She had her friend Claire over for dinner and asked her to text her when she got home, but she didn't, and then my mom couldn't get a hold of her." His jaw tightens. "And then it turned into a panic attack. She always worries people are going to get hit by a drunk driver."

Claire came to a hockey game with us recently. She lives in the southern part of the city. It'll take him an hour and a half to get there and then up to North Vancouver.

I'm buttoning my pants up. "I'll go to your mom's place."

He shakes his head. "No, I can go there after."

"Jamie, I'll take an Uber to your mom's place, and you can pick us up there after, or I can just take an Uber home if she's fine."

He stares at me, and something passes through his eyes. "Okay. Thank you, Pippa. I really appreciate this."

"No problem." I grab my phone and book a pet-friendly Uber before digging my headphones out of my bag and calling Donna.

"Pippa?" Her voice is high.

"Hey." I smile at Jamie, and my tone is warm and reassuring. "I'm going to pay you a visit while Jamie drives out to Claire's, and I'm bringing Daisy. Maybe we can take her for a walk around the neighborhood."

"Okay." She sounds hesitant, and her breathing is thin. "I could do that."

"I'm going to stay on the phone with you until I get there," I tell her, pulling my hoodie on.

I've been reading online about panic attacks. Some people who get them recommended distractions as a way to calm down.

"That would be nice." She sounds relieved. "I'm so sorry, honey. I just got all worked up and then—" She cuts herself off. "I don't know what happened."

"It's okay. Tell me about your day."

While Donna talks, Jamie stares at me like he doesn't know what to make of me, and I gesture at him to go. He nods and stalks out of the room, and moments later, I hear the front door close.

———

"Is that Orion?" I ask Donna, pointing up at the stars while Daisy sniffs a rosebush.

Donna cranes her neck. "I thought that was the Big Dipper."

We talked on the phone the entire way here, and by the time I arrived, her breathing was almost back to normal. Jamie called to explain that Claire's phone was dead and she couldn't find her power cord. As Donna and I wander her neighborhood, I can hardly tell she had a panic attack within the last few hours.

"Huh." I point over to the east. "I thought *that* was the Big Dipper."

Donna laughs. "I have zero knowledge of astronomy, so don't ask me."

"Me neither."

We both laugh, and she gives my shoulder an affectionate squeeze. "Thank you so much for coming up here on short notice, honey." She rolls her eyes at herself, looking embarrassed. "I'm so sorry I took over your evening."

"It's fine." I shake my head, smiling. "Honestly. We don't want you to be stuck up here all by yourself."

"Don't say that to Jamie or he'll try to move in with me again."

I snort. "He can be stubborn when he wants to be."

An image of him flashes into my head—arms folded over his chest, t-shirt straining across his shoulders as he glares down at me using the toy. My skin feels hot, and I turn away so Donna can't see whatever expression is on my face.

"I pictured her in a car accident, like Paul," Donna says quietly. "Jamie's father. And then I couldn't *stop* picturing it. It was like the thoughts took over and I couldn't get a hold of things. They're normally triggered by the smell of alcohol." Her eyes meet mine, and she searches my expression for something. Judgment, maybe. "Sometimes driving. But never out of the blue like this."

I make a noise of acknowledgment. "Lots of people have panic attacks. There are doctors who specialize in this."

She shakes her head hard. "No. No way. No doctors, no medication." She lets out a bitter laugh. "I've been there and I'm not going back."

I think about what Jamie said at dinner tonight, about how his mom had depression when he was a kid, and that's why he knows how to cook. My heart aches for them. I can see why Donna isn't interested in revisiting the past, and I don't even know the whole story.

"That looks like Scorpio," Donna says, pointing at a cluster of stars.

I squint at them. "Yeah. I think you're right."

We both laugh, because we have no clue.

While we walk, we chat easily, but my mind slips back to Jamie and what we did in my bed. I can't believe how easily things happened for me once he made me sit in his lap. That was the first time I was able to come with a guy. Maybe it was the way he felt against me, maybe it was the way he knew what he was doing, or maybe it was that exercise he did, where he asked me what I felt. Or maybe it was all of it combined.

Jamie isn't just the hot hockey player I had a crush on in high school. He's so much more. Under his surly, chiseled exterior, he's kind and caring and protective. He cares more about the people in his life than about himself. He encourages me in music like no one else has. I'm becoming friends with his mom, and I love taking care of his dog.

Hesitation rises in my stomach, and my mouth twists to the

side. Zach used to think I was special, but the shine wore off. I can't bear the idea of Jamie losing interest in me like Zach did.

At just the idea of it, I feel sick. I can't go through that again.

———

When we get back to Donna's place, Jamie is already inside. I texted him earlier that we were out on a walk.

"Hi, honey," Donna calls to him as he strides over to her, studying her face.

He scans her, worry in his eyes, and my heart twists. This is a lot for one person to deal with, and it must be tough to watch his mom struggle. He wraps her in a tight hug, and she sighs with exasperation.

"I'm completely fine," she says. "Just ask Pippa."

Jamie's eyes find mine over her shoulder and he gives me a look of gratitude. I just smile and nod.

For the next half hour, Jamie hovers while Donna makes tea and I sit at the kitchen table, making conversation with her. Finally, Jamie is convinced his mom will be okay on her own, and she shoos us out the door.

The drive home is weirdly tense, and I sneak glances across the car at him. His jaw is tight. Our eyes meet.

"Thanks for tonight, Pippa," he says, voice low and serious.

"Don't mention it."

He glances back at the road, looking frustrated. "I, uh. I would be so screwed without you."

"I know."

He huffs, amused. "Humble."

I look at him with my eyebrows raised, smiling. "Don't mention it. Honestly."

He nods and turns back to the road, but tension still lingers in his expression. When we arrive home, Daisy can barely keep her eyes open as she heads upstairs. She sleeps in Jamie's room when he isn't traveling.

Jamie and I exchange a glance. Now that we're alone again, I'm thinking about what we did earlier, how hot it was, how I want to do it again.

But we can't. I know that. I can't keep my emotions out of it the way Hazel suggested.

"About tonight," he starts. His throat works and he rubs the back of his neck.

"I don't think we should do it again," I blurt out, and his eyes shoot to mine. Is that disappointment or relief? I can't tell. "You have your mom and I have..." I trail off, shaking my head. I can't tell him the truth.

I have a very breakable heart and a big crush on him.

"Right." His intense gaze roams my face, studying me, and his jaw ticks again. "I'm sorry if I made you uncomfortable."

"No." I shake my head. "You didn't. It was great. Like, really great." Okay, I'm blushing now. "I work for you and we have a good thing here."

He nods, still watching me with that careful gaze. "Yeah. We do."

My throat feels thick when I swallow. "Great." I glance at the stairs. Through the giant windows of the living room, the ski-hill lights in the mountains twinkle, and I know I'm going to be staring at them for hours, replaying the entire night. "I should get to bed."

"Good night, Pippa." His voice is low, and there's something in his eyes that makes me want to hug him.

"Good night."

Inside my room, I lean against the closed door and gather my thoughts. Jamie doesn't have room in his life for me—tonight was a huge reminder of that. It wasn't Jamie's fault; it was just bad timing, but I know he's downstairs blaming himself for it. It's going to keep happening, and he's never going to choose me over his mom. He can't. She needs him too much.

The whole situation has a neon warning sign over it that says *DANGER*, blinking, with giant red arrows pointing to it. If I let it continue, I know exactly how it'll end for me.

WE'RE PLAYING Calgary again a few nights later. Alexei Volkov has the puck, but after he shoots, Miller crosschecks him. The puck hits the pipe, and the fans at the other end of the stadium jump to their feet, calling for a penalty. Play continues, and the booing begins.

When the Cougars' goalie catches the next shot, the whistle blows, and the refs and the linesmen take a moment to discuss before breaking apart.

"No penalty," the announcer calls, and the entire arena boos.

Miller grins at the fans, arms wide open as he skates down the ice. They're furious, slamming fists on the glass, and he revels in it. He takes his glove off and flips them the middle finger, and the boos get louder.

Now the whistle blows, and he gets a penalty.

Jesus fucking Christ. I barely recognize him. He used to be so disciplined and focused, like me. He used to love hockey, even with his dad watching his every move and berating him after games about what he did wrong.

I grab my water bottle and make eye contact with Pippa. She smiles, and I nod back. Hazel's with her tonight, drinking a beer and looking bored. The few times play has stopped near my net, Rory's eyes went straight to them.

Pippa's laughing at something Hazel said. She winks at me with a pretty smile, and my cock twitches. I thought the morning after would be awkward, but Pippa's been completely normal. Almost as if nothing happened.

I should be relieved she isn't upset. I should put it out of my head and move on. Instead, I can't stop thinking about the other night.

She was right that we shouldn't be messing around. What happened with my mom was a warning shot, a reminder of what can go wrong if I'm not there for her.

It doesn't mean I'm happy about it.

I'm desperate to make Pippa come again, but if we start messing around, we won't stop. I'll make her mine, over and over, every morning, afternoon, and night. Probably in the middle of the night. She's too fucking sweet, too soft, too special, and I can't get enough of my pretty assistant. She's so much more than the pretty girl from high school, and the closer we get, the more my resolve around her crumbles.

She deserves so much more than me, anyway. Someone who can make her their full focus, give her everything. I hate the idea of another guy in her life like that, but I want her to be happy.

Play resumes, and I tear my gaze away and pull myself back into the game.

———

After the game, I head up to the box. Pippa spots me right away and gives me a small wave as I walk over.

"Hi." I clear my throat, glancing around. "Where's Hazel?"

"She went to the washroom. She'll be right back." She smiles up at me. "Great game."

"Thanks."

Our eyes meet and my gaze drops to her lips. My blood is still pumping hard from the game, adrenaline flowing through my veins, and the only thing I want to do right now is drag her home and do more of what we did the other night.

"There she is," Miller calls as he approaches Pippa. He gives her a big hug, lifting her off her feet, and she lets out a peal of laughter.

My nostrils flare and I fold my arms over my chest, glaring at them. "What are you doing here?"

He sets her down and tugs on the end of her ponytail. My fists clench, and I feel the urge to hit him. "Just saying hey to my pal Pippa."

She grins at him. "Hey."

He wiggles his eyebrows at her. "Hey," he chirps back, and they laugh.

I hate this.

"Players from the other team aren't supposed to be in here." My tone is sharp, and my chest feels tight. They shouldn't be smiling at each other like that. She's mine, not his.

He rolls his eyes and tilts his chin across the room, where Calgary's goalie is talking with our second line forward. "Thurston's basically trading plays with your guy. No one cares." He beams down at Pippa and throws his arm around her shoulder, and rage surges in my blood. "How ya been, kid?"

She snorts. "You're two years older than me."

"Yeah, but you're short."

"I'm a normal height."

I hate the way she's tucked into his side like that. She should be tucked into *my* side. Not his. Never his.

"You're just ridiculously tall," she tells him.

My jaw hurts from clenching. I swallow past the knives in my throat as my pulse beats in my ears. Why am I so fucking worked up right now?

Hazel appears at Pippa's side, giving me a cool nod. "Hi."

"Hazel." I nod at her.

Her gaze goes to Miller, with his stupid arm still thrown around Pippa, and she makes a face of disgust.

I knew I liked Hazel.

"Hi, Hartley," he says. He's looking at Hazel with a confident smirk, but something predatory flashes through his eyes. "Remember me?"

You've gotta be fucking kidding me.

Hazel's distasteful expression intensifies. "Nope."

"Yeah, you do."

Pippa glances between them. "You know each other? You were in different years."

Miller's looking at Hazel like she's dessert. "We had a couple classes together. Hartley's a real brainiac."

"Right." Pippa nods at Hazel. "I forgot you took summer classes to get ahead."

He lets Pippa go and takes a step toward Hazel, still wearing that confident smirk that I want to wipe off his face. At least he's not directing it at Pippa anymore. "How you been, Hartley? Pippa says you're working for the team."

Hazel regards him over the rim of her beer as she takes a sip. "Yep."

"You always did have a thing for hockey players."

Pippa winces at me. My eyebrow arches, and she mouths *tell you later*.

Hazel stares at him like he's a squished bug on the floor, and if he wasn't hitting on Pippa moments before, I'd have the urge to laugh. I see the hockey gossip. Women don't usually look at him the way Hazel's looking at him.

From the gleam in his eye, it doesn't seem like he minds, though. "You grew up well," he tells her.

She just stares at him, and he gestures at himself.

"Aren't you going to say I grew up well, too?" His eyes glitter with amusement.

"Congratulations. You now seem like the kind of guy who owns a really expensive sex doll."

"Her name is Diane." He grins openly at her, and I can tell he loves this.

Pippa and Hazel gag in unison. "You shouldn't name them, Rory," Pippa says, and he shakes with laughter.

"Does your sex doll have a head?" Hazel asks him.

His eyes don't leave her face. "She did, but I removed it." His tongue taps his upper lip.

"That's worse."

He just grins at Hazel like he wants to keep her. Pippa shoots me an amused smile. It feels private, and my chest squeezes.

Hazel says something to Pippa and she turns her head to listen. Her ponytail brushes my arm, and I'm transported to a few days ago, when she sat between my legs, shaking against me as she came in my arms. I can still feel her hair against my chest as she writhed. I can't *stop* feeling it.

"You should come out with me and Pippa when she shows me around," he tells Hazel.

She stares at Pippa. "What is he talking about?"

Pippa rolls her eyes. "Rory needs someone to show him around Vancouver, even though he grew up here and doesn't live here anymore."

Rory tries to push Pippa behind him, and she dissolves into laughter. "Don't listen to her, babe." He smiles again at Hazel. "You should join us."

"I'm busy." Hazel scowls. "And don't call me babe."

"Sorry." He places his hand on his heart with remorse. "Ba*by*."

She stares at him before turning to Pippa. "You know he's going to try to lure you into a threesome, right?"

Pippa laughs. "I've never been in a threesome."

"You're not having a threesome," I snap, and all three of them look at me like I've grown a second head. "And you're not sleeping with Miller."

I can hear myself, but I can't stop.

Pippa nudges me with her elbow. "We're just kidding," she tells me before turning back to Miller. "When are you in town next?"

"I'm here for a couple more days, actually. Free tomorrow if you are."

His eyes are practically fucking *twinkling* at her. Rory Miller is *twinkling* at my Pippa. Everything about this is wrong, and a possessive rage rushes through me.

The idea of him trying something with her makes me feel sick. I just glare down at her, wishing I could pull her out of here so we could be alone.

"Tomorrow's perfect," Pippa tells him.

Miller's looking at me like he won something. He's challenging me, but I can't do a fucking thing. I've already drawn the line with Pippa and crossed it a few times.

That fucking *fuck*. I hate him for playing this stupid game with me. I hate myself for getting this jealous over a woman I can't have.

"Great." He sends me a broad smile. "It's a date."

WHEN I LEAVE my room the next evening, Jamie's pacing the apartment with a thunderous expression. I walk into the living room, and he stops short, glaring at my outfit.

Sparks ignite in my stomach, and I wonder if this was a bad idea.

I know Rory isn't interested in me. Even if he joked about threesomes, we're just hanging out as friends. I was with the same guy since the *tenth* grade, though, and after Jamie blew my mind with the toy, I realized how much I was missing out on.

I want to go out and have fun. I want to meet new friends and have new experiences. For two years, I followed Zach around on tour, working my ass off, and before that, I followed him to university. All my friends were actually *his* friends.

Besides, beneath his cocky bravado, Rory wants to be friends with Jamie again. He just doesn't know how, other than getting on Jamie's nerves.

"That's what you're wearing?" His nostrils flare and his deep green eyes flash.

I glance down at my wool mini skirt and band t-shirt from a show Hazel and I saw a few summers ago. Over the t-shirt, my open knit sweater nearly reaches the hem of my skirt. "What's wrong with this?"

He glowers at my legs, arms crossed. "You're going to be cold."

A shiver runs down my spine at his bossy tone and I turn away, checking the time on my phone to hide my flush. Rory will be here any minute.

"I'm wearing boots." I pull them out of the closet and step into them.

I love these boots, and I don't wear them enough. They go all the way up to my thighs and make my legs look amazing.

When I turn, Jamie's eyes are on the slit of bare skin between the boots and my skirt, and his jaw is razor sharp with tension.

"Jamie," I sigh, laughing a little. "Rory and I are just friends. You're just mad because he scored a goal on you the other night."

Daggers shoot from his eyes, and I can practically feel the prickle of his gaze on my thighs. "When he sees that skirt, he won't want to be *friends*." He lifts his gaze, and his eyes flash with frustration. "What if there are photos?" he bites out. "We told everyone at the wrap party that we were together."

"No one's going to take photos of us. We're going to this really dim secret bar on Main Street that has amazing cocktails. People in that neighborhood are too cool to take pictures of a hockey player."

My phone buzzes on the table, and *Front Door* flashes across the screen. I buzz Rory up and set the phone down.

I turn and bump into Jamie, and my hands come to his chest to steady myself. When I meet his gaze, my pulse lurches.

His eyes are wild.

"What's going on?" I ask, searching his dark eyes as he glances at the door and then back to me.

His mouth crashes into mine. I groan against him as his tongue slides between my lips, stroking me. He walks me backward until I bump up against the wall, and his hips pin mine.

My eyes go wide, seeing nothing. All I can feel is him pressing into my stomach, fully hard. My pussy aches, and I let out a soft moan.

"We agreed not to." My words are a regretful whisper against his lips, and he breaks the kiss, resting his forehead on mine, breathing hard.

"I don't care."

Honestly? Me neither. I can't remember why we even agreed not to do this. It's too good.

His mouth drops back to mine and he kisses me so hard I'll bruise. I'm lost in his kiss, the feel of his mouth taking mine, his hands on me and my hands in his hair. When I give his hair a soft tug, the resulting groan that rips out of his throat sends a thrill between my legs, and I can feel wetness pooling in my panties.

Oh god. Jamie is mouth-fucking me moments before Rory shows up, and I don't even care. I can't stop.

"I can't stop thinking about this," Jamie grits out, just as angry as before, but the heat in his eyes makes my core clench up with need.

He wants me so badly. All I can do is nod.

"Tell me to stop, Pippa," he says against my mouth.

I moan as he sucks my tongue. No freaking way.

A knock on the door beside us makes me jump, and his arm shifts to rest on the wall above my head, caging me in. My nerves are rippling with excitement.

"That's Rory," I whisper.

Jamie's free hand comes to my neck, gently holding me in place.

"Stay right there," he murmurs, and I shiver again.

His other hand drops to my thighs, and he runs his knuckles over the bare skin between my skirt and my boot. I can't breathe, and my heart races. My breasts feel full and tight, and when Jamie's hand drifts to the hem of my skirt, pushing it up, my hips tilt involuntarily.

He lets out a breathy chuckle, and when Rory knocks again, Jamie leans down until his mouth brushes my ear. "Tell him you'll be a minute."

He can't mean—

My pulse pounds between my legs.

He gives me an emphasizing, bossy look. His expression is clear.

*Do it. Now.*

"Just a second," I call, voice warbling while my eyes stay locked on Jamie's.

His hand trails up farther. The air crackles between us, but I can't look away. He strokes a soft line up my inner thigh, and with his other hand, his fingers tense around the base of my neck.

My eyes flutter closed as he brushes over my underwear, and pleasure jolts through me when he presses against my clit. My mouth falls open and I gasp.

"Fuck," I whisper.

"Shh." The corner of his mouth tips up but his eyes are so dark, like he's getting off on torturing me like this. "Does this feel good?"

I nod.

"You want me to finger you?"

I nod again, hands tensing on his broad chest. More than anything.

He raises an eyebrow. "Say please."

"Please," I whisper.

"Good girl." He stares down at me, searching my face as he

moves my panties aside and strokes his long fingers over me, circling my clit. I press my lips together to hold in a moan as he glides over my sensitive nerves. I'm breathing hard, wincing, and he dips one finger inside me.

"Fuck," he mutters, and my eyes fall closed at the delicious, tight feeling. "So fucking wet for me, Pippa."

I nod, resting my head against his chest.

"No, no, no," he whispers, "eyes on me."

I swallow another moan, biting my lip as I lift my head to look at him. His hair has fallen into his eyes, and even through my clouded, horny haze, I find that so endearing. He pushes another finger inside me, stroking in at an unhurried pace designed to make me insane, and I cling to his neck, practically hanging off him.

Rory knocks on the door again, and I startle, tightening up on Jamie's fingers. I forgot he was there. Jamie shoots me a dark, pleased smile.

"Pippa," Rory calls through the door. "This is boring. Let's go."

Jamie leans down. "You're mine," he murmurs in my ear, crooking his fingers toward my navel to rub against my G-spot.

I let a quiet moan slip out. "Just a second," I call back, and my voice breaks as Jamie bumps his thumb against my clit. Pressure and heat build low in my belly, and I feel like I did the other night, with Jamie pressing the toy to my clit.

I feel like I'm going to come.

"You want to come?" he asks with that satisfied, powerful smirk.

I nod frantically, eyes rolling back as he works my pussy, biting back the moan of pleasure.

"I'm right there," I breathe, staring up at him in awe. How is he so good at this?

"I know."

There's a smug, determined tone to his voice, and it sends more heat pooling around his fingers. My breath is coming out in short little gasps, and I cling to his gaze as the pressure at my center intensifies.

"There," he mouths, watching me intently, and his hand speeds up. His thumb brushes my clit, and the wave inside me rises. "Quiet," he whispers as I start to shake.

I clamp my lips closed, wincing as I clench up on his fingers. Intense, mind-bending light floods my body, curling, swelling, coursing, flowing through every inch of me, expanding from where Jamie's long fingers stroke me. I can *hear* how wet I am while sparks burst across my nerves. As I ride out the last of my orgasm, I let my head fall against his chest.

"Perfect," he whispers in my ear. "Fucking perfect."

I'm still catching my breath when he lifts his fingers to his mouth and sucks me off his hand. Another ripple of heat moves through me, and my clit throbs. He leans down and presses a soft kiss against my mouth, and I can taste myself on his lips.

There's another knock on the door, and Jamie's hand is on the doorknob. I scramble to straighten my skirt while he pulls the door open.

"About fucking time—" Rory stops when he sees Jamie, and he breaks into a cocky grin. "You going to crash our date, Streicher?"

"Yeah. I am."

THIS HAS BEEN the most awkward dinner ever.

We're sitting in the dim bar on Main Street, within walking distance of the apartment. It's a speakeasy with a secret entrance disguised like a seventies accountant's office, but the inside is all lush maroon velvet, bizarre and fascinating artwork, and a bright, hedonistic mural of people lounging around naked in nature.

I sip my chai whiskey sour and glance at the back hallway, where the washrooms are. There's probably a back door I could sneak out of.

I'm still buzzing from what Jamie and I did back in the apartment, and every time I think of it, my face feels warm. Beside me, Jamie's back to his glowering self. I know we shouldn't have messed around again, but the second he touches me, all the thoughts just fall out of my head. It's too electric between us. Too intense, too good.

God, his fingers inside me... A shudder rolls through me.

"Pippa." Rory leans back in his hair. "What's this I hear about you playing guitar for everyone?"

I roll my eyes. "It's just for fun."

Beside me, Jamie makes a low noise of disapproval in his throat.

"It is," I tell him with an indulgent smile, and he frowns down at me.

"She's good," he tells Rory. They're the first words he's said to him since we got here. "If she wanted to, she could work in the music industry."

A block of ice forms in my stomach. "It's not just about talent."

"No, it's not." Jamie's gaze is hard. "It's about hard work and believing in yourself. You're just missing the last one."

An ugly, hesitant feeling rises in me, and my hands twist in my lap. I'm about to change the subject when Rory cuts in.

"Sounds like you have a fan," he says, flicking a grin at Jamie.

No teasing. No overconfident smirk. Just a smile.

"Her biggest fan." Jamie's words don't have the bite they usually do when he speaks to Rory.

They look at each other for a long moment, sizing each other up.

Alright, enough of this.

"Why aren't you guys friends anymore?" I blurt out.

Jamie just glares at Rory, who shifts in his chair. There's a flash of vulnerability in his eyes before he blinks it away.

"He's the guy I'm scoring against." Rory's smile is sardonic. "Why would I be friends with a guy like that?"

Jamie folds his arms over his chest. "Sounds like a lesson from the Rick Miller school of hockey."

"Yep." Rory's eyebrows bob once, and there's a humorless slant to his lips as he surveys the bar.

There's a long moment where it feels like they both want to say more.

"Your dad is Rick Miller?" I ask Rory, eyebrows rising to my hairline.

Rick Miller is one of the greats in Canadian hockey. He'd be one of my dad's favorite players if he didn't have such a reputation for being an asshole to the press and to fans.

Rory levels me with a dry look. "The one and only."

"Wow."

He shrugs. "Don't be impressed, Pippa. He's just a regular guy."

I think about Jamie and how intimidated I was by him back in high school, and even a few months ago, and how kind, sweet, and protective he is beneath his surly exterior.

Something tells me Rick Miller isn't kind and sweet, though.

"We should get going." Jamie glances down at me. "I have early training, and your interview is tomorrow."

My stomach knots. Right, the interview for the marketing position. I've been preparing for it for two weeks, going over all my school notes, rehearsing with Hazel, and fending off excited phone calls from my parents asking if I'm ready.

"Songbird." Jamie's using the voice he only uses when we're together, like he's forgotten Rory is sitting on the other side of the table. "You'll kill it, if that's what you want."

That's not what I'm worried about, but I don't see any other path. Any other options are—

No. Just no.

I force a quick smile, and across the table, Rory's watching us with a curious look. The server passes behind him, and Jamie lifts a hand to get her attention.

"Can we have the bill, please?" he asks her.

She smiles. "It's already settled up. Have a good night." She leaves, and we look to Rory, who just winks at me.

"Thank you," I tell him. "You didn't have to get our dinner."

He lifts a shoulder, getting up. "It was the least I could do."

I'm not sure what he means by that, and I wonder if it has something to do with the way things ended with him and Jamie.

Jamie clears his throat, clearly uncomfortable with Rory paying for anything for him. "Thanks," he mutters, and I hide my grin as we leave.

Outside the bar, Rory tips his head down the street. "My hotel is this way."

"Okay." I smile at him. "Thanks for the fun hang."

He gives me a warm squeeze and a quick kiss on the cheek. I don't have a brother but I'm pretty sure this is what it would feel like.

"Let's do it again, okay?" He pulls away and grins down at me.

I nod. "You bet."

He turns to Jamie, who's staring with irritation. "And Streicher, you were there too, I guess."

Jamie's nostrils flare. I roll my eyes, say good night to Rory, and pull Jamie with me. We walk through the streets to the apartment in silence until he glances down at me.

"Thanks for letting me crash your hangout," he says.

My smile is teasing. "You didn't ask."

He snorts, and I know he's thinking about when he demanded I move in with him.

"And it wasn't a hangout. It was a date." I turn away from him, smothering a smile as he makes an unhappy noise in his throat.

"Not. A. Date."

I chuckle. I love teasing him.

We pass the guitar store, and a sigh slips out of me as my gaze lands on my dream guitar. I pause as I admire it.

Jamie stops at my side, folding his arms as he studies it through the window. "You love this guitar."

"I do." I gaze at it, memorizing the details of the wood. I can imagine just how the strings would feel.

"Next time we pass it, you should go in and play it."

I shake my head with a smile. "If I play it, I'll want it even more," I admit.

"Would that be such a bad thing?"

Yes, because then I'll want other things even more. I'll start picturing things. I'll start dreaming again, and the last time I did that, it didn't end well.

"In another life, maybe, but not this one. Come on. Let's go home."

When we open the front door, Daisy sprints over, and Jamie reaches down to give her scratches.

"I'm going to walk her," he says, lifting her into his arms.

Our gazes meet, and my mind is on what we did hours ago against the door. His eyes darken, and I know he's thinking about the same thing. A pulse of heat hits me low in my belly.

I'm tempted. I'm so fucking tempted.

The night Donna had a panic attack, though, after Jamie used the toy on me, he was about to let me down gently, and I quickly cut in because I couldn't bear to be rejected again.

I bet that's the expression he'll wear when he tells me we can't do this anymore. It's only a matter of time. He'd never dump me the way Zach did, I realize. He'd do it the right way. He'd do it to my face, with care and respect.

I flinch, picturing it. Why does that feel worse?

Because that's exactly the reason I like him. He's kind, and he would never hurt someone on purpose, but that doesn't mean he wouldn't hurt me without meaning to.

"I can't do casual," I tell him.

My words hang in the air, and my message is clear. We *need* to stop this. Even if it's fun. Even if he's giving me the best orgasms I've ever had. Even if we can't keep our hands off each other.

He stares at me for a moment before his Adam's apple bobs. "Yeah."

My chest feels funny, tight and strained, with an unwelcome pressure. "Good night."

He nods, looking so serious. "Good night, Pippa."

*In another life*, I said to him about the guitar. Maybe that applies to him, too.

OUTSIDE THE BUILDING that holds the team's marketing office, I check the time on my phone. There's a missed call from my parents' house. I have a few minutes, so I call them back.

"Hi, sweetie," my mom answers. "We just wanted to wish you luck before the big interview!"

My stomach wobbles. She sounds so hopeful and excited.

"Hold on a second. Ken," she says, calling to my dad. "Grab the other phone. It's Pippa."

A moment later, my dad is on the line. "Hi, honey. Good luck today. We know you'll do well."

I force a weak smile, even though they can't see me. "Thanks."

"We're so proud of you," he says, and I picture his wide smile and bright eyes.

"So proud," my mom adds. "Once you get this job, everything's going to fall into place. You just watch." She sounds so certain. "Within a couple years, you might even be able to afford an apartment outside the city."

I don't want to live outside the city. I don't even want to think about buying an apartment yet.

"You should ask about the benefits," my dad says. "Ask what retirement options they have."

"Oh, and ask about orthodontics."

"Definitely ask about orthodontics," my dad confirms. "Not all health plans cover them."

I frown. "I already had braces."

"Not for you," my mom says, "for your future children."

My future children?! I cringe as my mind begins to race. I can barely picture myself at this job in a few years, let alone, like, fifteen. Good lord. This conversation is making things so much worse. I'm going home for Christmas in a few weeks, and I have a feeling this interview will be the main topic for the entire time I'm there.

"I have to go," I tell them. "I'll talk to you guys later."

"Okay, bye, sweetie! Good luck!" my mom chirps.

"Don't forget to tell them how reliable you are," my dad says as a goodbye.

I sigh and stare at the door to the building. I don't want to do this, but I don't have another option.

# CHAPTER 43

# JAMIE

WARD WHISTLES as I step off the ice the next morning.

"Got your ass kicked today," he comments, and I make a noise of agreement.

My focus is shot today. My muscles ache, and my limbs feel heavy. All night, I tossed and turned, thinking about Pippa riding my hand, the sweet, soft moans she tried to muffle into my shirt as she came.

I've never been the jealous type, but around Pippa, I lose my mind thinking about her with other guys. I hated the idea of her going out with Miller.

Fucking hated it.

An unwelcome thought wanders into my head. Erin would hang out with guys all the time, and I never felt like this.

Alarm races through me. No more messing around. For real, this time.

I picture her getting ready to go last night and stifle a groan. Fuck, those *boots*. Fuck me.

Pippa Hartley has no fucking clue how gorgeous she is.

"Streicher, are you listening?"

"Hmm?" I snap back to reality. Ward's staring at me with a strange look. "Sorry, what?"

"The charity gala. You haven't confirmed yet."

I refrain from rolling my eyes. The Vancouver Storm is one of the main donors for the local children's hospital, and they're holding a gala event at the end of January in Whistler, a ski resort town two hours north of Vancouver. The team will be there along with the other donors. It's going to be a bunch of celebrities who I have no desire to spend time with. I support the charity, I attend the events at the hospital, and I even donate anonymously, but I hate going to the galas.

My thoughts are written all over my face, clearly, because Ward gives me a hard look.

"Attendance is mandatory, Streicher. I'm not asking."

Fuck.

I rein it in, because keeping Ward happy is part of staying in Vancouver. I've been playing well—even better when Pippa's sitting behind the net, a fact I hate admitting—and I'm not going to give the guy a reason to trade me.

"Okay," I tell him. "I'll be there."

"Are you bringing a plus one?"

I'm about to say no. I *should* say no. Pippa can stay in Vancouver with Daisy, and if something happens with my mom, she can get over there fast.

The idea of going with Pippa makes it bearable, though. I picture her in an evening dress, feeling gorgeous. Her hand on my arm. Sipping champagne, laughing.

"Yes. I'm bringing a date."

He studies me, the ghost of a smile forming on his mouth. "Good. Happy to hear it."

I spend the rest of the afternoon in the gym, trying to keep my mind off her and the way she said I *can't do casual.*

There it is—confirmation of exactly what I thought before. Pippa wants more than I can give her, just like Erin did. I'm older now, and I know better than to toy with someone's emotions. Guilt stabs through me when I think about how I torched Erin's career. She's working on some local low-budget TV show when she wanted to be a supermodel, and that's my fault.

I won't make the same mistake with Pippa.

My mind wanders to her interview, which should be over by now.

*How'd it go?* I text.

Typing dots appear before her text pops up. *Great. Nailed it!*

My eyes narrow. I believe her, but I'm not buying this cheerfulness. She hasn't said she doesn't want the job, but there's something there, something lurking in her words. When she plays her guitar and sings, light spills out of her, filling the room, brightening everything. It's such a stark contrast to the muted version of Pippa I see when she talks about this marketing job.

*Let's go for dinner tonight*, I suggest before I can think too hard about it. I want to hear about the interview. I want to spend time with her.

We won't be fooling around anymore, but I can't seem to stay away from my pretty assistant.

THAT EVENING, we're at a Mexican restaurant a few blocks from the apartment, sharing chips and guacamole. Christmas is coming up in a few weeks, and gaudy holiday decorations are strewn around the space.

"We should find out when Daisy's birthday is," I say between sips of my margarita.

"She's a rescue, so she probably doesn't have an official birthday."

My heart sinks. "Everyone should have a birthday."

His gaze rakes over my face, so soft and gentle I can almost feel it. "You're right. It's unacceptable." He pulls his phone out and frowns at his calendar app. "Mid-January? We can have a party."

"A party? *You* want to have a party."

His eyes spark. "Only if you're there."

"Oh, I'll be there. You know you have to wear a dog costume, though, right?"

He rolls his eyes, and I laugh.

"There's something I want to ask you." Hesitation passes over his features as he glances at me. "There's a charity gala at the end of January, and the team is expected to go. It's in Whistler."

I *love* Whistler, and I haven't been in years, probably since Hazel and I were teenagers.

"Okay." I lick the salt rim of my drink before taking a sip. "I'll watch Daisy for the weekend." The marketing job isn't supposed to start until February at the earliest. If I get it, that is.

His gaze drops to my mouth, flashing with heat. I think about last night, how hot it was as he towered over me while Rory waited on the other side of the door. The way his eyes darkened with possessiveness as his fingers pressed inside me.

We can't do it again, but that doesn't mean I can't think about it.

"No, uh." He looks away from my mouth, blinking. "I want you to come with me. As my assistant."

"No problem." My voice sounds happy and chipper, but inside, I deflate a little. I shouldn't, because we both know we can't be anything more than this, but a little part of me popped when he said *as my assistant*.

"I'll book us a suite and take care of getting a dress for you," he adds.

"Great." I finish my drink, and as the server passes behind Jamie, I gesture for another.

The conversation drifts toward the upcoming holidays. For the week between Christmas and New Year's, I'm visiting my parents in Silver Falls, the small town in the interior of British Columbia they relocated to for retirement.

I've been trying to think of a Christmas gift for Jamie, but he's impossible to buy for.

"Are we going to talk about the interview?" he asks, cutting through my thoughts.

I suck in a sharp breath as my stomach churns. "It was fine."

His eyebrow goes up, and I feel the weight of his gaze as I look away, glancing around the restaurant—at the multi-colored bottles behind the counter, the backsplash tiles behind the bar, the other tables, anywhere but his eyes.

I'm finally ready to admit it—when I picture myself at the marketing job, a little piece of me dies.

"Pippa," he says, and my resolve crumbles.

"It went well." My mouth is dry.

Jamie stares at me, waiting.

"I'm probably going to get it," I say to the ice in my glass.

"You say it like it's a bad thing."

I flatten my lips, dragging in a breath, and I'm quiet because I have no fucking clue what to say. It *feels* like a bad thing.

"Songbird."

Another chunk of my resolve falls away, and I wish he wouldn't call me that, because I like it too much. It's impossible to pretend with him when he calls me that.

He shakes his head. "You don't want that job, Pippa. Admit it."

"Fine," I burst out, and I feel like I'm about to barf. "I don't want the job. My parents make it sound safe, but..." I pinch my bottom lip between my teeth. What I'm about to say sounds so stupid.

Jamie's eyes are bright. "Safe is boring."

The breath whooshes out of me. "Exactly."

He studies me for a long moment before his expression softens. "Good."

"*Good*?" I lean forward, giving him a bemused look. "Are you listening? This is a fucking disaster, Jamie."

His eyes are steady on my face. "It's not a disaster."

Everything my parents worked so hard for, down the drain. All the things they scrimped on so they could afford for me to go to university, all the high hopes they have for me, down the drain. I think about my mom teaching ballet classes, a daily reminder that she failed to make it to the professional level.

*Failure hurts*, she once said to me.

Jamie leans forward, searching my gaze. I feel the urge to climb into his lap and cling to him like a koala, burying my face in his neck and inhaling him. That's the only thing that'll make me feel better right now.

"What about music?" he asks softly.

"What about it?" My heart beats hard, and just saying the words hurts. They feel insincere. They feel cruel and like a betrayal of myself, which makes no sense, because it was never an option anyway.

*You don't have it*, Zach told me.

Anger grows inside me, and my fists clench. What if I do, though? The desire to take control, to stop being this girl that things happen *to*, wraps around my throat and squeezes.

"You have the drive, Pippa." His tone has a frustrated bite to it, and his gaze pins me. "You're so fucking talented, and the only person who doesn't see this is you."

I roll my eyes with a bitter laugh. "Zach didn't see it."

"He saw it," Jamie spits out. "He definitely saw it."

Our surroundings fall away as our gazes lock. I see everything in his deep green eyes; I see that he wants this for me, that he hates what Zach did to me, and that he's furious that my parents have this unknowing influence on me.

"What about my parents?"

His jaw tenses like he's upset. "What about *you*?"

My eyes close for a brief moment. I picture their disappointment, and I feel like I'm crumbling. "It'll kill them."

His eyes ignite, focused and furious. It's the same look I've seen on game recaps, in close-ups of his face at the height of action. "They love you, and they'll get over it." He says it like a threat, like he'll make sure it works out like that, and my heart beats harder. "Do you know how many people told me I wouldn't make it?" His brow furrows with frustration. "Just ask Owens, or Miller, any other professional athlete. Anyone who has done anything bold has naysayers. Shut out those voices. The only opinion that matters is yours."

"Your opinion matters to me," I say, truthfully.

His nostrils flare. "Well, I know you can do it, so why don't you listen to me?"

I want to believe him. I think I might, too. I don't know if I'm ready to fail hard at something that matters, but there's a tiny, stubborn part of myself that isn't ready to give up yet.

When Jamie says things like *I know you can do it*, that stubborn part thrives. Across the table, he's studying me with a serious expression, and my heart tugs.

Jamie is so kind. I wish everyone else knew this side of him. I wonder if his ex ever saw it.

"What happened with you and Erin?" I ask softly. It's none of my business, but I'm curious. He said he only does casual, and I wonder if it has anything to do with her. It must.

He blinks and tears his gaze away.

"You don't have to tell me," I rush out. "If it's personal."

"No." He frowns. "It's fine. It's personal, but—" He looks across the table at me, really *looks* at me, and in this moment, I feel like we're so much more than we are. "I want to tell you. I've wanted to tell you for a while, but I wasn't sure how." He folds his arms over his chest. "She thought she was pregnant."

My heart stops. "You were nineteen."

"Yeah." His throat works. "It was my rookie year, and her career was just taking off." He glances at me. "She was a model."

I nod, not wanting to disclose how much I've Googled her.

"Her period was two weeks late, and when she told me she

might be pregnant, she looked so happy." He sucks a breath in as guilt moves over his features. "I was freaking out."

"Of course." I can't even imagine being pregnant at nineteen. I'd be terrified.

"Whenever I had time off, I'd fly home to visit my mom." His stare goes unfocused, like he's back there in his memories. "I thought things between me and Erin were casual, but she thought we were more."

"What happened?"

He lets out a long sigh. "She wasn't pregnant, but after she saw my face when she thought she was, it was different. We broke up." His gaze lifts to mine, so full of regret and worry. "And I saw online a week later that she left modeling. She had all these contracts for Fashion Week and she pulled out. She had a really promising career and walked away, and I know it was because of me." He shakes his head. "I fucking crushed her, Pippa."

My heart aches for Jamie, because I can see how torn he still is about this. "Jamie." Our gazes meet, and I give him a soft smile. "That's a lot of blame to put on yourself. People go through breakups all the time."

"Zach dumped you and squashed your confidence."

My lips part and I blink, scrambling to defend myself, but he's right.

"I can't do that again," he says.

This is why he doesn't do relationships. The realization makes me so sad. Jamie's been beating himself up about this for years.

"Maybe Zach broke my heart and told me I wasn't good enough to make music my career, but that doesn't mean I believe him. I did, but I don't know if I still do." I offer him a small smile. "And you have a lot to do with that. Did you ever talk to Erin about what happened?"

He studies me for a long moment. "No."

The song in the restaurant changes, and my thoughts screech to a halt as I listen to Zach sing the opening lyrics. My stomach drops through the floor.

"What's wrong?" Jamie's voice sounds very far away.

The lyrics float around me, and my lips mouth the chorus as Zach sings. I'm vaguely aware that Jamie's hand is covering mine on top of the table, but all I can focus on is Zach singing my song.

*My* song. The one I played for him and his manager. The one they laughed at.

They said it wasn't good enough before they took it.

**NAUSEA RISES UP MY THROAT.**

"Pippa." Jamie's sitting beside me now, arm around my shoulders, concern all over his face. "What's going on?"

"This is my song." My voice is flat. "This is my song," I repeat.

Some of the lyrics are different. The verses are a different tune, but the chorus is all mine.

Jamie flags the server down before pulling a bill out of his wallet and handing it to her. "Can you change the song, please? Right now."

A moment later, Zach's voice cuts off abruptly, replaced by the opening notes of a different song.

He laughed at me. This entire time, I thought I wasn't good enough.

*He saw it. He definitely saw it*, Jamie said about Zach.

"Pippa," Jamie murmurs, and his hand is on the back of my neck, warm and solid and comforting. The contact drags me back to the present, and I blink up at him. He looks furious and concerned, a hard set to his jaw and fire in his eyes.

I'm confused, shocked, and so, so angry, but having Jamie

here somehow makes it better. Jamie, who believes in me. Who's furious on my behalf.

Months ago, I cried in the airport and just wanted to disappear. Tonight, though, there's a tiny flame burning inside me. Something stubborn and pissed off.

Zach's ruined so much, but I don't want him to ruin this evening.

"I'm okay," I tell him, and I think that might be the truth.

"Come here," he says, wrapping me in a big hug, and I let myself lean into him.

My pulse returns to normal as I rest my cheek against Jamie's chest. His hand strokes down my back, and I inhale his warm, spicy scent.

"I hate him for what he did to you." I feel his low words rumble through his chest.

"Me too," I whisper.

"You want to go home?"

I shake my head. "I want to stay."

I'm done with Zach, and I'm done with letting the past weigh me down.

Minutes later, I'm filling my stomach with another order of tacos Jamie insisted I eat, and his phone lights up with a text. The background image makes my heart jump into my throat. It's one of the photos I texted him of Daisy and me at the park, sitting on one of the giant logs. I asked someone to take it.

He made it his background. My pulse gallops. I don't dare let myself hope. He sees where my eyes go, and he slips the phone into his back pocket before leaning his elbows on the table, watching me.

"Promise me you won't let this hold you back. Promise me you'll get back up on stage."

I blink, and that old hesitance lifts its head inside me.

"Promise me," Jamie says, and his eyes plead.

What did I say earlier? No more letting the past weigh me down.

"Okay," I tell him. "I'll do it."

A COUPLE DAYS before I leave to visit my parents for the holidays, I sit on the couch with my guitar, thinking about what I promised Jamie. My notebook lies open on the coffee table with a pen in the crease. My mind flicks from the song I heard in the restaurant to the way Zach laughed at me to the way he asked, *"Have you met Layla?"* the night of the wrap party.

I glare out the window at the moody gray sky. What a dick.

Anger knots in my stomach, and I begin to write a song about getting mad. The lyrics halt and flow as I find my footing, but within a few minutes, I have half a page of lyrics and a few chord progressions.

*"Betcha thought you'd get away with it,"* I sing quietly, but I cringe.

That doesn't sound right, so soft like that.

I try again, but this time I belt it out. Sparks crack and pop under my skin as I smile big.

There we go. That's the right feeling.

The added attitude opens something up inside me, and the words tumble out faster than I can write. I'm pissed off, but the song isn't about being stepped on—this song is about getting back up. It's about getting revenge but in my own way, by letting him go. Saying goodbye to the guy who hurt me, but vowing to prove him wrong. It's about all the discomfort and pain being worth it because I'm going to be so much better and brighter than before.

Writing this song feels fucking fantastic. My eyes well up with emotion as I smooth over the chorus, connecting with the next verse, and when the song is polished enough, I set my phone on the coffee table and record a version so I don't forget the tune. I feel like a kid again, sprinting down a hill without a care in the world. This feels right, like this is my purpose.

I love this song, and I'm proud of myself for writing it. I think Jamie would be proud, too.

On a whim, I text the recording to him. My heart jumps around in my chest, and I suck in a breath. Was that weird, that I sent it to him? He's probably busy in a practice or training. I stare at the phone for a moment before tossing it aside and jumping up to take Daisy on her lunchtime walk.

When we get home from the walk, I see a text from him.

*Thatta girl,* the message reads, and something warm bursts in my chest. *You should play this one when we go to the Filthy Flamingo next.*

*Maybe,* I text back, smiling.

*You will,* he says, and I chuckle.

*Bossy.*

He responds with a winking emoji, and I bite my lip before catching myself. What did I *just* tell myself a few weeks ago after he made me come against the door?

Absolutely no falling for Jamie Streicher. He's damn near perfect, and I can't bear to watch him turn into an asshole like Zach. If we're just friends, he can't hurt me.

*I have a training session starting,* he says. *I'll talk to you later, songbird.*

Every time he calls me that, I get a rush of happiness

through my chest. I picture him smiling at me, that rare, broad, sparkling smile that makes me want to stare at his face forever.

It's not fair that he's so hot. It's not fair that I have to see him every day.

A tune pops into my head and I giggle.

"*It's not fair that you're so hot,*" I sing, playing a few chords, and I laugh again.

I write a song about how hot Jamie is. I'm laughing the entire time, scribbling down lyrics and trying different combinations, and within an hour, I have the outline of the song.

By late afternoon, I have a handful of rough songs. One is about wanting someone but knowing they're wrong for you. One is about struggling with people's expectations and choosing what makes you happy in the end. One is about really, really good sex with someone new. I like that one—it's seductive and playful, and I wrote it thinking about sitting between Jamie's legs while he made me come.

I'm fueling that flame in my chest, adding kindling to make myself burn brighter. This is the pretend album I always daydreamed about writing when we were on a flight to a new city on the tour or when Zach was in the studio recording.

One song is about how Jamie takes care of everyone but himself, and who takes care of him? It's serious and protective. There's a lyric in there that just fell out of my mouth, and I'm not sure how I feel about it.

*I'd do it forever if it wouldn't break my heart.*

My throat feels tight as I swallow, reading that line. I should scratch it out, but I can't. The best songs are honest.

Daisy's staring at me, wagging her tail, so I take her out again for a long walk. The whole time, my mind is on Jamie, and on the songs I wrote.

The forest is dark, so we stick to the lit streets. The trees along the sidewalk are decorated for Christmas with pretty twinkling lights, and worry hits my stomach. I *still* haven't gotten Jamie a present.

Anything he wants, he can buy. He has a beautiful apartment. He doesn't need clothes or hockey equipment. He seems to enjoy cooking, but what am I going to get, a whisk? I cringe. That's so lame, and it feels wrong for our relationship. I work for him, but we're friends, too.

If I asked him, he'd tell me not to get anything, but that's because he doesn't realize that he's worth it.

We pass the guitar store, and my eyebrows snap together. My dream guitar is gone, replaced with a black Fender electric.

Something sinks in my chest. I couldn't afford it, so I don't know why I'm so disappointed.

Jamie's bright eyes and his determined expression appear in my head. Once I figure things out—however that will look—I'm going to save for a new guitar. Something special, just for me. Jamie will be happy to hear that. He'd be proud of me if he knew I spent the whole afternoon writing.

A realization hits me.

I wrote that album for Jamie. I thought about him the entire time, and when the impostor syndrome crept in, I remembered his words of encouragement and his warm looks of affection, and it spurred me on. I've never written even one song for someone, let alone a collection of them, and no one has ever encouraged me the way Jamie has.

It's like he thinks I can do anything.

The truth is obvious, and no matter how hard I deny it or try to compare him to Zach, it's not going away.

I have major feelings for Jamie Streicher.

Now I just have to figure out what to do about it.

CHRISTMAS WAS FOUR DAYS AGO. I'm at my mom's house, sitting on the couch with Daisy, watching the video of Pippa again. A cheeky smile lingers on her mouth as she belts the lyrics out, her foot taps in the air as she plays the guitar, and her eyes glitter with mischief, like she isn't supposed to be singing about getting mad at her ex and moving on to something better.

She's so beautiful like this. She's always beautiful, but especially like this, singing her heart out, looking so happy.

It's day five of not seeing Pippa, and I'm going out of my mind. We text constantly, but it's not the same as having her right in front of me. Within arm's reach is the best place Pippa can be.

After five days, it's obvious. I have feelings for the pretty songbird, and I'm tired of telling myself no. Just thinking about her makes me happy.

I reach for my old excuses, but something cuts through them. What if I could find a way to make this work?

She and Hazel flew out to Silver Falls last week, and because my flight from Minnesota to Vancouver was delayed due to bad weather, she left before I got home. I didn't get to say goodbye or give her the Christmas presents I got for her. I could have overnighted them to Silver Falls, but I want to see her face when she opens them.

What if I visited her? What if I did the impulsive thing that I never do and just went to her?

Something lifts in my chest, but my mind wanders to the time Pippa and I hooked up and I had a ton of missed calls from my mom. I wasn't there when she needed me. I was off getting distracted. I scrub a hand down my face, pushing the daydreams away. I'm not going to Silver Falls. I'll see her next week when she comes home.

A shadow passes over me, and my mom leans over the back of her couch where I'm sitting, mooning over my goddamned assistant. I pull my headphones off.

"Is that Pippa?" she asks before I can tuck my phone away.

I nod.

She gestures at my headphones. "Play it out loud."

When I press play after disconnecting the headphones, Pippa's voice fills the room while we watch her on the screen. Daisy readjusts on the couch, resting her head on my arm, and she lets out a long sigh.

My mom gives Daisy a scratch. "She misses Pippa."

Daisy and I look at each other. *Me too, buddy.*

My mom gives me a side-long look, studying me with a curious sparkle in her eyes. "I can watch Daisy if you want to go out on New Year's."

The only person I want to see on New Year's is Pippa. "It's fine."

"Jamie." She studies me, and there's a flicker of sadness and something else in her eyes. Embarrassment, maybe.

"It's fine," I repeat. "I'm not really into partying." And I'm needed here, I don't say.

She watches me for a long moment. "I started looking for a therapist."

My head snaps up and I turn to get a better look at her. "What?"

She nods, spinning one of her rings around her finger. "Pippa mentioned it that night you two were over. She made it sound kind of normal."

My heart bursts with pride and affection for my Pippa. "It is normal. Lots of people get therapy."

She shrugs again. "I haven't found someone yet, but I'm looking."

"That's great." That heavy weight in my gut lessens. "I'm really happy to hear that."

"I thought you might be." She takes a seat beside Daisy and combs her fingers through Daisy's fur. "What's Pippa doing for New Year's?"

"She and Hazel are going to a bar."

I imagine Pippa in the busy bar, her hair loose and wavy like at the wrap party. Maybe she's wearing a dress, but more likely, she's dressed casually because it's a crappy bar in a small town, and she doesn't want to stick out. When she told me that, I laughed, because there isn't a single room where Pippa wouldn't stick out.

An unwelcome image pops into my head of a guy leaning on the bar, talking to her. Smiling at her. His gaze dropping to her mouth, her tits. Maybe he reaches out and tucks her hair behind her ear, says something teasing. My nostrils flare.

I hate that idea. I hate it so fucking much. My knee bounces as I stare at nothing.

"Jamie?"

I snap to attention. "Hmm?"

My mom shrugs, nonchalant. "Why don't you go visit Pippa? Silver Falls is lovely, honey, and I bet she'd love to show you around her hometown."

My knee continues to bounce as I consider it. I'm crawling out of my skin without her.

In the past few weeks, my mom *has* seemed better. She seems less worried, less anxious, like she has more control. Maybe she'd be fine.

Miller's mom lives a few minutes from here, and I'm certain he's spending the holiday there. I have a weird feeling he'd be over here in a heartbeat if I asked.

And she's looking for a therapist. That is a huge step.

"Okay." I nod. "I'm going to Silver Falls."

THIS HAS BEEN the longest week of my life.

"Pippa." Hazel opens her eyes from the chair beside the window overlooking the backyard. She's in her pajamas and has major bedhead.

I'm draped across the couch, also in pajamas with major bedhead, staring limply out the same window at the snow-covered trees. They're pretty, but I don't even care. "What?"

"I'm trying to meditate but you keep sighing." She gives me a look that's both irritated and amused.

I wrinkle my nose. "Sorry."

She raises an eyebrow, and my stomach tightens. New Year's Eve is tomorrow, and then we fly home the next day.

I have absolutely no idea what to do about my crush on the guy from high school, which has expanded into full-blown swoony feelings. I like him. I might even feel more than that, but I'm not looking in that direction right now. I'm just trying to figure out what to do.

My gut tells me he feels the same way, but after what he admitted about Erin? He might not be ready to hear it. That would be the ultimate devastation, telling him and having it fall flat.

I'm torn, so I'm sitting here, staring out the window, getting on Hazel's nerves while I deliberate.

My phone lights up with a text.

*Hey.*

There's a burst of excitement in my chest. I can't help it. It's just my body's reaction when he texts me. We've been texting *a lot* over the break, and part of me hopes that he's just as bored and miserable without me.

*Hi,* I respond, eyes glued to my screen, watching as the typing dots appear.

*I've been thinking about taking a trip.*

*Oh, yeah? Somewhere warm?*

*Somewhere cold.*

Dumb, naive hope twirls and spins in my chest. The typing dots pop up, disappear, and pop up again.

*I've never been to Silver Falls,* he texts.

My heart leaps into my throat and I beam at my phone.

"What is going on?" Hazel asks, smirking at me.

"Nothing." *It's gorgeous this time of year,* I text. *You'll freeze your ass off.*

*Perfect. Can I come say hi?*

*Yes, please.*

*Great. My flight lands in two hours.*

My mouth falls open. *What?!*

*I'm at the airport. Is that okay?*

*Of course!* My smile stretches from ear to ear.

Hazel drops down beside me, peering at my phone to read the texts. "What?" she repeats. "What's going on?"

I don't care that my emotions are written all over my face. "Jamie's coming to visit."

She sighs, but she's smiling. "Of course he is."

———

The doorbell rings, and I leap up from the couch before taking a deep breath in front of the door. Hazel snorts from the kitchen, where she's on her laptop.

I open the door, and he's standing there with a barely perceptible smile, which means he's just as excited as I am. God, he's so tall. I'm speechless, staring up at him with a doofy grin on my face.

"Hi," I say stupidly.

His cheeks are flushed from the cold. He's wearing a green toque that brings out the color of his eyes. Maybe it's wishful thinking, but he's looking at me like I'm the best thing he's ever seen.

"Hi," he says, and the low tenor of his voice sends a shiver down my spine.

The tension runs between us, and his gaze drops to my lips. He looks like he wants to kiss me, and my stomach wobbles in the best way.

"We're home," my dad calls from behind Jamie, and we take a step apart.

My parents climb the steps, chatting, and stop short when they see Jamie. They were visiting friends, and I thought they'd be out later.

My dad's eyes go wide like he's seen a ghost. "Oh my god." He thrusts his hand forward with a big, friendly grin. "What the heck is Jamie Streicher doing on my front step? Ken Hartley."

Jamie shakes his hand. "Nice to meet you, sir." He offers my dad a smile, and from her spot in the kitchen, Hazel glances at me in confusion.

*Sir?* Hazel mouths and I shrug.

"Oh, this is the hockey player!" My mom claps her hands. "We've heard so much about you."

He smiles again at her, and my face burns. They haven't

heard *that much* about him. So I mention him once in a while. So what?

"Hi, Mrs. Hartley," Jamie says, shaking her hand.

She pulls him into a hug. Her head barely comes to his shoulder. "Call me Maureen, honey. Let's go inside. You're going to catch a cold."

We pile inside, and my dad remarks again about what a surprise it is to have *the* Jamie Streicher in his home, which is both cute and totally embarrassing, but Jamie doesn't seem to mind. He just smiles and answers my dad's questions.

Hazel walks in and Jamie nods at her. "Hazel."

Surprisingly, she doesn't glare at him. "Hi. You made it."

He nods. "I did."

Hazel glances at me, and she seems pleased. "Good."

"Everyone, sit down," my dad says, gesturing at the living room. "I'll bring out some snacks. Jamie, do you want a beer?"

Jamie's head dips. "A beer would be great."

"What's your preference?" I have a feeling that whatever Jamie said, my dad would run to the store to buy it right now.

"Whatever you have on hand," Jamie says. "I'm not picky."

"Miller Lite okay?"

"Perfect."

"Good man." My dad disappears, and weirdly, Jamie smiles again.

As we sit down in the living room, my gaze flicks to the outdated furniture and decor, the knickknacks on the shelves, and the dorky pictures of me and Hazel as kids. Jamie pauses in front of my grade two picture. In the photo, I'm smiling wide, ear to ear, pigtails sticking out on either side of my head. I'm missing my two front teeth.

Jamie tilts his head at the picture. "You get hit with a puck, Hartley?"

I groan, and my mom laughs.

"I forgot it was picture day," she tells him. "You should have seen my face when Pippa came home and told me."

Jamie's eyes linger on the picture, and I think he's smiling again. "Very cute."

My dad hustles into the room with a tray of drinks and insists Jamie sit in the comfy La-Z-Boy chair where my dad usually sits while watching hockey. Internally, I'm cringing my face off, but Jamie is polite and friendly and indulges my dad in all his questions and conversation revolving solely around hockey.

Half an hour later, my mom checks the time. "I should put the chicken in the oven." She looks at Jamie. "Do you eat chicken?"

"Uh." He looks at me. "Yes?"

I send him a smile. "I hope you didn't think you were leaving without staying for dinner."

"You *have* to stay for dinner, Jamie," my dad scoffs.

Jamie chuckles. "I'd be happy to. Thank you."

"Where are you staying?" my mom asks.

Jamie runs a hand through his hair. "I don't know yet. I saw a hotel on Main Street. I'm going to try there first."

My dad's eyes go wide. He's so dramatic sometimes. "You don't have a room booked?" He shakes his head in dismay. "It's not going to happen. Everything gets booked up this time of year."

My mom nods. "You have to stay with us."

"What?" I choke. Jamie's used to staying in five-star hotels with king-sized beds and HBO on the TV, not homes with furniture older than me. Hazel's and my beds are from when we were teenagers, and the guest bed is even older. "Jamie doesn't want to stay with us. We can find him an Airbnb or something."

"At this time of night?" my dad asks, looking at me like I'm crazy. "Pippa, it's almost five in the evening. I know it's not much," he says to Jamie, "but we have a guest bedroom with your name on it."

I open my mouth to protest again, but Jamie nods at my parents. "I'd love to stay here." I stare at him, and he glances at me with amusement in his eyes. "If it's okay with Pippa."

"Yeah." I blink at him. "Sure."

"Great." My dad jumps up. "I'm going to help Maureen with the chicken and then I'll be right back. Another beer?"

Jamie nods. "Sure, thanks, Ken."

My dad beams at him, and I know it's because Jamie called him by his first name. I stare at Jamie in shock, but my heart is dancing around in my chest.

Who is this version of my grumpy goalie?

THAT EVENING, my mom pulls my dad away to give Jamie a break, and Hazel's upstairs in her room, so it's just Jamie and me in the living room, watching *Elf*. We're drinking hot apple cider, a yearly tradition in our family, and the cinnamon, nutmeg, cloves, and star anise make our home smell amazing.

"Let's make this at home," Jamie says, and I melt.

I love the way he says *home* like that.

I love that he flew out to Silver Falls.

I love hanging out with him, just sitting in the living room like this, even if I'm in sweatpants. He seems more content and relaxed than ever.

"Is this okay?" I ask, gesturing around us at the shabby living room. "We can go to a bar or something."

Jamie nudges me. "This is exactly where I want to be."

On screen, Will Ferrell jumps up and down in an elf costume, shrieking about how excited he is to meet Santa, and I laugh.

"My mom's looking for a therapist," Jamie says.

I light up. "She is? That's great."

He nods with relief. "Yeah." He rubs the back of his neck, glancing at me. "That's because of you, you know."

"We don't know that."

"It is. She told me it was because of the conversation you had."

My throat closes up with emotion. "Really?"

He nods again, soft gaze traveling over my face. "Thank you."

I want to climb into his lap and hug him. "I'm really glad, Jamie. Seriously."

"Me, too."

His hand slips around mine and he gives it a squeeze. Something sweet and sparkly dances in my stomach, and I glance at his mouth. I can practically feel his lips against mine, demanding and unrelenting. His eyes darken, and pressure and warmth thrum between my legs.

"I want to give you your Christmas present," he says suddenly, pulling his hand away, eyes darting to mine like he's nervous. "Is that okay?"

"Of course." I blink. "Yours isn't ready."

He shakes his head. "It's fine."

"I mean, it's mostly ready. Ready enough to show you tonight." I bite my lip, and now *I'm* nervous.

What if he hates it? What if it's too much? My stomach thrashes with butterflies, like they're trying to escape.

Jamie gives me a quick smile, slips his shoes on, and heads to his car. Moments later, he's back with two boxes—one huge and one about the size of a shoebox. He has to turn the big present sideways to get it in the door. They're wrapped beautifully in bright paper and shiny red bows.

"Oh god." I stare at them in horror. They're going to blow my gift out of the water. "Can I go first?"

He shakes his head with a laugh as he clears the coffee table off and sets it down. "No. I'm nervous." The corner of his mouth curves up as he hands the smaller gift to me. "You first."

I blow a long breath out and study the present while nerves tap-dance in my stomach. Jamie raises his eyebrows and looks at his watch in an exaggerated way, and I laugh.

"Stop it," I tell him before untying the bow. His knee bounces while I open it, and when I pull the lid off, I burst into a big grin. "You got me my own jersey?"

He studies my face with a funny look. "You like it?"

I pull the navy and white jersey out of the box, turning it to read the back. *STREICHER* is stitched in bold white lettering, and my body hums with something pleased, proud, and possessive.

"You don't have to wear my name on your back," he says quietly, watching me carefully. "We can take that part off."

"Don't you dare." I hold his gaze as my insides melt into a puddle. "I want to wear your name."

"Okay." The corners of his mouth hitch, and his eyes warm. "I want you to, too."

I can't tell him the truth—that wearing his jersey, having his name on me, makes me feel like we're so much more than we are, and that I love it. I love every inch of this present.

He tilts his chin at the bigger box. "Next."

Curiosity fires around in my brain as I unwrap it with care. The size of the box is a lot like—

Nope. I don't even want to get my hopes up.

"I hope it's a motorcycle." I wiggle my eyebrows at him.

His eyes gleam like he's enjoying this, watching me open presents he gave me. I don't know what to make of that. It makes me feel special and cared for, and there's another hard thump in my chest. I pull the last of the wrapping away, and my breath catches.

"Jamie," I whisper, staring at the box. My throat feels tight.

His finger brushes the back of my hand playfully. "Open it."

I press my lips into a flat line, wavering, before I flip the lid off.

Yep. There it is, but instead of in the front window of the guitar store, it's sitting on the table.

It's *so* beautiful, but it's more than that. This guitar is something I thought I couldn't have, and yet, here it is. My eyes well up with emotion and I blink fast to clear them.

"It's too much." I can't look at him. If I look at him, I'll cry. Or kiss him. I'm not sure.

"It's not too much."

"It's too expensive." My feelings for him grow by the second, expanding like a balloon.

"Pippa." His voice is firm, leaving no wiggle room. "I'd buy you every guitar in the city if I thought you'd let me."

Shit. This guy's going to break my goddamned heart.

When I finally look at him, his expression is so proud, and I know he's telling the truth about buying every guitar he could.

Shit.

"Saying thank you feels like not even close to enough. You're spoiling me." I run my fingers over his name on the jersey.

He shrugs his big shoulders. "So let me spoil you."

"Thank you," I say, leaning forward to hug him, and his arms loop around me. I lean into his shoulder, inhaling his warm, spicy scent. One of his hands threads into my hair, the other holding me tight against him.

"You are so welcome, songbird." I feel his low voice against my chest, and I wish we could stay like this forever. "Alright, time to take it for a spin."

I pull back and study the guitar. "It's too nice to play."

"No way. Don't you have to break guitars in?" His mouth quirks.

I burst out laughing. "That takes years."

He gestures at the guitar. "Better get started, then."

Nerves shimmer through me. I'm hesitating, but it's now or never. "I'd like to give you your present first." From the side table, I grab my phone and open a folder, sharing it with him.

His hand brushes my lower back. "You didn't have to get me anything, Pippa."

"I knew you'd say that." His phone pings in his pocket, and I nod at him with a smile. "That's from me. Open it."

When he opens the email, his laugh is surprised and pleased. The sound melts into my heart. His face lights up while he scrolls through the professional photos I had taken of Daisy at the dog beach, and his eyes are bright.

"I'm having them printed," I explain. "I was going to frame one and put it in the apartment."

He grins big at the one of Daisy mid-jump, tongue hanging out with wild eyes. "These are amazing. I love them."

He lands on one of me and Daisy.

A flash of embarrassment hits me, and my face warms. "I wasn't going to print the ones with me in them. That's the entire folder, so there are going to be some extras in there."

He's still smiling at the one of me and Daisy. "I love it."

I bite my lip, nervous about the next gift.

"There's something else," I tell him, pulling out my phone again. My hands are shaking. I've never done something like this.

Jamie's hand covers my knee, and the warmth of his big hand bleeds through the fabric, pulling me back to the present. He's smiling at me, that soft, handsome smile that makes me want to kiss him.

"I wrote an album," I blurt out, and his eyebrows shoot up. "What?"

I nod. "Yeah. I wrote an album for you. I mean—" I tilt my head back and forth. "I wrote it for me too, so I hope it doesn't suck that we have to share this gift, but you encouraged me and made me feel like I could do it, so I kept writing because I wanted to have a full collection of songs to show you."

His eyes glint with pride. "Show me."

I huff a laugh at his tone.

"*Now*, Pippa."

I laugh again, opening another folder on my phone. "Hold on a second. So impatient."

His hand hasn't moved from my knee, and his thumb strokes back and forth as I share the videos with him. I would normally record them as audio only, but I liked the way the light looked in the living room during golden hour, and then I just left the video running. After I was done, I cut the full songs into their own clips.

Jamie's phone lights up, and a moment later, my voice rings out in the living room. His mouth curls into a pleased smile again, and he tilts a glance at me.

"You wrote an album," he says softly.

My chest is bursting with pressure and giddiness and disbelief. "I wrote an album."

He shakes his head in wonder, still watching me while my song plays. "Fucking incredible. I'm so proud of you."

I smile down at my hands in my lap. "Thank you." My throat feels thick as I swallow, reaching for my new guitar. When I lift it up, my heart pounds.

There's something perfect about this guitar—its weight, the way the neck feels in my hand, the curve of the body over my thigh as I settle it in my lap.

"This guitar is my soulmate," I tell Jamie, and he smiles.

"You going to play the rest of the album for me?"

"If that's okay with you."

He leans back against the armrest of the couch, facing me, tucking his hands behind his head as I play. I'm playing these songs, and Jamie's smiling at certain lyrics because he knows exactly what I'm singing about. Over the past few months, Jamie's become one of my closest friends, and playing guitar for him, singing for him, it feels intimate and special.

I finish the song about revenge, the one I sent him a few weeks ago, and my fingers hover over the strings.

The only song left is the sexy one. He lifts an eyebrow in challenge, like he can see my hesitation.

I should end it here. I should call it a night and go up to bed. I really should. It's about Jamie, and there's no way he isn't going to see that.

Something risky and bold thrills through me, and I start playing the song.

Some of the lyrics are, um, really specific. That's my favorite part about songwriting, how specific some of the lyrics are, about eating cherry chocolate ice cream and walking past your old high school or something, and you can totally picture yourself inside the song.

*I'll sit between your legs while you make me shake against you. Make my body feel new things, we both want to.*

Facing me, Jamie stiffens, and his eyes go hazy. I stop playing.

"Songbird," he warns, lifting a brow. There's a delicious slant to his cruel mouth, and my face feels hot.

You could cut the tension in this room with a knife.

"We should end it there," I mutter.

"Not a fucking chance." His voice is thick.

My gaze drops to Jamie's lap. He's fully hard, erection straining against the fabric of his sweats. Heat pulses low in my stomach, but I continue playing the song.

"You wrote that one for me?" he asks when it ends. He won't take his eyes off my face.

I nod. Our gazes hold, and tension cracks between us.

Jamie's gaze darkens, and his jaw tightens as I lick my bottom lip. Pressure gathers between my legs, and my skin feels warm. I want him so badly.

His eyes pin me with determination. "That was the best Christmas gift I've ever gotten."

"Me, too," I breathe.

A beat passes where we just stare at each other, but Jamie snaps his gaze away. "I should go to bed."

*No*, I want to scream, but instead, I nod. "Good night."

"Good night." He stands, adjusts himself, and heads upstairs without another word.

I sit on the couch for a few moments after, feeling hot and jittery, full of energy, before I turn out the lights and head up to my old bedroom, carrying my Christmas presents. In my room, I hold out the jersey and smile.

I love it. I'm going to wear it to every game, and I can already imagine Jamie's smile when he turns around and sees me behind the net, wearing it with pride.

"WHERE DID you and Jamie go today?" Hazel asks the next evening, sitting across the booth from me in the busy dive bar.

It's New Year's Eve, and the only bar in town is packed. I glance around, taking in all the people, the Christmas decorations still up, and Jamie waiting at the bar to get us another round of drinks. He catches my eye, gives me a quick wink, and I automatically smile.

"I showed him around town, and then we drove into the mountains." I bite back a laugh at the memory of his expression after I threw a snowball at him.

"He stuck up for you tonight," she says, glancing at him. A group of guys are talking with him while he waits for the drinks, stars in their eyes.

"He did." My heart squeezes. At dinner with my parents, they brought up the marketing job, and Jamie immediately told them how talented a singer and songwriter I was. They laughed and said it was important to have hobbies.

"*Pippa has what it takes to make music her career,*" he told them, and they were stunned until I changed the subject.

She leans forward, lowering her voice, and her eyes dance

with teasing. "Just try to keep it down tonight, okay? The walls are thin."

My eyes go saucer-wide, and I suck in a breath. "Nothing's going to happen." With everyone in the house? No way.

Her eyes roll back. "*Oh, Jamie.*"

I reach across the booth to cover her mouth, laughing. "Shut up."

"*Uhn, puck me harder with your hockey stick.*" She sounds like a porn star, and people glance over.

I gasp with laughter. "That doesn't even make sense."

She bats me away, grinning.

Two big male bodies flop down into the booth on either end of us, ending our conversation.

"Happy New Year, ladies!" Hayden throws his arm around my shoulder, jostling me.

A surprised laugh falls out of my mouth. Across the booth, Rory's grinning down at Hazel, who's staring at him like he's a cockroach that just crawled onto the table.

"What are you doing here?" she asks him.

"Streicher said he was taking a last-minute trip out here," Hayden tells us. "We thought we'd pay him a visit." At the door, half the team is piling in. "We begged the team to let us use the bus."

I burst out laughing at Jamie's confused expression as the guys surround him at the bar. They're drawing a ton of attention.

Hayden tosses a coaster at Rory. "And this fucking guy likes us more than his own team."

Rory won't take his eyes off Hazel, and I have a feeling he knew she'd be here.

At that moment, Jamie returns to the booth with drinks. He looks at me with a begrudging expression, like he's irritated that the players crashed our night but also secretly pleased, because they obviously consider him a friend.

"We have company," I tell him.

"I saw." He rolls his eyes before gesturing at Hayden to move.

When Jamie slips into the booth beside me, caging me in, he drapes his arm over the top, and his fingers brush my shoulder. Nerves skitter in my stomach and I hold down a smile. Around the bar, people glance over at us with curiosity.

"I don't understand why you hang out with these guys so much," Hazel is saying to Rory. She's putting on an irritated front, but her eyes are bright and she's having trouble meeting his gaze.

He's looking at her like she's the only person in the room. "I like these guys. There's no rule that we aren't allowed to hang out with our friends, even if they're on another team. I just don't talk about plays." He tips his chin at Jamie with challenge in his eyes. "Not that that would help Streicher here. The dude could get all my strategies ahead of time and I'd still score on him."

Jamie's hand tightens around his glass, knuckles going white as he stares at Rory. Rory's baiting him, trying to get a reaction from Jamie.

Half of me wishes they'd just talk about it. Or fight. Something to get it out of their systems. I doubt that would be good for either of their careers, though. Phones would be out within seconds, recording it, and it would be on the news.

My hand lands on Jamie's thigh, and his gaze drops to mine. His jaw ticks, and I give him a soft smile.

"Ignore him," I tell him.

He looks down at me with a small smile, and a moment later, his fingers brush my hair as he plays with the ends.

By New Year's Eve standards, sitting in a small-town bar and listening to the house band play while drinking cheap beer is mild. Sitting here, tucked into Jamie's side, though?

This is the best New Year's Eve I've ever had.

TWO HOURS LATER, I'm happily tipsy, surrounded by loud, boisterous hockey players. Jamie's glued to my side, and he's had a few drinks. There's a pink flush across his cheekbones, similar to when he gets out of the shower, and he even smiles a few times. A handful of players keep doing shots from the shot-ski, a series of shots taped crudely onto a ski so all participants need to drink simultaneously, and Hayden ordered a special shot that led to him currently getting spanked with a paddle by the bartender while the bar cheers. In the corner, a band plays, and as we approach midnight, the fun party energy in the bar heightens.

"You going to kiss me at midnight?" Rory asks Hazel.

She holds his gaze, wearing a smug grin. "Go kiss your sex doll."

"I left her at home."

I hold back a laugh, and Hazel looks like she's trying to as well.

He looks to me. "What about you, Pippa? Can I get a spot on your dance card?"

Beside me, Jamie stiffens. "No."

I glance at him. His arm is up on the booth, but I can feel

the heat from him. "My dance card's full tonight. Thanks for the offer, though."

Jamie glares at Rory, but before anything can happen, Hayden's at Jamie's side. "Streicher, you're playing pool with us."

Jamie glances between me and Rory, uncertain.

"Go," I tell him, tipping my chin at the pool tables. "Hazel will protect me with her sharp teeth."

Hazel bares her teeth at Jamie, and I laugh. Rory just gazes at Hazel with horny interest.

"Back in a bit." Jamie's hand brushes my lower back before he follows Hayden.

"So," Rory says across the table, "you two."

My smile is tense, and I shrug at him. "What?"

His gaze is curious and teasing. "He likes you."

I laugh to myself, and my face feels hot.

"It's true," he goes on, nodding. "He likes you more than anyone I've ever seen."

His words send a thrill through me, and I hide my smile. Maybe I have feelings for him, but I'm not ready to tell people. I haven't even fully admitted it to Hazel. "I'm just his assistant," I lie.

He makes a noise of disbelief. "You're his *something*, that's for sure."

Thankfully, more players arrive at our table with drinks, interrupting us, and I make conversation while I watch Jamie playing pool with Hayden and Alexei.

"Alright, folks," the lead singer of the band says into the microphone a few minutes later. "We're going to take a short break just before midnight, but we have a special treat for you."

Jamie and Hayden make their way back to our group through the crowd, and Jamie's eyes are on me.

"We've got another musician in the house, and she's going

to sing us a song," the lead singer says into the mic, and Jamie's mouth tips up.

My pulse stops.

"Everyone welcome Pippa Hartley!"

My eyes go wide as the bar cheers and applauds, half the patrons turning to look at me as I sit there frozen.

"What?" I ask Jamie as my pulse restarts at a gallop, whooshing in my ears.

He lowers his mouth to my ear. "Get up there, songbird. I want to hear my Christmas present live."

I meet his eyes, and my lips part. I blink at him, clinging to his gaze.

Performing at the Filthy Flamingo back in Vancouver, there were thirty people there, mostly the team. This place is packed. The crowd around the bar alone is eight people deep. Every chair and booth is full, and it's standing room only. There are at least two hundred people here.

I'm freaking out.

"I can't," I whisper, shaking my head.

Everyone is staring at me.

He holds my gaze, so strong, steady, and full of affection. His mouth curves into a gorgeous smile. "Yes, you can. I know you can."

I glance around the bar, meeting familiar gazes as they watch and wait. Jamie always thinks I can do it, and every time, he's been right. A funny feeling cuts through the panic and stage fright—determination. If I don't do this, I'll be proving that I'm not right for the music industry. That I'm just that girl who used to date the famous singer.

I want to prove them wrong, and more than anything, I want to prove Jamie right.

"Okay," I whisper, nodding at Jamie. "Okay."

His grin stretches across his face, and my pulse stumbles. "Alright."

God, I love making him proud like that.

I head up to the mic, savoring the brush of his fingers on my lower back as I pass him. The crowd applauds, and I take the guitar handed to me on stage, slipping the strap over my shoulder before I stand at the mic and stare out at the crowd.

It's just like the first time, when I stepped up to the mic in the bar after Jamie made me that deal. My heart's beating like a drum and I'm hyperaware of everyone waiting.

"I'm Pippa Hartley," I say into the mic, and my voice is strong and clear. "And this is a song about revenge."

The crowd whoops, excited and drunk, and I meet Jamie's gaze. He gives me a firm nod, still smiling, and I launch into it. I sing the song about getting back up after getting stepped on, the one that makes me feel strong and powerful. My voice rings out, and I dig deep, giving the song everything. On the last round of the chorus, I stop playing the guitar while I sing. The audience claps in time, and I beam back at them as I sing.

A woman near the small stage hollers in support and appreciation, and I wink at her. My chest bursts with energy and pride, and I'm flying high. I finish the song with full commitment, and when I play the last chord, the roof blows off the bar.

It's euphoria. I'm floating, gliding higher than ever, heart racing and skin tingling. I've never felt like this, and I already know I'm addicted.

THE BAR ROARS with drunken appreciation for Pippa, and I watch as she gives the crowd a shy smile, hands the guitar off, and makes her way off the stage.

Seeing her up there, it's so obvious: I'm head over fucking heels for this girl, and I have been for a long time. A lot longer than I realized.

Pippa Hartley has me wrapped around her little finger. I'll do anything for her, and I'm not even mad about it. I want to do terrible things to her, make her come with my mouth and my hands and my cock, make her scream my name and show her how fucking incredible sex can be. I know sinking into her tight, wet pussy is going to change my life.

It's not just the sex, though. I want to wake up with her, spend free evenings watching a movie on the couch, and go for walks in the woods with Daisy.

I don't know how, but we're going to figure this out. All the stuff with my mom, my concerns about hurting Pippa like I hurt Erin, I'm going to deal with it. I'm going to fix it. I don't want to be weighed down by it anymore.

I just want Pippa.

She reaches our group, and I gather her in my arms, burying my face in her hair, inhaling her warm scent.

"I'm in awe of you," I say into her ear, and when she pulls back to smile up at me, her eyes sparkle.

"Thank you for encouraging me," she says. "That was..." She trails off, shaking her head. "Incredible. I felt like I was flying."

My feelings hammer against my chest, wanting out. Nerves flash through me, and I search her eyes. Christ, she's so pretty and perfect.

She got up on stage in a packed bar even though she was scared, even though her fuckface ex tried to crush her. I'm always encouraging Pippa to be brave, and now it's time I take a fucking page out of my own book.

"I have feelings for you, songbird." My heart pounds, and the rest of the bar falls away. "I like you so fucking much. I don't want to pretend I don't anymore. I flew out here for you." Something expands in my chest, filling every corner with an intense warmth. Our gazes are locked, and my arms are still around her, keeping her close. "I don't want to fight this anymore."

Her eyes are bright and full of vulnerability. "Me neither."

"Really?"

She nods, laughing lightly like she's relieved.

I don't know what to do with this feeling ricocheting throughout me. It's like there are firecrackers in my blood. Fucking finally, I can stop fighting it.

"We're going to figure it all out together."

She smiles, and I fall a little harder for her. "I know."

I almost missed out on this. I tried to fight this for so long. Unbelievable.

"Ten, nine, eight," the bar around us chants, and I realize

it's seconds to midnight. Pippa blinks, looking around, before her gaze swings back to me.

"Happy New Year, Jamie," she whispers.

I draw her closer. Something has shifted in my chest, locked into place. This is right. This is the way it's supposed to be. I thought about her for all those years, and we found our way back to each other.

"Three, two, one," people count before the bar erupts in cheers again.

"Happy New Year, Pippa," I murmur before sinking my hand into her hair and pulling her mouth to mine.

"DO YOU HAVE EVERYTHING YOU NEED?" I ask Hayden later that night in my parents' living room.

The guys didn't have a place to stay because Hayden's a twenty-three-year-old rookie who's terrible at planning. We couldn't let them sleep on the bus—they'd freeze—so they're staying at my parents' place. The drunkest players are already snoring on the floor, covered in blankets that I dropped over them.

My dad is going to lose his mind with excitement tomorrow. I bet he'll make everyone pancakes.

Hayden waves me off. "We're good." His gaze flicks over my shoulder to where Jamie's waiting.

My stomach flutters. Everyone saw us kiss at midnight. After, Rory gave me an *I told you so* look.

"Okay." I give Hayden and Rory, who's on the couch, a wave. "Good night."

Rory winks. "Night, Pips. Don't let Streicher keep you up all night."

My face burns red as we head up the stairs, and my body hums with wound-up energy. I've been buzzing with anticipation for hours.

I hide a smile as we reach the upstairs landing, and his hand slips into mine. Outside my bedroom door, we pause, and the tension in the air grows as he looks down at me with a hot look.

"Hi," I whisper.

His eyes warm, and he presses a kiss onto my mouth. His tongue parts my lips, and I lean into him as he strokes into me, so warm and careful. He walks me back until I'm against my bedroom door, and when his hand comes to my hair, he angles my head back so he can get deeper.

Arousal thrums between my legs.

He breaks the kiss with a low noise of frustration and leans his forehead against mine.

"We can't," he murmurs. "Not here. Your parents are in the other room."

"We can be quiet." I bite my bottom lip, swollen from kissing him, and offer him a mischievous look.

"Maybe you can, but I don't know if I can." He drags in a deep breath, and for a moment, I think he's going to cave, but he shakes his head. "We can't, songbird. I want to so fucking badly, you have no idea." He takes my hand and puts it over his cock.

He's fully hard, and when I stroke him over the fabric, his eyes close.

"Fuck," he breathes before he pulls away from my touch. "No." He drops a firm kiss on my lips. "Good night."

I arch a brow at him, and he points at my bedroom door.

"Now," he says in a firm tone, although his eyes are full of amusement.

I let out a silent chuckle. "Good night, bossy."

A minute later, I'm getting undressed, about to put my pajamas on, when the jersey catches my eye, and instead of sleeping in an old t-shirt, I pull the jersey on over my bare skin.

That low-lying arousal simmering under my skin begins to boil as the jersey brushes my nipples, and they prick. I ignore the ache between my legs and climb into bed.

Through the wall, I hear the squeak of the bed in the guest bedroom as he settles in, and picturing his feet hanging off the end makes me chuckle.

*Something funny?* he texts.

I grin at my phone. *I'm sorry you're in the world's tiniest bed.*

*It's fine.*

*Thank you again for the jersey. I love it.*

I open my camera app and snap a pic of me wearing it before sending it to him. Only my shoulders are visible because I'm tucked under the blankets.

Through the wall, I hear a low groan. *You're wearing it to bed? Fuck, songbird. I'm trying not to get turned on in your parents' house.*

Lust shoots through me, and my gaze flicks to the wall separating us. I picture him lying there, doing that eyes closed, deep breathing thing he does when he's trying to control himself. Heat gathers low in my belly, and I squeeze my thighs together.

After flying high tonight from singing on stage and Jamie and I telling each other the truth, I feel bold and brave.

*It's all I'm wearing,* I respond.

*Jesus Christ. That's so fucking hot. That isn't why I bought it for you... but now that's all I can imagine.*

My mouth twists into a coy, pleased smile. There's a long pause before another text pops up. *You're sure you can be quiet?*

*Yes,* I text back while my heart slams against the front wall of my chest.

I listen to the bed creak as he gets up and softly pads down the hall to my room. My door opens and he steps inside, leaning against the closed door. He takes me in, lying in bed, wearing a jersey with his name on it, and his gaze rakes down the bed before returning to my face. The thick ridge of his hard cock under his sweatpants sends a thrill through me.

"Hi," he murmurs.

"Hi." I bite my lip, and his gaze follows the motion, darkening even more. He strides over to the bed, and it dips as he places his hands on either side of my head, hovering over me with a heated look in his eyes.

Between my legs, the ache intensifies, and I can't look away from him.

"You need to be very, very quiet, songbird. Not a single noise." His breath tickles my face. "Understand?"

I nod, sighing out a breath. I'd say anything to get his mouth on me again.

"Good."

He leans down to kiss me.

SHE LETS out a silent sigh of relief as my tongue glides into her mouth, and I move so my knees are on either side of her.

"Fuck," I whisper into her mouth, so warm and welcoming. She tastes so sweet, so right, I can barely contain myself.

I pull the covers back to look at her, and my mind goes blank as I stare at Pippa wearing only my hockey jersey.

A feeling rushes through my chest.

*Mine*. Pippa is mine. I'm never giving her up.

I'm wordless as I rake my gaze up her body. I'm never going to forget the sight of Pippa's soft thighs, smooth skin, the peek of cleavage over the neckline of the jersey. The scatter of freckles along her collarbone.

Her thighs press together, and I drag my hand up her inner thigh.

"You look so fucking good like this."

Her hands skim up my chest until they brush up my neck, and I shudder under her soft touch. I told her to be quiet, but I'm the one biting back a groan as her fingers thread into my hair. She tugs my hair in that way that makes me even harder.

I push the hem of the jersey up, and my heart stops when I see what she has on underneath.

No. Panties.

I stare at her perfect pussy.

"You've ruined me," I tell her, shaking my head before I reach between her legs and drag my fingers from her entrance to her clit. Her hips shake, her lips part, and when I feel how wet she is, I let out another curse. "Soaked, Pippa. You're fucking soaked."

She bites her lip, watching my every movement. I stroke over her, circling her clit. She tenses up as I brush the tight bud of nerves, and a dark grin hitches on my mouth. I love how sensitive she is. I love that I make her feel like that, that I can do this to her.

I keep my voice low and my eyes on her. "Were you going to touch yourself in here?"

She nods, and I reward her by pushing one finger inside her, finding her G-spot and crooking my finger. Her back arches but her wide eyes stay on me, and I fucking love that.

"Oh, shit, Jamie," she whispers, panting.

"Shh." I stroke her, watching as she presses a hand to her mouth, brows furrowed. I settle between her legs, and her eyes widen. "Did he ever do this for you?"

She shakes her head. "He tried but I wasn't into it."

Competition beats in my blood like a drum, and I push in and out of her tight entrance at a languid pace. "You want to try again?"

She hesitates, and I crook my fingers against her front wall, loving how her eyelids fall closed. "Um." She sighs as I thrust into her. "If you want to."

"I do." I watch where my fingers enter her, watch how her pretty pussy sucks them in. "I really fucking do. I think about it all the time."

She nods with a dazed look. "Okay."

I press kisses to every freckle on her inner thighs, slow and soft, warming her up until I lower my head and kiss her clit. My tongue brushes over her, and I bite back a groan at how sweet she is. She arches, tightening up as I stroke into her, covering her hand over her mouth. She's trying so hard to be quiet, my little songbird, and I love it.

While I drag my tongue over her clit, again and again, listening to her pretty little muffled gasps, my free hand drifts to her ass and I grip her soft skin, pushing her against my mouth while I give her swollen clit a long suck. Her thighs shake, and a moment later, her fingers are in my hair, tugging.

"You like that?" I whisper, and she nods feverishly. "You want me to do it again?"

"Please," she gasps.

Need rushes through me. I love how badly she wants this.

"Shh." My pulse beats in my ears as I watch her. "You need to be quiet."

She nods, and when I stroke in and out again, her lips part as she mouths my name. I feel like a king.

I push my jersey up her stomach so I can see her tits. Jesus fucking Christ, Pippa looks so good lying there, chest rising and falling fast. Her skin is so soft, her nipples are pinched and puckered, and I raise up to pull one into my mouth. Her hands return to my hair as I lave the peak with my tongue.

Telling Pippa how I feel was the best idea I ever had, and flying out to see her is a close second.

Her breath comes out in pants, and I grin as I press a kiss between her breasts. "You want to learn something new, songbird?"

"This feels pretty new to me." Her voice is thin as I dip my finger into her again. "Oh god," she whispers.

I huff a laugh, letting my stubble scrape the soft skin on her stomach on my way back down between her legs. "You're going to tell me what you want." I kiss a trail across her skin, down her thighs, anywhere except where she wants it.

"Please, Jamie," she whispers.

"Tell me."

"Do what you were doing just a second ago."

"Which was?" My voice is low and teasing. "Say it, songbird. You can do it."

Her frustration peaks. "I want you to lick my pussy."

I crook a grin at her. "There we go, baby." When I pull her clit between my lips and suck on it, a low moan slips out of her. "You gotta be quiet."

Around my finger, she clenches up, and I can feel how badly she needs this. I want to be the guy doling out her pleasure, watching her unravel because of me.

"I can't," she whispers, breathing hard as I slick my tongue over her clit again.

I freeze. I'm rushing her, I realize.

"Tell me what you feel." My mouth returns to her thighs. She's so wet—

"No." She sinks her hands into my hair and pulls me back to her slick center. "I can't be quiet but I don't want you to stop. I need to come so badly. Please, Jamie."

Smug, primal satisfaction courses through me. I wasn't rushing her. She's desperate to come.

"I'm not going to stop." I return to her clit, licking, sucking, dragging her own arousal over her sensitive, swollen skin.

"Oh, fuck." Her head tips back. "Jamie, I can't hold off."

I bury my face in her pussy. Her muscles flutter around my fingers as I work her G-spot. She's close. With my free hand, I reach up and cover her mouth. One of her hands stays in my hair, but the other clutches my arm as she tightens on my fingers.

"Coming," she moans against my hand over her mouth, and I latch onto her clit, sucking hard. Her legs snap against either side of my head as she shakes beneath my mouth, thighs pressing against me, arching off the bed to ride against my face while she lets out muffled whimpers. My cock is so hard it hurts as she soaks my face with her release, breathing hard.

She collapses back, catching her breath, staring at me like she can't believe it.

"Nice work," she whispers, and I chuckle against her inner thigh, pressing a kiss against her skin before lifting up so I'm hovering over her.

My Pippa. So fucking hot. Such a perfect angel, all flushed from her own orgasm. I run my thumb across her bottom lip.

Her gaze drops to the front of my sweatpants, where my cock strains against the fabric. A wicked gleam enters her eyes.

"Not tonight," I tell her, knowing I'm going to regret it. "If we mess around more, Pippa, I'm going to break your bed."

She opens her mouth to protest, but I cover it with a kiss, stroking into her mouth the way I want to with my cock. I give myself five more seconds of her mouth before I pull away, stand over the bed, and frame her jaw with my hands.

"You're so perfect," I tell her. "So fucking perfect."

She watches me with that sweet, drowsy smile. It feels special, discovering sex with Pippa like this. Like we're both discovering how it can be, because it sure as hell has never been like this for me.

She is so fucking *mine*.

I pull the covers up around her, smiling as she settles into the pillows, still wearing my jersey, hair fanned out, all messed up from my hands in it.

I love her. The words are right under my vocal cords, but I hold them back, because this is all so new. They beat through my blood, they weave through my heart, and I'm sure they're written all over my face.

"Good night, songbird," I say instead.

# CHAPTER 55

CAN WE TALK?

Ten days after New Year's, I stand at the kitchen counter, staring at the text I just received from Zach.

My mouth goes dry as I read it again and again. It can't be real, and yet, that's his number. The last texts we exchanged were back in August, a couple days before he dumped me, when I was picking up coffee for myself and wanted to know if he wanted anything.

Disgust stirs in my gut. He had the audacity to take my song, and now he wants to talk?

I block him and delete the text history.

Jamie opens the door of the apartment, and I jump. He shoots me that handsome, disarming smile I'm addicted to, and thoughts of Zach vanish.

The second Jamie flew home from Silver Falls, he had to leave for a ten-day away game streak, but now he's back. I rush over to hug him. At our feet, Daisy does her excited tippy-taps on the floor, tail wagging a mile a minute in excitement.

"You're home," I say into Jamie's neck while he presses a kiss to the top of my head. His arms around me, pulling me into his hard chest, is the ultimate comfort.

"Finally." He presses another kiss to my temple, and when I lean back to look up at him, his eyes go soft. "I've been wanting to do this for ten days."

He kisses me, and I sigh into him. His mouth on mine is pure relief, sweet and careful, until he groans and sweeps his tongue between my lips. His stubble lightly scratches me, and heat pulses through me.

"Missed you," he murmurs against my lips between kisses. "I love coming home to you."

My heart soars like it did on New Year's Eve, when I sang on stage. Like when we told each other we have feelings for each other. It can't be healthy to experience heart palpitations like this so often, but I don't care.

Jamie pulls away, looks down at Daisy, and picks her up. "Missed you, too," he tells her. She licks at his ear, wiggling in his arms, and he grimaces while I laugh.

This man with a dog is almost too cute to be legal.

"I was just about to take her for a walk."

Daisy hears the word walk and her head whips to me. Jamie smiles and gives her another scratch.

"I'll go with you."

Twenty minutes later, we're walking through Stanley Park. Vancouver is experiencing a cold snap, and snow falls lightly around us, coating the towering emerald trees. People hate driving in the snow in Vancouver, so except for our boots crunching on the snow, downtown and the park are quiet.

"Your mom seemed really good the other day." Hazel and I took Daisy for a walk with Donna a couple days ago, before it snowed.

He makes a pleased noise in his throat, smiling at the ground as we walk. "She has an appointment with a doctor on Tuesday."

I light up, smiling at him. "She does? For medication?"

He nods, relief spreading over his features. "Yep."

"That's great." God, I'm so happy to hear this. Not just because Jamie has spent so long taking care of her. Donna is a really lovely person, and she's been through so much. She deserves to feel better and have the tools to deal with her panic attacks.

We walk in comfortable silence for a while before Jamie nudges me.

"The video has over three million views."

My stomach wobbles. "I know. Don't remind me."

Hayden took a video of me singing on New Year's Eve and, after asking me, he posted it on his TikTok. It went viral, but I'm pretending it doesn't exist. Just thinking about that many people seeing me sing one of my own songs makes me sick with nerves. I made the terrible mistake of reading the comments on the video, and while most of them were complimentary, I can't shake the few ugly ones out of my head.

*She's nothing special. This is boring. She's not even playing the guitar. That's just for show. This song sucks. They only let her up there because she's hot.*

I couldn't write music for months because Zach hurt my feelings. How could I ever have a career with thousands of Zachs out there, saying even worse things? Maybe saying them to my face, every day?

"Hey." Jamie stops walking and reaches for me, putting his arm around my shoulder and pulling me to his side. "I'm proud of you. That took guts, getting up there."

I nod with a noise of acknowledgment, but my anxiety about the whole thing bleeds into my forced smile. He watches me for a long moment.

"We do a visualization exercise with one of the sports psychologists on the team," he says, studying me. "She has me picture the game. I imagine the other team's forwards trying to score on me and what the puck feels like in my glove or hitting my blocker. I picture each of their guys and every scoring configuration I can think of. The more specific I am, the better." He arches his brow. "I think you should try that, but with music."

A frown slides onto my face as I think about enduring mean comments for the rest of my life. "I don't really want to picture people booing me." A light laugh scrapes out of me to hide my discomfort.

"Not that. Picture the career you want. Picture your dream, songbird." His hand slips from my shoulder down to my gloved hand, and he gives it a squeeze. "You've been stuck in this loop for months. It's time to picture something new."

He's right, I realize. All I do is think about the past, and it's holding me back. Every time I even consider music, I think about what happened to warn myself away. I keep putting my own barriers up in my path.

My throat is thick as I swallow, glancing up at him with hesitance. His warm, confident expression bolsters me, and I nod. "Okay."

"Close your eyes."

I glance around. It's just us and Daisy, who's busy sniffing the side of the path. I take a deep breath and let my eyes fall closed.

The forest is almost silent except for Daisy's sniffing. Cold flakes land on my cheeks and nose, and the air smells clean and crisp.

I picture myself on stage. It's a small show, and I'm opening for a bigger artist. There are a couple hundred people in the crowd.

No. I catch myself, opening my eyes, blinking up at Jamie, who's still watching me with a small smile on his face. I want more than being the opener. My eyes close and I try again.

I'm on stage in an arena. I'm the headliner, and my dream guitar is slung across my chest. I'm touring with my new album that I recorded with my dream producer, Ivy Matthews. She's known in the music industry for being eccentric and picky as hell, but she's supremely talented at creating unique and authentic musicians. Behind me, a hand-picked band of kind, talented musicians is ready. I'm wearing something that makes me feel gorgeous and strong, and my hair is loose around my shoulders.

"*I'm Pippa Hartley,*" I say into the mic, and they cheer. Every person in this arena bought tickets to see me, but I like to introduce myself at the beginning of every show. It's my thing.

I glance to the wings. Jamie's standing there, looking proud, and I smile at him.

"*And this is a song about falling in love.*"

In my mind, I launch into the song, the band begins to play, the arena fills with sound and light, and it's fucking spectacular.

My eyes open, and I beam up at Jamie. Tears well up in my eyes, because what I just imagined was so sweet. My chest aches for it.

"I don't want the marketing job." My voice is hushed.

He nods, serious. "I know."

A weight settles in my stomach. When I told my parents I passed the second interview with flying colors, they could hear the false cheerfulness in my voice.

I wish they could be proud of me. I wish I didn't have to shove myself into some job I don't want to gain their approval. My throat tightens with the ugly realization. I know their intentions are good; they tie happiness to financial stability, because it's what they lacked growing up.

I didn't, though. Working a job I don't like won't make me happy, even if it does pay my bills. My heart twists in my chest, and like he can feel it, Jamie's hand is on my back, rubbing slow, calming circles.

I got swept up in what they wanted, just like with Zach. Jamie looks at me right now the same way he looks at me every time I'm about to step up on a stage—like I can do anything. The flame in my chest is a pilot light, fueled by memories of singing on New Year's and recording songs that I wrote in the living room. That fire is my love of music, the way I feel like I'm flying when I sing my heart out. It's the reason I can't walk away from the music industry even though I tried. Something sharp and glowing rushes through my blood, and I suck a breath in.

I'll figure out how to tell my parents. The idea of letting them down makes my stomach clench, but it's what I need to do.

"You want to tell me what you pictured?" Jamie's mouth tilts. "You don't have to."

Jamie isn't Zach. He'd never laugh at me, never tell me my dreams are stupid or that I should stay in my lane.

"I want to."

I tell him everything, and when I'm done, his eyes are bright with affection and excitement.

"Would you ever reach out to her?"

I blanch. "Who? Ivy Matthews?"

He nods.

"Um." I blink. My instinct is to say no, but I catch myself again.

No more putting up roadblocks for myself. No more letting what Zach said weigh me down. If I want what I imagined just now, I'm going to have to do scary things... like send my music to people who could reject me.

"I guess I could." Determination pours into my blood, and I nod at Jamie. "Yeah. I'm going to do it."

His smile is so broad, it makes my heart break open. "Good girl."

I laugh, and he slings an arm around my shoulder as we keep walking.

While Jamie is at the gym that afternoon, I study Ivy Matthews' website. There's an email address, but no information about whether she takes submissions. She probably wouldn't want to work with me unless I'm signed by a record label. She didn't even want to work with Zach. His manager tried to arrange something with her and she turned them down. He was so angry about the rejection.

This is such a long shot, it's not even funny, but I told Jamie I'd do this. I write a brief, professional message about my experience in the music industry and attach links for my viral video and the songs I wrote for Jamie for Christmas.

Hesitation rears its ugly head again and again, but shoving it away gets a little easier each time.

I hit send and blow out a long breath. Even if nothing will come of it—and I'm certain that's the case—I tried. I took one step forward.

———

That evening, I'm about to feed Daisy dinner when my phone rings with an unknown number, and I answer.

"Is this Pippa Hartley?" a woman asks.

"That's me." I drop the cup of dog kibble into Daisy's slow-feeder bowl, and she races to eat it.

"My name is Marissa Strong. I'm Ivy Matthews' assistant."

My brain stops working.

There's a pause. "Are you still there?"

"Yes," I say quickly. "I'm here. Just wondering if I'm hallucinating."

She laughs. "Yeah. I get that response sometimes. I saw your submission and passed it along to Ivy. She's in town recording, and the band has wrapped up early, so she's free tomorrow. If you're free, she'd like to record a demo with you."

I'm staring at nothing. I don't think I even have a pulse right now.

"There's absolutely no guarantee anything will happen with the demo," Marissa continues, all business, but her tone changes to something thoughtful. "There's something interesting about you, though, and she's curious."

Something interesting about *me*. My pulse kicks in, and I try to breathe.

"I'm free," I say, feeling breathless. I can't believe this. "I'll be there."

IVY MATTHEWS SKEWERS me with her gaze in the lobby of the East Vancouver studio, and my skin prickles with self-consciousness.

Why did I wear sneakers? I look like someone's babysitter. Nerves pinch in my stomach, and I fight the urge to chew my lip.

Ivy Matthews is famous for a closed studio with as few people as possible, so we're alone. No receptionist, no Marissa the assistant.

Right now, I wish there were others here to take the attention off me. Being her sole focus is a lot, and I have no idea if I'm messing this up or not.

This is my big shot. I can't mess it up.

I wish Jamie was here, but he's at practice.

"Did you eat?" Her voice is sharp and no-nonsense, such a contrast to the sweet freckles scattered over her dark skin. Her salt-and-pepper hair is pulled back into a tight bun, she's wearing black from head to toe, and her glasses have thick, fluorescent orange frames. She looks like a stern art teacher.

I nod quickly. "Avocado toast with a poached egg." Jamie

made it this morning, insisting I eat despite my rolling, nervous stomach. "And a coffee."

She studies me for a long moment. "Good." She crosses her arms over her chest, and I suppress a smile as I get a flash of Jamie doing the same thing.

She asks me about my history in the music industry, and I give her a quick summary of my music training and my time on tour with Zach. I mention his name so she understands the scale of the tour, but I don't tell her the context of our relationship.

At Zach's name, her nose wrinkles. "I never had a good feeling about that guy. He didn't sing like he meant it." Her gaze slides to mine, studying me through her orange frames, and a hawk-like smile tips up on her mouth. "You, though. You mean it. I feel it." She nods, watching me, cataloging me, and I feel like there's a spotlight on me in this quiet lobby. "And I always trust it when I feel it."

Even though I'm scared, even though I feel every ounce of pressure weighing on my shoulders, I want to prove her right.

I want to prove I'm nothing like him.

A feeling hits me square in the chest. This moment isn't for him; it's for *me*. I want to show her who I am, what I can do, and I'm going to do that by doing what I do best.

I'm enough, and if she doesn't see that, this isn't the right moment. I'll keep trying, though. I meant what I told Jamie the other day—I'm ready to try to make music my career. Terrified, but ready.

I straighten up, pushing my shoulders back, and give her a warm smile, just like I did to Jamie the day I showed up in his apartment. I feel better already. Just because she's intimidating doesn't mean I have to cower in fear.

"Shall we do this?" I ask brightly, and she blinks at me before she barks out a laugh and gestures at the studio space.

"Get in there, honey." There's a surprised tone to her words, but she disappears through the door of the sound booth, and it's time for me to go to my side.

———

"Good," Ivy says two hours later into the microphone that plays into my headphones. "Again."

I take a sip of water before launching into the song again. I have no idea how this is going. I'm just playing my songs and doing my best, because that is the full extent of my control. I'm trying not to fangirl over how professional this studio is—everything from the mics to the lighting to the acoustics is top quality, and I see why she loves to record here. In the control room, Ivy's expression through the glass gives me nothing while her sound technician records. Sometimes, I see her mouth moving as she instructs him on the console. Mostly, though, she just watches.

Strung across my body, my dream guitar feels like an extension of me. The fact that Jamie bought it for me makes this moment just a little more special, like a perfect circle. This moment feels like one of those snapshots from the mental exercise Jamie had me do in the forest yesterday. It's almost too good to be true.

"Good," she says again when the song ends. "Next."

I drag in a breath, gaze falling to the carpet as I decide what song to play. I settle on the one I wrote about Jamie, about how he takes care of everyone but himself.

When I play the song this time, it feels different, because now that Jamie's mom is getting better, it seems like he's going to be okay. He can live his own life now that she has hers under control.

*"I'd do it forever if it wouldn't break my heart,"* I sing. My throat tightens as the words spill out, and my voice catches.

It feels different, because I know Jamie isn't Zach. Things have changed between us. It's so new and I'm terrified to think forward to the future with him, but that doesn't mean I can't hope.

I close my eyes, because I don't want to see whatever Ivy's expression is. It's unprofessional to get emotional in the studio.

I keep my eyes closed the entire song and let myself feel all the feelings. Jamie wanders into my mind, and I smile to myself, because his encouragement is the reason I'm even here, and I'll always be grateful for that.

"Beautiful." Ivy's clipped voice comes through the mic, and my eyelids fly open.

Jamie stands beside her in the sound booth, arms folded over his chest, watching me with that intense, bright gaze, and the corner of his mouth curves up. So serious, even when he's smiling.

He's here, and I'm so stunned and pleased that all I can do is let the grin stretch across my face as my heart flips over in my chest.

He's here, and I fall a little deeper in love with Jamie Streicher.

———

"Interesting," Ivy says in the lobby that evening after she's decided we're done. It's eight o'clock and I'm starving, but I'd stay here for days if she asked me to. She studies me for a long moment, barely glancing at Jamie. "Very interesting. Thank you. We're done for today."

And then she's gone, disappeared back into the control

room. From her reaction, I can't tell if I impressed her or bombed, but I don't see how I could have done better.

"Songbird." I feel Jamie's gaze on my face like a brush of his fingers. His eyes are soft like velvet, and my heart squeezes as I smile at him. "You did it."

Emotion floods me, and I smile wider at him. "I think I did."

Something between us. All these feelings I'm experiencing for the guy who has become so much more than *Jamie Streicher* pulse in the air, demanding attention. His gaze drops to my lips, and it's not just heat I see in his eyes, but more. His eyes lift to mine again, and he gives me that proud smile.

"Let's get you fed," he says, and I nod. "And then home."

# CHAPTER 57

# JAMIE

WE GET HOME that night after dinner and then taking Daisy
for a late walk, and I've never been more in love with my pretty
assistant.

She's so brave. She sang her heart out in that sound booth,
just opened up her chest and let everyone see the heart beating
behind her ribs, even though she was afraid.

She got back on the ice, like I told her to all those
months ago.

"Thank you for coming today," she says as she kicks her
sneakers off.

"Like I'd miss it." I almost skipped practice to go, racing to
the studio as soon as the whistle blew instead. "I'm so proud of
you, songbird."

Her eyelashes flutter, her gaze still on my face. Her lips are
so pretty, so lush, and my fingers itch with the urge to trace
them. "I love it when you call me that."

My pulse jumps as something big expands in my chest.
The nickname is my way of telling her I love her, I realize. I've
been doing it for months, long before the reality sank in. The
words are on the tip of my tongue, but I hold back.

It's new, and I don't want to rush her.

A rueful smile twists onto my mouth. "I love calling you that."

I stare down at Pippa, into her mesmerizing blue-gray eyes. I'm never going to find someone like Pippa Hartley. She's one in a million, and after what I saw today, she's finally realizing it.

"There's something I want to ask you." I tuck a lock of her hair behind her ear.

I've been thinking this over since New Year's Eve, when my feelings for Pippa hit me like a freight train.

"I want to reach out to Erin." Erin's devastated expression appears in my head, and guilt weaves through me. "I want to make things right with her. I—" My words cut off as I look down at Pippa, so open and curious. Jesus, I love her. I'd do anything to prevent crushing her like I crushed Erin. "I want to fix things."

Pippa gives me a sad smile. "You always want to fix things."

I nod. "This is important. Is it okay with you?"

"Of course."

I knew she'd be fine with it, but now that we're whatever we are—together, in a relationship, dating, all these phrases that feel too mild and watered down for what I feel for Pippa—I want to be as open with her as possible.

I press a kiss to her temple, and her eyes fall closed. Her skin is warm and soft, and I brush my lips over her cheek, over the shell of her ear. Her scent is intoxicating, comforting, and fucking arousing.

"We should try something," I say, because I haven't touched her properly since New Year's Eve. I was traveling for games, and then last night, she was practicing her guitar and songs in her room until after midnight.

Her breath catches as I softly nip her earlobe. "What?"

My fingers tangle into her hair and I tilt her head back to look at me. "I want to make you come twice."

Pippa's eyes widen, and her lips part as she searches my gaze. "I've never—"

"I know."

"I don't think I can."

My eyebrow quirks as smug satisfaction weaves through me. She can. I can make it happen. I know I can.

I'll do anything to make it happen.

"You say that a lot, but I can't remember the last time you were right."

Worry wavers through her gaze. "I don't want you to be disappointed."

I shake my head, because she couldn't be more wrong. "Pippa, that's not how this works. Touching you is a goddamn dream. I'd only be disappointed in myself if you didn't enjoy it. Not in you, baby. Never in you."

The worry fades from her eyes, leaving only lust and want, and my own need surges.

"Okay," she whispers, and my mouth falls to hers.

OUR KISS IS urgent as I carry her up the stairs. Her thighs squeeze my waist, and I grip her ass, giving it a sharp slap. Her moan vibrates into my mouth, and when she sucks on my tongue, fucking hell. I groan back into her, pinning her against the wall upstairs.

"Oh my god," she whimpers as I hit the perfect spot with my hips. "Oh my god."

"Right there, huh?"

She nods, eyes closed and lips parted, and my blood beats with the primal need to please her.

"Jamie." Her eyes open with that fucking perfect dazed look as I rock against her clit. "Need to touch you."

I move to carry her into her bedroom.

"No," she says, and I stop. She gives me a shy, embarrassed smile. "Your bed."

Jesus *Christ*, I like that.

A moment later, I lower her onto my bed, yanking my shirt and pants off, then supporting my own weight on my elbows on either side of her head as I kiss her. Another shred of control falls away as my tongue strokes against her, urgent and demanding.

My blood sings with the truth: Pippa is mine.

"You like being in my bed?" I murmur as my fingers trail beneath her shirt, skimming up her stomach. Her skin is so soft.

"Yes." Her breath catches as I brush the skin beneath her bra, teasing, knowing what she wants but holding back an inch.

"I like it, too."

Her back arches into my touch. I pull away to tease her, and she growls, hand coming to my arm.

"What's the matter?" I ask in a low voice, smiling at her. I shift so I'm on my side, watching her.

"Jamie." The way she says my name, irritated and aroused, makes my grin turn wicked.

She sits up and pulls her shirt off, and I'm face to face with her perfect tits, pushed up into something incredible in a white lace bra embroidered with flowers.

Lust floods my body. "Not fair," I murmur, trailing my fingers over the lace.

I circle the lace over her nipple, feeling the stiff peak beneath the fabric. Her eyes glaze and her lips part before I move to the other one. I'm fully hard, lying here with Pippa, playing with her, teasing her, working her up.

It's heaven.

"Let's talk game plan, songbird." My voice is low as I brush back and forth over the sensitive peaks covered in lace. "How are we going to do this?"

Her cheeks are flushed. "I think you should go down on me."

My eyebrow arches. "Oh, really?"

She nods, and we're both thinking about a few weeks ago in her parents' house, when she wore my jersey.

"You liked that, did you?" She nods again, and something electric crackles in the air around us. "So did I."

Surprise passes through her eyes, and my pulse beats harder.

"Did you doubt that, Pippa?" My fingers brush over the swells of her breasts, just above her bra. "Did you doubt that your pussy was one of the sweetest things I've ever tasted?" I dip into her bra cup to find a stiff nipple, and she lets out a soft moan. "Because it was, baby. I think about it every time I stroke my cock, how wet you were. How you sounded, moaning for me while I licked into you."

She arches into my touch again and unhooks her bra. My mouth falls to her breast, circling the pinched point with my tongue. The noise that scrapes out of her throat, needy and relieved at the same time, makes my balls ache with want.

"Are we using the toy tonight, Pippa?"

She shakes her head.

"No?" I arch a brow as I suck, and her breath catches.

"I want to try without," she whispers, biting her lip.

She looks at me like she thinks I can do it, make her come again without the toy. My cock surges, straining in my boxers.

"This is driving me crazy," she says as I pinch and roll the other peak. "Touch me."

I grin down at her. "I am touching you."

"More," she demands.

"You don't want to tell me five things you can feel?"

Her frustrated glare makes me shake with laughter. I've never *laughed* during sex. My songbird is horny and furious, and I'm in heaven. In this moment, I feel like she's my best friend, and yet I'm rock hard, thinking about pleasing her. Sex has never been so playful, and I can't think of another time I felt so comfortable around someone.

This is what it's supposed to be like, I realize.

"Stop. Teasing. Me." Her teeth are clenched as I brush her nipple as softly as I can, watching her reaction.

"Beg me."

When her gaze simmers with heat and a sigh falls from her lips, my blood sings.

"Please, Jamie," she whispers. "Please make me come."

Heat burns down my spine, pooling around the base, and I drag in a breath, holding on to the last remnants of control.

"When you beg like that, I lose my fucking mind."

Her eyes are glazed with lust but certain. "So lose it."

I get her fully naked within seconds. My hands settle on her inner thighs, pushing them apart as I lower myself between her legs.

She's wet, soaked, glistening with damp thighs, and pride courses through my veins. I did that. I make her feel good. No one else.

Pippa is mine.

The first stroke of my tongue up her wet center makes Pippa arch off the bed.

*This.* The taste of Pippa ignites my hunger all over again, sets my greed for her on fire, and the possessive need inside me intensifies. I bury my face between her legs, licking, stroking, sucking the tight bud of nerves. The noises slipping out of Pippa's mouth are rough, breathy, unfiltered, and my cock pulses with the need to fuck her hard.

When I slip a finger inside her and find the ridged spot, her thighs slam tight around my head.

"Jamie," she chokes out, and my chest beats with pride.

"You looked so fucking hot in my jersey," I say before I suck her clit. Her thighs shake on either side of my head. Her pussy's so wet I can hear sucking sounds as I push my finger in and out. "So fucking hot. Do you know how it makes me feel to see my name on your back, Pippa?"

I suck her clit again, and her hands drift to my hair,

clutching and tugging. The sensation shoots more heat down my spine. My length aches, dripping pre-cum.

"It makes me feel like you're mine," I tell her.

Her eyes go hazy. "It makes me feel like that, too."

My pulse whooshes in my ears, and I've never felt this feral need, this primal, out of control, instinctive want. The sight of Pippa lying beneath me, splayed open for me, hair spilling over my bed, hands in my hair as she holds on tight, it slices away any hesitation.

"Oh god, Jamie," she moans when I add another finger and rub her G-spot.

I know that tone. I've memorized it, replayed it over and over again as I fucked my fist, thinking about her.

"You're close," I say before swirling my tongue over her clit. She jerks a nod, eyes closed tight. "Uh-huh."

Something hot and smug settles in my chest, and I close my lips over her clit, sucking and working the nerves with my tongue as my fingers stroke in and out. She tightens around me—her abs, her legs around my head, her pussy around my fingers.

"Say my name when you come like a good girl."

"Fuck," she chokes out, and I can feel her tipping. Her hands grip my hair so tight it hurts. The pain sears my scalp and I love it. "Jamie."

She shakes all around me, crying out my name, coming and coming, and I don't let up until I've wrung every drop from my pretty assistant's pussy. As her orgasm subsides, I press sucking kisses to her clit. I can't tear myself away from her.

Her legs fall apart as she catches her breath, hands still in my hair. Her fingers comb my hair out of my eyes as she stares at the ceiling.

"Jamie," she whispers. "What the hell?"

I chuckle and kiss her inner thigh, coated with her arousal.

My tongue runs along the soft, sensitive skin there, and she lets out a high, tight noise when I reach her clit.

"Sensitive," she gasps.

"Sorry, baby." I crawl over her, hovering with my elbows on either side of her head, caging her in. I tip her chin up and kiss her, and her breath tickles my face as she lies there in a puddle. "Can't help myself." I press kiss after kiss to her face, to her cheekbones, to her forehead, to her nose, to her eyes, to her soft, pliant, warm, inviting mouth.

She's perfect, my Pippa.

Her hands trail up and down my arms, over my chest. Her nails scrape the stubble down my neck, through my chest hair, over my abs, over the ridges of my back. I'm so hard it hurts, but I wouldn't interrupt this moment for anything. I love her like this, sated and pleased and calm.

In this moment, we're the only people in the universe. Nothing else matters. There's no family drama, no exes, no worries about careers or the future or getting our hearts broken.

It's just us.

"Songbird," I whisper, because I love her.

Her eyes meet mine, full of affection, and for a moment, I think she might love me, too. I kiss her deeply, sinking into her warm, pliant mouth, and while I'm caught up in my pretty songbird, mooning over her, she reaches down and pulls my straining cock out of my boxers and gives it a firm stroke.

"Oh, fuck," I groan into her mouth before yanking my boxers off. "Hold on a second, baby."

I'm too close to the edge, and I want this to last. It never lasts with Pippa, and I want as much out of this as I can get.

My cock settles in the cradle between her thighs. Her pussy is still wet, so warm, and electricity travels up and down my spine, numbing my brain, letting the base instincts take over.

I drag my cock through her wetness, and the urgent need to come beats all the thoughts from my head.

Nirvana. I've reached it. It's between Pippa's legs.

"Do it again," she coaxes, tilting her hips, dragging friction and arousal down my length.

Oh, fuck. This is too good. My cock aches and I can't stop from sliding against her again. Her pussy is soaked, warm, coating me in wetness.

"Oh my god," she moans, staring up at me like I'm a god. "That feels good. So good."

Power thrums through my blood, and I do it again, sliding my cock through her, against her clit. Her eyes roll back, and my pulse pounds in my ears.

"Like this?" My voice is ragged. I don't know how long I can do this for. It's too intense.

"Yes," she gasps, writhing as I keep stroking against her. "Jamie. Like that. Shit." Her last curse is in surprise, like she can't believe it.

"When I finally fuck you, Pippa, I'm going to come so fucking hard inside your tight pussy." I find a rhythm, stroking myself against her.

I don't tell her that when I finally fuck her, it's going to break me. She'll ruin me. I think she already has.

"I want that," she gasps out, hips canting to meet mine.

"I want it, too. You have no fucking idea how long I've wanted it for."

Her nails dig into my back, and pleasure sparks at the base of my spine. Her moans pitch higher, breathier, and her eyes go wider.

"Oh, fuck. Jamie. Please."

"Please what?" I'm holding on for dear life here as I slide against her again.

"Please fuck me," she breathes. "I need it, Jamie."

Her expression is pleading and filled with affection and love.

I love this girl. I'm not ready to tell her, because it feels dangerous and risky, and more than anything, I want what I have with Pippa to last.

I can't tell her that I love her, but I can show her.

My jaw is tight as I jerk a nod. "Okay." The word scrapes out like sandpaper. "Yes."

Finally, fucking *finally*, I'm going to show Pippa who she belongs to.

# CHAPTER 59

# PIPPA

MY HEART BEATS SO HARD I can hear it. Jamie reaches for a condom from the bedside table, and once he's rolled it on his thick length, he positions himself at my entrance.

He hesitates, watching my reaction, and I smile, because Jamie's sweet, kind, and caring. My hips tilt against his in encouragement, and his jaw is tight as he pushes inside me, searching my eyes for any sign of discomfort.

Oh *god*. A moan slips out of me as I stretch around his thickness. He's careful as he slowly feeds his cock into my body, and every swear word I can think of flickers in my head at the pleasurable ache between my legs.

"So fucking tight," Jamie manages. He's only halfway in.

"It's been a while." The pressure grows, and I gasp as he hits every nerve inside me.

"There you go." His voice is a low, comforting murmur, but his eyes flash with heat as he keeps pushing. His hand drifts to my breast, toying with my nipple as he slides in farther.

The sensation of him inside me is mind-bending, DNA-altering, and we're both shaking.

He bottoms out, and my thoughts fall out of my head. Sensitivity courses through my body, radiating out from where we're joined. Our hips are pressed tight against each other, my legs wrapped around his waist, and another moan of pleasure slips out of me as heat races up my spine. God, he smells so good.

"Good girl." He brushes a lock of hair off my face. "Such a good fucking girl, taking my cock so well." His voice is strained, and a flush spreads across his cheekbones. "You okay?"

I nod, meeting his eyes, and his gaze is hot, desperate, and admiring, all in one.

I'm already addicted to him looking at me like that.

"Does that feel good?"

"Yes," I say, but it's mixed with a moan. "It's really tight."

"Mhm. I know." His cock throbs inside me, and my breath catches as I ache around him.

"I was right," I whisper, and he arches a brow at me. "You're a little too big for me."

His mouth slants into a wicked grin, and I bite my lip. "I've been thinking about this for so fucking long, Pippa." He presses a soft, intimate kiss to my lips, and his hair brushes my forehead. "Are you ready for me to move? We can stay like this as long as you want."

He's trembling above me, and with how hard he is inside me, I know he's holding back. Even like this, he's so controlled and careful. I tilt my hips against him, inching back and forth on his cock, and just the small movement has me dizzy with need.

"Ready."

He pulls out, slowly, so torturously slowly, before he pushes back in. I moan at the delicious ache, and when he bottoms out again—so fucking deep—I gasp.

"Good?" he manages, neck corded.

My nod is vehement. "Good. So good. Again." I'm not even

putting full sentences together. That's what Jamie Streicher's dick does to me.

He thrusts again and we both groan.

"Holy fuck, Pippa."

He strokes in and out of me with care until I adjust, then he finds a faster pace. Watching him move over me with that clenched jaw is fascinating, with that gorgeous, cruel mouth, those deep green eyes that burn hot for me. I don't even want to blink.

Being fucked by Jamie Streicher is a religious experience. Pressure swells inside me, but the pleasure is deeper, lower, a slower build than when Jamie's mouth was all over me earlier. Instead of a sharp peak of sensation, the feeling expands throughout my body. My body doesn't even belong to me in this moment—it's all his. And he's wielding it exactly how he wants.

"I can't believe how good this feels," I gasp, and he falls into a faster, more punishing pace. The heat behind my center intensifies, and my world narrows down to me and Jamie, here in his bed, connected like this.

He was there for me today at the recording studio. He's been there for me all along. My throat works as I gaze up at him. Emotion surges inside me, mixing with the climbing heat and pressure between my legs, and I might reach heaven before we're done here.

It's never been like this before.

"Pippa," Jamie grits out, and it seems like he's losing control. "I need you so bad. I've always needed you."

The expanding base of pleasure spreads, and I'm close. I'm so fucking close.

His eyes glaze but he won't take his piercing gaze off me. "You think you can come again?"

I don't have the capacity to say *god yes,* so I just jerk a nod, and his hand drifts between us, stroking my clit while he watches my reaction. So watchful, this guy, in every aspect of his life. So careful with me.

A fresh wave of arousal floods between us, and as he touches my clit in that perfect fucking way of his, so soft and fast, my muscles tighten around his thick cock.

"I'm almost there," I manage as my back starts to arch.

"Yes," Jamie urges me with a wrinkle of focus between his brows. I'm still climbing, the pleasure is still rising, and I feel suspended. Jamie's thrusts are turning erratic. "You're there. I know you are. Show me. Need to see it."

My body pulls taut as the intense waves start, radiating out from where Jamie drives into me. My pussy spasms, gripping him like a fist, and my legs shake around his waist as pressure bursts low in my belly. I hear a high moan, gasping, Jamie's name, and I realize it's me. I'm falling, clutching his hard chest and shoulders as I come, repeating his name over and over again as I tear apart at the seams. I'm vaguely aware of the fire in his eyes as he watches me lose my mind, the pleased, dark look in his eyes as I shatter around him.

Later, I'm going to write a song about this moment—being so connected to someone, feeling like nothing exists but me and Jamie.

His expression turns agonized, incredulous, and pained, and I feel him swell inside me.

"*Fuuuuck.*" He buries his face in my neck. "I'm going to come so fucking hard."

I reach up and lightly scrape my nails down his back. The pleasure has peaked inside me but I'm still shaking, still riding it out as his hips rock against mine.

"Coming." His voice is thick as he pounds into me, and I memorize the moment when Jamie Streicher gives himself over to me completely. He groans, fucking me so hard my breasts bounce, until his thrusts slow and his breathing turns deeper.

Nothing has ever felt so real and right.

"Holy fuck, Pippa." His mouth is against my neck, breathing me in, and I trail soft lines up and down his chest, his arms, his back.

He presses a kiss to my cheekbone, and I'm floating.

His mouth meets mine, and we smile against each other's lips.

I can't believe I ever thought I couldn't have this.

TWO DAYS after Pippa rearranged my entire state of consciousness, I approach the lunch spot where I'm meeting Erin.

"Mr. Streicher," the doorman says, opening the door, and I give him a nod hello.

To my total fucking shock, Erin was actually willing to talk to me. Thankfully, she's in town, and her show is on hiatus. The restaurant where I booked a table is known for being discreet and private, so we won't be bothered, even if we are recognized. The last thing I need is photos of us surfacing and rumors circulating. What Pippa and I have is still forming, and I don't want to cause problems early on.

Pippa. My chest eases the second I think of her.

My pretty songbird. My strong, beautiful, brave Pippa, who sings on stage when she's terrified and gets back on the ice.

Now that I have her, losing her isn't an option. I won't fuck this up.

The hostess leads me to the table, and Erin's already sitting there, texting. Her face has filled out, her hair is shorter, and her skin glows. My heart squeezes. I don't love Erin, but it's nice to see an old friend, even if I did hurt her.

And then the guilt hits again.

"Erin."

Her head whips up, and when she sees me, a big smile stretches across her face. She stands, and my gaze drops to her belly.

She's pregnant.

"Hey, you." She reaches for me, and I hug her. She still smells the same, like fruity shampoo.

We pull apart and take our seats, and I clear my throat as nerves rise.

"You find the place okay?" I ask.

She waves a hand with an easy smile. "Oh, yeah, I've been here with my agent."

A server takes our drink orders, and when he leaves, my pulse picks up. I'm just going to get right into it and not waste Erin's time. I take a deep breath, and across the table, it seems like she's doing the same.

"I'm sorry—" I start.

"I want to thank you—" she says at the same time.

We stare at each other with equally confused expressions.

She gestures at me. "You first."

"Okay." Another deep breath. Every ounce of guilt and regret tightens into a knot in my stomach. "I want to apologize for what happened between us. I know it was a long time ago and we were young, but..." I fold my arms over my chest, thinking about how I told myself *no* for so long. "These things can have a lasting effect." I lift my gaze to hers. "I wasn't clear with you about what I could handle in a relationship, and that's my fault."

She wrinkles her nose in confusion. "Huh?"

"The way I reacted when you thought you might be—" My gaze drops to her stomach. The internet said she was married, and there are a set of rings on her left hand. I bet her husband didn't stare at her in horror when she told him she was pregnant. "I shouldn't have reacted like that. I shouldn't have led you on about what we were. I ruined everything for you. Erin, I saw what they said about you." My heart twists with pain. "You were going to be a supermodel until I broke your heart."

She stares back at me, frozen, and there's a weird prickle in my brain.

My eyes dart to hers, suddenly unsure. "Right?"

Across the table, Erin bursts out laughing.

I blink, confused, as she shakes with bright, surprised laughter.

"Jamie." She shakes her head, eyes glittering. "You didn't ruin *anything*."

I frown as I flick through my memories. Her excitement at the potential pregnancy, her devastation at my reaction. Her pulling out of her upcoming fashion shows, dropping off the face of the earth for years. Her IMDb profile with a list of low-budget productions.

"First," she starts, "modeling made me miserable. You read that I was going to be a supermodel, but all I read about was how I was too heavy, too skinny, too ugly, too tall, too short." She swallows, and I see the pain in her eyes as she shakes her head. "I was never enough." The corner of her mouth turns up in a humorless smile. "When I realized how late I was for my period, my first thought was *now I get to leave modeling*. That's fucked up, right? That's not a great reason to have a kid."

A memory comes back to me of Erin skipping dinner because she was meeting with a designer the next day.

Her hand rests on her bump, and she shoots me a funny smile. "I already love this kid more than life itself, but at nineteen, being pregnant and having a kid would have been *tough*."

My mind is reeling. "You disappeared."

She shrugs. "I had to get away. I was a teenager with this

insane life and more money than I knew what to do with. I didn't even like most of my friends, I was hungry all the time, and I hated my life. So I bought a beach house in a small town and did yoga for a few years. I didn't have the internet or cable, so I read, painted, and hung out with the retired women on my street." She smiles again, and this time, it feels real. "When I was ready to go back to real life, I did, but it was on my terms."

There's a long pause where I take all this information in. I picture her life in the beach house, and my heart squeezes for her. She was miserable, and I didn't see it.

"Look," she continues, adjusting the position of her water glass. "You're not the first person to feel bad for me because I'm on a crappy cable show." Her expression turns wry. "I like the show, though. Josh and I love living in Vancouver, and the hours are really good. I'm home for dinner every night and I have weekends off. The cast and crew are cool, and they've been super accommodating with my pregnancy."

When I swallow, my throat is tight. "I'm sorry I didn't see how unhappy you were."

She offers me a sad smile. "You had your own stuff going on that year. And besides, if you saw it, you'd have tried to fix it, and the only person who could fix it was me."

Her words sink in, and I nod. She's right, I would have tried to fix her situation without any idea of how.

"How's your mom?" she asks.

"Better." It's been a few weeks now, and my mom avoids talking about therapy, but that's fine. I'm giving her space. She'll give me details when she's ready.

"Good." Erin smiles at me. "I'm glad."

We sit there a long moment in silence, and when I go back to that old guilt over what I did, I find nothing.

A weight lifts.

I didn't break Erin. I didn't crush her. The woman across

the table from me is a stronger, happier version of the girl I thought I hurt.

Erin is more resilient than I realized. She struggled, and she came out on top. Over the past few months, Pippa has conquered her fears again and again. I imagine her on New Year's Eve, singing on stage. The moment I realized I was in love with her. A bright, warm sensation expands in my chest.

"Wow," Erin says, blinking at me in mock-surprise. "A rare smile from *the* Jamie Streicher? Must be my lucky day."

I snort and smile wider. "Very funny."

"Enough about the past." She studies me. "What's new with you?"

"I met someone."

I say the words without thinking. Pippa is the biggest, brightest part of my life, and I'm excited about us. Telling Erin feels right.

Her eyes turn soft and she smiles. "Is this the girl I saw on the sports news?"

A laugh scrapes out of me. After my last game, the sports networks showed clips of me smiling at Pippa behind the glass.

*Streicher shut out after a Streich-ing smile!* they said.

It was the first time they'd seen me smile in public, the sports anchors joked.

"Yeah." I nod at Erin, and a smile twitches on my mouth. "That's her."

She just studies me with that kind, affectionate smile, and I know she's happy for me. "Tell me everything about her."

We spend the rest of lunch in a flurry of conversation. I show Erin the video from New Year's Eve, tell her about the guitar I bought Pippa, the trip out to Silver Falls, and show her every photo of Pippa and Daisy on my phone. She shows me photos from her wedding in Bali last year. When I tell her about the upcoming charity gala and how I'm going to take

Pippa dress shopping, she pulls out her phone and sends me a list of recommendations.

"That's where I go for dresses," Erin tells me about one place close to the apartment. "If you call the owner, you can arrange to have the store to yourselves." Her eyes twinkle. "Really make her feel special, you know?"

"Perfect." Something sparks in my chest at the thought of the gala. There's no way Pippa and I can walk into that place without people knowing we're together, and I'm strangely excited about that.

After lunch is over and I give Erin a hug goodbye, I walk home through the streets of Vancouver in a lighter mood than before.

This thing with Pippa is going to last. I can feel it.

IN THE MORNINGS, Jamie Streicher is warm, sleepy, and sexy as hell. He wakes me up with his lips on my neck, pressing soft kisses there as his hands roam my body. I pull back to see him smiling, so relaxed and at ease.

I love seeing him like this.

His gaze falls to my mouth, and there's an aching throb between my legs as lust flares in his gaze. His hair is unruly from bedhead, his eyes are puffy from sleep, and dark stubble spans his jawline. I can imagine exactly how that stubble would feel against my inner thighs.

In bed like this, Jamie Streicher looks supremely fuckable. Jamie's hand tangles in my hair and he pulls my mouth to his, letting out a hum against my lips that sounds like relief.

"Let's have a shower," he whispers, and I nod.

Minutes later, under the hot spray, Jamie makes me come with his fingers buried inside me.

"That's it," he murmurs as I start to tip, gasping into his chest, clenching up around him. "Ride my hand, songbird. Ride it out."

When I'm done, he reaches for the condom he left on the

windowsill beside the shower, turns me around, puts my hands on the shower tiles, and pushes inside me. He's a bit too much for me, but it sends waves of heat through my body as we come undone together.

"I can't get enough of you." His words are a desperate whisper in my ear, and I flutter with happy, sated warmth.

I feel the same way.

Jamie insists on washing my hair, massaging my scalp in slow, firm, drugging movements.

"How's this?"

"I'm a puddle," I tell him, eyes closed, melting as he works the muscles at the back of my neck. His low laugh makes me smile.

"Good."

I could get used to this. I could get used to this so hard.

———

"Remind me why I need to eat breakfast sitting in your lap?" I ask, turning to Jamie between sips of coffee. Daisy's eating her breakfast, I'm reading news from the music industry, and Jamie's watching old game tape against Calgary. They have another game tonight, which is why he has the morning off, and I know he's antsy about playing Rory again.

"It's good for you," he lies, giving my hip a squeeze.

"Good for *you*, you mean," I laugh, and he rewards me with one of those sweet kisses on my temple.

We eat in content silence for a few minutes before his hand rubs across my back.

"Any word from Ivy?"

"Nope." The first few days, I checked my email incessantly, but being on edge constantly was exhausting, and now I only check a few times a day. "That's okay, though," I tell him, and it's the truth. "I'm just happy I did it. I can't control what happens on her side, but if she was interested, others could be, too."

Jamie watches me, listening.

I shrug and smile to myself. "I'm proud of myself for doing it. It was hard and scary, but I did it."

"You did." His tone is pleased as he tucks a lock of my hair behind my ear. "I'm proud of you, too." He glances at the time on his phone. "We should get going."

I send him a curious look. "Go where?"

He grins. "To buy your dress for the gala."

------

The tiny store is empty when we arrive except for a woman in her forties with a dark pixie cut and a big smile. From the outside, the shop appears modest, with just one dress artfully arranged in the window, but inside, jaw-dropping gowns cascade from the ceiling, adorned with feathers, sequins, beading. Some dresses are simple, with flowing, smooth fabric. Some are works of art, with thousands of tiny flower buds sewn onto their skirts. One has a neckline that goes to the navel, and that dress scares me.

"Welcome," the woman says, striding toward us. "You must be Pippa."

She introduces herself as Miranda, the owner. "Jamie, can you please lock the door?" she asks. At my confused look, she explains, "Your gentleman has requested we have the shop to ourselves this morning."

Jamie winks at me. When he said he wanted to buy me a dress, I thought I'd go by myself and buy it on the card he gave me. I didn't expect *this*.

"Every dress is unique and special." Miranda's eyes sparkle. Her voice has this lovely calm energy, like when Hazel's teaching yoga, and I immediately feel at ease here. "Shall we find a dress as beautiful as you?"

I blush and give her a quick nod. She leads me into the back, where a mirrored area is curtained off with thick red velvet. A brown leather couch sits outside the changing area. A few dresses hang, waiting for me. One catches my eye—a blue-gray piece, a few shades darker than my eye color. Dark, moody flowers flow down the skirt, giving the illusion that they're pouring out of the bodice. On the hanger, it's hard to tell the dress's shape, but the rich colors glow under the store's warm lighting.

Miranda has pulled a few dresses that she thought might suit me and the event, so Jamie takes a seat on the couch while I step into the dressing room and slip my clothes off. She pops in from time to time to add clips to adjust the sizing, help me with a zip, or help me out of a gown, but nothing feels quite right.

I save the blue dress for last, but the second I slip it over my head, I know.

The fabric is soft against my skin, and something about the weight of the dress feels divine. In the mirror, I study the details, the bold slices of color, the delicate shape. This *dress*. The bodice is velvet, and when Miranda zips me up, it's a perfect fit. The giant flowers make me feel pretty, special, and happy. This dress is an elevated version of the one I wore to the wrap party. Miranda leaves the dressing room, and my heart bursts with excitement as I think about walking into the gala in this dress with Jamie.

"Pippa?" Jamie's low voice comes from outside on the couch. "Show me."

I slip out, and the second he sees me, his gaze flashes with heat. I'm suddenly shy, but I can't ignore the sparks skittering over my skin as he takes me in. Miranda is nowhere to be seen, giving us space.

"I like this one," I say lightly.

He stares for a moment longer before closing his eyes, like he's sobering himself. "Fuck," he mutters, adjusting himself. "Pippa." He says it like a curse.

I chuckle. "What?"

His gaze is back on me in the dress, and his jaw tenses as he stands up. My heart flutters as he walks over to me, gaze locked on mine, before he presses a soft, loving kiss to my lips.

I can't get a full breath, and my head is spinning.

"You're beautiful," he says quietly.

I smile up at him. "You make me feel beautiful."

He looks at me like there are a thousand kind, loving things he wants to say. But instead, he just smiles. "Good." He glances pointedly down at my dress. "Do you want this dress?"

"How much does it cost?" I ask first.

He snorts and shakes his head with amusement.

"Tell me," I insist.

"No." His eyes are full of laughter, and a smile lifts on that mouth I used to think was cruel. "Do you want this dress?" he asks again.

The guitar already cost so much money, and now this? I'm torn.

"Pippa." He dips his head to catch my eyes, and his fingers come to my chin, tilting my face up to his. "I don't think you understand." His eyes are steady, warm, kind, and serious. "Anything you want, songbird? It's yours. Where you're concerned, money is no object, because making you happy is worth it."

I shouldn't love this. I'm not a material person, and money isn't important.

Jamie being generous and wanting to please me, though? It makes me melt.

"I'm buying you the dress, and you're not going to argue. I'm going to buy you more things, and you won't argue about those, either." His eyes hold mine. "Okay?"

I nod wordlessly, trying not to smile at his satisfied, posses-sive expression. Bliss—I think that's what this feeling is called.

"Good." He steals a kiss before returning to the couch, and for the thousandth time, I admire how he moves with such power and grace. I don't think I'll ever get sick of that. He tilts his chin at the change room. "Now go change so I can take you for lunch."

I smother a smile. Miranda pops back in to mark and pin alterations before helping me out of the dress. I'm tying my sneakers up when my phone pings with an email. It could be Ivy Matthews, so I check it, but when I see who sent the message, my stomach drops.

*Can we talk? I texted you but I think you changed your number.*

My hands shake, gripping the phone as I read his message over and over again.

"Pippa?" Jamie's low voice travels through the curtain. "You okay?"

I realize that I've been in here for a while. How long have I been staring at his message, frozen? My throat knots as I swal-low. I'm still shaking with anger.

"Can I come in?"

It's like he can sense when I'm upset.

"Yes," I say quietly.

He steps into the small space. "What's going on?"

His voice is so caring, so concerned, that I just break.

"Zach emailed me," I tell him, showing him the phone.

Anger and resentment tear through me, and I blow a frustrated breath out. "He texted me the day you got back from traveling but I blocked him." My heart pounds as Jamie glares at the phone, reading the message. "I don't want to talk to him. I don't know why he's messaging me." I shake my head hard. "I don't want this."

"Why didn't you tell me?"

"I blocked him. I thought he'd go away." I suck in a deep breath, trying to shove all this Zach-related anger away, but it doesn't work. "It was the day before I recorded with Ivy. I just wanted to forget him and focus."

He sighs. "Yeah. I understand that." He turns his full attention to me. "You can tell me about this stuff. We can figure it out together."

I look up at him, and his eyes search mine with worry. "I know." I grab my phone, open my email, and block his email address. "There," I tell Jamie with a firm nod. "We'll have to keep the windows closed in case he tries carrier pigeon next."

A sharp laugh scrapes out of his throat, and he drops a quick kiss onto my cheek before we go settle up with Miranda. Neither of them will tell me how much the dress costs, and Miranda and I set a time for me to pick the dress up after the alterations are finished.

As Jamie and I thank her and say goodbye, she leans in. "Undergarments will be included with the dress." She winks conspiratorially, and I give her a funny smile. Miranda's lovely, but I'm not sure if I want her to buy me underwear.

After lunch, we head home so Jamie can nap before the game, and I text with Hazel about the event in Whistler. As part of the team, she's going, too.

*Uh. We have a problem*, she texts me. *I just saw the guest list.*

*???*, I respond. Last I checked, they were still finalizing it.

*Forwarded you the email. They're still trying to sell the last tables. Table 16 is going to be an issue.*

My email pings. That familiar nausea rises when I see who's sitting at Table 16.

Zach Hanson.

THAT EVENING, the arena's energy is tense. The players, the coaches, the fans—everyone's on edge, including me.

He *texted* her. The memory of Pippa's face this morning replays in my head, and my blood pounds with fury. Pippa is *mine*, and he has the fucking audacity to reach out to her.

Before the game, she reluctantly showed me the list of attendees. He's going to be at the gala, and I know it's because of her.

*You don't have to go,* I told her. My attendance is mandatory, but hers isn't.

Instead of cowering, her nostrils flared, she tilted her chin up, and determination flashed in her eyes. *I'm going,* she said. *I'm not going to let him scare me away.*

My fucking heart. Pippa has it in the palm of her hand.

On the ice, the other goalie catches the puck and the whistle blows. My shoulders tense as I watch Miller and Volkov exchange heated words.

I don't know what Calgary's coach is playing at, but our team has been taking nasty hits all night. The refs don't seem to notice, which only fires up the fans and our team even more. Miller's back to his usual cocky, fight-provoking self.

The bad energy hangs in the air like a mist. There's going to be a fight, I can feel it.

One of Calgary's defensemen crosschecks our third line forward long after he passes the puck.

Still no whistle.

Volkov yells something at the other team's player, and the tension bubbles into a boil. Miller skates between them, grinning like a sly cat, but there's no humor on his face. He's different tonight. Colder. Unhappy. Pissed off.

He looks like his dad, who's a rich, miserable asshole, and as I watch Miller get in Volkov's face, I wonder how much of that got passed on.

Play resumes. Our team tries to get the puck in the Calgary net, but Miller wedges his stick between Owens' legs. The fans are on their feet, booing and calling for a penalty.

The whistle blows as Calgary's goalie catches the puck, and I turn to get a drink of water, locking eyes with Pippa behind the glass. She smiles and gives me a small wave, and I nod at her, spraying water through my mask, thinking about how good she looks in that jersey. My jersey. My chest pulls tight at the sight of her, here, supporting me, wearing my name proudly.

This girl is everything to me.

The players line up to resume the game, and I get into the ready position. The whistle blows, and Miller trips one of our guys.

It's like he's not even trying. Like he doesn't care about hockey. When he cares, he's unstoppable, and that's probably why he's still on the fucking team. The spark he used to have for the game is gone, though.

Finally, he's thrown into the penalty box, and the arena hollers and jeers. People slam their fists on the glass, and he shakes his glove off before flipping them the bird.

I inhale sharply. I see it now. He used to pull this shit when we were teenagers. His dad would say something to upset him, and he'd hit the ice in a mood. He antagonizes players, he fires up the fans, he makes himself the villain so everyone will see him like he sees himself. The guy hates himself, and he's flailing out here, hoping someone will give him what he deserves.

When his two-minute penalty is over, he skates back into the game, capturing the puck immediately and heading straight to my net. He slaps the puck at me. It pings off the pipe—fucking lucky—and a moment later, he crosschecks me.

My temper ignites, and my blood whooshes in my ears. The whistle is distant because fans roar around us, rattling the glass.

"What the fuck?" Owens bites out, getting in Miller's face.

Miller's eyes challenge me. The energy cracks around us, sparking and buzzing with tension.

"What's the matter, Streicher?"

"You're in a fucking mood tonight." I tap Owens, indicating for him to move out of the way, and he skates back, watching us. The rest of the players are circling, waiting, watching.

"*Fight, fight, fight,*" the fans chant from behind the glass.

The fight I felt in the air—it's me and Miller.

We've only fought once. We were sixteen. He showed up for practice in a foul mood after something his dad said, and he pulled all the same shit he pulled tonight.

"What?" He cocks an ugly, hateful grin at me. "You going to hit me? You, up in your ivory tower? Jamie Streicher, the most responsible guy in the room."

The noise around us fades away as I glare at him, gritting my teeth at his baiting.

"Come on," he spits at me, eyes flashing. "I deserve it, don't I?"

My fists clench. *He* was the one who changed. He was the

one who turned into a fucking asshole. He used to care about hockey. Now it's a big fucking joke to him.

Everything's a joke to him.

"Go on," he goads.

Blood rushes in my ears. In the NHL, both players need to agree to a fight, or the player who instigates will get a penalty while the other doesn't.

All the anger I've held inside for years at the guy who used to be my best friend bubbles to the surface, overflowing, and I rip my gloves off.

The crowd roars. Goalies almost never fight.

I pull my helmet off, and the glass behind me shakes from the fans. The refs and linesmen circle us, ready to break up the fight when it goes too far. Until then, they'll let us deal with it, because this is how the score is settled in hockey.

I don't dare look at Pippa. I can hold my own in a fight, but I don't want her worry and concern in my head as I do this.

"Fucking finally," Miller snaps, and I remove my goalie pads and toss them aside.

I skate at him, and his fist flies. I block his punch before throwing my own. It connects with his jaw, and a second later, his fist sears the outer corner of my eye.

It hurts, and it feels good.

Chaos breaks out around us. Fists fly as players let the pressure off, clutching each other's jerseys as they land punches. The energy in the arena boils over. I've never heard it this loud in here. My blood beats hard, flooded with adrenaline as Miller and I take out our aggression on each other.

The fight is all instinct, all primal rage. I'm gripping his jersey, he's gripping mine, and we're hitting each other. The pain feels cathartic, and my face is wet. There's blood in my mouth and more trickling down from Miller's eyebrow.

Whistles blow left and right, and it's a tangle of limbs,

helmets rolling around on the ice, guys sitting on each other, jerseys getting ripped.

The fans are going nuts.

I land one more punch and wait as Miller straightens up, the linesmen struggling to pull us apart. The fight dies from his eyes as he catches his breath, watching me.

"Done?" he asks.

He means the fight, but I think he means this seven-year tension. I wipe the back of my hand over my mouth. Blood smears over my skin. My chest heaves for air, and adrenaline whistles through my veins.

Something shifts between us, and my anger deflates. I don't want to be angry anymore. I just want to move on. I glance at Pippa, who's peeking through her hands with a worried expression, and my heart clutches.

I don't want to hold a grudge, because life is too short and sweet. I give Pippa a nod to say I'm okay.

On the bench, I expect Ward to be livid as players get hauled into the penalty boxes, but instead, his smile stretches from ear to ear.

"Yeah," I tell Miller, meeting his gaze. "Done."

# CHAPTER 63

"YOUR EYE," I gasp when Jamie finds me in one of the staff hallways at the arena after the game. My hand automatically drifts up to his cheekbone, careful not to brush it. The area around his eye is swollen and bruising, and his lip is cut.

"I'm okay, songbird." The untouched corner of his lip quirks up. Despite the bruises, he seems lighter than before the game, less stressed. "Do I look hideous?"

"You're too handsome to look hideous. You look even hotter with the black eye."

His eyes spark with amusement. "You think I'm handsome?"

"You know I do. Bossy and demanding, but unfairly handsome."

His smile lifts even higher, and I don't miss the way his hand comes to my lower back as he leads me down the hallway to the parking garage. I look up at him again, so tall, his hair still damp from his shower. My gaze falls to his lip and I can feel the worry all over my expression.

He chuckles and stops walking. "I promise you." He pulls my hand to his chest, flattening his palm over mine so I can feel the steady thump of his heart. "Feel that?"

His eyes are on me, watching me with affectionate amusement. I nod, and I can't look away.

"Still beating." He studies me, and it feels like he wants to say more.

"What happened out there tonight?"

His thumb strokes over the back of my hand absently as he looks away. "Miller and I settled what's been building for a long time."

I've never heard the arena like it was tonight. The fans were livid and bloodthirsty. Watching Jamie fight tore my heart out, but it also tugged on something between my legs. He looked like a warrior, all power, strength, and brutality.

It was hot.

He strokes my skin again, and I remember the other night, him moving on top of me, and the agonized expression on his face as he came. My center flutters at the idea of it.

"Let's go home." His eyes trail over my face, and my gaze snags on his cut lip again.

Tonight, I'm going to take care of my goalie.

———

Jamie frowns at the huge bathtub piled high with bubbles. His bathroom smells like my vanilla chai bubble bath. He's shirtless, dressed in only low-slung athletic pants, and I'm trying not to get distracted by the deep-cut V muscles leading into the waistband.

"Get in," I tell him, gesturing at the tub.

His eyebrow goes up, and he winces. The bruise around his eye is getting darker. "You want me to have a bubble bath." His tone is flat.

"Mhm. It'll help you feel better."

His gaze flares with heat, and I get another glimpse of him

from last night, mindlessly thrusting into me, moaning into my hair. His gaze drops to my lips, and his tongue slides over the cut on his mouth.

"Only if you get in with me."

The flutters between my legs intensify and heat crawls up my neck.

"Fine," I say, and a dark look flashes through his eyes.

When he slides his pants and boxers off, he's already hard, jutting out thick and proud. There's something in his eyes that I like, a little bit of pride, a lot of arousal, and a possessiveness that sends a shiver through me. His muscles move as he gets into the tub—his thick thighs, the ridges of his abs, his rounded, strong shoulders as he lowers himself into the water. He settles back and his gaze sharpens, pinning me.

"Your turn," he says, and the way his mouth tugs up feels dangerous.

Anticipation pumps in my veins. I pull my jersey off, laying it on the counter before I start to take my sweater over my head.

"Slower."

He props his elbow on the side of the tub as he watches, and although his body language is relaxed, his eyes are determined. Watchful, cataloging me. This is what he looks like on the ice, watching every move.

My clothes come off slowly, and heat clenches between my legs as his eyes darken. Finally, I'm naked, and a muscle ticks in his jaw.

I step one foot in the tub, and my breath catches.

"It's hot," I whisper.

"Come here." He leans forward and guides me between his legs, back against his chest, just like the time with the toy. His cock rests against his stomach, pressing into my backside, sending thrills through me. I sigh in comfort as he locks his arms across my collarbone, pulling me against him. "That's better."

I feel his low voice through his chest, and we sit there in comfortable silence as the bathroom fogs up. My fingers trail a slow path up and down his thighs, and he relaxes around me, breath turning steady. Eventually, his hands slide over my skin to my shoulders and his thumbs dig into my traps, working out the tension in the muscles.

"How's your face feeling?"

His laugh is low. "Hardly feeling it right now." He drops a kiss onto my shoulder, and I smile. "You're the perfect distraction."

He brushes the skin between my breasts, light as a butterfly, but my nerves dance with his touch, and I feel it everywhere. I've never done this with a guy, just sit in the bathtub and explore each other's bodies. His fingers drift to my nipple, circling it, and the breath whooshes out of my lungs at the sharp ache between my legs.

Against my lower back, his cock pulses, and he drops another kiss to my shoulder.

"You're supposed to be resting," I whisper. He tugs and rolls the peak before moving to the other, and it's making my head spin, it feels so good.

"How does this feel?" he asks in a low voice, ignoring me.

"Good." My eyes fall closed as he pinches me, and my center clenches around nothing. The water is so warm, his hard body is so comfortable against mine, and my head fits perfectly against his shoulder as I melt into him.

His mouth is on my temple. "Where do you feel this, songbird? Tell me."

"My chest." I sigh as his fingers work, lulling me into a delicious, hazy state of arousal.

"Mhm. Where else?"

God, his voice is so fucking sexy, murmured in my ear like that. "Between my legs."

"Really." He says it like he's not surprised.

I nod, eyes closed, and sigh again as his big hand cups my breast, weighing it, massaging.

"I can't stop thinking about last night," he tells me, lips brushing my ear, and I shiver.

"Me neither," I breathe. "And this morning."

"Seeing you come is a dream, Pippa. I'm addicted to it." His hand drifts down my stomach, trailing light touches that I feel in every nerve ending. "I've pictured making you come in a thousand different ways. Bent over the kitchen counter. In the back seat of my car. In my bed. In your bed." At the brush of his hand over my clit, I jerk, muscles tightening.

He cups my pussy, and on instinct, my hips tilt, seeking friction. My clit aches as my legs press outward into his.

"Needy." Without moving his hand, his teeth nip my shoulder and my hips tilt again. "So fucking needy."

"You're playing with me."

His laugh is low and pleased. "What do you need?"

"Touch me. Fuck me. Fill me, Jamie."

I can't believe the words coming out of my mouth. I've never said these things before, but then again, I never felt this way before.

He lets out a hoarse groan. "That mouth. That pretty, dirty mouth." His mouth traces the shell of my ear. Heat builds low in my belly, and I know that whatever he does, it won't take long to make me come. "Now what? Show me."

My hand covers his, and I slide it lower, pressing on two of his thick fingers near my entrance. He pushes them inside me, and I gasp, arching against him at the delicious stretching ache as I accommodate him.

"Like that?" he asks, smug.

"You *know* it's like that," I manage as he strokes in and out.

"What else? What else do you need to get there?"

"Clit." My voice is thin and strained, and I'm clutching his thighs, trying to breathe.

His palm presses against my clit, dragging over it with the movement of his fingers, and my eyes roll back. My head spins at the intensity.

"There we go," he murmurs against my temple, and his pleased tone makes me flush. "Such a good girl for me. Such a fast learner. Are you ready to come?"

I nod frantically.

"Use your words."

"Please." It falls from my lips as a moan. "I need to come."

His groan vibrates through my back, and his cock presses into me insistently. "Love it when you beg me."

He crooks his fingers inside me, finding the spot that blanks my thoughts out. His fingers are just a little too thick, but the light, aching sting nudges me closer to my release. His other hand settles around my neck, gentle but possessive, and I only want to be his.

I cry out at the first tremors.

"Yeah." His tone is smug, and I wish I could see his face. "That's it right there, isn't it?"

I shake as intense pressure builds. When he touches that spot, my body floods with bright, intense sensation.

"Jamie," I whimper.

It feels too good. Too much. The friction on my clit, his arm around my waist, anchoring me to him, his lips against my temple, his thick fingers punishing me—electricity courses through my muscles as the wave gains strength.

It peaks, and I crash.

"I'm coming." The words are puffs of air as I shake, suspended while pleasure pulses through me from my center.

I'm clamping down on his fingers, pressed into him from head to toe, writhing under the pure fucking ecstasy that is a Jamie Streicher-induced orgasm.

"So good," he murmurs as I come. "Good girl. Perfect. Just like that, baby. You're so tight around my fingers."

I fade back, and Jamie's hand smooths up and down my thigh while I catch my breath.

He lets out a ragged sigh. "I love doing that."

"You're very, very good at it," I say lightly, and when he brushes my clit, I jerk, laughing. "Too sensitive."

His laugh is low against my hair, and it puts a dumb, goofy smile on my face as he settles me back against his body.

When we get out of the tub, Jamie insists on drying me off. He's still hard, and as he pulls the towel around my back, tipping a small grin at me, I reach for his gorgeous cock.

He groans, and I smile up at him as I draw my thumb over his tip, over the bead of liquid there. I lift it to my lips, and my eyes fall closed at the taste. When I open them, his expression is agonized, dark eyes glazed and jaw tight.

I'm growing to love this moment where I hold complete power over him.

I get an idea and bite my lip before reaching for my jersey on the counter. Anticipation lights me up, because I think he's going to like this. With the jersey in one hand, I lead him to the bedroom.

"What—" His words cut off as I pull it over my head, and his eyes travel down my form, flashing with lust. "Fuck."

I sink to my knees, and his eyes darken.

"*FUCK*," Jamie mutters again, jaw tightening.

Lust and affection weave together in my chest as I stroke him, watching his focused frown. Jamie's so special, and he deserves to be taken care of the way he takes care of everyone else. And with the expression on his face right now, so trusting and desperate for me?

I love this guy so much.

His hands sink into his own hair as I play with his length. His cock is undeniably perfect—thick and long, smooth and hard, and when I lick the liquid off the end, more appears.

"You're going to wear my jersey while you suck my cock." He says it like he can't believe it, and I smile again.

"Yep."

I slide my lips around him, watching his eyes gleam with intensity and focus. He's thick in my mouth, a snug fit, and my intimate muscles squeeze. I take his length as far as I can before my cheeks hollow out with suction, and his head falls back with a tortured groan.

I smile around him before I do it again. Slow, so slow. I know he's had blowjobs before, but that flame in my chest that's gotten brighter these past few months wants this to be the best fucking blowjob of Jamie Streicher's life.

I suck Jamie's cock at an agonizing pace. I want him to think about this one for a long time.

"Songbird, you're killing me here." His voice is guttural, and torturing him is making me wet all over again.

"You said slower, earlier."

He huffs out a sharp, pained laugh. "Fuck."

I keep my pace slow and steady, running my tongue over his tip each time I pull back before taking him all the way to the back of my throat.

He groans, and his fingers settle in my hair, so gentle but flexing each time I add suction. "Jesus fuck. This is going to make me come so hard." His gaze falls to my jersey. "You sucking my cock while wearing my jersey is the hottest thing I've ever seen."

Pleasure twists through me, and I smile around him. I *love* this. I love making him feel this way. I love having this man at my mercy.

He lets out a low moan, and he pulses in my mouth. I don't speed up, though. I just keep this pace, keep taking him to the back of my mouth, keep dancing my tongue over him. The noises he makes are incredible—low moans of anguish like he's wounded, like he'll never recover from this.

"Yes," he gasps, moaning again, watching me with fascination. "Yes. Now. Going to come, Pippa."

My gaze is encouraging as I hum in approval, and he tenses, abs rippling.

"Fuck, baby, fuck. Yes," he grits, spilling salty liquid into my mouth. His fingers twitch against my scalp. "Pippa. Fucking love this."

He fills my mouth and I swallow it down. He watches like

I've stolen his soul, and he's not even mad about it. He pulls back, heaving for air, gaze still on me as I drag my finger over my lips, catching any spillover.

In a rush, he hauls me to my feet, and his mouth is on mine, tongue stroking into me, hands in my hair, walking me back to the bed.

"So fucking good," he growls against my mouth between kisses. "That's the hardest I've ever come. My legs are shaking. Get this off." He lifts the jersey over my head before he lowers us to the bed and tucks me into his chest, one arm under me and one locking around me.

We look at each other for a long moment.

I want to say it, but now that we're in this, the thought of losing him terrifies me. I know he'd never do any of the things that Zach did, but there's no guarantee what we have right now won't fade away one day. Telling him I love him would make a breakup so much worse. I'm frozen like I'm standing on a crumbling cliff, rocks breaking off around me, and any sudden movement will bring the whole thing down.

Tomorrow, we drive up to Whistler for the charity gala. I can picture it—his hand on my lower back, the private smile he reserves just for me. My heart aches. I want it to be real and forever.

Jamie's eyes flicker with an emotion I can't pin down.

"I want to tell you something," he murmurs.

My heart stutters.

"I—" He stops himself, searching my eyes.

I wait, and it feels like I'm standing on that cliff edge again, clinging to it. I'm equal parts terrified and excited at whatever is about to fall out of his mouth.

He blinks like he's pulling himself back, reining it in. "I'm really looking forward to going to the gala with you."

*Even if that asshole is there*, we're both not saying.

"Me too," I whisper.

His lips press to my forehead, and we fall asleep like that.

THE NEXT DAY, Jamie pulls up to the hotel in Whistler, and I gape at the elegant, chateau-style building. It's the highest-rated luxury hotel in Whistler, where all the celebrities stay, and with the whimsical winter lights and snow-topped trees, it looks like something out of a fairy tale.

Anxiety weaves into my mind, because Zach's going to be there tonight. Maybe he's even staying in the hotel. My stomach tightens. This morning, my phone buzzed with an unknown number, but I ignored it. They didn't leave a voice-mail, but I have a cold, sinking feeling that it was Zach.

I really, really don't want to run into him, but more than that, I don't want to bail on Jamie. He bought me a gorgeous dress, we arranged for Donna to watch Daisy all weekend, and this feels like our first trip together. I don't want my dickhead ex to get in the way of that.

"Welcome, Mr. Streicher," the valet says, taking Jamie's keys when he steps out of the car.

Jamie thanks him, and when the valet walks around to open my door, Jamie shakes his head. "I got it, thanks." He opens my door and lifts his eyebrows at me, the corner of his mouth tipping up.

I climb out and give him a shy smile. "Thanks."

His eyes are soft. "Don't mention it."

"We'll take your bags," the valet says. "I hope you and your wife have a wonderful stay."

I open my mouth to correct him.

"Thank you," Jamie tells him, guiding me to the front door. I look up at him in surprise, and he just winks at me.

Wife?

I've never even considered that word. I'm only twenty-four, but hearing that word in Jamie's vicinity makes my breath catch. Wife. Jamie's wife. My mouth pulls into a smile and I bite it down. The warning thoughts at the edge of my mind jump around for attention, but I pretend I don't see them.

After we check in, Jamie leads us upstairs to the top floor, and when he opens the door of our suite, my jaw drops.

"Wow," I say stupidly, staring at the cavernous lodge-style suite with floor-to-ceiling windows, cozy decor, and an incredible view of the snowy mountains. The fireplace is on, adding to the cozy vibe, and in the room off the living room, a king-sized bed with a fluffy white duvet begs me to flop down onto it.

The corner of Jamie's mouth twitches, and his eyes are full of amusement.

"Is this the kind of place you stay in when you travel with the team?" I ask.

He huffs. "No. I'm usually rooming with another player. I upgraded once you said you'd be my date."

Something sweet fizzes in my chest, and I cock a teasing look at him. "There's only one bed."

His eyes flare with heat. "Mhm." He steps toward me, and his hands come to my upper arms. "Is that okay?"

Our eyes lock, and it's hard to get a full breath under the intensity of his sharp green gaze.

"Totally okay." I bite back a grin and gesture at the giant L-shaped couch. "The couch looks big enough for you."

A laugh bursts out of his chest, and I get one of those rare, intoxicating Jamie Streicher smiles. We've been sleeping in the same bed since the day of the recording session.

His phone buzzes, interrupting us.

"Hi," he answers, pausing a moment to listen. "Ready anytime. Thanks." He hangs up and lifts his eyebrows at me. "The massage therapist will be here any minute."

Oh. I didn't realize he had booked himself a massage. A hesitant feeling flares. "A woman?"

His snort is derisive, like it's obvious. "Yes."

I hate the idea of a woman touching him. I *know* she's likely a professional, and that he's sore and in pain after yesterday's game. A massage will make him feel better.

I still don't like it. Jamie's gorgeous and ripped. Head to toe, he looks like a god. I don't even like the idea of a woman *thinking* horny thoughts around him.

He glances at me, gaze falling to my chest. I'm wearing one of his hoodies; it's huge on me, but he stares at my body like he did earlier this morning in the shower.

"I'm a patient guy, Pippa, but I don't want another guy touching what's mine."

My face screws up in confusion. Does he mean, like... his dick? We're at the nicest hotel in Whistler. I doubt they'll give him a rub and tug.

"Jamie, a professional massage therapist isn't going to give you a happy ending," I blurt out.

He stares at me, equally confused. "I fucking hope not." His eyebrows knit. "The massage is for you."

"Oh." I let out a high laugh, and my face burns. "Sorry."

He tilts his head, eyes narrowing.

"What?" I ask, turning to hide how red I'm going, but his

hands land on my shoulders and he turns me back around.

"You're jealous," he says, studying my face with a twitching mouth.

I roll my eyes. "Stop it."

"You are." His eyes are so bright. Smug. So fucking smug. "You're jealous because you thought a woman was going to give me a massage."

I shrug, and he pulls me against him.

"So fucking cute," he mutters. "Like I have eyes for anyone else."

A moment later, there's a knock at the door, and Jamie opens it to let her in.

"Hair and makeup arrives at four," he tells me as she sets up, dropping a kiss onto the top of my head. He smiles at my baffled expression, stepping away to gather his things for a light gym workout. "Just wanted you to feel special."

"I do," I tell him truthfully. "Thank you."

"Don't mention it." He's at the door but doubles back to me, kissing me again like he can't help it. "If I don't leave now, I never will."

I smile against his mouth, gently pushing on his chest while laughing. I'm overflowing with delight, and I can't stop smiling.

He leaves, and later, as the massage therapist works on my traps, I let myself replay the past few weeks with Jamie.

Something thrashes in my chest, desperate to get out. What if I told him how I felt? The damage is done; I'm in love with the guy. I've been telling myself that keeping it a secret will keep me safe. It'll hurt less if it ends.

Is that true, though? Or will not telling him how I feel be one of my biggest regrets?

I think about how he's encouraged me over the past few months. What's the point of learning to push myself out of my comfort zone if I don't do it for the things that matter?

Jamie matters. I think he might matter more than almost anyone.

*Touching what's mine*, he said earlier, and something stirs in my chest.

Floating in this blissed-out, happy, in-between zone is starting to not be enough for me anymore.

I need to tell Jamie how I feel.

———

Jamie gets back just as I finish putting the undergarments on that Miranda provided for my gown.

Okay, I wouldn't call them undergarments.

They're lingerie. I'm wearing lingerie. Lacy, expensive, seductive-as-hell lingerie made in France. My hair is loose around my shoulders in polished waves, and the makeup artist did a soft yet sexy look that makes me look like a Victoria's Secret model.

I'll admit it—I look insanely hot.

"Pippa?" Jamie calls, and I hear his footsteps.

"In the bedroom."

Until moments ago, I was the only one here, so I didn't bother closing the door. Jamie appears in the doorway and stops short at the sight of me.

"Hi." I smile at him, embarrassed that I'm standing here alone, staring at myself in lingerie. "I was just getting dressed."

"Fucking hell, Pippa." His eyes darken, gaze moving from my face down my body, and then back up. "Stay right there."

"What are you—"

He strides over, sinks to his knees in front of me, and yanks my panties down.

"Oh—" My words cut off as he licks a firm line up my pussy. "Do you, should I..." My eyes roll as his tongue swirls around my clit in fast circles. Wow. It's hard to think when he does that. I'm already wet. "Do you want me to lie on the bed?"

"No." He groans, burying his face deeper between my legs. He hooks a big hand around the back of my thigh, pulling it over his shoulder, and my hands fly to his hair for balance. "Don't want to mess up your pretty hair. We should probably do it like this."

"Okay," I sigh, eyes falling closed as he slides two fingers inside me.

Later, after I come all over Jamie's mouth, I happily reciprocate.

"You're going to wear this again," he says, catching his breath, nostrils flaring as he runs his fingers over the strap of my garter.

"Fine by me." I kiss him and rake my hands through his thick hair. "We should probably finish getting dressed."

After I'm finished getting ready and Jamie's showered and dressed, I walk into the living room in my gown. My breath catches at the sight of him standing by the big windows, gazing out at the snow-covered mountain with his hands in his pockets, looking so handsome and strong in his tux. He turns at the sound of my footsteps.

"Pippa." He says my name like a prayer, taking me in. He blinks at me like I'm a dream. "You're so beautiful." He pulls his hand out of his pocket, holding a small black box. "I got you something."

He flips it open, and my lips part. On a delicate silver chain, a blue-gray stone catches the light, sparkling brilliantly. It's the same color as my dress. Something warm floods my chest and it's hard to get a full breath.

"It's beautiful." I glance up at Jamie, and he's watching me with interest. "It's too much," I tell him, because my heart is exploding into confetti right now.

"Do you like it?"

I nod, gazing at the necklace. I can't help but smile. It's gorgeous. "I love it."

"Then it isn't too much." He gently lifts the necklace out and unlatches the clasp with impressive dexterity. It's so funny, seeing his big hands hold something so dainty. He tilts his chin at me. "Turn around, songbird." His voice is low, and a shiver runs down my back.

I do as I'm told, and Jamie drapes the necklace over me. More shivers run down my spine as his fingers brush the back of my neck.

"There," he says, and I turn. His gaze drops to the necklace, and when he gives me that small, serious smile, my stomach does a slow, warm roll forward. "Beautiful."

"Thank you." I bite my lip, looking down at the necklace, running my fingers along the fine chain. "I love it."

"Good."

My smile is shy as I glance down at my dress. Everything about today, about my life right now, feels like a fairy tale. The princess goes to the ball in a beautiful dress, swooning over the handsome prince.

It's not just the dress, or the necklace, or the lingerie, or the hair and makeup. I feel beautiful around Jamie. I never felt more special and beautiful than I did sitting on Jamie's lap the other morning, with no makeup, with wet, messy hair, wearing his old hockey hoodie. The confidence he's helped me build over the past few months has seeped into my veins—every time he said *you can do it* or *I believe in you* or *you're so talented, songbird*—and now it's a part of me.

I give Jamie the brightest smile I have. "Let's go, handsome."

He laughs in surprise, and I can tell he likes that nickname.

OUTSIDE THE BALLROOM, Jamie's hand slips into mine, and his serious, watchful gaze searches my face.

My heart is pounding. In the elevator, he didn't want to mess up my makeup, so he kissed a soft, torturous line down my neck as I watched our reflection in the mirror, breathless. Part of me wanted to stay in that elevator forever so I didn't have to face Zach. Part of me couldn't believe the gorgeous, towering guy in a tux was mine. And part of me roared with anger and resentment for Zach pushing his way back into my life like this after what he did.

Jamie's thumb strokes against my hand. We're about to encounter the person who hurt me, and his protective instincts are flaring, just like at the wrap party. Except this time, it's worse, because Zach stole my song and made it his.

I drag a deep breath in, looking up at him, counting every dark eyelash rimming his green eyes. His eyes tell me everything—Jamie won't let anyone hurt me tonight.

I remember Jamie's words outside the wrap party about getting back on the ice, and how every time I was scared to do something bold, I shocked myself with my bravery.

"I know you'll never let anything happen to me," I whisper

to Jamie. An energized, strong, stubborn feeling fills my chest, and I stand a little straighter. "And I won't, either."

I can stand up for myself now. Jamie helped me develop that skill, and now it's flourishing.

"We're going to pretend he isn't there," I tell Jamie. His jaw tightens, and I smile at him. "I got all dressed up for you, and I'm not going to let him ruin this."

His face looks like he wants to argue, but his expression softens. "Okay."

"Come here, handsome." When he leans down, I press a kiss to his cheek before leading him inside.

"Wowza, Hartley," Hayden says as soon as we enter. He's in a tux like Jamie, wearing his own black eye. "Babe alert."

I laugh, and Jamie growls.

"Careful, Owens," he tells Hayden, but Hayden just grins and slaps him on the shoulder.

Other hockey players find us, and we're surrounded. I feel like a baby elephant in the circle of giant adults, peering around them in short glances, on the lookout for Zach. I've never seen so many beautiful people in one place. The ballroom is packed with hockey players in tuxes, and I spot familiar faces from the Vancouver and Calgary teams, most of them wearing evidence of last night's fight. I recognize a few celebrities, actors and musicians. My heart stops at a woman with long, platinum blond hair, but she turns and I let the breath out. It isn't Layla. It's a woman from a reality show.

Hazel finds me, and I light up at her magenta gown. "You look lovely."

She gestures at me, eyes bugging out of her head. "*You* look great."

I nudge Jamie at my side. "Someone hired hair and makeup to get me all pretty for tonight."

He glances down at me, the corner of his mouth curling up before he nods. "Hazel."

"Jamie." She glances between us. Jamie's hand is on my lower back, reassuring but possessive, and she smiles to herself as she looks at him with approval. "Nice work, Streicher. I'm still going to beat the crap out of you in physio, though."

He nods. "I figured."

They smile at each other like they're friends, and my heart flips over.

"Good," she chirps before looking at me, expression sobering. "I haven't seen him yet."

I lean in and lower my voice. "Which one is Table 16?"

She indicates a table across the room. "We're on the other side of the room, thank fuck." She shakes her head, nostrils flaring. "When I see that guy, I'm going to fucking destroy him."

"Get in line," Jamie tells her, eyes flashing.

"No one is going to destroy anyone," I tell them, and I'm smiling because I love both of these people. "We're not going to make a scene, because we'll look like assholes." I straighten up and lift my chin. "We're going to ignore him."

"But—" Hazel starts.

"Ignoring." I nod and smile at her.

Her eyes narrow, and after a long moment, she relents. "Let's get some booze."

Minutes later, Hazel, Jamie, and I are at our table, chatting with players and sipping champagne, when Rory approaches.

Purple bruising surrounds his left eye, and there's a red scrape across his jaw. Even with his wounds from last night, he cleans up nicely in his tux and fresh haircut.

"Hey, Pips." He wraps me in a big hug. "You look so much better when you aren't wearing that ugly Vancouver jersey."

A laugh bursts out of me before I can stop it. I spare a

glance up at Jamie, and he rolls his eyes. The corner of his mouth twitches, though.

Rory pulls back and nods at Jamie. "Streicher." He tucks his hands in his pockets, studying the damage he did on Jamie's face. "Nice shiner."

Jamie tips his chin back at him. "Likewise."

A beat passes, and I wait for the familiar tension that runs between them, but it doesn't show up.

Jamie clears his throat. "We go to Hazel's hot yoga classes on Sundays," he tells Rory. Hazel's just out of earshot, talking with Alexei. "It might help you get in better shape."

Rory laughs. "You fucking asshole."

Jamie almost smiles at that. I glance between them, fascinated. Men are so weird.

"Hartley?" Rory raises his voice, gaze straying to Hazel. His mouth tips into a teasing grin, but there's more to his expression. Sincerity, like he wants to make sure she wants him there. "That okay with you, if I join yoga?"

She studies him before shrugging with a cool expression, like she doesn't care. "Whatever."

In one hand, she holds a drink, but the other is at her side, her pointer finger rubbing the pad of her thumb in quick circles. Her nervous tell.

She likes him. Excitement flutters in my stomach. Hazel *never* likes guys, preferring to use them and cast them aside.

Rory's eyes are soft as he watches her. His expression is a lot like how Jamie looks at me.

"You look beautiful," Rory says to her in front of everyone, and there isn't a lick of teasing in his tone.

She blinks, taken aback by this side of him. "Thanks." She's flushing and can barely meet his gaze, and I hide my smile by turning to look at Jamie.

He shoots me a quick wink. He sees it, too.

The emcee asks guests to take their seats, and dinner begins. Over at Table 16, there's an empty seat. Zach hasn't arrived.

My hands twist in my lap. Maybe he bailed.

There are speeches, a presentation about the charity's work this year, and a video of players and other celebrities at the local children's hospital. At one point, Jamie appears on screen, sitting on a tiny chair, letting a little girl put a tiara on him, and it's so freaking cute that my heart hurts.

His hand comes to my lap as we listen to the last of the speeches, and he gives me that quiet, private smile.

My heart flutters, and I know I have to tell him how I feel. Soon. When the time is right.

When the speeches are over, the real party starts. Music plays, and drinks flow. I eat all the desserts Jamie keeps bringing me, and Hayden makes me and Hazel laugh so hard we can't breathe. Zach's seat at his table remains empty, and I relax more. I glance over at Jamie, and he's talking with Coach Ward, who looks too handsome in his tux to ever have been a hockey player. Jamie's at ease, surrounded by all these guys who clearly admire him, and I feel a rush of gratitude that he has them.

I finish the last of my champagne and catch Jamie's eye, motioning to him that I'm going to use the ladies' room. When I step out of the washroom moments later, Jamie's leaning on a nearby table, waiting patiently.

"You didn't have to accompany me," I tell him.

He shrugs. "You were looking a little wobbly there, songbird."

I giggle. "I'm not drunk. I'm just feeling a little silly tonight." Zach didn't show, and I feel like a weight has lifted. My head buzzes pleasantly, but I'm not drunk.

"You can be both. I don't care." He reaches up and brushes

my hair off my shoulder. Amusement glitters in his eyes. "I'll hold your hair back while you barf."

My chest shakes with laughter. I love this silly side of him. "I'm not going to barf." I loop my hand around his arm, feeling floaty and happy. Zach didn't show up, and this gala has been so fun. I feel beautiful and special.

Just outside the doors leading into the ballroom, someone steps in our path, and my pulse flatlines. In an instant, the floaty, happy feelings evaporate, leaving me hollow.

Zach.

I can't breathe. Beside me, Jamie stiffens.

"Pippa," Zach says. His eyes move over me in wonder, like he sees me in a new light.

The new Pippa. Instead of sneakers and jeans, I'm wearing an expensive dress, with my hair in glamorous waves, with a professional hockey player hovering over me. Zach looks at me like my value has gone up.

Anger flickers in my stomach, because none of this matters. The dress doesn't matter, the hair and makeup don't matter. It doesn't even matter that Jamie's a professional athlete, because he's so much more than that.

*I'm* so much more than all of this. Jamie cared about me long before tonight. I remember the way he looked at me after I played that song for him in his living room in the middle of the night. That's what matters to Jamie. The real stuff. Not all of this artifice.

"Can I talk to you?" Zach spares Jamie a glance, lip curling. "Alone?"

"No," Jamie and I say in unison.

My hand slips into his, and he gives me a reassuring squeeze. I give him one right back.

"Okay." Irritation flashes across Zach's face, and the familiarity of it makes me feel sick.

In my head, I scramble for the calm, cool game plan I laid out hours ago. *Ignore Zach. He doesn't matter. Don't make a scene.*

Rage drums in my blood, and my molars grit. This guy made me feel like I wasn't enough. He broke my heart, and then he invited me to that *stupid* wrap party so he could shove it in my face. *Have you met Layla?* He took something I created, *laughed* at me, and then made it his.

"All that stuff with Layla," Zach starts, shaking his head. "It's not working out. I made a mistake." He shifts on his feet. "She's not you."

Something splinters through my rage. She's not me—is that because she stood up to him? Did she want to be treated as an equal, instead of some groupie muse solely for his use?

I thought this moment would be sweeter than it is. I thought I'd feel vindicated, but instead, I'm sad for Layla.

I'm also really fucking angry.

My eyes narrow as I study him, watching him get more and more uncomfortable. He expected me to wilt and fold for him, no doubt.

*I made a mistake,* he said, but I wonder what he thinks the mistake was.

He's not sorry for hurting me. He's not sorry for what he did. He's just sorry it didn't work out the way he wanted.

"What's going on?" Hazel's standing ten feet away, gaze darting from Zach to me to Jamie.

"Pippa's handling it," Jamie tells her, and when I meet his eyes, I see that he believes it.

Jamie knows I can stick up for myself.

Hazel folds her arms over her chest and stands on my other side. She and Jamie are like two bodyguards, hovering.

"Let's try it all again." Zach's words rush out, tinged in

frantic desperation. "It'll be different." His throat works again, and he clings to my gaze.

Shit, he must really be in trouble. I do the mental math. The tour is over and his record label is likely planning the next one. And in the meantime, he'll be recording a new album.

Oh. There it is. He doesn't have someone to feed him ideas without wanting credit.

Too bad I'm not that girl anymore. That rage from before echoes through me.

"You took my song." My voice is confident, and I channel Jamie's glare. "I heard it. The song I played for you? You made it yours."

Zach rears back, bemused. "What, *that*? That wasn't a song, Pippa. That was a mess, and we cleaned it up."

The anger pours back into my blood, and I blink at him.

He waves me off. "Artists take from each other all the time. Nothing in art is original."

He says it in such a condescending way, like I have no idea how the music industry works. My heart pounds, and I've never been so pissed. All the hurt from the past few months swirls in me like a whirlpool, gathering energy. I feel like I'm about to breathe fire and torch this whole hotel.

Hazel makes a furious noise in her throat. "Finish him," she says under her breath, like in the video games we used to play as teenagers.

Something strong courses through me, and I let it free.

"You don't want the best for me," I tell Zach, a wry smile twisting onto my mouth. "You want the best for *you*. You always have."

He blinks, stunned.

"We were never equals." Even though my hands are shaking, my shoulders slide back, and that flame in my chest flickers brighter, hotter. "And we still aren't, are we? You think you're doing me a favor."

He blanches before scoffing, and he's never looked uglier than when he's looking down at me like this, like I'm nothing. "I *am* doing you a favor." He snorts, and it hurts. "What are you doing now? Nothing in music."

"She recorded a demo with Ivy Matthews," Jamie cuts in with a sharp tone.

His words hit their mark, because Zach looks stunned all over again. Ivy is his white whale, and I got her. Even if nothing comes of my demo with her, she chose me and not him.

I give Zach a sad smile. I don't want to be mad at him anymore, because while this anger energizes me, it's going to leave me drained. I just want to be rid of him, to move on to a better life.

"Goodbye, Zach." I look up at Jamie and see the pride in his eyes. "Let's go," I tell him and Hazel, and Jamie's arm comes around my shoulders.

I don't look back as we walk away.

I'M in awe of Pippa.

*You don't want the best for me. You want the best for you. You never saw us as equals.*

I love this woman, and I need to tell her. When we lay in bed last night, I almost said it, but I held back. Now, in the elevator up to our suite, I can barely keep from blurting it out.

I love taking care of Pippa, but she doesn't need me. She can take care of herself, and I love her for that. In my mind, I see our future together, and I want it too badly.

Pippa's my forever person. I know that now. I think I always knew it.

"You're incredible," I tell her, and a smile lifts on her face.

"Because of you."

"No." I shake my head. "That was all you, songbird." I walk her back against the wall, holding her eyes. Electricity simmers around us, and I love the way she looks up at me, so trusting and sweet. "Have I told you how fucking beautiful you are?" I murmur, brushing her hair back before kissing her neck.

She laughs quietly under my touch. "Yes."

"Good." I nip her shoulder. Her breath catches, and I love the sound of it.

I'm so gone for this girl. I love every sound she makes.

The doors open on our floor and I take her hand, leading her to the suite. Inside, her gaze roams the space. The fireplace is on, there's a bottle of champagne waiting in an ice bucket, and through the windows, the ski-hill lights twinkle.

She presses her hands together in front of her chest with a dreamy look on her face. "I never want to leave this place."

I'm buying a place in Whistler, I decide, for weekends. A place just like this—cozy cabin style—where Pippa and Daisy and I can come to relax. What's the point of making millions if I don't spend it on the people I love, doing the things that matter?

This is what matters.

In the bedroom, I lace my fingers in hers, heart pounding as I kiss her, sinking into her warm, welcoming mouth, loving every catch of her breath, every quiet moan. I work her zipper down, letting the dress pool at her feet.

Pippa stands there in that lingerie, looking fucking delectable. Every cell in my body sings for this goddess. I run my hand through my hair as desire pulses in my blood.

"Fuck," I breathe, memorizing how her tits swell over the lace, how the panties hug her curves, how her perfect pink nipples are barely visible. I brush my thumb over one of the peaks, and her eyelids fall halfway.

There's a lingerie store near our apartment—I've passed it and thought about her a hundred times. I'm going there tomorrow, I decide, to buy half the store for Pippa. My jaw tenses as I picture Pippa wearing panties I bought for her. Her gasping as I tear them off.

Jesus Christ, that is fucking hot.

My pretty Pippa undoes my bowtie, and I feel a twist of affection. Undressing each other feels familiar, and I think back to when the valet referred to her as my wife.

I liked that. My mouth tips up as she undoes my shirt buttons. I liked that a lot. I picture this woman with my ring on her finger, and something possessive beats in my chest.

I like that image, too.

She pushes my jacket and shirt off, and they fall to the floor before her hand slides over my cock.

"I love how hard you get," she breathes, watching her hand work me over my pants before glancing up at me with a playful smile.

Oh, yeah. She's getting a ring. A big one. Loud and flashy. Disgustingly over-the-top. She'll hate it, I'm sure, but I want people seeing it from a mile away. From space. I want it to signal to everyone that she's taken.

"What are you grinning at?" she asks me, smiling.

She's so pretty. I won't force her to wear a ring she doesn't like. I could never do that. She can wear whatever ring she wants.

I rest my forehead against hers as she strokes me. Need tightens in my body, and my blood beats for her.

"Wait."

Her hand stills. "What is it?"

My nostrils flare as I drag a breath in. My feelings for Pippa swell and pitch, crashing like waves on a stormy ocean, desperate to get out. Without telling her the truth of how I feel —all of it—intimacy between us feels incomplete. I pull back and search her eyes.

"I love you." My words are a quiet murmur as I watch her reaction, and my heart slams against the front wall of my chest. I've never said those words to a girl. I've never felt this way, and it's exhilarating and terrifying. "I love you so fucking much, Pippa. I'm in love with you. I want everything with you."

Her lips part, and her chest rises and falls fast as my words sink in. *Please feel the same way*, I pray to the universe.

"You're everything to me." My Pippa. My distraction, the girl I've always been powerless against. "I want you in my life. You make me so, so fucking happy, songbird, and I hope I make you happy, too."

"You do," she says immediately, and her hands slip into the back of my hair. "You do make me happy. You're everything to me, too. I love you, too," she whispers.

My heart bursts open, expanding in my chest. "I was hoping you'd say that."

My mouth falls to hers, and the soft noise in her throat has my blood humming. She loves me, and I don't have to keep it in anymore. She loves me, and we're doing this.

She loves me, and this is forever.

My hands fall to her chest, and my thumbs rub twin circles on her nipples over the fabric of her bra. She arches into my hands, swaying on her feet. A dark chuckle rumbles out of me, and I slip one hand into her panties.

Her pussy is soaked. She moans, wincing with pleasure as I stroke through her, dragging slow, delicate friction over her.

"Shit," I breathe. "You're so wet."

She nods, looking up at me like I'm a lifeline. She clutches me for stability, and I wrap an arm around her shoulders to hold her upright while I touch her. She's so soft, so wet, so warm, and I can't get enough.

"You've come twice today," I tell her in a low, teasing tone. "Look how worked up you are."

She nods again, wetting her lips, and it's that flash of her tongue that has me dripping with pre-cum. I pull my hand out of her panties and watch her expression glaze as I suck the wetness off my fingers. I groan at her taste, giving her a wicked smile, reveling in her look of disbelief and awe.

"Need you naked, songbird," I tell her, unhooking her bra and slipping her panties down. "Need you bare for me so I can make you come again." I guide her down onto the bed near the edge, hovering over her and seeking one of her pinched nipples with my lips, working the other with my fingers.

"That always feels so good." Her words are a low, strained whisper, and my balls ache with need at the desperate, pleasured tone in her voice.

I *love* pleasing Pippa. I love making her feel good, and I love being the only man to have done it so well. Her hair is spread out across the pillow, and it's one of the most breathtaking things I've ever seen, Pippa beneath me, looking up at me like this. It makes my heart ache.

"Open your legs for me, baby," I whisper against her breast. "Open your legs so I can keep making you feel good."

She obliges, and a dark satisfaction weaves through me at her following my instructions so obediently. So trusting, like she knows I'd never hurt her.

Her abs tighten as I rub her clit.

"Jamie," she moans in frustration, and I chuckle before lowering my mouth to her.

Her taste hits my tongue, and I groan into her, pushing her thighs wider so I can get deeper. My tongue sweeps up and down her slit, circling her clit, dipping into her tight center, slicking over every sensitive nerve ending until her hands are in my hair, tugging.

"Can't get enough," she gasps.

"Good." I suck her clit, and her back arches off the bed. "Neither can I."

While I work my tongue over her, I unbuckle my belt and pull my cock out, giving it a few hard strokes.

Jesus. I'm close. I'm too close.

"You're playing with me." Her voice is thin, breathy, accusing. "You're teasing me."

"You fucking bet I am." I draw slow, light circles on her clit before sucking hard, and her hips tilt, pressing her further onto my mouth. "You're mine to play with. Isn't that right, songbird?"

She nods, pulling my hair, and the sensation shoots down my spine. I suck her clit in a pulsing rhythm, and her thighs shake around my head. Around my fingers, her muscles flex.

"Use your words, baby. Say it so I can hear you."

"Yes," she moans as I rub her G-spot. "I'm yours to play with. I'm yours."

"Good girl. That's what I like to hear. You want to come?"

Her hands tighten in my hair. "Yes."

"Ask nicely."

"*Please*," she begs. "Please make me come. Please, baby."

I relent, sucking hard on her clit while dragging my tongue over it, working her G-spot in the steady, pulsating rhythm that makes her lose her mind.

My free hand drifts beneath her, between her cheeks, teasing, and her head lifts so she can see me.

"Did he ever touch you here, songbird?"

The pad of my finger drags across her back entrance, wet from her arousal, and she squeaks, shaking her head.

"Do you want me to?" I circle the tight bud, rubbing gentle friction.

Her eyes close as she lets out a high, desperate moan I've never heard before. "Yes, please."

I ease my finger inside her ass, so slow and cautious, and as I begin to stroke, she tightens up around me.

"Good?" I ask, smiling.

She's frantically nodding, breathing hard, saying things like *please* and *yes*. I slide my tongue over her clit again, sucking, and within seconds, she bows off the bed, letting out a high, desperate moan and clenching up all over my fingers. My face is soaked with her arousal as her thighs tremor around me, and I'm so hard it hurts.

"Jamie." She reaches for me, chest heaving while she catches her breath. "I need you here."

I kneel on the bed, settling over her, kissing a trail down her neck and chest.

"You came three times today," I tell her, smiling.

Her eyes spark and she smiles down at me. "You *made* me come three times today."

Pride pulses in my chest. "Fucking right, I did," I bite out, and I lower my hips, sliding my cock against her slick center. She shakes when I rub against her clit, and her legs fall open wider.

She reaches down to angle me at her entrance, and I'm already mindlessly pushing inside her, my cock throbbing at how tight and wet and warm she is.

"Oh my god." Her hands are in my hair and the look of agonized bliss on her face makes my balls tighten. "Oh my god," she repeats.

A shred of sanity slices through.

"Condom," I groan. I'm not wearing one. I'm halfway inside her and shaking with need, but I'd never do this without her green light.

"I'm on the pill." She sobers, and her tongue darts out to lick her lips. "I've never gone without a condom before."

My brain stutters, and every base instinct roars to life. More than anything, I want to come inside her. I want to make her mine, fully and completely.

"Me neither," I tell her, swallowing. My cock pulses inside her, and her breath catches.

She nods, urging me on, and her hips tilt, seeking more. I sink in the rest of the way, and every thought in my head burns away.

Fucking Pippa bare is the highest plane of heaven. The noise that rips through my throat is unearthly. When I pull out and push back in, she lets out a low moan.

"Do we need to do that thing?" I ask through clenched teeth as I thrust. Her scent wafts into my nose, and it only makes me harder. She's so wet I can hear myself moving in and out of her, and the sharp pinpricks of pain from her nails digging into my back shove me closer to my release.

I can't hold on for much longer.

"What thing?" she gasps.

"The—" I scramble for the words, but all I can think about is how fucking incredible she feels around me. I didn't think it was possible to feel this heightened sense of pleasure. It's sharper than any pain from any injury. Coming inside her is going to tear my brain out of my skull. "Where you get stuck in your head," I manage. "The grounding thing we do."

She's shaking her head, and the movement is erratic. "I don't need help. I'm close, Jamie."

Thank *fuck*, because I can't handle this for much longer. Heat coils low inside me, twisting and pulsing. "Touch yourself. Show me what you can do. I want to see you make yourself come while being fucked."

Her hand falls between us to where we join, and my breath is a hiss as she clenches up on me. Her fingers work her clit in soft, fast circles, and her expression is glorious— wincing with pleasure and desperation as we chase our releases.

Her lips make an O as she stares up at me like she can't believe it. My control slips, and I stroke into her harder. The necklace I bought her bounces with her tits as I fuck her, and pride pounds in my blood.

"I love you so much." My voice is rough. The pressure at the base of my spine builds rapidly. "So fucking much, Pippa."

She's nodding, over and over again. "I love you. Oh my god." Her mouth falls open. "I'm going to come."

On a choked gasp, she clamps down on my cock, and my release barrels toward me. My world narrows to her—her full breasts, her plush lips, her beautiful blue-gray eyes, clouded with lust and clinging to my gaze. I drive into her, uncontrolled and claiming, as my release closes in on me.

I shatter into a million pieces, coming inside Pippa. My forehead falls to hers, and I'm moaning as my vision goes white. The most intense pleasure of my life cuts through every cell in my body as I fill her, gritting out her name.

My world comes back into focus, and I heave for air, staring down at Pippa in disbelief. "Holy fuck."

A laugh bursts out of her, and then I start laughing, and then we're laughing together. That was the most intense physical experience of my life, and we're giggling with each other.

I love this girl. With Pippa, I've never felt so complete. Everything I secretly wanted, I have.

I'm never letting her go.

I WAKE up the next morning in a huge, comfy bed, tucked against Jamie's chest. Sunlight streams in through the windows, and my body feels both relaxed and deliciously sore from what we did last night... and again in the middle of the night.

"Morning," Jamie murmurs into my hair, and I smile against his skin, tracing my fingers down the trail of chest hair leading into his boxers.

"Good morning." My voice is soft and a little shy after last night.

He said he loved me.

I said it back.

I peek up at him. He's looking down at me with his own smile, and my heart flutters. I hope that thrill will never go away. I brush my fingers around the bruise on his eye, studying the shades of green in his eyes as he gazes back at me.

"How are you feeling?" he asks, and his hand slides over my hip.

The way he asks it, and because it's *Jamie*, who turned out to be relentlessly caring, I know he's asking about everything—Zach, the sex, the *I love you*s.

"A little sore," I admit, "but I don't regret a thing."

"Good." He studies my face like no one else has, and I realize he's been doing this since the day I stepped into his apartment all those months ago.

My fingers wander up his chest, and goosebumps break out over his muscles. "You?"

His Adam's apple bobs, and there's a flash of vulnerability across his face. "Just one regret."

I freeze.

"I wanted to ask you to grad," he says before I can let myself deflate. "Back in high school."

My brows snap together and I can feel the shock all over my face. "No."

Grad is the big dinner and dance for all the graduating students, the Canadian version of prom. The grade twelve students are allowed to bring dates.

"Yes," he emphasizes, and the way he blinks and looks away makes me think he's a little flustered. "I'd look for you at parties, Pippa. I went to all the band concerts just to watch you sing and play. I asked around about whether you and Zach were together, but no one knew. I thought there was a chance you were single, and I mustered up the courage to ask you to grad, and then I saw him holding your hand."

In my mind, I'm back there in the high school cafeteria as Zach slips my hand into his out of the blue, and my heart twists.

Jamie makes a frustrated noise in his throat, and his brow furrows. Cute. So freaking cute.

"I let it go, but I thought about you for years after that." His mouth tips up. "When you showed up as my new assistant, I thought I was hallucinating."

This all sinks in, and a surprised laugh falls from my lips. "You were going to ask me to grad?"

A flush spreads over his cheekbones like he's embarrassed,

and I love him. I love this guy so much. A broad smile pulls at my mouth, and my chest is about to explode with happiness.

"I had the biggest crush on you in high school," I tell him.

He frowns. "No."

"Yes." I shake my head at him, smiling. "Jamie, you have no idea what you look like, do you?"

He laughs, a sharp, bright, joyful laugh of relief and amusement that goes straight to my heart. "Come here." He pulls me on top of him, and my legs fall on either side of his hips, straddling him.

We look at each other for a moment, his hand in my hair and mine in his, brushing it off his forehead.

"Do you remember when I spilled the Slurpee on myself?" I ask him.

He chuckles. "Yes. I was about to go get napkins to try to help you, but you ran off."

If I had stayed a few seconds longer, maybe everything would have been different. But then I wouldn't have learned some tough but important lessons with Zach.

I lean down to kiss Jamie, and I feel his smile against my lips.

"Songbird?"

"Mmm?" My lips skate over his stubble, and the sensation makes me sigh.

"I love you so much."

When I open my eyes, I can see the truth of it in his gaze. My heart squeezes for the guy I never thought I'd get.

"I love you, too." I drop a kiss on his mouth. "Handsome," I add, and in a split second, he flips me onto my back as I yelp with laughter.

# CHAPTER 69

# JAMIE

PIPPA and I are driving home on the winding Sea to Sky Highway, listening to music, talking, and admiring the forested mountains and clear blue lakes.

I've never been so fucking happy. I've never felt like this, and when I think about how hard I tried to resist her, I laugh.

"What are you grinning at?" Pippa asks from the passenger seat.

I'm laughing at the fact that I thought I could ever walk away from her. I'm laughing because I somehow thought pining after her for the rest of my life was a better option than this. Better than being together. Better than telling each other how we feel.

"Just happy," I say, and she smiles back at me.

"Me, too."

"Good."

My phone rings through the car's Bluetooth. It's my mom's number.

"Hi," I answer. "We're on our way home. We should be there in an hour and a half."

"Is this Jamie?" a woman's voice asks, and Pippa and I frown at each other.

Alarm rises in me, flooding my veins. "Yes?"

"I'm calling from the emergency room at Lions Gate Hospital," she continues.

The alarm blares, and my mouth goes dry. That's the hospital in North Vancouver. We're approaching a lookout point on the highway, so I pull off to park.

"Your mom had a panic attack. She's okay, but we'd like someone to pick her up."

My mind reels as I white-knuckle the steering wheel. She's better. She has a therapist, and she was looking into medication. She hasn't had a panic attack since that night that Pippa and I went over. We're past this.

She's better.

Pippa's hand is on my shoulder, and her eyes are full of concern.

"Okay," I say, because I don't know what else to do.

"Her car has been towed to a local shop," the woman continues, and something in my chest crumples.

"She was driving?" I stare at Pippa with shock. She's worrying her bottom lip with her teeth.

"It seems that she had a panic attack while driving, and then hit a police officer's car."

My stomach drops. I can't believe this. This doesn't feel real.

"Fuck," I mutter, raking my hand through my hair. "What about her medication? Did she not take it today?"

There's a long pause, and my stomach sinks further.

"I'm not aware of any medication," the woman says. "She didn't list any on the intake form."

She lied to me. All the avoidant conversations where I thought she just needed space. She never got medication. A headache grows behind my eyes. This is so much worse than I could have imagined. She was driving and hit a *cop car*. She's supposed to be taking care of Daisy—

My pulse explodes. "Was there a dog in the car?"

If something happened to Daisy, I couldn't bear it. I'd never forgive myself.

"No," the woman answers. "She said the dog is at home."

Pippa and I look at each other in relief. That's something, at least.

"We'll be there as soon as we can," I tell the woman.

We hang up, and I look over at Pippa. I feel lost and confused, and suddenly, I'm ten years old again, coming home from school to my mom sleeping at three in the afternoon, blinds drawn closed. There's a sinking feeling of disappointment and dread in my gut.

"I thought she was better," I tell Pippa. "I thought she had a handle on it."

"I know." She nods, still wearing that worried look. "I did, too. Getting better won't be a linear process, though."

I'm silent, because I don't want to point out that maybe she was never getting better to begin with.

Over the next hour and a half, we drive in silence as I turn over everything I thought to be true.

I thought my mom was better and that she didn't need me micromanaging her life.

I thought I could handle everything.

For once, I thought I could have something for myself.

———

"I'm sending you home," I tell Pippa as we approach the hospital. I'm vibrating with stress, worry, and frustration. "I need to deal with this alone. I'll order you an Uber."

From the passenger seat, she stares at me in disbelief. "No."

"Yes." Tension knots in my gut. My instincts to take over and fix things are at an all-time high. Even I can see, though, that what I've been doing until now isn't working.

I'm so fucking lost. I don't know what to do.

"I'm not going home," Pippa says, folding her arms. Her tone is stubborn, and I blow a long breath out.

If my mom can't make progress, or even *try*, I don't see how Pippa and I will work, and that's breaking my fucking heart. Maybe it won't hurt our relationship right now, but eventually, it will. I can't do that to Pippa. I can't continue to choose my mom over her. I can't put every ounce of my energy toward worrying about my mom.

Pain twists in my chest. Everything we told each other yesterday was for nothing.

"Fine." We're pulling into the hospital parking lot. "Stay in the car, then."

Hurt flashes in her eyes. "*No.*"

I don't have the energy to argue with her. "Fine."

Inside the ER, the front desk nurse gives us directions to my mom's room, and we hurry down the hall.

We reach the door, and Pippa touches my arm. "I'm going to wait outside," she says. "I'm here if you need anything."

I steel myself for whatever shitstorm is waiting inside this room. "Thank you."

In her room, my mom is chatting happily with the nurses, laughing and smiling. It's a fucking party in here. She sees me and sighs, rolling her eyes.

"Oh my goodness." She looks to the nurses. "Candace, I told you not to call him!" She winces at my black eye. "Ugh, look at that thing. How was your trip?"

I stare at her in disbelief, and something angry and frustrated drips into my blood.

"Can we have a moment alone?" I ask the nurses, and they filter out.

When we're alone, my mom shifts under my gaze. "Honey, I'm fine—"

"Don't say you're fine." I feel sick. "Don't say you're okay, that it was nothing, that you don't need help."

She laughs in surprise, but there's no humor in it. "I *don't* need help."

"You hit a police car."

It's quiet for a moment, and we just stare at each other. There's a shift inside me, and when I reach for that endless patience, it isn't there. Instead, I find betrayal and frustration.

Something needs to change, and until now, it's been me. With my mom, I'm always the one who bends. I've been encouraging Pippa to stick up for herself, put herself first, do what's best for her career and her life, but I haven't been following my own advice.

"I moved here for you," I tell her, but I'm saying it to myself, too.

She waves a hand. "You moved here because you missed Vancouver."

"No." I fold my arms over my chest. I can feel how hard my heart is beating. "I moved here for you because you started having panic attacks and you clearly couldn't handle it yourself."

She blinks like I've slapped her, and although my heart pinches to see her hurt like this, she needs to hear the truth. She's been running from it for so long.

"You had a panic attack and got into a car accident, so I moved my entire life back here to take care of you."

Her jaw tenses as she stares at the floor, and it's like looking in a mirror. A knot unties in my chest as I tell the truth. Her fingers go to her bracelet, turning the beads. She won't meet my eye.

"The nurse on the phone said you weren't on medication."

"I don't need that stuff," my mom mutters. "I tried it." She's referring to years ago, when her depression was at its worst. "It made me all loopy."

"That was fifteen years ago." My voice is rough. "There are new meds now and new research. Doctors who specialize in anxiety." I pause, about to ask a question I think I know the answer to. "Did you find a new therapist like you said?"

She stares at the beads as she spins them. "It didn't work out."

"So that's a no." I blow a breath out.

I see it so clearly, all laid out in front of me. She's going to keep getting worse, and I'll chip away at my life until there's nothing left because I don't want to hurt her feelings. And in the meantime, I'll tell myself I can't have the woman I love because I don't have time for her.

My heart hurts. I love Pippa, and I don't want to give her up. I love my mom, and I don't want to see her get worse.

"Why were you driving alone?" I ask softly.

A muscle ticks in her jaw, and her eyes stay on her bracelet. "I needed something from the store. It was just a quick trip."

She could have seriously hurt herself, or someone else. If Daisy was in the car—

I can't even think about that. I love that dog so much.

"You know you get panic attacks while driving, and yet you got behind the wheel. How is this any different from what Dad did?"

Her head snaps up because I've hit a nerve. Good.

"Jamie." Her tone is sharp.

I've never spoken to her like this. We never talk about him.

I take a step forward, folding my arms over my chest.

"You're ignoring the problem, and it's getting worse. You lied to me about finding a therapist."

Her mouth flattens. "I looked." Her voice is small. "I looked and then I just—" She freezes up, shaking her head. "I couldn't."

"Why?"

She throws her hands up, discomfort radiating off her in waves, but I don't care. "I don't want to talk about this anymore."

My pulse races. "You never want to talk about it."

"This is not your problem. Let me deal with it."

My head is about to explode.

"I don't want you to shoulder this alone, because I love you and I owe you everything, but you have to give me *something*." I scrub a hand down my face, and my chest sinks further in defeat. "I don't know what to do anymore. If you can't take care of yourself, if I'm always worrying about you, I can't have a normal life. You know what I told myself for years, Mom? I told myself that I can't meet anyone or get married until I retire from hockey because I need to focus on my career and taking care of you."

Pain flashes through her eyes.

"I'm in love with Pippa." My voice softens as I think about the woman outside this room. "I love her, and I want to be with her, but I worry that it's going to get in the way of taking care of you." I rub the ache in my chest. "I don't know what to do."

My mom's face falls, and she looks so heartbroken.

I swallow past a thick throat and take a seat beside her on the bed. "I love you so much. It kills me to watch this happen."

She runs her fingers along the beads on her wrist and takes a slow, deep breath.

"I felt so much guilt for what happened with your father,"

she whispers, squeezing her eyes closed with the pain. "If you had been in the car, I never would have forgiven myself."

"I know." She's never said this out loud, but somehow, I know it.

"I have never been the mother you needed." A tear leaks out of her eye, and she wipes it away fast before she shakes her head to herself. "I thought that stuff was behind me." Her eyes are watery when she meets mine, and her throat works. I know she means the depression and anxiety. "I wanted it to be behind me so badly."

"You always felt guilt because you never made Dad get the help he needed, right?" I ask.

She meets my eyes and nods.

"How is what you're doing any different?" My voice is soft because this is going to be the hardest truth to stomach. "You know deep down you need help and you're ignoring the problem."

In her eyes, I see it all: guilt, worry, regret, self-hatred, and resignation.

"Yeah," she says, deflating. "You're right."

"I don't want to be right."

A rueful smile ghosts over her face. "It's hard admitting that there's a problem." She stops herself. "That *I* have a problem."

"I know."

Her gaze lifts to mine. "I want you to have everything."

"I want you to get a therapist and tackle this like I know you can." I think about Pippa and the stuff she's been through with her ex, how he tried to decimate her confidence, but she rose up stronger and brighter. "Having these issues doesn't make you weak. It makes you stronger, and I know you can do this."

A moment passes where we just look at each other. Things have changed for the better. I can feel it.

"You love Pippa?" she asks softly, eyes roaming over me with warm admiration.

I huff. "That's what you got from all of this?"

She laughs lightly and sighs. "I'm going to get a therapist, I'm going to talk to them about medication, and I'm going to give this a serious try. Because I don't want to drown in this anymore, and I want you to be happy." Through her sadness and shame, her eyes spark with teasing. "So, you love Pippa?"

I smile and my heart expands, filling every corner of the room. "Yep. I love Pippa."

"And she loves you?"

"Yep," Pippa calls from the hall.

We both burst out laughing.

Pippa pokes her head in the door with an embarrassed smile. She's blushing. "Sorry."

My mom waves her in. "Come in, come in."

Pippa wanders into the room and leans against the table near the door.

"Did you two have fun at the gala?" my mom asks.

Pippa and I look at each other, smiling.

"Yes." She smiles wider, and I wonder what part she's remembering. "Jamie looked very handsome."

"And Pippa looked very beautiful." I lift my eyebrows at her. "She always does."

"I want to see photos," my mom says, glancing between us with a pleased smile. "And you love each other?"

I hold Pippa's gaze while my heart does backflips. "Yep."

My mom makes a happy humming noise. "I hoped that would happen."

"Me too," I admit.

My gaze falls to Pippa's left hand, and I wonder if it's too soon to think about buying her a ring.

Probably.

But maybe not.

We leave the hospital and drive my mom home, and when Daisy sees us, she races over and jumps into my arms, wiggling like crazy with excitement as Pippa and my mom laugh.

Pippa wouldn't leave my side today, even when I stubbornly demanded to send her home in a flurry of panic and shame. She's been there for me since day one, even before we were together, and I know that even if my mom's recovery takes longer than expected, I'm not alone in it.

Pippa isn't just the love of my life; she's my family.

A MONTH LATER, my parents, Hazel, Donna, and I head up to the box at the arena after one of Jamie's games. We sat behind the net, and when Jamie waved at us through the glass, I thought my dad was going to start crying from excitement.

Jamie had suggested my parents come out for a visit, insisting on putting them up in a nearby hotel. Last night, he took us all out for dinner. It's like he wants to get to know them better.

I rescinded my application for the marketing job, and Jamie spoke with the team to extend my contract until I figure out a plan with regards to music. There's been radio silence from Ivy Matthews, and although I'm disappointed, it's not holding me back from writing more.

I've played six open mics around the city in the past month. I'm doing this, and I'm going to give it everything, because it matters.

Nerves buzz in my stomach as we step into the box. I'm stalling on telling my parents all of this because I know they won't react well.

In the box, my mom chats with Donna, Hazel, and a few

others. The players who visited Silver Falls for New Year's greet my dad like an old friend and thank him again for the breakfast he made for everyone, and the players he hasn't met introduce themselves immediately. When Jamie finally arrives, he doesn't look surprised to see my dad deep in conversation with Ward about the defensive plays tonight.

"Hi, baby." Jamie drops a kiss onto my lips, and I smile.

"Hi. Did you tell everyone to come say hi to my dad?"

The corners of his lips curve up. "Yep."

This man. Seriously. He's perfect. "Thank you."

His gaze is so warm and pleased as it roams over my face, my hair. "For you, songbird? Anything."

I flush with pleasure. I'm so happy with this guy.

Donna and my mom cackle with laughter. "They're getting on like a house on fire," I whisper to Jamie, smiling, and his eyes warm as he regards his mom.

After the car accident, Donna got serious about tackling her anxiety and panic attacks. Twice a week, Jamie drives her to counseling, patiently waiting in the car, and afterward, they go for lunch. If he's out of town, I drive her. He's even joined a few sessions at the request of Donna's counselor, and although they have a lot of ground to cover, it seems like they're making progress. Donna talks more openly about her issues now. I heard her mentioning it to my mom during the game.

I smile up at Jamie. "Thank you for putting my parents up in a hotel."

"Happy to." His lips brush my ear as he lowers his voice. "I don't want you to be quiet tonight."

A shiver runs down my spine as I bite back a cheeky grin. My thighs squeeze together, thinking about his tongue between my legs last night, and then him taking me against the wall after, with my legs wrapped around his waist. Telling him I loved him unleashed something in Jamie, and he's been showing his love for me in many, many ways.

I'm not complaining.

"We're going to the bar," Hayden cuts in. He points at my parents. "Ken? Maureen? Donna? You're coming with us, right?"

My dad is about to faint with happiness.

———

The Filthy Flamingo is full of noise, laughter, conversation, and music, punctuated by the occasional drink getting knocked over. The team's all here, even Ward. He's still in conversation with my dad, but his eyes linger on Jordan behind the bar.

Jordan's casual sex guy is on the small stage, playing guitar and singing, and I listen to the new song he's trying out. It's about wanting more from a girl who isn't interested, and his eyes *also* linger on Jordan the entire time. He really needs to tune his guitar.

"Folks, I'm going to take a short break," he says into the mic, and his eyes meet mine. "But I'm hoping our friend Pippa can play for you in the meantime."

My eyes go wide as everyone turns to me. Hazel gives me an encouraging nod.

"Yeah, Pippa," one of the players cheers. One of the drunker players howls like a wolf.

My parents stare at me in confusion. They know about me performing on New Year's Eve—everyone in Silver Falls does—but they don't know it's a regular thing.

They haven't seen me play live in years. My pulse picks up as nerves dance in my stomach. They call it a hobby, and they still think I'm going to have a career in marketing.

If I want to be in the music industry, though, I have to play in front of people, even if I'm scared.

I stand, and the people around me cheer. My parents look baffled at the response. My pulse drums in my ears as I make my way up to the stage. I know what song I'm going to play because it's all so clear now. When I wrote song after song about Jamie, that was me telling him I loved him. When I wrote a song about struggling with the expectations of others, that was me thrashing against the cage placed around me.

"Hi," I say into the mic, strumming the guitar. "I'm Pippa Hartley."

A few people chuckle, because I'm friends with everyone in this room.

I launch into the song, and when I look at my parents, they're listening with rapt attention. My mom wears a sweet yet sad smile, and my dad looks at me like I'm an NHL player. Something aches in my chest. My mom reaches for my dad's hand, and he murmurs in her ear. She nods and smiles again.

I sing my heart out. I sing about wanting more, wanting to believe in myself, wanting to break free and be my own person. I sing about going for what I want because I don't want to regret a single moment. I don't want to waste a second doing something other than following my passion and purpose.

Being up here is where I'm meant to be. Even if nothing comes of it. Even if I play dive bars for the rest of my life.

Jamie watches me sing with a proud look, like I'm everything to him.

I sing about how taking the risk might be worth it, and when I'm done, the bar erupts in cheers and applause.

Back at the table, my parents are speechless. They haven't seen me perform since high school, and back then, I'd only perform cover songs, never something I wrote. I take a seat, and

Jamie glances between me and my parents, ready to jump in if needed, but I shake my head.

Jamie stood up for himself to his mom, and I can stand up for myself to my own parents. If I want a career in the music industry, I'm going to have to get used to standing up for myself.

"I'm not taking the marketing job," I blurt out to my parents.

My mom's expression is guarded. "Was the offer too low?"

"You need to negotiate." My dad leans forward. "They expect you to negotiate the salary, Pippa."

"No." I shake my head. "Please, let me finish."

Concern passes over their features. Beside me, Jamie waits, letting me handle this.

"They didn't make an offer because I rescinded my application." I take a deep breath, watching them process this. My mom is freaking out, but she's hiding it. I can tell from the look in her eyes. "I don't want that job."

My dad blinks. "You said you wanted it."

"I don't think I did." I wince. "I thought it was the right thing to do." I gesture over my shoulder at the stage, and I think about that thought exercise Jamie had me do in the forest and all the incredible moments I pictured. "That's what I want to do. I want a career in the music industry. I want to write my own music and go on tour around the world playing for people. It makes me happy." I meet Jamie's steady gaze. "And I can do it. I'm talented and I work hard."

My parents are silent as this sinks in.

"I'm so grateful for everything you've done for me," I continue. "You worked so hard to pay for my school, and I'm going to pay you back. Every penny."

"No," my dad says quickly, frowning. "We don't want that."

"Agreed," my mom adds. "That money was so you had options."

"Exactly. We always wanted you girls to have options." My dad glances at Hazel a few tables away. "We wanted you to have everything because we didn't have that."

My mom takes a deep breath, shifting in her seat, looking uncomfortable. I know she's thinking about how she didn't get into the ballet company in her twenties. She spent three decades teaching dance when it wasn't her passion.

"I know what you're thinking," I tell her, and she raises an eyebrow. My pulse races because I hate being in conflict with them like this. "I'm taking a really big swing, and there's no guarantee it'll work out. The odds are against me."

There's a beat where she just studies me, and it's the most serious I've ever seen her. "It's going to be hard, Pippa."

"I know."

"It's going to be the hardest thing you've ever done, and there's a *likely* possibility that you'll end up teaching music to five-year-olds." Her tone is matter-of-fact, like she's explaining a recipe to me. Pain flashes through her blue-gray eyes. "It's hard to fail at something you love. It hurts so much."

My chest strains for her, and my hands twist. "I know, but I still need to try, or I'll regret it forever."

She considers this for a long moment, and I worry that she's unconvinced, but then she looks at my dad. Something passes between their gazes, some silent communication honed over decades of marriage, and her expression softens.

"We don't want you to work a job you hate," she admits. "We want you to be happy." She glances up at the stage. "Being broke is really hard, honey."

"She'll never be broke," Jamie cuts in, and the look he sends me tells me he means business.

I try not to laugh at his protectiveness.

"I'm okay with things being hard," I tell them. "It'll be worth it."

We're all quiet amid the bar noise.

"You're really talented, sweetheart," my dad says with a wistful look in his eye. "We've never seen you like that. While you were playing, I said to your mom, she looks like a pro up there."

My mom nods, and she smiles at me like she sees me in a new light. "You looked like you belong up there."

Something unwinds in my chest, thread by thread, until I feel free. "I do belong up there."

Jamie's hand covers mine in my lap, and I lace my fingers into his. He sends me a quick wink, and my heart jumps. "She recorded a demo with a producer," he tells them.

"You did?" My dad looks between us.

I nod, smiling and squeezing Jamie's hand. "Yep. I did."

My parents exchange a look. "We don't say it enough," my dad says, and there's a catch to his voice. "We're proud of you. No matter what."

"We really are." My mom nods. "We love you so much."

Their words are everything I wanted to hear, and I blink away the sting in my eyes.

"Love you, too," I whisper, smiling.

My dad stands. "Group hug." He gestures to Hazel a few tables away. "Hazel, honey, you, too. Get over here."

I laugh, and my dad pulls all of us into a warm embrace.

"Hey, you two." Jordan's behind us, gesturing to me and Jamie. She's holding a Polaroid camera. "Come here. I want to take a photo of you."

Jamie pulls me against him, and the blinding flash goes off just as he presses a kiss to my temple, making me smile.

The camera spits the photo out, and a minute later, the image of us appears.

The photo is snatched out of my hands. "I'll take that," Jordan says before she walks behind the bar and tacks the photo to the wall.

"We look happy," I tell Jamie, and he smiles at me.

"We are, songbird."

———

That evening, I'm in front of the bathroom sink, getting ready for bed, when my phone pings with an email. I read it, and my heart jumps into my throat.

"Pippa," Jamie calls from our room. "Are you coming to bed?"

I read the email again, hands shaking.

It's happening. It's actually happening.

Footsteps approach and Jamie appears at my side. "What's wrong?"

I smile up at him, dazed and elated. "Nothing's wrong. Everything's amazing."

A laugh bursts out of me because Jamie is so gorgeous and handsome standing here in just his tight black boxers, and Ivy Matthews has offered me a recording contract with her new record label.

I don't even recognize my life anymore.

When I show Jamie my phone, a huge smile breaks out on his face.

"Songbird." He says it the same way he says *I love you*.

Emotion wells up in my eyes, and I'm smiling so hard it hurts. "Yeah."

"You did it."

"I did it because of you." A tear spills over. "Because you showed me I could."

"You always had it in you." His hands are in my hair as he tilts my face up to him. "Always."

I sigh as he kisses me, and my heart is so complete. I'm going to write a song about this moment.

"I love you," I tell him for the tenth time today.

He pulls back to look into my eyes, and his gaze is full of affection. "Pippa, I've loved you for a lot longer than I realized."

In a rush, his hands are on me and I'm over his shoulder as he walks to the bedroom. I laugh upside down and give him a slap on the butt.

He gives me a squeeze. "Let's go make up for lost time."

# EPILOGUE
## PIPPA

*SEVEN MONTHS LATER*

"*READY ON PIPPA'S INTRO,*" the stage tech says in my earpiece.

The arena buzzes with energy. Against the blinding stage lights, I can see the twinkle of phones in the crowd. My blood hums with a million emotions at once, and I take a deep breath, grounding myself. Throughout the tour, I've found a ritual in the moments before the show starts.

The last seven months have been insane.

Ivy Matthews started her own record label, and we recorded an album together.

My dream guitar is slung across my body, my fingers resting on the strings and the neck. A low hum pulses as the cheers die down. Everyone's waiting, watching.

We released the album, and then everything went nuts. Two of the songs picked up speed on the charts, and Ivy pulled some strings in the industry to get me the opening spot on this tour. It normally takes years to make this kind of progress, but Ivy was determined.

There are nineteen thousand, seven hundred seats in this

arena, and tonight, every single one is full. Sure, they're here to see the artist I'm opening for on this tour, but I'm standing on stage in a pretty blue dress, playing music that I wrote.

A broad smile stretches across my face, and my heart swells. I'm here, living my dream, and I'm so grateful.

"Good evening, Vancouver," I say into the mic, and the crowd cheers. "It's so good to be home. I'm Pippa Hartley."

The crowd cheers again, and I glance to the wings, where Jamie watches with a VIP pass hanging from his neck. The affection and pride in his eyes sets me on fire. He's been following me on tour all summer, but the opening game of the season is later this week in this very arena, so we'll do long distance until November, when the tour is over.

I brush my fingertips over my necklace, the one with the blue-gray stone. When I'm on stage or he's on the ice, this is how I tell him I love him. I find myself doing it constantly, even when he's not around.

"And this is a song about falling in love."

The crowd roars, and I smile at Jamie.

"*Pippa and band on five, four, three.*"

*Two, one.*

The band and I begin to play the song I wrote about Jamie, and my heart is so full.

———

Two evenings later, we're back in the same arena, except the floor is covered in ice instead of a sea of music fans. Jamie and the other players finish warming up, and I'm waiting by the entrance to the ice, microphone in hand. The hockey fans are brimming with excitement after last season. Although the Storm were eliminated in the first round of playoffs, they had a better season than usual, and Coach Tate Ward has won over the Vancouver fans.

"Ready?" the opening coordinator asks, and I give her a confident nod. My stomach tumbles with the familiar excitement I always feel just before stepping on stage, but it energizes me.

She says something into her earpiece, and the lights in the arena dim. The crowd cheers as the players line up in their spots.

"*Please stand for the opening anthem,*" the announcer says.

The coordinator gestures to me. "Ms. Hartley, that's your cue."

I glance down at myself in Jamie's jersey, wearing his name on my back, and smile.

"*Our talent tonight is homegrown,*" the announcer continues. "*Please welcome Pippa Hartley!*"

I step onto the red carpet, and the crowd cheers. As I head to my mark, I catch a glimpse of myself up on the Jumbotron, grinning from ear to ear.

Jamie stands on his skates closest to my mark, shuffling on the ice to stay warm. I flash him a broad smile and give him a quick wave before my hand automatically brushes my necklace. Under his goalie mask, his eyes are bright. He's happy to be back on the ice, I can tell. It's been incredible having him with me on tour all summer, but this is where he belongs.

I take my spot, and once the camerawoman is in her position, I nod to the coordinator. A moment later, the music starts.

My voice is strong and clear as I sing the Canadian national anthem. My heart pounds harder than ever, and it feels incredible. It's a moment I'll never forget, and when I'm a hundred years old, I'll think back to standing here on the ice, singing my heart out into the mic while Jamie looks on proudly.

I belt out the last notes, and when I'm done, the arena

erupts. The Vancouver players are whooping and cheering way more than is appropriate, and I can't help but laugh.

Jamie and I look at each other, and we're wearing matching ear-to-ear smiles. He mouths something to me.

*Songbird.*

"*Please give it up for Pippa Hartley,*" the announcer says, and I wave at the crowd before walking to the entrance, off the ice. "*Pippa, if you could just stay right there a moment.*"

My brows snap together in confusion, but I stop walking. At the entrance, the coordinator is smiling at me, holding up a hand, mouthing *stay there.*

The arena hums and I look around, confused.

"Pippa."

Jamie's at my side, no longer wearing his helmet or the goalie pads on his legs, and I blink up at him. In his skates, he towers more than normal.

"What's going on?" I ask, pulse stumbling. Everyone in the arena is watching, murmuring.

His Adam's apple bobs as he swallows, and his jaw ticks again. He's been acting weird all day. Nervous, a little jumpy. I scared the daylights out of him earlier when I walked into the bedroom too quietly.

He takes my hands. The arena lighting makes him look even more handsome, with his sharp jaw, thick lashes, and strong nose.

"First," he says, low enough so only we can hear, "you were the girl I had a crush on in high school. The girl who didn't see how pretty, talented, special, and interesting she was." His throat works. What the actual hell is happening right now? "And then you were my assistant, the distracting woman who demanded her job back and called me a dickhead."

A laugh bursts out of me, and Jamie's eyes dance.

"I don't think I used the word *dickhead*," I whisper.

Seriously, what is he doing? The entire arena is watching.

"You did," he says. "You definitely did. And now you're my girlfriend." My eyes are locked on his and I can't look away. "But I want you to be my wife, and I want to be your husband. I want us to be a family and live long, happy lives together."

Understanding rushes at me like a freight train, and Jamie drops to his knee to tie his skate—

He's not tying his skate. My heart pounds. He's looking up at me, holding a small, black velvet box. It fits right in his big palm, and there's something very sparkly inside. His free hand slips into mine, and he gives me a warm, reassuring squeeze.

I can already hear the song I'm going to write about this moment.

A rush of noise, cheering, whooping, applause swells around us, and my gaze snaps back to Jamie's. It quiets down as the arena waits.

My heart is in my throat, and my eyes are welling up. "I want that, too. All those things."

"I know we're young." His eyes search mine. "And that we haven't even been together a year." The corner of his mouth pulls up. "I don't care, though. I love you, songbird. There's no doubt in my mind that you're the one for me."

I can't even speak. I'm just smiling at him, blinking, while my pulse gallops. This doesn't feel real. This feels like the best dream I could ever imagine. I'm so glad he isn't mic'd for this. Even though everyone is watching, it feels like this moment is just for us.

"I think we should try something new," he says, mouth twitching. His eyes are the brightest green I've ever seen. His expression is so soft, so sweet, so loving. "We should try being married." His expression breaks and he huffs with amusement. "You should see your face."

"Uh." I'm laughing. "I'm busy looking at something else." I

can't get a full breath as I meet his eyes. I think I'm crying. I'm not sure. "I love you, too." It flies out of my mouth. Telling Jamie I love him is like breathing, it's so effortless and true. A tear spills over, and his hand lifts to wipe it away. "I want to marry you."

Jamie's chest swells and his expression melts into something gorgeous. So proud and happy and at ease. "I was hoping you'd say that."

He stands, and his mouth finds mine immediately. Our kiss is soft, intimate, and loving. Around us, the crowd is screaming, cheering, hollering, stamping their feet, rattling the glass, whistling.

I don't even care that thousands of people are watching. Probably more, because this is being broadcast on TV.

Everything was worth it, all the heartache, all the pain, all the scary moments. They were all worth it for this, and I'd go through it a thousand times so I could end up with Jamie Streicher.

"You should probably look at the ring," he whispers against the corner of my mouth.

I glance down at the box he's holding, and I melt all over again.

"It's like my necklace."

A striking blue-gray stone sits on a white gold band, with tiny diamonds scattered around the perimeter of the large center stone. It's delicate, unique, and perfect.

"Mhm. I wanted it to match, so you can wear this every day, too." He gently pulls it out of the box. "You want to try it on?"

I can't take my eyes off this ring. I've never seen anything like it. "Yes, please."

Jamie's deep chuckle makes me smile, and I flush with pleasure as he slides the ring onto my left ring finger. The arena explodes with noise, and I swear the ice is shaking under my feet from the volume. The players are tapping their sticks on the ice, grinning and whooping for us.

"I love it." I bite my lip as my chest squeezes with a million warm, fluttery emotions.

Jamie holds my hand, and when I look up into his eyes, I see it all in front of us. This is just the beginning, and I can't wait to see where our incredible life goes.

"You ready to be mine?" I ask.

"Songbird." He smiles down at me with that breathtaking smile that's just for me. He smiles at me like I'm adorable, and like he loves me more than anything. "I always have been."

———

Hazel and I are in the box upstairs with Donna, waiting for the third period to start. Donna keeps grabbing my hand and grinning at the ring before tearing up.

She's so excited. It's adorable.

Hazel's phone buzzes, and she unlocks it. Around us, other staff members are pulling out their own phones as notifications chime. Hazel's eyes move across her phone screen, and she goes rigid.

"Hello." I nudge her.

When her eyes meet mine, she looks like she's about to be sick. Or faint. I'm not sure.

"There's a new trade memo," she says quietly. The team staff get an email every time a new player is traded to the team so each department can prepare.

The emotionless tone to her voice makes me pause. "Who is it?"

Her movements are swift as she shoves her phone into her back pocket. "Rory Miller."

At her side, her fingertips brush in fast circles. Her nervous tell.

The season is about to get interesting.

———

**Want a bonus spicy scene with Pippa and Jamie?**
They have the team's box to themselves after Pippa's been on tour, and Jamie is determined to show his wife exactly how much he missed her.

To receive the bonus scene, sign up for my newsletter at www.stephaniearcherauthor.com/jamie or scan the QR code below.

**Can't wait for Rory and Hazel's book?**
***The Fake Out* is out now!**

And if you're looking for a spicy, small-town, fake-dating romantic comedy, keep reading for an excerpt from
*That Kind of Guy*.

There was the tinkling sound of someone clinking their glass, and the entire restaurant quieted down. Emmett stood at his table with his glass raised.

Oh my god. My gut wrenched with panic, my lungs constricted, and I remembered the conversation we had a few days ago, right after I woke up.

I had forgotten about it.

My mind raced. Here? No. Tonight? He was going to do it *tonight*? But we had only talked about it a couple days ago. There was supposed to be more planning involved. The guy could have given me some warning.

I spun around, intending to sprint back into my office, lock the door, and slide the filing cabinet in front. Max, however, the little brat, blocked me again.

"No, you don't," he said, turning me back around. He locked his arm around my shoulders to hold me steady.

"What are you doing?" I hissed at him. "Whose side are you on?"

He continued smiling at Emmett while whispering to me out of the corner of his mouth. "Emmett slipped me a hundred bucks to make sure you were here for this."

That bastard. A tiny fraction of me was impressed. I shouldn't have been surprised. The guy was always strategizing, always scheming. The deal we cooked up? It had come to him so naturally. He had everything figured out before I even said yes. Of course he had this timed to the minute.

"Most of you know me," Emmett was saying to the restaurant. "I was born and raised here in Queen's Cove, and you know my parents, Elizabeth and Sam." He tipped his glass to them and smiled. "This town means more to me than most of you will ever know. I've traveled all over, but I've never met a finer group of people."

Wow, he was laying it on thick. My pulse picked up speed. Maybe this was just a toast to his campaign.

"I love this town, and I love the people who live here. That's why I'm running for mayor. The people of Queen's Cove are important, and I'm going to do everything I can to protect them, including upgrading the electrical grid so those power outages are a thing of the past."

People started clapping, and he waited for them to finish. I rolled my eyes. In Emmett's head, he was Jesus Christ himself, here to save our sad little town. Annoying.

Emmett nodded. "You know me as the Queen's Cove boy who caused trouble with my brothers, you know me as the upcoming mayor, but there's a side of me you don't know."

Emmett, the showman he was, let this last sentence settle in the room. There was a ripple of curiosity throughout the restaurant. My stomach was in knots, twisting and churning, and adrenaline dripped into my bloodstream from the anticipation. His family exchanged curious glances.

"I'm also a man in love."

Every woman in the room except me swooned. My face tingled, and I couldn't tell whether it was from exasperation, nerves, or nausea. Diners watched me with big smiles. They must have seen Miri's photo of us online.

Emmett gave them all a bashful look. "That's right. I've

fallen head over heels for the last person I expected." He set his wine glass on the table and reached into his pocket.

I closed my eyes. Why, *why* did I agree to do this? This was mortifying. No one was going to believe it. They'd take one look at my face and know it was a complete load of crap.

Emmett pulled out a small, navy-blue velvet box, and a chorus of gasps rose up around the room. He looked straight at me, and Max's grasp on my shoulders tightened in response. My throat was thick. Even as Emmett inflicted this mortification on me, I couldn't look away from him. He was an anchor. He was the only person who knew the truth, and we were in this together.

He gave me a soft smile and walked across the restaurant to me. The slow thump of his boots echoed on the hardwood as everyone held their breath.

Max shoved me forward to the center of the restaurant. Everyone could see me.

"Avery," Emmett said, and behind him, Elizabeth clutched her hands to her mouth in elation. "I know you're scared, and you wanted to keep us a secret." He reached out and took my hands. "But baby, I'm crazy about you, and I want to tell the world. You make me a better man. I want to spend the rest of my life with you." He dropped down to one knee and more gasps rose up around the room.

"Oh my god!" Max squealed behind me.

My head was about to explode. A nervous laugh sat right below my vocal cords, ready to bubble up at any minute. My stomach twisted back and forth. My hands shook in Emmett's. Everyone stared at me. Every single person I considered a friend was here tonight, watching me, watching this happen.

On bended knee in front of me, Emmett opened the box.

My mouth fell open.

It was a vintage diamond ring from the 1920s, Art Deco

style. I'd seen similar styles online. It sparkled brilliantly, catching the light from every angle. The center diamond was a soft gray, just like the color of Emmett's eyes. A halo of tiny white diamonds encircled the larger diamond, with baguette-style gems cascading from the halo.

It was gorgeous. It was complicated, unique, over the top, and yet delicate. My heart squeezed.

How did he know what I would like? The only person I had told about this was—

My gaze cut to Hannah, who gave me a soft smile while biting her lip in anticipation. She wiggled her eyebrows at me.

I swallowed again and my gaze returned to Emmett. His money and influence knew no bounds in this town, it appeared.

"Avery Adams, will you marry me?" he asked, loud enough for everyone to hear.

The whole restaurant was silent, waiting for my answer. Emmett watched me with a gentle, reverent look on his face. I was frozen. My thoughts moved through Jello, slow and sluggish. The longer I was silent, the more the tension grew. Shit, what was I doing? I had to say something. I had to say yes.

Out of the corner of my eye, Chuck fidgeted in his seat before checking his phone, like he was bored.

The restaurant. I was doing this so I could get the restaurant. Emmett and I were in this together, and I always kept my word. I always held up my end of the bargain.

Uncertainty flickered through Emmett's eyes as he waited for my answer. His Adam's apple bobbed.

"Yes," I whispered.

"Yes?" His eyebrows shot up, and I could tell he was relieved I didn't fuck it all up. "Yes?"

I nodded and smiled despite myself. It was fun, playing with Emmett's sanity and emotions like this. "Yes."

He slipped the ring on my finger, stood, and before I realized it, stepped into my personal space and put his mouth on mine.

I stopped breathing.

His arms wrapped around me. Emmett was kissing me.

Around us, applause and cheering exploded. Emmett was kissing me. A champagne bottle popped behind the bar. Emmett was kissing me.

His mouth was warm, soft, and I felt the lightest scrape of stubble on my skin, which sent a little shiver down my spine. I could smell his masculine scent, and my hands instinctively came to his chest. I shivered again when his fingers tangled into my hair.

Before my brain could make sense of what was happening, he pulled back and smiled down at me. "Nice work," he murmured into my hair.

**That Kind of Guy is in Kindle Unlimited, paperback, and audio!**

# AUTHOR'S NOTE

Thank you so much for reading Behind the Net! If you enjoyed, I would love if you could write me a review or rate it on Amazon, or share it with your friends.

Someone pointed out that I write a lot of female character who are discovering or developing in their careers. Love is important, but feeling worthy and proud of yourself because of the work you put into something you love? That's important, too. No one can take that kind of thing away from you. I hope you know, reader, that you're worth pursuing something you love. Your dreams are valid. Ignore the people who say differently, and listen to the people who believe in you.

And now for a few words of gratitude! This book was so, so fun to write. It's only because of Brittany Kelley and Grace Reilly that this book isn't called *Bent Over the Boards* or *Pucked Between her Crease*. Thank you both so much for encouraging me and patiently listening when I plot-panic. I love you both.

A million thank you's to my wonderful, insightful, hilarious betas: Jess, Esther, Marcie, Ycelsa, Brett, Sierra, and Wren. Thank you all for making this book so much better, and for letting me kill off the hot mess sister (sorry, Esther, I know you loved her, I might use her again one day).

Thank you to Chloe Friedlein for another stunning illustration, and Echo Grayce for the perfect typography! Both of you are endlessly patient with me and I appreciate it so much.

To my superwoman assistant, Ally White, whose organized

brain works on a whole other level, and whose excitement for hockey romance kept me going. Thank you so much for everything you do.

To my soulmates: Helen Camisa, Bryan Hansen, Alanna Goobie, Sarah Clarke, Anthea Song, and Tim, who legitimately thought hockey romance was one woman vs the entire team. I love all of you so freaking much and I'm lucky to know you.

And lastly, thank you, readers! You're the reason I get to live my dream of being a romance author. Your excitement for my characters, my covers, and my future books makes my heart explode with sparkles and rainbows. I'm so grateful for all of you.

Until next time,
xo Stephanie

**Turn the page to discover more spicy, laugh-out-loud romances from Stephanie Archer.**

**The best way to get back at my horrible ex?**
**Fake date his rival.**

Being the team physiotherapist for a bunch of pro hockey players is challenging enough without my ex joining the team. He's the reason I don't date hockey players.

Vancouver Storm's new captain and the top scorer in pro hockey, Rory Miller is the arrogant, flirtatious hockey player I tutored in high school. And he's just agreed to be my fake boyfriend. I get sweet revenge. Rory gets to clean up his image. It's the perfect deal.

Faking with him is fun and addictive, though, and beneath the bad boy swagger, Rory's sweet, funny, and protective.

He teaches me to skate. He sleeps in my bed. He kisses me like it's real.

**What if he was never faking it at all?**

The Fake Out *is a pro hockey fake dating romance. It's the second book in the Vancouver Storm series but can be read as a standalone.*

**My arrogant fake fiancé? I can't stand him.**

Cocky and charismatic Emmett Rhodes isn't a relationship
kind of guy, but now that he's running for mayor of our
small town, his bachelor past is hurting the campaign.

**Thankfully, I'm the last woman who would
ever fall for him.**

We're total opposites—he's a golden retriever and I'm
a black cat, but he'll co-sign on my restaurant loan if I
play his devoted fiancée. Between romantic dates, a
prom night re-do, and visits to a secret beach, things
heat up, and the line between real and ruse is lit on fire.
I'm starting to see another side of Mr Popular, and now
I wonder if I was all wrong.

**We can't keep our hands off each other,
but it's all for show . . . right?**

*A hilarious, enemies-to-lovers, fake-dating romantic comedy
with an HEA. This is the first book in the Queen's Cove series
and can be read as a standalone.*

**The hot, commitment-phobe surfer is the only one I can turn to . . .**

In my small-town bookstore, I'm surrounded by book boy-friends, but I've never had one in real life. At almost 30, I've never been in love, and my bookstore isn't breaking even. Something needs to change, and I know exactly who's going to help me: Wyatt Rhodes, the guy everyone wants.

**He agrees to be my relationship coach, but his lessons aren't what I expected.**

Between surfing, mortifying dates and revamping my store, his lessons are more about drawing me out of my shell than changing me into someone new. But when we add praise-filled 'spice lessons' to the curriculum, it's clear he wants me. He's leaving town and I'm staying to run my store, so it can't work, but that doesn't seem to matter to him.

**He's supposed to find me someone to fall for but instead, we're falling for each other.**

*A hilarious, small-town, friends-to-lovers romantic comedy with lots of spice and a guaranteed HEA. This is the second book in the Queen's Cove series but can be read as a standalone.*

**The deal is simple: the grumpy guy will pay off my debt if I find him a wife.**

Holden Rhodes is grouchy, unfairly hot, and has hated me for years. He's the last person I'd choose to inherit an inn with. As we renovate the inn and put his dating skills to practice, though, I see a different side of him.

**What if I was all wrong about Holden?**

When we add 'friends with benefits' to the deal, our chemistry is so hot the sparks could burn down the inn. Holden's a secret romantic, and I'm secretly falling for him.

I'm terrible at bartending, a video of a bear stealing my toy went viral, and everyone in this small town knows my business, but Holden Rhodes is so much more than I expected.

**I don't want him to find love with anyone but me.**

*A grumpy-sunshine, friends-with-benefits, small-town romantic comedy with lots of spice and an HEA. This is the third book in the Queen's Cove series but can be read as a standalone.*

**The guy who broke my heart is now an arrogant, too-hot firefighter . . . who's hell-bent on getting me back.**

This summer, I have one goal: field work. I need it to finish my PhD. I never expected Finn Rhodes to offer help. He broke my heart twelve years ago, and now that he's back in town, I want nothing to do with him. The only problem? He insists we're meant to be together.

**I'll pretend to date him, but actually? I'm trying to get him to dump *me*.**

Between hiking the back country and cringe-worthy dates designed to turn him off, I begin to remember why we were best friends. Despite how hard I try, Finn isn't interested in dumping me . . . and now I'm not sure I want him to.

**Finn's always been trouble. The kind that might break my heart. Again.**

*Finn Rhodes* Forever *is a spicy, second romantic comedy. This is fourth book in the Queen's Cove series but can be read as a standalone.*